WITNESS

Books by E. G. Lewis

The Seeds of Christianity™ Series

WITNESS

DISCIPLE

MARTYR

Commercial Fiction

PROMISES

LOST

About the Author

Writing has always been a major part of E. G Lewis' life. A former newspaper editor and publisher, his articles have appeared in many national and regional magazines. He also wrote and directed corporate training films.

He has a graduate degree in Economics from Ohio State University and worked in management and corporate planning before deciding to become a fulltime novelist.

He and his wife, Gail, also a writer, live on the Southern Oregon Coast with more pets than they need.

WITNESS

Book One of The Seeds of Christianity™ Series

A Novel

by

E. G. Lewis

Cape Arago Press
North Bend, OR
www.capearagopress.com

Witness is a work of fiction. Events, characters, and incidents in this book are the product of the author's imagination, or are used fictitiously. Any resemblance to real persons, living or dead, is purely coincidental.

Copyright © 2009 by E. G. Lewis
All rights reserved. Except for short phrases used in a review, no part of this book may be reproduced, distributed, or transmitted in any form or by any means without prior written permission.

Scripture texts are taken from the *Revised Standard Version* of the Bible, copyright 1952 [2nd edition, 1971] by the Division of Christian Education of the National Council of the Churches of Christ in the United States of America. Used by permission. All rights reserved.

Quotes of Flavius Josephus are taken from *The Works of Josephus* Complete and Unabridged New Updated Edition Translated by William Whiston. ©1987 Hendrickson Publishers, Inc. PO Box 3473 Peabody, MA 01961-3473 and are used by permission of the copyright owner.

Cover: *The Newborn Lamb*, by William Adolphe Bouguereau, 1873, lunagirlimages.com.

ISBN: 978-0-9825949-0-2

1. Fiction: Christian—Historical 2. Ficiton: Christian—Biblical

Printed in the United States of America

I want to offer my heartfelt thanks to the many people who facilitated my research by graciously sharing their knowledge and expertise, who answered questions as they arose, and supported my goal of accurately depicting everyday life in the era during which Christianity came to be.

This book is dedicated to my children—
Crystal, Randy, Elizabeth, Scott, and Emily

The Birkat Kohanim

May the Lord bless and keep you.
May the Lord cause his countenance to shine upon you and be gracious unto you.
May the Lord favor you and grant you peace.

Historic Personages Mentioned in WITNESS
Name, Meaning, Biblical Reference, Modern Equivalent

Yeshua's Family
Yeshua: The Lord is Salvation...Jesus
Mother: Miryam...Wished for Child...Mother of Jesus...Mary
Foster Father: Yosef...He Will Add...Jacob's son w/Rachel...Joseph

Others
Annas: Former High Priest and Caiaphas's Father-in-Law
Athrongeus: Judean Messianic Pretender
Avraham: Father of Many...Hebrew Patriarch...Abraham
Caiaphas: High Priest at the time of the crucifixion
Daniyyel: God is My Judge...Prophet...Daniel
Judas the Galilean: Messianic Pretender, founder of Zealot Party
Moshe: Deliverer...Led Jews out of Egypt...Moses
Pontius Pilate: Roman Prefect in Palestinia
Quintillius Varus: Governor of Roman Syria

Fictional Characters in WITNESS
Name, Meaning, Modern Equivalent

Rivkah's Family
Rivkah: A snare...Rebecca
Her Father: Yaakov...Supplanter...Jacob/James
Her Mother: Hadassah...Myrtle Tree...Esther
Her Uncle: Chayim...Life...Hyam
Her Aunt: Tamar...Palm Tree...Tamar
Her Cousin: Ruth...Companion...Ruth
Her Cousin: Elisheva...God is Abundant...Elizabeth
Her Cousin: Yonah...God is Gracious...John
Her Oldest Son: Yo'el...Yahweh is God...Joel
Her Oldest Daughter: Hadassah...Myrtle Tree...Esther
Hadassah's Husband: Hebel...Breath...Abel
Her Middle Son: Yaakov...Supplanter...James
Her Youngest Daughter: Channah...Grace...Hannah

Fictional Characters Continued

Shemu'el's Family
Shemu'el: God has Heard...Samuel
Father: Yo'el...Yahweh is God...Joel
Mother: Sarit...Lady...Sarah
Brother: Yhonatan...Yahweh's Given...Jonathan
Yhonatan's wife: Miriam...Wished for Child...Mary
Brother: Caleb...Dog...Caleb
Caleb's Wife: Avigail...My Father is Joy...Abigail

Others
Friend Rachel: Ewe...Rachel
Rachel's Husband: Binyamin...Son of Right Hand...Benjamin
Rachel's Son: Nahum...Comforter...Nahum
Rachel's Sister: Nava...Beautiful...Nava
Nava's Betrothed: Uri'el...God is My Light...Uri
Friend Devorah: Bee...Deborah
Devorah's Husband: Shaoul...Asked For...Saul
Friend Gavriel: Strong Man of God...Gabriel
Friend Simeon: Hearing...Simon
Father's Friend Sidonius: Man of Sidon
Sidonius' Son Tyro: Man of Tyre

Book Club Members

Do you belong to a reading club? *WITNESS* makes a great book for group reading. Go to www.capearagopress.com to download a free Discussion Guide and/or to arrange a visit to one of your club meetings by *WITNESS* author E. G. Lewis. Cape Arago Press offers a discount for six or more copies with No Shipping or Handling Charges when delivered to a single address.

WITNESS

~ 1 ~

I would have seen the lion if those clods of dirt flying past my head had not distracted me.

There I was, relaxing on a hill, bothering no one. The sheep poked around the sparse pasture for the last clumps of edible forage while I sang Psalms and wove a basket. The summer sun had browned the grass and baked the Judean hills, turning them tan as barley bread.

My tongue swept around my mouth tasting the gritty dryness of the afternoon as another clod sailed overhead. It struck the ground in front of me and broke apart in a spray of dust.

All sorts of strange objects took flight whenever I tended the sheep. Overripe figs, half-eaten pomegranates, sticks, and now clods of dirt had sprouted wings and flew through the air.

The boys did it to upset me, to make me cry. Once upon a time it had worked, but no longer. If I cried, they won. And I would *never* let them win.

Jumping to my feet, I spun around to face them.

Two more clods headed toward me.

Ducking under them, I rested my hands on my hips and glared across the ravine at the boys throwing them. "Stop, or you will be sorry," I yelled, adjusting my headband.

Like the bigger shepherds, I carried my *shebet*, a small club, and my sling tucked in my sash. I tugged the sling out and stooped to gather stones. Imagining myself David, I threw my shoulders back and rolled the stones in my hand. Seeing their startled faces when one of these rocks bounced off their forehead would do my heart good.

But there would be no rocks to the head this day, I thought with a sigh. No matter how angry they made me, there was little I could do. On Mt. Sinai, the Lord gave Moshe the stone tablets containing the Law which commanded, *Thou shalt not commit murder.* The boys had nothing to fear and they knew it. Gavriel and Simeon could throw things, call me names, and torment me without fear of retaliation.

"Go sweep floors, little maiden," Simeon hollered. "Comb wool, weave cloth, bake loaves."

"Perhaps you should go to Jerusalem and apprentice yourself to a fuller."

Simeon's head snapped back. His eyes popped open wide.

Beside him, Gavriel snickered at the idea of seeing his friend removing lanolin from wool cloth by plodding knee-deep in a vat of stale urine.

Simeon's face reddened.

Gavriel's snickers became laughs. They grew louder until he doubled over, holding his sides and choking.

"Go away! You do not belong here," Simeon shouted. He stuck out his tongue and did a little dance, daring me to do something about it.

"Do too belong here. I am tending my flock." The smooth stone slid between my thumb and fingers.

Where to hit him?

"Sheep are for shepherds." He gestured toward his loins. "Shepherds. Understand little girl?" He spat on the ground, clearing his mouth of the despicable word *girl.*

"There are shepherds and there are shepherdesses, you evil little boy. Take a look. What do you see? A shepherdess with her flock. Now go away, you are making the sheep anxious."

A rock to where he pointed would give him good reason to dance. I gritted my teeth in frustration. Not only did Yahweh's law rule my life, but Abba's did as well. My father would never approve of me hitting a boy in the loins with a stone.

Abba's stern voice echoed in the back of my mind. "Rivkah, my little dove, will you never learn? A gentle answer turns away wrath, but harsh words stir up anger. Do not fight with the boys.

Exhibit the comely behavior and feminine demeanor befitting a daughter of Avraham."

Easy enough for him to say.

"There is no such thing as a shepherdess," Gavriel hollered.

I shook my fist at him. "Did an unclean spirit turn you into a *goy*?" He glared at me for calling him a gentile, not that I cared. "What about Laban's daughters, Leah and Rachel? Have you never heard of Jethro's seven daughters, of Zipporah the shepherdess and wife of Moshe?"

Behind me the sheep bleated nervously. I ignored them. The boys and their dirt balls not only upset me, they bothered my sheep as well. Sometimes they threw things into the midst of the flock scattering them. It took a lot of effort to chase after those sheep and bring them back together.

We stared daggers at each other across the narrow gully.

I fit a stone into the pouch of my sling and let it dangle at the end of its straps. Shepherds used their slings to drive off small beasts and vermin. Gavriel and Simeon qualified.

Swinging it up in a practiced arc, I whipped it around in a tight circle. The whirling blur above my head buzzed like a hoard of locusts.

The boy's mouths dropped. They glanced at each other nervously, at me, and then at each other again.

My warning shot smacked the ground in front of their feet, boring into the dry soil and scattering dust over their bare toes.

Gavriel laughed. "Ha! You shoot like a girl, little shepherdess. You would miss the side of a camel if it were standing right in front of you." He stuck his fingers in the corners of his mouth and made a face.

"May the Lord will your face to remain like that for the rest of your life," I said.

There were several more stones in my left hand. If they wanted war, war they would get. The boys jumped when they saw me reloading my sling.

But I never threw that second stone.

Shemu'el appeared behind them while they scoured the ground for ammunition. He is three years older than we are, almost twelve and soon to become a man. Shemu'el is tall, and stronger than Gavriel and Simeon put together. And, most importantly, he is my friend. It upsets him when the boys bother me.

They were so busy hunting for rocks, his footsteps went unnoticed.

Taking long strides, he marched up behind them and grabbed each of them by a shoulder.

I grinned when the boys winced and howled as he shook them.

"Go take care of your sheep, you little fools. They are beginning to stray." He spun them around and gave them a shove.

Today's battle may have ended, but our war had not. The boys shot me a look that promised revenge, then slunk away.

Shemu'el swung out his staff and gave them a spank as they left. Turning, he glanced up at the ridge behind me and gave a start.

The expression on Shemu'el's face made my stomach quiver.

He studied the hillside a moment longer, then, quick as a gazelle, leaped the ravine and ran to where I stood.

"Look, Rivkah," he whispered. "A lion."

~ 2 ~

Shemu'el dropped to one knee and rested his hand on my shoulder. He pointed across the dry meadow to an outcropping where a large, yellowish animal crept along the ridge.

Tales went around the campfire of lions carrying off sheep, but I had never seen a real one before. The hair prickled on the back of my neck. He was much larger than those in my imagination.

"What are we going to do?"

"We can drive him off. When a lion stalked our flocks, my older brothers defended the sheep."

"But we do not have Caleb and Yhonatan here to help us." I swallowed hard, struggling to control my rising panic.

Even though the lion's tawny coat blended into the dry soil, the ewes noticed him. They bumped against each other, softly bleating. So it was not the boys who made the sheep nervous after all.

"Where did this lion come from?"

"He came out of the mountains. My father says they range from the Negev north all the way to Galilee and east into Syria."

"From the tales they tell around the campfire, I expected more fur around his neck."

"His mane is not yet full because he is still young and small."

Small?

"Why is he here?"

"Most likely he was driven by hunger. Game becomes scarce in the hills during the dry season."

"What if he plans on eating us?"

Shemu'el chuckled and shook his head. "They seldom attack people. He came to raid your flock." He gave me a reassuring pat on the shoulder. "Our job is to stop him before he can."

I wished for his confidence.

The lion inched along the slope, using the scrub and dried

brush for cover.

"The lion is concentrating on the sheep," Shemu'el whispered. "If we stand still, he may not notice us."

My eyes scanned the parched meadow, determining the lion's target. Shemu'el and I saw the young lamb at the same moment. A look of understanding passed between us. The lamb with one brown leg had found a treasure, a patch of green growing in the shade of a boulder. She continued eating, oblivious to the predator stalking her.

My hands moved one around the other as tears welled in my eyes. Why, oh why, had I let those boys distract me? A single moment of carelessness might cost Abba one of his lambs. Maybe Simeon and Gavriel were right. Perhaps I was not cut out to be a shepherdess after all.

"You stay with the flock. I will go and retrieve your lamb."

Shemu'el adjusted the heavy *shebet* tucked into the band of rope wound around his waist. About two cubits of hard, old grapewood, his shepherd's rod had a large knob at one end.

Mine, much smaller, was mostly for show. When there was nothing else to do I used it to smash bugs.

Eyes on the ridge, Shemu'el set out on a curving path to the lamb.

I scurried down the hill toward the flock, walking on the sides of my feet to avoid slipping. Bits of soil and dislodged pebbles tumbled ahead of me. Like Shemu'el, my eyes remained on the predator creeping along the ridge.

The lion had the advantage. A few quick steps and a long leap would put him on top of the lamb. It dropped into a low crouch and inched forward, muscles taut and tail twitching.

Shemu'el broke into a run.

Whispering a prayer, I loaded a stone into my sling. Shemu'el counted on me for help and I could not let him down.

Crashing over the last cubits of hillside, Shemu'el flared his cloak and gave a throaty snarl.

The surprised lion snapped out of its crouch.

Shemu'el beat his staff through the brush with a defiant shout, sending branches and dry leaves flying into the air.

The lion showed its teeth and growled.

Swinging with all my might, I loosed my first rock. It slammed against the top of the big cat's shoulder.

The lion flinched and retreated a step, grumbling and snarling. His head swiveled, searching for the stone's source. An instant later its yellow eyes honed in on me standing in the midst of my sheep.

A shiver of fear rippled through me. I imagined the lion deciding which made the better meal, me or the lamb. A voice inside my head screamed, *"Run!"* My legs twitched, begging to go, but I held my ground. If Shemu'el had the courage to face a lion, so did I.

The lion's gaze moved to Shemu'el, then to the lamb.

It might be confused, but we knew what to do. Two slings whistled in the air. Two rocks flew toward the lion. Shemu'el's larger stone smacked its head.

The lion jerked its head and staggered back. Rearing up, it clawed the air. Its angry roar echoed around the narrow canyon.

We both hit him again.

Confused, and tired of being pelted by rocks, it vented its frustration on the leafless branches of a nearby bush.

Shemu'el sensed the tide of battle turning in our favor and hurled his staff at the lion like a spear. He jerked the rod out of his sash. One well-placed blow could shatter the lion's skull. Shemu'el held the rod high, ready to strike, and inched his way closer to the cowering lamb. He scooped up a fist-sized rock, hurled it at the lion, and broke into a run.

The rock made a hollow thud when it struck the animal's side. The lion growled over its shoulder and slunk away.

In one swift motion, Shemu'el snatched the lamb and tossed it over his shoulder.

I continued lobbing stones at the lion to speed him on his way. The lion had disappeared by the time Shemu'el returned with the lamb. Now that the danger passed, my body shook like a leaf in the wind.

"You were brave," Shemu'el said, placing the lamb in my shaky arms. "Your father will be proud of you."

He smiled. "You are a good shepherdess, Rivkah. Do not let the boys convince you otherwise."

He turned to leave, then stopped. "In the excitement of the lion, I almost forgot why I came."

He dug in his leather pouch and handed me a short piece of carved and polished wood.

I turned it in my hand, enthralled by his artistry and the swirling grain of the wood. Shemu'el had trimmed away a portion of the branch, allowing him to create a wreath of delicate flowers curling around its entire length. I studied it closer, noting the angled cut at one end and row of neat, evenly-spaced holes set between the blossoms.

Seeing my confusion, Shemu'el took it out of my hand. "It is a *shrika*. I chose olive wood because of its fine tone. Here, let me show you."

He put the whistle to his lips and blew. It made a pleasant, melodic sound. He lifted his finger, uncovering a hole. The tone changed. He vibrated his finger above the hole.

I looked on in amazement. It was not only beautiful to look at, the *shrika* made beautiful music, too. The trilling sound he made reminded me of the small yellow and gray-feathered serins that flitted from bush to bush.

When he handed it back I drew a big breath and blew into one end. Instead of music it made an embarrassing squeal. My cheeks warmed when he laughed.

"Takes a little practice," he said, with a wink. "You will learn."

The strong muscles in Shemu'el's shoulders moved under his tunic as he trudged back up the hill. At the top he turned to grin and wave good-bye.

My heart swelled until I feared it would burst. Clutching my precious *shrika*, I raised my hand high above my head and returned his wave.

As I watched Shemu'el leave, it became clear to me why he came, why he always stopped the boys from pestering me and why he brought me gifts. He planned to take me for his wife.

As a young maiden, not even a woman yet, some would say

it was too soon for me to be thinking about these things. But what other explanation could there be?

Most days I enjoyed being alone with the sheep. Today it unnerved me. The slightest sound worried me. What if the lion returned and Shemu'el was not there to help? Better to take them home to the sheepfold.

I watched the shadows, jumping at the slightest movement as we walked home. The sheep sensed my uneasiness and reacted to it. They clustered around me, jostling for position as we walked.

Together we drove off a lion, I thought, smiling. It felt like a dream. Shemu'el said we could and we did. He said I had been brave. We both knew better. He was the courageous one.

Someday Shemu'el would be my husband and the father of my children. It gave me a secure feeling knowing this most important matter had been decided.

~ 3 ~

Abba was up on a stool picking plums when I returned. He gave me a surprised look and hopped down.

"You are home early, is anything wrong?"

"A lion..." All the way home I promised myself I would not cry when I told Abba what happened. Yet as soon as the word *lion* came out of my mouth, I broke down and bawled like a lost lamb.

He pulled me into his arms and kissed the top of my head to make me feel better. "You have no injuries, which is more important than any lamb. Tell me about it."

"If Shemu'el had not been there to help me, the lion would surely have eaten one of our lambs."

"Shemu'el is a fine young man. I will tell his father about this good thing he did."

His words warmed my heart. Abba thought Shemu'el was a fine young man. He would be proud to have him for a son-in-law when Shemu'el asked to take me for his bride.

"Which lamb was it?" Abba asked.

"This one," I said, walking over to the flock and picking out the ewe lamb with one brown leg.

"Very good. Now come sit beside me, my brave little shepherdess."

He had something on his mind. Was he upset with me for neglecting the sheep? I snuggled against Abba's strong chest, hoping he was not.

"Hungry?" He offered me my choice of plums from the pot he picked into.

Choosing a nice one, I cleaned it on my cloak and took a big bite. Sweet juice dripped out of the side of my mouth.

He caught the drip with his finger up and smiled.

When Abba smiles like that it makes me feel good all over.

He studied his sticky finger for a moment, then popped it into his mouth and licked it off. "I think the time has come for you to have a sheep of your own."

I jumped up and down and clapped my hands for joy. "Which one...which one?"

"The one you saved. She owes her life to you, so we will make her yours."

"Do you mean it?"

I frowned into Abba's soft brown eyes. He sometimes made jokes and played tricks on me. Do not let this be one of those times, I prayed. Please do not let this be a joke. It must not be.

"Of course I do. You are ready to start your own flock."

Throwing my arms around his neck, I hugged him with all my might and kissed his scratchy cheek. "Oh, thank you, thank you, thank you."

"My father gave me my first lamb when I was about your age. It is a way for a boy to build a flock for the day when he must provide for himself and his family. Since I have no sons, I will do it for you instead. This will furnish you with a dowry." He stopped and glanced down at me. "Are you listening to me?"

"Of course." My mind sometimes wandered, but not this time.

"We will add an extra notch to her ear meaning *this sheep belongs to Rivkah*. When your ewe is bred, all her offspring will become yours." He raised a cautionary finger. "Now understand, you will be responsible for the offering of the first fruits. After that, if she drops ewe lambs, you may keep them to increase your flock. If she brings forth rams, we will take them to the Temple along with mine."

He offered me an important privilege. The sheep vendors in Annas' market at the Temple in Jerusalem paid the best price for lambs. Only approved shepherds could sell to them and, even then, they inspected each animal for blemishes. Abba's father and his father's father had provided sacrificial lambs to the Temple. He and his brother, Chayim, inherited this right when they came of age. Now my lambs would also be eligible.

What about my husband? Could he sell to the Temple too? You worry too much, a little voice inside my head told me. Shemu'el's father, Yo'el, sold his lambs to the Temple just as we did. I imagined being grown up and married to Shemu'el and walking beside him when we led our lambs to Jerusalem.

Abba's voice jerked me back to reality. "Are you paying

attention to everything I've been telling you?"

"Yes. Oh, yes." Well, I had been thinking about lambs...sort of.

"When we take your lambs to Jerusalem, I will pay the road tolls and the livestock tax at the Sheep Gate. We will deduct it from the sales price when I give you your money."

Money? Did he say, "*Money*?" Having a sheep of my own was such an exciting prospect that the thought of money never entered my mind.

"When we are paid for our lambs at the Temple Treasury, you can place your tithe into the offering bowl. It will be up to you to set aside an equal part for second tithes. After that, the rest will be yours to keep."

I leaned against Abba and tugged his big arm around me. Soon there would be a new flock in our little settlement. Not a shepherdess, heh? What would Gavriel and Simeon say about me now?

After supper Abba said our evening prayers and put a single lamp in the niche for our nightlight. Abba always said the sleep of a laborer is sweet. He fell asleep right away. Shafts of moonlight shone through our window while he snored.

Even though it had been a tiring day, my mind refused to let me rest. When not remembering the lion or thinking about my new sheep, my thoughts returned to Shemu'el.

A few weeks before, in the shade of the orchard, my friend Rachel and I took turns braiding each other's hair. We found a scrap of blue ribbon and tied the ends with it, pretending we were getting ready for our wedding day. While we worked we speculated on what it would be like to have husbands.

I piled my braids atop my head and spun around for Rachel to admire. "Do you think Shemu'el would like my hair pulled up like this?"

"Do you really believe Shemu'el will take you for his wife?"

"I am certain of it."

"What if he chooses someone else."

Just the thought of Shemu'el choosing someone else made me sad enough to weep. "Do not ever say that, Rachel. Shemu'el will take me for his wife. He will...he must."

"And will you kiss him?"

"Well, of course," I stammered, trying to sound very confident.

Rachel giggled. "When you are betrothed you must let Shemu'el kiss you right on the mouth the way lovers do."

"How do you know so much about lovers?" She always seemed to know more about these things than me.

"My older sister, Nava, is to be married soon. One evening I followed her and Uri'el, her betrothed, while they walked in the vineyard."

"They let you do that?"

A devilish gleam twinkled in Rachel's eyes. "I hid between the rows. They spent all of their time staring at one another." She clasped her hands and pretended to swoon.

I scooted over so as not to miss a word.

"They never noticed me. I watched them put their arms around each other. Uri'el stroked Nava's cheek and sniffed her hair. They lay down on the grass side-by-side and kissed each other on the mouth over and over. They were so close I couldn't tell where Uri'el stopped and Nava began."

Rachel leaned over and whispered, "The following day I overheard Nava tell a friend she had incited Uri'el's lust in the vineyard. She said his wonderful kisses made her weak."

We thought we understood the part about inciting his lust, though neither of us knew for sure. As for kisses making you weak, Abba often kissed me. Always on the cheek or the top of my head. It made me feel happy inside and secure when he kissed me. Is that how Uri'el made Nava feel, happy inside?

The only person who ever kissed me on the mouth was my little cousin, Yonah. He was still learning to walk and called me Rivvy. Whenever I picked him up, he grinned and gave me a wet, slobbery kiss right on the mouth. Would a lover's kisses be messy like that?

How would it feel to kiss Shemu'el?

Abba snorted in his sleep making me jerk.
Could he somehow know my thoughts?
He coughed and moved in the bed. After a deep sigh, he resumed snoring.
Easing my arm out from under the covers, I brought my hand to my mouth. I closed my eyes and kissed the back of my hand pretending I was kissing Shemu'el.
That was not how kisses would feel. There should be some lips pressed against mine. The next time I put my first two fingers against my lips.
Too bony.
How could I ever know what it felt like? I would die rather than ask Shemu'el to kiss me.

But if it was his idea...

~ 4 ~

Aunt Tamar was not pleased when she heard about me starting my own flock. It seemed like she complained to Abba about me every chance she got. Said I spent too much time with the sheep and not enough time learning household tasks. The household tasks were just an excuse. She needed me to care for my young cousins, Yonah and Elisheva, so she had more time to gossip at the well.

Not that I minded caring for my cousins. Women's work was fine too, but I liked being with the sheep as well. She and Abba reached an agreement allowing me to split my time between the sheep and the house. After we prayed, I spent the rest of each *Shabbat* with the sheep since the Law forbade housework.

More importantly, I got to stay in the fields all night with Abba during lambing season. It was my favorite time of the year because I loved babies, all kinds of babies. Baby lambs, baby goats, baby birds...even baby people. My cousins were young, but not babies anymore. I loved them just the same.

Some birds nested in one of the olive trees beside my uncle's house. Every few days I checked the eggs to see if they hatched. Once they did, I looked in on my baby birds every afternoon to see how they were getting along.

Gavriel and Simeon noticed and asked about the birds. It surprised me that they would be interested in baby birds. I offered to let them climb up and take a look, but they said, "No, thanks. We are happy just letting you tell us about them."

Aunt Tamar saw me up in the tree and talked to Abba about it.

"You must stay out of the tree, my little dove," Abba said. "It is not proper for a young maiden to be climbing."

"Why?"

"Because you must lift your clothing when you climb. A young maiden should not expose herself in such a manner. Tamar noticed the boys staring up your tunic while you were in the tree." He paused to let me think about this then asked, "Were you wearing a loincloth?"

My stomach quivered and my cheeks burned. "Yes, Abba," I said, lowering my head. "Always."

He hugged me. "Then you have nothing to be ashamed of."

And that was that.

Not having a mother meant my father and I sometimes had to discuss embarrassing topics. My mother, Hadassah, died a few days after I was born.

The same thing sometimes happens with our ewes. They have a lamb and then turn right around and get sick and die. You can never tell. It happens the other way, too. The mother survives and the lamb dies. But it all evens out in the end. We put the motherless lambs with another ewe and she raises them.

My father's brother, Chayim, is also a shepherd. He and his family live in the house next to ours. They took me in as a newborn, making me and their oldest daughter, Ruth, milk-sisters. His wife, my Aunt Tamar, nursed me until my father took me back at three years of age.

Aunt Tamar opposed the idea, saying it was not a good thing for him to do. Better I should stay with her and learn the womanly work of keeping a house. After all, who wanted a wife who herded sheep and could not cook and sew?

But he insisted, and so back I went. It has worked out all right. I learned how to cook and keep house. Everything in our little home gets taken care of and Abba never complains. We have each other and that is all we need. The Lord looks after us and we look after the sheep.

If I was such a disgusting person, why did Gavriel and Simeon want to look up my tunic? They told me they were interested in knowing how my baby birds were doing. Ha! They had no interest in birds at all. No more climbing for Rivkah.

I spent a lot of time thinking about it and the same thought kept running through my mind. Gavriel and Simeon were the ones who misbehaved, not me. So why did it feel like I was the one being punished? Who committed the transgression, Bathsheba taking her bath and bothering no one, or King David sneaking around his palace and peeking out the window at her nakedness?

Aunt Tamar said I should not waste my afternoons watching birds when there were useful chores to be done. She taught me to spin wool into thread. Making clothes is more than just sewing cloth. First we sheared the sheep, and then I carded, or combed, the wool to remove any dirt in it.

In the evenings, while Abba said our prayers, I took handfuls of carded wool and rolled them on my thigh, twisting them into coarse yarn. Since I started doing this, my hands were no longer rough and scratchy like a shepherd's. The lanolin in the wool made them nice and soft. Very womanly.

Aunt Tamar wanted to teach me how to spin my coarse yarn into finished thread. We placed the balls of yarn in a special bowl with guides to keep it from becoming tangled. I attached one end to a spindle, turned my back to the bowl and raised my arm. Then, holding the thread between my first finger and thumb, I dropped the spindle.

The spindle twirled as it fell, spinning the coarse yarn into finished thread. You controlled the thread's thickness by how fast you let the spindle drop. When it hit the floor, I wrapped the new thread around the spindle and repeated the process.

My aunt did two at once, one strand in each hand. Each time I tried to keep track of two of them, I got confused and made a mess of them both. My thread never came out as fine as hers either. I tried to explain, because I am short, her spindle had farther to fall than mine.

Aunt Tamar said it was because I am hopeless.

I worked extra hard spinning several skeins of very nice thread to impress her. I planned to dye it red and use it to weave stripes into a bolt of cloth for Abba's cloak. One day, while she shopped, I decided to dye it myself and surprise her.

Everything went just the way it should. I ground dried madder roots, put them in a pot of water, and heated it. Then I strained the roots out and soaked my thread for a long time over a low fire before letting it cool.

No one told me to use a stick to lift the yarn out of the dye. When the time came to remove it, I reached into the pot, squeezed out the excess dye and put the thread into a cool rinse. My arms turned bright red all the way up to my elbows.

Aunt Tamar screamed so loud when she saw me that everyone in our little settlement came running.

"I thought you were bleeding to death," she said, patting her heart and fanning the air in front of her face.

Abba heard the noise and hurried over to check. He patted my head and chuckled. "This is how we all learn," he said. "The next time you will know."

"There may not be a next time," Aunt Tamar said and made a nasty face.

For two weeks every time Gavriel or Simeon saw me they jumped back and waved their hands in the air shouting, "Unclean! Unclean!"

It made me wish I had some terrible disease just so they would catch it.

~ 5 ~

Shemu'el and I sat side-by-side on the hillside scarcely breathing. A few feet away, a chickadee hopped from branch to branch in search of berries.

We stared into the bush without making a sound and communicated with our eyes. A hush settled around us and I listened to the faraway hum of a beehive. A fly landed on my arm. I gritted my teeth and stifled the urge to bat it away. To do so would startle the tiny feathered creature we were watching.

Shemu'el sighed with pleasure when the bird flew away.

An impromptu merging of his flock and mine, grazed in the meadow below us. Shemu'el often led his flock to fields adjacent to where mine grazed. It gave us time to spend together talking about whatever crossed our minds. We enjoyed each other's company and spent many days this way. Because I was young, and he not yet a man, no one paid much attention.

When it came time for the midday meal, we shared what was in our sacks. I usually slipped little treats and tidbits into mine to give to Shemu'el.

After we ate, we lay on our backs and stared up at the sky. Raptors soared high above us, nearly as high as the clouds it seemed. I saw a scattering of storks sweep past. The return of the storks signaled the beginning of their annual migration. Soon our skies would be filled with flocks of migrating birds.

Shemu'el unwrapped the cloth. "I love the wood's beauty," he said and handed me the bowl.

Beauty? What beauty? All I saw was a crude bowl, rough and splintery. I slid my tongue along my lips trying to decide what to say. Would his feelings be hurt if I spoke the truth?

Shemu'el read my face and grinned. "You do not see it, do you?"

Lowering my eyes, I shook my head. "I am sorry, but I do not."

Rather than taking offense, he surprised me by laughing. "No wonder. There is little, if any, beauty there yet. I look at it with my imagination, not my eyes." He touched the side of his head. "I sometimes forget you cannot see what is in here. Hopefully, I will transfer what I hold in my mind to the bowl you hold in your hand."

"Where did you get it?"

"When we take lambs to the Temple, Abba lets me visit Leandros the woodworker," he said. "He attaches the block of wood to a device called a lathe that turns it like a wheel. As it spins, he gouges out the center and shapes the sides." Shemu'el smiled. "And then he gives it to me."

"After all that work, he *gives* it to you?"

"To finish, carve and polish. Then I return it to him and he pays me three *denarii* for my work."

"He is very generous."

Shemu'el gave a self-conscious chuckle. "Do not grieve for Leandros. Rich men pay him well for my bowls. But not this one. When this bowl is finished, I plan to give it to Imma."

I envied his mother receiving such a beautiful gift. Shemu'el covered his lap with a piece of hide. Placing the bowl in the center of it, he began working on it with a curved scraper. Sweat beaded on his brow as he scraped. Every so often he stopped, brushed an arm over his forehead and dumped out the thin curls of wood that accumulated inside the bowl.

A week later Shemu'el removed his materials from his bag and arranged them in a straight line. The last item out was the bowl.

He offered it to me for inspection. "Well, what do you think now?"

I hardly recognized it. His scraping had shaved away all the gouges, splinters and chips.

"It is lovely," I said, turning it in my hands. I ran my fingers over the wood, feeling its grainy texture.

"It still must be smoothed," Shemu'el said, reading my mind. He filled the bottom of a clay dish with light gray powder.

"What is that?"

"The Romans call it *pumicis*. It is mined near the town of Herculaneum, at the base of Mt. Vesuvius, and crushed into fine powder. I get if from Leandros."

"Is it hard work to smooth the wood?"

"It is one of the easier steps. Would you like to try?"

I looked everywhere but at Shemu'el. "Oh, no. I might ruin your bowl."

He caught my hand and gave a playful tug. "Nonsense. Come, sit here. I trust you."

I sat cross-legged as I had seen him do and smoothed my tunic. He spread the hide across my lap and placed the bowl on it. I folded my hands in my lap and squeezed them together to keep them from shaking.

"We always start with oil and finish with water." Shemu'el removed the stopper from a small bottle of olive oil, added it to the gray powder in a dish, and stirred them into a paste. He handed me the dish and a pad.

I stared up at him, not knowing what to do.

"Would you like me to show you how?"

I nodded.

Shemu'el stood beside me for a moment chewing his lip, then said, "Uh...Rivkah, I do not want you to think I am taking liberties. Would you be offended if I reached around you? Just to show you how it is done, you understand."

"No," I said in a tiny voice. I swallowed hard. "You may do that."

He dropped to the ground and slid close. "First, dip the pad into the paste."

I did as he instructed.

"Now set the dish aside and place your pad into the bowl."

Shemu'el eased his arm around me, taking care not to brush me. He placed his hand atop mine. "Like this," he said, directing my hand. "Without too much pressure, swirl it in circles."

Together, our hands glided around the bowl in a slush of oily grit. Feeling his breath on my cheek made my heart pound. I forced myself to concentrate on the swirling pattern inside the bowl, though other thoughts kept intruding.

"Now begin to run the pad up the side each time we go around."

Shemu'el inched forward. When his chest brushed my back, I leaned back against him ever so lightly.

"Can I see it yet?" I would never look until Shemu'el allowed me to.

He unwrapped it with care and handed it to me. After our oil sanding, he sanded the bowl again with *pumicis* and water, then carved and stained the wood. The bowl was nearly done.

I squealed with surprise and delight. Graceful stalks of wheat circled the outside of the bowl. I ran my finger over them, marveling at their realistic beauty. "The wheat is unbelievable," I said, handing it back to him. "You should be a woodcarver, not a shepherd."

He shook his head. "I enjoy carving, but I was born to be a shepherd. All that remains is the polishing," he said and stretched for the pot he'd left warming in the sun.

"What do you use to polish the bowl?"

He tilted it for me to see. "My own recipe, sweet almond oil and beeswax. Taste it," he said, offering me the pot.

"Will it make me sick?"

He stared into my eyes, his expression serious. "I would never do anything that would bring you harm. Go ahead." With a happy chuckle, Shemu'el caught a dab on his fingertip and licked it off. "See. There is nothing in it to hurt you."

I took some and rubbed it between my thumb and forefinger, feeling its slipperiness. I sniffed, then put it to my tongue. It tasted sweet and nutty...surprisingly pleasant.

Shemu'el grinned when my finger returned to the pot a second time.

More than anything, I wanted to fix the taste in my memory...and with it this day. Even then, I somehow sensed how much this memory would someday mean to me.

~ 6 ~

"And in that region there were shepherds out in the field, keeping watch over their flock by night."
—Luke 2:8

I named my sheep Liat, which means *You are mine*. Having a sheep all my own made going to the fields much more exciting. I still did womanly chores with Aunt Tamar, but as soon as Abba returned with the flock, my feet flew out the door as I ran to check on Liat. Now I had two things to think about while sweeping, grinding meal and kneading dough, Liat and Shemu'el. Well, mostly Shemu'el.

But for a time there would be no more weaving and dyeing, sweeping and stitching for Rivkah. Lambing season had come and, as a shepherdess, my duty was to be with my flock. Abba and I would spend our nights in the field along with Shemu'el, his brothers and father and the other shepherds of our settlement. I danced with excitement as I scurried around the house preparing to leave.

Abba moved the sheep to the birthing pasture about the ninth hour, leaving me behind to gather the things we needed. My bag waited, stuffed with food. Knowing the fields grew cold at night, I threw in our fleece-lined cloaks. After tucking my rod into my sash, I glanced around the room making a final check. Ready to go. I tossed the bag over my shoulder, grabbed my staff and bid my cousins in the next house farewell.

My heart pounded with anticipation as I skipped down the path. The coolness of the coming evening settled around me on my way to the pasture. A surprisingly large number of people traveled the main road heading for Bethlehem. I threaded my way between them watching the setting sun paint pink and purple bands across the western sky.

I had slipped my *shrika* into my leather purse in hopes of playing it when we sang around the fire. A quick pat verified it was still there. My feet could not get me there fast enough.

By the time I reached the fields, the sky had turned dusky blue-gray and a delicate rim of moon peaked over the mountains behind me. Wispy ribbons of smoke rose from the valley; they had already lit the evening's fire. Abba noticed me walking along the crest of the hill and dashed up to meet me.

He was breathless from the climb. Good news. Our lambing season has begun, my little dove. Just before you arrived the first ewe dropped a pair of healthy rams."

"Perhaps those twins are the omen of a prosperous season."

"May the Lord make it so."

I took his hand as we walked. "Why are there so many pilgrims on the road? It is not a time for festivals, and *Pesach* is not until the month of Nisan."

"Those are not pilgrims, they are going to Bethlehem for the census." Sensing my confusion, he explained. "Some time ago Caesar Augustus ordered a count of the whole world. They do it by province, beginning in the west and moving to the east."

He shrugged. "Our turn has come. It is about taxation and gathering gold. Just another Roman scheme to squeeze the last drops out of a rag they have already wrung dry."

"Do they not have enough already?"

Abba rested his arm over my shoulder and lowered his voice. "Let me tell you something about gold, little one. It is best to have none at all. Once you begin to accumulate gold it makes your palm itch for more. Love of money is the root of all evil." He licked his lips. "So what have you brought for our supper?"

Other shepherds drifted in from the fields as I spread a cloth and sat out our meal. There was a large block of soft cheese with herbs kneaded in the way Abba preferred, barley loaves, parched grains in vinegar and oil with sliced cucumbers, dried fruits, and eggs cooked hard in water.

A man's voice from behind startled me. "Those apricots look tasty."

A large hand reached over my shoulder into my open package and stole an apricot. I jerked around in surprise and watched the thief, my Uncle Chayim, grin as he popped the fruit into his mouth.

Chayim was more than an uncle to me...almost a father. He called me his other daughter because I spent my earliest years in his household. Many of those evenings I crawled into my uncle's strong arms and fell asleep.

Chayim clapped my father on the back and dropped onto the grass beside him. "Twins, eh Yaakov. An auspicious start to the lambing season." He grinned. "You may be ahead for now, brother, but this season is far from over. We shall see who wins out in the end."

"And how are you, little shepherdess?" He rummaged in his pack for supper as he spoke. "Tamar sent honey cakes. There may be enough to share, although I feel hungry as a lion tonight." He bared his teeth, gave a low growl, then chuckled deep in his belly.

Abba grabbed a stick from the pile of branches the younger boys gathered that afternoon and poked at the fire, sending sparks soaring into the sky. He continued prodding the embers until flames re-appeared, then tossed on several more logs. The circle around the fire filled as the other shepherds drifted in from the meadows. The men shared food and talked among themselves. I sat with my head down, listening as I ate.

Shemu'el sat opposite me, on the other side of the fire with his brothers and father. We stole glances at each other through the flames. He and his brothers talked and laughed, making me wonder what they said. Each time our eyes met he smiled. The fire painted a glow on his face and its light sparkled in his eyes.

The hungry lion shared Aunt Tamar's honey cakes like I knew he would. They left my fingers sticky so I walked down to a nearby creek to wash.

"May I come down?" Shemu'el asked from the top of the hill.

"Of course." The cold water made my hands tingle.

Shemu'el's footsteps drew closer, then he plopped down beside me. "You do not mind me being here, do you?"

He understood that as the only maiden it was sometimes necessary for me to go away by myself.

"Oh no. Uncle Chayim brought honey cakes to share. I came

to wash my sticky fingers."

He rubbed his hands together and grinned. "This is your first season with your own flock. You must be excited."

I beamed with pride. "Yes I am, thanks to you."

Shemu'el and his brothers each had their own sheep. He had been building his herd for several years in anticipation of the day he would take a wife.

"You give me too much credit, Rivkah. I did not rescue Liat. We drove the lion off together."

Shemu'el always said nice things that made me feel good inside. He never belittled me the way the other boys did. *Stay and talk some more*, my heart begged. Knowing the other boys would tease us if we were gone too long, I forced myself to say instead, "We should get back to the fire."

Shemu'el rose and extended an arm. His strong hand grasped mine and he pulled me up. He continued holding my hand as we walked back to the campfire. I imagined walking this way everywhere we went after we wed.

"As your herd increases you may want to introduce new bloodlines," Shemu'el said. "My brother Caleb has a fine new ram. He would let you use him if I asked for you. I watched the ram search out and mount some of our ewes; he is a very aggressive breeder."

My fingers quivered in his hand. "How nice. I will keep that in mind." Aggressive breeding was the last thing I wanted to discuss with Shemu'el.

Our eyes met in the moonlight. Shemu'el noticed my embarrassment and let my fingers slip through his.

We walked the rest of the way in silence. Oh, how I hated that ram of Caleb's.

Abba and I rechecked the sheep before turning in. Like always, groups of shepherds kept watch in shifts while the others slept. If a predator appeared, or anything out of the ordinary occurred, they would rouse the others.

Those on the first watch left for the field and the rest of us took our places around the fire. The flames danced in the dark as the men began chanting *Ma'ariv*. I tugged my fleece cloak over me for a blanket and tucked it under my chin as they sang our evening prayers.

Using my arm as a pillow, I watched Shemu'el through the flames as he arranged his bedroll. I imagined us snuggled together and sleeping in each other's arms.

Myriad stars spread across the heavens above me. An unseen weight pushed my eyelids closed and I drifted into a deep slumber.

~ 7 ~

"And an angel of the Lord appeared to them,
and the glory of the Lord shone around them,
and they were filled with fear."

— Luke 2:9

"Look out, a star is falling on us!" I awoke with a start and squinted into the bright light racing toward us.

Abba hunched beside me staring into the sky.

The terrified look on his face gave me a chill. What was happening? Nothing frightened Abba.

The light drew nearer, growing larger and larger, until it surrounded us. I scrunched between the other shepherds, making myself as small as possible. The other shepherds? What were the other shepherds doing clustered around me? When did they move to our side of the fire? What became of our watchmen? Why had no one sounded an alarm?

Too many questions. No answers.

Struck dumb with fright, we sat like statues, our faces turned to the sky. What at first appeared to be a falling star gradually took shape. The light came from the creature at the center of it. Placing a hand along my brow to shield my eyes, I squinted up at him. His light washed over us, pure and clear. Everything stilled as this powerful being hovered above us.

"Do not be afraid."

I cannot recall what his voice sounded like, or if he even had a voice. His words became a part of my thoughts without me knowing how. An incredible sense of peace washed over me, better even than waking from a nightmare in my father's arms.

The others felt it too. All around me people smiled and sighed in relief. We had nothing to fear.

No matter what happened, we knew it would be good. Just four simple words. This mighty creature had said, "Do not be afraid," and we cast away our fears as easily as one tossed aside their cloak at the end of the day.

We came to understand he was one of God's angels sent to bring us a message. I snuggled under Abba's left arm and stared into the sky. With my fears gone, I could now look up at the angel without squinting.

"I bring you good tidings of great joy, which shall be to all people," the angel said. *"For unto you is born this day in the city of David a Savior. He is the Mashiach, the Lord. And this shall be a sign unto you; you shall find the babe wrapped in swaddling clothes and lying in a manger."*

Then the night sky opened.

I gasped as more and more of these marvelous creatures poured out of the heavens as rapidly as barley kernels spill from a split sack. This heavenly host gathered about us, swirling above our heads, praising God and singing, *"Glory to God in the highest, and on earth peace, good will toward men."*

And then, as quickly as they appeared, they were gone. The sky closed around them and we were left in darkness, staring up at the stars in wonder. The night never seemed darker than it did after the angels left.

"What was that light?"

"We have seen the *Shekinah*, the Cloud of Glory," Abba said. "The manifestation of the Most High God."

"And those creatures of light were his angels, cherubim or seraphim perhaps," Shemu'el added.

Shemu'el? How could I not have noticed him beside me?

Everyone grew quiet, thinking on this. All at once the men looked at one another and cried in a single voice, "Bethlehem. We must go to Bethlehem. Let us go and see this thing that has happened, which the Lord has told us about."

The men scurried about gathering their things and preparing for the trip.

"What about our sheep?" someone shouted. "Shepherds do not abandon their sheep. Have we forgotten there are ewes in the meadow about to give birth?"

The men stopped in their tracks and cast questioning

glances at each other.

Yes, I thought, what of the sheep?

"We shall leave the sheep in the hands of the Lord," Abba said. "He would not have sent his messengers to call us if He did not expect us to go."

So off to Bethlehem we went.

When men are in a hurry they take long strides, making it difficult for people with short legs to keep up. The shepherds led the way and I ran alongside. Each time I stumbled in the dark Abba's strong arm caught me before I fell.

No one knew what to expect when we arrived in Bethlehem. The angel gave us no directions, yet somehow we knew right where to go.

We turned the corner of Bethlehem's back streets and found a man sitting on the ground blocking the entrance to a stable. He had his coarse traveling cloak wrapped around himself as a blanket and his back propped against the post which framed the opening. He reminded me of a shepherd keeping watch in front of a sheepfold. Seeing his head resting on folded arms laid across his bent knees, I assumed he dozed.

As we drew nearer, he heard the scuffling of our footsteps and stirred. Pushing aside the cloak gathered about his face, he lifted his head and studied our little band warily.

He rose, stretched and rolled his shoulders before untying the straps of his *tefillin*.

These small leather pouches contained verses from the Law. Jews tie them around their forehead and on their left arm near their heart in obedience to the Torah, which said, "bind the commands, decrees and laws of the Lord to your forehead and to your heart."

He had been praying, not sleeping.

The man stood and combed his fingers through the tangles of his beard, watching us as we approached. Though clearly tired, his dark, intelligent eyes remained alert. I knew just about everyone in Bethlehem, but not him. He must have come to be numbered in Caesar's census.

He held his large hands in front of him, not threatening, but prepared to defend if necessary. Defend what? What needed guarding in this little room attached to the back of a small house?

He moved to the center of the doorway. "*Shalom Aleichem.* Peace be unto you," he said. "What is it you seek?"

"*Aleichem Shalom.* Peace to you as well," Abba replied. "I am Yaakov bar Yonah, a shepherd." Planting his staff in the soft dirt, he grabbed it with both hands and gently rocked from side to side as he spoke. "These are my friends and neighbors, other shepherds. We seek the one of whom the angels spoke."

The man's eyes widened. "Angels? I do not understand. I know nothing of angels."

Abba and the other men all spoke at once, chattering in excited voices as they tried to explain what had happened in the fields. The bright light that surrounded us, the angelic being and the heavenly host singing, "Peace on earth and goodwill to men."

Then they told him about the message the angel gave us.

"We know only what we were told. The hand of the Most High urged us to leave our flocks and come to Bethlehem. We came without understanding why," the men confessed, spreading their arms in bewilderment. "Can you help us find this wondrous thing of which the angels spoke?"

"You have come to the right place," the man replied.

Recalling their fright when the heavens opened and the heavenly host poured out, the men shrank back. But their fears quickly gave way to excitement. Regaining their courage, they inched forward toward the doorway, stretching and craning to see. His raised hand stopped them.

"You must wait here," he said, courteous but resolute. "The midwife and the other women just left. My wife is feeding her infant for the first time. They must not be disturbed." He smiled and motioned the men away from the entrance. "Come," he said, "we shall talk while we wait."

He seemed most interested in hearing about what happened to us in the fields.

"Tell me again all you saw and heard," he said, squatting. His eyes swept across the men circled around him. "Omit nothing."

He listened, interrupting to ask questions from time to time. Sometimes he made reference to one or another of the prophets. As Jewish men will do, the shepherds all replied at once, each giving their own interpretation, telling what this rabbi or that rabbi once said.

When they finished with the angels he asked about their new lambs. Were they healthy? Was the lamb crop good this year? He was a carpenter, he explained, from the North Country, from Nazareth in Galilee.

Laughing and nodding, the men discussed the kind of things men always talked about, tools and work.

Then, from inside the stable, a baby's cry pierced the quiet night.

~ 8 ~

"And they went with haste and found Mary and Joseph, and the babe..."

—Luke 2:16

The lusty cry of the newborn echoed in the night air. The men paused, listened, then grinned and clapped the man on the back, congratulating him.

Everyone ignored me so I tiptoed away from the men and back to the entrance. And, since no one tried to stop me, I went inside.

The family's animals had been tethered outside and the room, which usually housed them, had been cleaned and prepared for these travelers.

A young woman sat on a blanket laid over a bed of fresh straw near the back of the stable. Head down, she concentrated on moving her newborn from one side to the other. Adjusting the child in her arms, she tugged her cloak open and exposed her other breast. She brushed his cheek and he latched on, eating as greedily as a newborn lamb.

Watching her made me smile.

When he finished, she rested him on her lap and adjusted her clothing. She patted his back until he burped and then nestled him against her bosom.

I crept forward into the circle of light surrounding them.

Her head jerked up. The crinkling sound of my footsteps on the straw must have startled her.

I lowered my eyes, waiting for some signal she was not upset with me for being there.

"Hello. Who are you?" She lifted a finger and motioned me closer.

"My name is Rivkah. Shalom Aleichem."

"And to you." She smiled. "I am Miryam. That was Yosef, my husband, at the doorway."

"The baby's father."

For an instant an unsettled look clouded Miryam's face. She

didn't seem to know how to answer me.

She chewed her lip as she thought. Then a load seemed to lift off her shoulders. "Yes," she nodded, "Yosef will be the child's father."

"How are you feeling?" I asked, noting the fatigue in her eyes.

"Tired," she said. "Tired, but very, very happy."

She eased the blanket back and let me see the baby's face. It looked pink and slightly wrinkled, pretty much like every other new baby I'd seen. I reached out and brushed back a few stray hairs from the child's forehead.

Miryam seemed pleased.

New mothers enjoy having people fuss over their babies. Every time I see a baby I always try to act like they are extra special. Even the ugly ones. Not that this child was ugly; it was the sweetest baby I had ever seen.

"May I hold your baby?"

My request shocked her. New mothers are always nervous about letting people hold their babies. Some sheep are the same way. They get very protective when they have their first lamb and try to butt you if you come too close. But, just like the ewes, new mothers eventually get better. Time passes and they worry less.

"Will you be very careful?"

A part of me wanted to tell her I knew all about newborns. I had handled more baby lambs than you could ever count. Pulled them out when they got stuck, held them up to their mother's teat if they were too weak to nurse and cut the cord for ewes too weak to do it themselves. Many a cold night a new lamb slept with me nestled inside my cloak.

Of course there were also the babies of the shepherd's wives. My younger cousins, Aunt Tamar's children, needed my help every day. But Miryam was new at this, so I humored her.

I sat down and scooted back until we touched. Then she reached around and placed the infant in my arms. The first thing I did was loosen the wrap and peek in to check. The angels were right. It was a boy. When I glanced back over my shoulder, our eyes met and we shared a smile.

Every mother wants her firstborn to be a boy. It pleases her husband. By Jewish law the first boy child belongs to the Temple. Yosef and Miryam would have to go to Jerusalem and make an offering to ransom him back.

I re-wrapped the swaddling and leaned forward, putting my mouth very close to his little ear, and whispered, "*Shema Yisrael Adonai eleheinu Adonai ehad.*"

She liked seeing me do that.

The Shema is the first prayer of every Jew: *Hear O Israel, the Lord is our God; the Lord is one.*

He squirmed and made a whimpering sound in his sleep. Thinking he was uncomfortable, I adjusted him in my arms.

Miryam reached around me and put her arms under mine to help support him. "Here," she said, "let me help you."

Imagine. She worried about me dropping her baby. It was easy to see how she might think that, but given a little time she would learn.

Together, we rocked from side to side. He snuggled against me and I sang the Jewish lullaby, *Lailah Tov Motek*, Goodnight, my darling. His little lips made sucking motions as he dozed.

Shuffling footsteps and whispered voices came from the front of the stable. The men had finally come to see the baby. Yosef and Abba were in the lead. When they saw me sitting with Miryam holding the baby, they came to a halt. The surprised look on their faces made me grin.

Eight days later, when Yosef circumcised him, they named their baby Yeshua. Since they had to make trips to the Temple to ransom their son and then again for Miryam's purification, they remained in Bethlehem. They may have intended to return to Galilee, but one thing led to another and so they stayed on.

At first they knew very few people, so each time Abba made a trip to Bethlehem I tagged along. He would drop me off at Yosef's carpenter shop to visit with Miryam and Yeshua while he conducted his business.

Times were becoming hard for Abba and me. We paid taxes and duties and road tolls to Herod each time we took sheep to Jerusalem, plus the poll tax, the annual Temple tax, first tithes and second tithes. We paid and paid until Abba's purse was nearly empty.

Raising more lambs seemed to be the answer. One *Shabbat* we asked Uncle Chayim to watch our flock so we could go to the synagogue in Bethlehem to pray about it. Red streaks filled the eastern sky when we left the house. We talked and sang Psalms along the way.

Some people at the synagogue gave us unkind looks and whispered comments about smelly shepherds when we arrived. You might expect that in Jerusalem, but not in a farming town like Bethlehem.

Many of the people in Jerusalem lived very well. They grew proud and looked down on shepherds and country folk. Annas, the former high priest, and his family lived in homes made of cut block, each stone polished until it sparkled. Their lavish homes crowded the hills west of the Temple.

I had lived with this prejudice all my life. When you are a shepherd, you get used to people not giving you any respect. The scribes and the Pharisees murmur we shepherds do not keep all the rules of the Law. Well, perhaps not down to the last iota and dot.

We were shepherds, not Pharisees, after all. We did the best we could. When I was alone at night with the flock under the stars, I felt as close to God as any High Priest ever did in the Holy of Holies.

Yosef and Miryam were at the synagogue when we arrived. I squeezed in beside Miryam in the women's section, wishing her *"Shabbat Shalom."*

I got to hold my little friend, Yeshua. He brought the toy sheep I made for him. I cut a scrap of fleece, sewed it and stuffed it with barley husks.

He shook it and said, "Baa, baa, baa."

I pretended to be upset and tried to shush him, but I secretly enjoyed it.

A few weeks earlier I found a burl on a branch that Abba pruned from one of our olive trees. While Shemu'el worked on his bowls I whittled at my burl, squaring the sides and putting a point at the bottom. It would become a *dreidel*.

After I smoothed it, I planned to ask Shemu'el to carve the letters *nun, gimmel, hay* and *shin* on it. One letter on each of its four sides. They stand for *nes gadol hayah sham*—A great miracle happened here. When my *driedel*'s finished, I'll rub it with some of Shemu'el's almond oil and beeswax finish. I plan to give it to Yeshua and teach him how to make it spin.

Abba made a special mark on the left ear of all the twin ewe lambs. When he decided which to sell and which to keep, he selected the keepers from among the twins. He believed that a twin, when bred, was more likely to produce more twins.

At the synagogue I asked the Lord to bless our flock and let every ewe bring forth two lambs this spring so we would have enough money to pay our taxes. After our visit to Bethlehem life continued in a normal manner for a time, then strange things began happening.

~ 9 ~
"Rise, take the child and his mother, and flee to Egypt,…"
—Matthew 2:13

A few weeks after we went to Bethlehem the first ewes began dropping their lambs. Perhaps the Lord answered my prayer. It felt like we were getting more twins than usual. Not all twins, though. Maybe I asked for more than we deserved.

It was the middle of Shebat, the month of spring lambing and we spent our nights in the fields, looking after the sheep from a watchtower. Being up high gave us a bird's eye view of the field. We could spot predators long before they threatened our flock.

Constructed of mortar and stones gathered from the surrounding fields, these round towers had a lot in common with our house. Both of them had an outside stairway leading to the top. It was flat, like our roof, and they each had a low wall around them so no one fell over the side.

I stretched to my full height and pointed north. "Look."

Together Abba and I watched the far-off silhouette of a solitary wayfarer trudging toward us on the south road. I rubbed my eyes and squinted at the dark image. A man led a donkey piled high with…well, he was too far away to say.

It surprised me to see a lone traveler. Long strings of camels often slipped past in the moonlight while we tended our sheep. Merchant caravans preferred traveling at night when it was cool, but few others dared be on the road after sunset. Even pilgrims traveled during the day and in the company of friends or relatives. Bandits lurked in the Judean hills ready to pounce on the unwary.

A full moon hung low in the heavens, shimmering across the surrounding fields. The sheep gathered in tight clusters along the grassy hillside below us. They shone white in the moonlight, reminding me of the limestone boulders strewn along the road to Jerusalem.

The high-pitched, cackling laughter of a hyena reverberated in the darkness.

Jerking up, I cocked my head and listened. An eerie

stillness settled over the valley, a tense waiting.

Abba tossed his cloak aside.

My heart thumped. I leaned forward and scanned the brush for movement. What else might be out there? Even after two years, I had not forgotten the day Shemu'el and I drove off the lion.

The sheep stirred on the hillside below us.

Abba pulled his *shebet* from his sash. The knurled piece of ancient grapewood bore the stains of many a predator's blood. He rocked it in his hand as he counted the shadowy shapes scattered across the dark meadow.

Everyone accounted for. He gave a relieved sigh.

Most ewes go off by themselves when the time comes to deliver their lambs. A missing sheep often meant someone was giving birth. We had to track them down right away because she could be in distress and need our help. Jackals, wolves and hyenas became more aggressive during lambing season. They often stalked isolated ewes, waiting to steal their newborn lambs.

Abba left to soothe the sheep.

I rechecked the road. The man leading the donkey had gotten closer. What I imagined to be his pack of goods turned out to be a passenger, a woman. He took quick, measured steps, checking the moonlit road in front of him, then casting furtive glances over his shoulder.

When Abba returned I pointed out the man's odd behavior. "He looks like he is running away from something. Do you think he is being chased?"

The man led the donkey around a curve in the road and headed straight at us. He spent so much time checking the road behind that he failed to notice us watching from the tower. Moonlight flooded down on him. His distorted shadow, overly tall and stretched-out looking, moved along the grass with each step he and the donkey took.

My heart leaped in my chest. I recognized them! It was Miryam on the donkey and her husband, Yosef, leading it. They should be asleep in their bed behind his carpentry shop in Bethlehem. What were they doing out here all by themselves so late at night?

"Look, Abba. It's my friends, Miryam and Yosef. Can I say hello to them?"

"I suppose it would be all right."

I skipped down the stairway and began pulling up handfuls of grass.

"What are you doing?" Abba asked.

I stooped for another handful. "Gathering grass for Isaias, Yosef's donkey."

"Yosef named his donkey, Isaias?"

"No. I did." Why explain about the jokes I played on Yosef by giving his donkey a different name each time I visited? I ran toward the road waving my grass and hollering, "Miryam, Yosef, stop. It is me, Rivkah."

Yosef made an unpleasant face when he saw me. He pulled back on the donkey's rope, bringing the little animal to a halt. Miryam whispered something to him and Yosef's shoulders relaxed.

"Hello, Isaias," I said to the donkey. I still could not believe they were so far from home. "What are you doing out this night?"

I scratched the donkey's long nose and fed him clumps of fresh grass. He seemed happy to see me even if no one else was. Isaias raised his sad, brown eyes and stared at me as if to say, "It was not my idea to be out late at night. I was happy sleeping in my stall until Yosef roused me."

In back, Yosef muttered to himself while he checked the baggage. He rounded the side of the donkey shaking his head.

"Why must you always call him names? The poor creature has a weak enough intellect without you changing his name every week or two. It confuses him. And calling an animal by the name of so great a prophet is disrespectful."

I grinned up at him. "Maybe I will call him Caesar Augustus instead." The donkey took another mouthful of grass. "Or perhaps, King Herod."

"You are a foolish little girl. If a soldier heard you say such a thing, he would knock you down and kick you across the street."

It was not like him to be short with me.

"It was only a jest. I meant nothing by it." Lowering my head, I offered the donkey the last of my grass. "Here, nameless donkey." I dabbed at my eyes and scratched the donkey's nose while he chewed.

"She meant no disrespect," Miryam whispered.

Yosef's mouth formed a tight line. "I am sorry, Rivkah. I did not mean to upset you. We are in a great hurry and must not be delayed."

The bundle on Miryam's back began wiggling and making noises. She gave Yosef a loving look. "You have had little sleep today, husband, and you are tired. Rest here while I feed the baby. We have a long night ahead of us."

He gave a resigned nod. Giving the rope a sharp tug, Yosef led the donkey over to the side of road.

Abba appeared over the brow of the hill. His eyes went from me, to Miryam, to the man leading the animal.

"*Shalom Aleichem*, Yosef. You appear to be a man full of troubling thoughts. Is all well with you this evening?"

Motioning Abba aside, Yosef stepped away from the donkey. They turned their backs to me and conversed in hushed whispers. Whatever it was that upset Yosef, he did not want me to know about it.

I walked around to the side of the donkey, looked up and smiled. "*Shalom Aleichem*, Miryam."

"*Aleichem Shalom*, Rivkah. Ignore Yosef. He thinks of other things tonight." She glanced back over her shoulder, studying the moon. "And how are you this night?"

"Abba and I are watching the sheep. Lambing time again." I rested my hands on my hips and gave her a stern look. "Do you know how dangerous it is to travel alone at night?"

Miryam chuckled. "Sometimes, my young friend, a person must do what they must do. Fear not, God is with us. Yosef plans to join a caravan along the way. If not in Hebron, then surely by the time we reach Beersheba."

"Beersheba? Why are you going to Beersheba?"

She nibbled at her lip. Miryam's eyes flicked to Yosef, still in deep conversation with Abba, then back to me. She shook her head. Her expression said she could tell no more.

"Did I wake Yeshua?"

"Oh, no." She loosened the strap and swung the cloth bundle on her back around to her lap. "He has been awake for a little while now making hungry noises." She folded back his blanket. "Would you take him for a moment?"

She handed him down to me. At eighteen months, Yeshua was much heavier than the first time I held him. Miryam no longer worried because Yeshua and I played so often at their home behind Yosef's shop.

Miryam slipped off the donkey's back and onto the grass. As she stretched, her eyes searched the moonlit road a second time. She made no attempt to mask her concerns.

The men squatted by the side of the road whispering and scratching lines in the dirt.

"We have heavy cloaks in the watchtower."

At the sound of my voice, Yeshua blinked up at me with a toothy grin. I lifted him up to my shoulder and kissed him on the cheek. He hugged my neck and said, "Rivvy," the way my little cousin, Yonah, used to.

I sat on my cloak and offered Abba's to Miryam. Yeshua and I played grab my finger while she loosened her clothing. I listened to her hum *Lailah Tov Motek* as he nursed.

"I wish I had a baby like Yeshua to feed and care for."

Miryam smiled. "I remember watching women nurse their babies when I was a girl and thinking the same thing. Your womanhood will come upon you before you know it. Then a young man will knock at the door asking your father if he can take you for his wife."

"I already know who it will be."

She arched an eyebrow. "Do you now?"

"He is very handsome."

"I am sure he is."

"And he is strong and brave and brings me presents."

She paused, trying to decide what to say next. "Rivkah, you and I both know the marriage arrangements are made by the men in the family."

"No matter. Shemu'el will be the one."

"And you know this how?" She switched Yeshua to her other arm and closed her cloak over him.

"Because I love him. Better a meal of vegetables where there is love than a fatted calf with hatred."

"Time will tell, my young friend. Time will tell."

"But marriages are *b'shert*. If something is destined by the will of God, it must come to pass."

"True enough." Miryam hugged me tightly and kissed my forehead. "Keep in mind, God's ways are not our ways. In addition to happiness, God's plan sometimes brings heartache and sacrifice."

~ 10 ~

"And being warned in a dream not to return to Herod, they departed to their own country by another way."

—Matthew 2:12

I held Yeshua while Miryam settled herself on the donkey. He grinned up at me sleepy eyed. Putting my mouth close to his little ear, I whispered the *Birkat Kohanim*. This priestly blessing was repeated many times each day in the Temple, "May the Lord bless and keep you. May the Lord cause his countenance to shine upon you and be gracious unto you. May the Lord favor you and grant you peace."

"May it be his will. Blessed be the Lord God, the God of Israel, from everlasting to everlasting," Miryam responded for her young son.

I kissed him. "Good-bye Yeshua. Be safe while we are apart, *Yeki'ri*."

When we first began playing together I called Yeshua *my little king*. After all, the angel told us he would be the *Mashiach*. Miryam heard me do this and asked me not to. She said Yeshua would find his destiny in his own way and time. From then on I called him *Yeki'ri*, my precious one.

I dug in my bag and offered her the *dreidel* I had carved. "Here, I made this for Yeshua. I planned to give it to him the next time I visited."

She thanked me and tucked it away in a saddlebag. Then she said something that sent a chill up my spine. "It will be good for him to have something that reminds him of home."

"Home? Where are you going? When will we see each other again?"

Some questions, it seems, get no answer. Miryam adjusted the slumbering babe on her back and nodded her readiness to Yosef. She waved as the donkey plodded away. "All in God's good time, Rivkah. *Kol Tuv*, my young friend."

I returned her wish to *Be Well* with a heavy heart. They grew smaller and smaller until they became a speck on the horizon. I leaned into Abba and he rested his hands upon my shoulders.

"Where are they going?"

"For Yeshua's sake, it is better that you not know."

"I do not understand."

He dropped to one knee and held me by my arms. "Yosef has been warned. The child is no longer safe in Bethlehem."

I looked at him with questioning eyes.

He shook his head. "I can tell you no more, my little dove. In time, perhaps things will become clear. For now, know this, you must forget you ever saw them. Say nothing of this night to anyone."

Though it made no sense at the time, as a good daughter I would do what my father asked.

He took my hand. "Come, time to check the ewes."

Hours later the sound of hooves roused me. I snapped awake in an instant, my heart pounding. It was dark and cold, the bone-chilling cold which came just before dawn. My cloak was damp, heavy with dew.

"Listen, Abba. Horses," I whispered. "Many horses, coming toward us."

He grabbed his rod from where it rested against the tower's low wall. "Stay here. I will see who it is."

"No. I want to go with you." I jerked my little rod out of my sash and rose, ready to fight.

He opened his mouth to speak, but shook his head and gave an angry grunt instead.

I followed one step behind. By the time we reached the roadway an entire cavalry had drawn into a line in front of us.

Never had I seen such finery. They looked like a royal escort. The war horses, one indistinguishable from the next, were black as night, sleek, broad-chested and muscular. Their harnesses, bridles and saddles gleamed with silver buckles and trim. Even their saddle blankets matched, deep blue with a white star at one corner. These massive stallions tossed their heads and pawed the ground, blowing and snorting.

Each of the riders wore a plumed helmet and a blue cape drawn around pure white tunics. Their heavy leather breeches extended to their ankles and an armored coat of silver scales protected their upper body. They carried a sword on their right side, holstered in a heavy scabbard, and a javelin slung along the horse's flank. A hammered shield, emblazoned with gold lions and eagles, hung from the left side of each saddle.

Farther down the road a group of pack camels plodded toward us. Three riders pushed through the formation of horses and reined their mounts to a stop. A uniformed man leaped off his horse and gathered the leads as the three men dismounted.

Instead of a soldier's uniform and armor, all three wore rich brocades and silks. Their tunics were long and loose, with gold tassels around the hem. Their purple cloaks were as beautiful as those worn by the High Priest. Elaborate turbans, each secured with a jewel, encircled their heads.

Our shepherd's rods were of no use against such an overwhelming force. Abba sank to his knees and bowed low. I dropped down beside him, quaking.

"Arise. You have nothing to fear from us," their leader said in heavily accented Aramaic. "We are on a mission of peace and diplomacy."

The man was tall and thin with bushy white eyebrows above his welcoming eyes. He towered above his two companions. I stared up at his gaunt, deeply-lined face as I rose and smoothed my tunic.

"Are you kings?" I asked.

He stroked his white beard and gave me a benevolent smile. "No, my child, we are not kings." He turned to Abba. "Pardon my rudeness. I am Melchior." He swept his arm in the direction of the others. "My companions...Gaspar and Balthasar. In our country they call us *Magoi*, the Great Ones of the Upper House of the *Megistanes*. We are advisors to Phraates, ruler of the Parthian Dynasty."

The man called Gaspar studied us for a moment. "You are

Jews, yes?"

Abba seemed to stand taller as he replied, "We are shepherds, children of Avraham who worship the one and only God of the universe."

"We came to your king bearing gifts," Balthasar said.

"You have seen Herod?"

"Indeed. We paid a courtesy call to Herod, the Idumean pretender." Melchior spat on the ground. "With his army away on maneuvers, he tolerated our presence and feigned hospitality. We expected little more. After all, forty years ago it was the Parthians who killed his brother, Phasaelus, drove Herod from this land, and restored Hasmonean rule. The only thing Herod hates more than Parthians is the thought of a rival to his throne. We found the king we sought, the true King of the Jews, in Bethlehem, not Jerusalem."

"Did the angels tell you where to find him?"

"Angels?" Melchior chuckled and shook his head. "No, my child. Not angels, prophets."

"Prophets?"

"Your prophet Daniyyel, the man Nebuchadnezzar renamed, Belteshazzar. He once held a position in the court of Babylon and is still revered by my people. His scrolls and others like it have a place of honor in the Royal Library. They foretell the birth of a King who will be your *Mashiach*, the Rock not cut by human hands. Our mathematicians calculated the dates and predicted his birth. Our astrologers studied the night skies." He pointed into the dark, pre-dawn sky. "We followed a star that led us to the babe."

I danced with excitement. He meant Yeshua. They had been to see my little king. "Abba! Abba, does he know—"

My father clamped his large hand over my mouth.

Melchior gave him a reassuring smile. "Do not worry about her unwittingly betraying confidences, my friend. We, too, have been warned."

My father's eyes sent the old man a message and he said no more.

All these secrets were getting worrisome.

Melchior dropped to one knee and took my hand. "You wonder why we have come, and I will tell you. There are still many of your people in our Empire, descendants of Jews who, many hundreds of years ago, chose to remain in Babylon rather than return to Jerusalem."

He lifted his eyes and gazed far off. "We are on a diplomatic mission. Someday this King, this *Mashiach* of yours, will crush all the kingdoms of this world. He will conquer not with war, but with peace and love. When he does, he will find allies among the Parthians."

"How may we serve you?" Abba asked.

"We planned to take on water and provisions at Jerusalem before heading east from whence we came. Our plans have changed. We will not be going to your holy city. Still, we must replenish our waterskins and allow our animals to drink their fill."

"My daughter will lead your men to water."

Melchior stepped aside and conferred with one of his chiefs for a moment. The man turned, barked a command in a strange language and the soldiers dismounted as a group.

As they formed into a line, Melchior said, "The Parthians and the Romans maintain an uneasy peace sustained by mutual distrust and our cavalry's consistent ability to outflank their legions. We wish to draw as little attention to ourselves as possible. Despite our worthy mission, Caesar would not appreciate so deep an incursion into his territory."

The chief of the guard snapped to attention in front of me. "We await your command," he said with a bow.

I pointed the way.

A long line of men, horses and camels stretched out behind me as I led them down the trail to the lake where we watered our sheep. Leaving them there, I traipsed back up the hill. The first rays of daylight were breaking over the peaks of the Judean Mountains.

Abba knelt beside the road with a soldier at his side. Melchior, Gaspar and Balthasar bent over with hands resting on their knees and looked over his shoulder while Abba scratched a map in the dirt.

He pointed in the direction of the rising sun. "Due east of here, on the other side of those mountains, is Lake Asphaltitis." His stick skipped over the long row of upturned points representing the Judean mountains and came down in the center of a large oblong shape.

"Do not go there. Its waters are dead. Neither man nor beast can drink of them. Pillars of pure salt rise from its depths." He raised his eyes to the man at his side.

The man nodded in understanding.

"To the south of us is Herodium, one of Herod's retreats. Here." The point of his stick poked into the dust, marking it. "It has a small garrison of troops." He moved the stick closer to Jerusalem and poked again, this time into one of his peaks. "Hyrcania, a Jewish city in the mountains. Best to thread your way between them. Here is the pass," he said, tracing a squiggly line between the peaks.

"Can a camel train make it through?"

"Some of the defiles are narrow, but they can advance single file. It is safe, there are no troops anywhere near there. This route will bring you out near the top of Lake Asphaltitis. Follow the shoreline north past Secacah, a peaceful community of the Essenes — devout Jews who spend their days in prayer and meditation. Beyond Secacah you will encounter the sweet water of the Jordan River. Perea lies east of the river, Nabatea to the south and The Decapolis to the north."

"We can retrace our steps from there," the soldier said.

He retrieved a quill and inkhorn from his saddlebag and copied the drawing onto a scroll. He handed it to my father for his approval. They rose smiling and dusted their knees.

"For your trouble," Melchior said. The gold coins he placed in Abba's palm sparkled in the morning sun.

My father contemplated them for a moment, then shook his head. "Thank you for your generosity, but no. Our Law demands we provide hospitality and assistance to the sojourner. I have done nothing to merit payment and we are not beggars."

"As you wish." Melchior returned the coins to his bag.

Turning, he said something in another language.

A camel driver rummaged in one of his packs. He returned with a large, square package wrapped in a type of papyrus and tied with twine.

Melchior removed a sword from one of the men's scabbards and sliced the twine. Motioning me forward, he leaned down and handed it to me.

Inside was the biggest block of Persian candy I had ever seen.

He watched my face light up and smiled.

~ 11 ~

"Then Herod,...sent and killed all the male children in Bethlehem and in all that region who were two years old or under..."

—Matthew 2:16

I pestered Abba to tell me more. Several days later, when Miryam and Yosef were safely away, he told me where they went.

"Yosef planned to hide during the day and travel at night until they left Gaza."

"Gaza? Where were they going?"

"Egypt. From Gaza they will follow the *Via Maris*, the road that runs beside the Great Sea, to Pelusium. Then around the Nile delta to Memphis, and back up to the sea at Alexandria."

This was awful. I would never see little Yeshua again if they lived in Alexandria.

"Why go to Alexandria? Bethlehem is nice enough. Did you remind him our people ran away from Egypt once before?"

Abba laughed and pulled me into his arms. "Do not look so troubled. Your friends will be fine. Alexandria is a great metropolis, second only to Rome itself. And, unlike Rome, almost a quarter of the Alexandrians are Jews."

"Bethlehem has nothing but Jews," I said, pouting.

"Be happy for them." He put fingers at the corners of my mouth and pushed up.

It was hard to frown when Abba did that.

"They will have a good life. There are many fine synagogues and much work for a craftsman like Yosef. Alexandria also puts Yeshua well beyond Herod's reach."

"What do you mean, Herod's reach?"

He brought a finger to his lips and shook his head. "Patience, my little dove. Patience."

Would the secrets never end?

One horrible day made it all clear. Yosef's fidgety behavior, his constant glancing back, Miryam's evasiveness, their whispered conversations with Abba...even the Magoi, made sense to me now.

Herod's soldiers began north of Bethlehem. They scoured the countryside moving from farm to farm, searching for infants. They came unannounced, stopping to ask for a cup of water, a handful of dates, directions perhaps. Once they received what they requested, the Centurion opened a conversation.

"Have you gotten enough rain?" he would ask. "How are the crops? Are your children well? Splendid! May I see them?"

Anytime someone presented a small child for him to admire, one of his soldiers ripped it out of its mother's arms and stripped away its clothing. They returned the girls without explanation and moved on to the next farm. They dashed the boys to the ground and ran them through with their *gladius*. One thrust of the soldier's short fighting sword ended the youngster's life.

Word spread quickly. By the time the troops reached Bethlehem, the town was in a panic. Too late then. The soldiers sealed all the roads so no one could escape. They beat mothers who tried to shield their children. Fathers died protecting their sons. After they found an infant hidden in a wheat bin, the soldiers ransacked every home.

"Go! Do not worry about your things, just leave," Abba shouted. He grabbed Aunt Tamar's hand and hurried her out the door. "There is no time. The soldiers could be here any moment, take the children and run. Chayim waits beyond the tree line."

My Uncle's family was the last to leave our settlement. They stayed longer than they should have. Seeing Abba so agitated made me nervous.

I tried to calm myself by sitting in the side yard and combing wool. I imagined weaving a new cloak for my husband, Shemu'el. And, though it shamed me to admit it, I took guilty pleasure in the knowledge that the soldiers were searching for infants. Shemu'el was safe. The thought of soldiers harming him would have been unbearable.

A dark shadow blotted out the sun. I looked over my shoulder and found myself eye to eye with a Roman Centurion. The soldiers had come to our settlement just as Abba warned.

He smiled. "How are you this fine day, little maiden? I see you are hard at work combing wool."

"*Shalom Ale—*" I stopped half way through my greeting. He was a Roman, not a Jew. "*Ave,*" I stammered. My hands refused to stay still in my lap.

"You need not fear me," he said. The Centurion squatted beside me and pointed to Uncle Chayim and Aunt Tamar's house. "Where is the boy who lives in that house?"

Fear rolled in my stomach. I began to shake. It would be easy for the soldiers to catch up with Aunt Tamar. She had my cousin, Yonah, with her. How could I save him?

"I do not know," I blurted out.

My hand was on the comb when I saw the flicker of satisfaction in the Centurion's eyes. In an instant everything became clear. He had tricked me into giving the wrong answer. In my turmoil I forgot that he could not have known a boy lived there. My answer should have been, "*No boy lives there.*"

Having talked with Yosef, Abba knew of the impending danger and warned our neighbors. Families with young boys abandoned their possessions and fled. The remaining shepherds divided their sheep and goats among them, each adding a few to their flock. Older women, well past childbearing age, moved into the deserted homes.

My foolish tongue undid all his hard work. Without intending to, I had betrayed my cousin Yonah. Sweet Yonah whom I loved dearly. A little boy who never hurt a soul would now die because silly Rivkah fell for Roman trickery. I buried my face in my hands and sobbed.

The Centurion grabbed the back of my garments and yanked me to my feet. "Look at me," he shouted.

Horrified at what I had done, I kept my head down. Tears rolled down my cheeks, making my nose run. My lips quivered.

He shook me until I looked into his face.

"Just as I supposed, a boy *does* live there. Where is he?"

"I do not know."

"Do not lie to me!"

He jerked me back and forth as easily as I snapped out a damp towel.

I continued weeping hysterically, shaking my head and crying *I do not know.*

Then I heard my father's voice ask, "Is this necessary? I understood you sought boys, not girls."

I collapsed like a pile of rags when the Centurion let me go.

"She refuses to tell me where the boy is," he said, pointing at my Uncle's house. He stepped toward Abba and took out his flagellum. The whip's metal tips clinked against each other as he held it in front of Abba's face.

Sniffing and hiccupping, I scooted along in the dirt. The effects of my blunder had spiraled out of control. Not only had I endangered Yonah, but now Abba might be beaten.

"What boy?" Abba asked.

He was so brave. As brave as I wished I had been. I curled up in a little ball, covering my face.

The Centurion pointed at my uncle's house. "The one who lives there."

Abba shrugged. "No boy lives in that house."

"You lie."

"I do not. My daughter is easily frightened and just as easily confused. You asked where the boy was, not if a boy lived there. She gave an honest answer. She did not know the family moved to Emmaus."

Lying on the ground, I watched the two men eye each other.

Hearing the commotion, Dinah, the old widow who temporarily moved into Uncle Chayim's house, peeked out the door.

Abba smiled. "A widow woman lives there now. Ask her yourself if you do not believe me." He raised his arm and motioned to her. "Dinah," he called, "this Roman refuses to believe that Chayim and Tamar moved to Emmaus. Come tell him so he will leave us in peace."

Beaten at his own game, the Centurion holstered his whip and stormed away.

Still sobbing, I ran to the safety of Abba's arms.

The soldiers who came to our little settlement, never knew that the birds had flown the coop. When the danger passed, our friends drifted back and their neighbors returned the goods and livestock they safeguarded for them.

King Herod had sent his soldiers to kill Yeshua. Unsure of who or where he was, they killed every boy child they found. Everyone mourned the loss of those innocent children.

We later learned Herod gave an order to kill all males two years or under. But the soldiers wasted no time counting birthdays, some boys as old as four perished beneath their swords.

~ 12 ~

"...for those who sought the child's life are dead."

—Matthew 2:20

They say bad news travels like wildfire. That day good news flew across the countryside as if carried on the wings of eagles. Herod, the king, had died. After reigning almost 34 years, he left this earth the winter following the massacre of the innocents, in the month of Tebeth. When the news of his death reached us, we danced and wept tears of joy.

Whether we rejoiced or mourned, we expressed our feelings through the Psalms. There was never a time I had not known them. My earliest memories consisted of sitting cross-legged with Aunt Tamar and my cousins, listening to the men sing. Their deep voices wrapped around me like a fleece blanket. Even now, the memory of those warm feelings brings me comfort.

We were moving the flocks to new pasture and, like always, sang Psalms as we walked. They were such a part of our lives that speaking the first line brought the entire Psalm to mind. If, for instance, I wanted to refer to Psalm 23, I could say, "The Lord is my shepherd; I shall not want." Everyone knew the rest.

It was a time of rejoicing over the death of an evil man, and Abba chose Psalm 36. "transgression speaks to the wicked deep in his heart," he sang, in his rich baritone. His voice seemed to float across the meadow ahead of us, spreading joy. "There is no fear of God before his eyes."

"For he flatters himself in his own eyes that his iniquity cannot be found out and hated," I sang in response.

Other shepherds joined us. "The words of his mouth are mischief and deceit; he has ceased to act wisely and do good."

Then Abba sang again. "He plots mischief while on his bed; he sets himself in a way that is not good; he spurns not evil."

When the Psalm ended, the men walked in silence. I listened to the bleat of the sheep and wondered what lay ahead for us now. The men turned to discussing Herod's sins. Horrid tales of the king's wickedness burned my ears.

Even on his deathbed, Herod's evil hand struck out. Four days before he died, he had his son and designated heir, Antipater, executed. The caravans told us Herod named another of his sons, Archelaus, to succeed him. They also said his sons, Herod Antipas and Herod Phillip, planned to lay counterclaims before Caesar.

These traveling merchants believed Caesar would decide who ruled the Jews. They failed to comprehend that God, not Caesar, determined who ruled his chosen people.

We came to a fork in the path. Some of us led our flocks to the right; others went to the left. We waved, knowing at day's end we would gather again. Beside me, Uncle Chayim sang the opening lines of Psalm 37. "Fret not yourself because of the wicked, be not envious of wrongdoers! For they will soon fade like the grass and wither like the green herb."

As he neared the end of his verse I glanced over at Shemu'el. Our eyes met and we nodded to each other. When the time came, together we sang, "Trust in the Lord, and do good; so you will dwell in the land, and enjoy security."

We expected better times after Herod died. Alas, the Lord willed otherwise. A fever pitch of revolt swept across the land like a summer sirocco. Herod's death did nothing to quench the anger over his killing of the men who pulled down the eagle from the Temple wall. The people petitioned his successor, Archelaus, to punish those responsible for their murder. Instead, he sent delegates to tell them his father had acted lawfully.

His answer inflamed the people. Their anger simmered like a covered pot until the Feast of Unleavened Bread. Then, with the temple full of pilgrims, it boiled over.

Abba and Uncle Chayim left early that morning taking lambs to the Temple. They were gone longer than usual. The afternoon waned, but still they did not return. I grew more concerned each time I checked the road and did not see them. Our little house felt emptier and emptier with each passing hour.

Supper time came and went. The sky began to darken and still no Abba. I sat on a stool wringing my hands and trying to guess what terrible tragedy befell him. Knowing that anxiety weighs down the heart, but a good word cheers it up, I put my supper in a pot and knocked on Aunt Tamar's door.

But she and my cousins had no good words for me. After we said our evening prayers Aunt Tamar had us join hands and ask the Lord to protect our fathers. "We will sing a Psalm to lift our spirits." She began, "He who dwells in the shelter of the Most High, abides under the shadow of the Almighty,"

We sang our hearts out, but our spirits refused to lift. Little Elisheva wept when her turn came. My lips quivered and I stuttered my way along, "A thousand may fall at your side, ten thousand at your right hand; but it will not come near you."

The next thing I knew, we were all hugging and sobbing, convinced something terrible had happened to the men in our family.

They returned the next evening, ashen-faced and exhausted, wearing dirty, blood-stained clothes.

"I knew it! I knew it," Aunt Tamar cried. She ran with open arms. "Chayim, where are you hurt? Come, let me help you."

His raised hand stopped her. "You must not touch me. Neither Yaakov nor I have injuries, but we are unclean. We will explain later."

They washed as the Law required and burned their clothing. They returned with hair and beards still dripping and told us their story.

"Mounted soldiers stopped us on our way to Jerusalem," Abba said. "They had blockaded the city and held us prisoner there with our lambs."

"Horsemen also surrounded the pilgrims camping outside the city, preventing them from going to the Temple," Chayim said.

"Why?"

"Some of the worshippers staged a protest. Archelaus panicked and sent in his soldiers."

"When did the soldiers release you?"

"As dusk came upon the land," Abba said. "It was too late to go to the Temple then, so we led the lambs to fresh pasture and spent the night with them."

"But you had no food or heavy cloaks."

My father smiled. "Do not worry, my little dove. We survived." He smiled. "See, here we are safe and sound."

"The next morning, hungry, cold and tired, we delivered our lambs," Chayim said. "The priests inspecting the lambs told us of the previous day's events, but nothing could have prepared us for what we saw."

Both men lowered their heads and beat their breasts.

"Was it bad?" Yonah asked.

Chayim sighed. "May you never live to see such a scene."

Aunt Tamar clapped her hands over little Yonah's ears. "Later, Chayim. The children do not need to hear this."

"Yes they do," Abba said. "Let them hear the truth when it is spoken. The Temple was in shambles when we went to the Treasury with our tablets. Bodies of the guilty and innocent alike still lay scattered across the Court of the Gentiles."

"It was awful." My uncle ran his eyes around the room, seeing it all again. He buried his face in his hands. "Women moved among the bodies wailing and tearing their clothes as they searched for their loved ones."

Tamar's hands shook, causing her to spill the wine she was pouring.

"Our hearts were moved with pity," Abba explained. "We stayed to help them search among the dead for their husbands."

Elisheva's hand went to her mouth. "If you touched a dead man, you are both unclean."

"Save those words for the Pharisees who tiptoed between the bodies with their cloaks hiked-up around their knobby knees," Chayim said. "We touched more corpses than you can count."

Abba read our shocked faces.

"Do not be concerned for us, my dears. We performed a *mitzvah*, a good deed. We did what we did, Law or no Law. How can the God who defends and sustains the widow not be pleased?"

While his countrymen mourned 3,000 dead, Archelaus and his family left Jerusalem and sailed for Rome. All of Herod's sons followed, each arguing their cases before Caesar.

No matter who won, God's chosen people would most certainly lose.

~ 13 ~

"This was foreseen by Varus...so he left one of those legions which he brought with him out of Syria..."

—Josephus, Wars of the Jews, Book 2, 3:1-40

"Is it not just as I said?" Even though the troops in the valley were half a mile away, Shemu'el kept his voice to a faint whisper.

"You were right. They seem to go on forever." What I saw frightened me so that I, too, spoke in whispers. "Who are they?"

Shemu'el and I lay on our stomachs at the edge of a bluff, hidden among the weeds and scrub pines. We stared down into the valley below where a thousand campfires glowed in the darkness. The pinpoints of firelight formed a precise grid.

"It is one of the Syrian Legions," Shemu'el said.

"Why do you think they have come?"

Muffled, disconnected sounds from the valley floor drifted up to us, the whinny of their horses, braying of asses, the clang of the smith's hammer against metal, an occasional muffled shout.

"My father says Quintilius Varus, the Governor of Syria, sent them. You know that with King Herod dead all three of his sons have traveled to Rome?"

Yes, I knew.

A sliver of moon shone above us. Watchers in the Temple had spotted the new moon just two days before. One of the priests blew the *shophar*, the ram's horn trumpet, and signal fires transmitted the message throughout the countryside. It was *Rosh Chodesh*, the first day of the month, of Sivan. The month of wheat harvest and *Shavo'ut*, the Feast of Weeks—Pentecost.

"Caesar sent a procurator named Sabinus to administrator Herod's domain until they return. I overheard my father talking with some of the other men. They think Sabinus is afraid the Jews will outnumber his troops during the upcoming Feast and stage a revolt. He petitioned Varus for additional men."

Transfixed by all the activity, we watched for several more minutes before slipping away.

We returned the following afternoon. All we saw were the

scattered remnants of their perimeter fences, a wide expanse of trampled grass and a grid of blackened rings left by their fire pits. The troops had broken camp and marched on to Jerusalem.

We stood side-by-side gazing down at this scene with no understanding of the events about to overtake us.

Over the next week the cares of day-to-day living pushed the memory of the Syrian legion to the back of my mind.

The sun was to Shemu'el's back and, when I stared up at him, I noticed soft whiskers running from his ear down along his jaw. Looking closer, I saw a shadowy line of dark hair bordering his upper lip. It was fitting for him to go to Jerusalem and present himself to the teachers, I thought. Truly, Shemu'el was becoming a man.

"The sun allows me to see your beard," I said, smiling.

He frowned. "It is as soft as down on a newly-hatched duckling." Shemu'el rubbed his hand along his cheek, then brightened. "But Yhonatan says that is how it starts."

"Before you know it you will have the luxuriant beard of a scribe."

He gave me an uncertain look, hoping my words were true, but not really believing them.

"I wish I could go to Jerusalem with you," I said.

"I do too, but they would never allow it."

"Everyone is giving you presents and I have nothing for you."

"Your friendship is worth more to me than any present."

An idea occurred to me. I did have something for him. Digging into my bag, I removed the *shrika* he made for me and placed it in his hand. "Here, take this with you when you are examined by the rabbis and scribes."

"You do not wish to have it any longer?" His words were tinged with disappointment.

"It is the most valuable thing I have ever owned. More precious to me even than Liat. Take it with you to Jerusalem. It will remind you I am thinking of you, praying for you, believing in you. It will be my way of being there, if only in spirit."

He studied the *shrika* for a moment then smiled and dropped it into the shepherd's purse. "I promise I will return it."

I started to leave, but Shemu'el's voice pulled me back.

"Rivkah?"

I turned. "Yes."

"Can I tell you something?"

Hour by hour, most of our lives pass unnoticed. Then there are those special instances when time seems to stop. When events rush in and change us in profound ways, transforming us into something, someone, we never were before. These are the moments we remember not for just a day, a week, or a year, but for a lifetime. I knew in my heart this was such a time. Swallowing my concerns, I nodded.

"I have always thought you were different from the rest of the girls here in our settlement."

Different? What did he mean, different? Aunt Tamar thought I was different. Simeon, Gavriel...a lot of people said I was different. My face must have revealed my confusion.

"I meant I always considered you very pretty."

"And I think you are strong and handsome."

What had I done? Without thinking I spoke the first words that came into my head. A young maiden was not supposed to be so bold in her speech. Blood surged into my cheeks setting them on fire.

He stepped closer. "I have imagined someday taking you for my wife."

In his eagerness Shemu'el, too, had spoken from his heart. I knew all about having a secret hidden deep within you. Sometimes it refuses to stay put. Words must be spoken and feelings shared.

Happiness washed over me like a mountain waterfall. Shemu'el wanted me just as I wanted him. It was not the childish dream my friends said it was.

"I have prayed you would."

Shemu'el made a clumsy, disjointed reach for me.

Frightened by what I knew was coming, I turned into a stone statue.

He grasped my arms and brought his face close to mine. His breath smelled of cinnamon from the spiced apricots we had shared at our noonday meal. Bending, he pressed his lips against mine.

Joy surged through me.

Shemu'el's lips were against mine for only an instant, then he whisked them away.

His actions left me speechless. Feeling his lips touch mine for even the briefest of moments made my knees wobbly. I leaned against him, resting my head on his chest.

His arms tightened around me in a hug.

I pressed myself against him, listening to his heart thump in his chest. When I lifted my face to look up at him, Shemu'el kissed me again. Longer this time. I attempted to kiss him back.

Shemu'el released me and took a step back.

I stared at the ground, nervous and afraid, unsure what to do or say.

He cleared his throat and, in a husky voice, whispered, "I love you, Rivkah."

I raised my eyes to meet his. "I love you too, Shemu'el."

We both took a deep breath. The tension between us drained away.

The first time, Shemu'el had not known what to do; the second time he did and I did not. This time, when he took me in his arms, we both knew what we wanted. We held each other and shared the lover's kiss Rachel talked about. A lover's kiss sweeter than any honey. A lover's kiss repeated over and over until we were both flushed and shaking.

This physical connection between us felt new, strange and incredibly exciting. Unlike anything I imagined. At last I knew what Rachel's sister, Nava, meant about a man making you weak.

I thought myself very womanly, with understanding in the ways of love. The coming years would teach me how little I had known of love...and life.

~ 14 ~

"Since therefore the Romans were sorely afflicted...they set fire to the cloisters...whereupon (they) were encompassed by flame, and many of them perished therein...and others dispersed by the terror they were in..."

—Josephus, Wars of the Jews, Book 2, 3:3-50

Shemu'el knocked at our door the following morning. I opened it to find him standing there with a grin and a new *tallit* over his arm. His father, Yo'el, and his brothers waited on the road.

"I wanted to say good-bye. We are leaving for Jerusalem."

"Is that the *tallit* you will wear in the Temple?"

"Yes. Imma made it especially for this day."

A few feet away his older brothers, Caleb and Yhonatan, frowned and pawed the ground like restless camels. The longer we talked the more impatient they became.

Ignoring their angry expressions, I asked, "Can I see it on you?"

Shemu'el unfolded the prayer shawl and kissed the *atarah*, the collar band, on which his mother had embroidered the *tallit* blessing. He held it above his head for a moment, eyes closed and praying, then draped it around his shoulders. He opened his eyes, blinking in the sunlight, and smiled at me.

I longed to tell him how handsome he looked wearing it, tell him again that I loved him, kiss him one last time. Instead, I said, "It is quite nice, just the right size."

"Imma worked very hard on it." He removed the *tallit* and carefully refolded it. He hesitated, licking his lips as he cast a furtive glance at his waiting family.

"Rivkah," he whispered, "when I return I will be a man. At that time I shall ask your father if—"

The look on my face stopped him. In some places girls were betrothed before their womanhood, but not in our settlement. Such an act would be highly irregular. Why court the wrath of our elders?

"I love you more than life itself," I whispered in reply. "But we must not speak of this now. It is too soon. We are both young." I hated myself more as each word left my tongue. Love and logic, it seemed, occupied different worlds.

"I would never do anything to draw shame upon you. All I need to know is that you will wait for me."

I stared into his eyes. "Shemu'el, I would wait for you until the end of time."

A quick glance at his brothers' angry faces told us our time together had come to an end.

"Well, everyone is ready to leave. I will tell you all about it when I return."

I leaned against the doorframe watching them walk away. Just before they disappeared over the rise, Shemu'el looked back and waved.

That was how I remembered him...smiling as he waved, his eyes bright and sparkling, a glow of happiness lighting his face. I grinned and waved, then turned back into the house wondering how I would pass the time until his return.

All the way to Jerusalem Shemu'el's brothers took turns testing his knowledge of the *Torah*—the Law, the *Nevi'im*—the Prophets, and the *Ketuvim*—the Writings. He gave thoughtful replies to each question they asked.

After what seemed like an interminable wait, the city finally came into view. The Bethlehem road circled the Hinnon Valley and deposited them in front of the Gennath Gate adjacent to Herod's palace.

The magnificent edifice, half the length of the Temple courtyard and equal to the city wall in height, now sat empty while Herod's sons argued over who would succeed the dead tyrant. Like everything Herod built, the palace was constructed of mammoth blocks of white Melekeh limestone quarried from the same caves where Solomon had gathered material for his Temple.

Once inside the city gate Shemu'el's party headed east, taking the most direct route to the Temple. When they brought sheep, they remained on the main road and continued around the Temple Mount. It was a familiar trek, one Shemu'el had made with his father many times. Past the Roman garrison, Antonia Fortress, then along the Maccabean wall, the city's northern boundary, and on to the west side of the Kidron Valley. There, near the Pools of Bethesda, were the holding pens where the priests inspected sheep.

The street they walked paralleled Jerusalem's original north wall. The wall Nebuchadnezzar's army leveled when they sacked the city and Nehemias rebuilt after the remnant returned from Babylon.

Shemu'el's group joined the throng of worshippers heading toward the Temple. By the time they reached the former Palace of the Hasmoneans the crowd's progress slowed to a crawl. Impatient, Shemu'el craned to stare over the heads of the crowd. He delighted in watching the river of worshippers thin as they flowed onto the tall viaduct spanning the Tyropean Valley.

"Look, Abba," Shemu'el said as they crossed, "we must be higher than six houses stacked on top of each other."

He glanced over the side down into the valley floor. At the base of the Temple Mount, eighty feet below, shops and vendor's stalls, sellers of scrolls, incense and souvenirs lined the busy thoroughfare.

He looked up at the Temple entrance and took a deep breath. At last they were here. As unbelievable as it seemed, his dream was about to come true. Shemu'el's excitement increased with each step.

He heard the hum of a thousand conversations buzzing around him like bees in a distant hive. Shemu'el and his father and brothers topped the stairs and crossed into the Court of the Gentiles. They had large crowds, on this first day of *Shavo'ut*.

The buzzing grew louder. Jews from all over the world had returned to Jerusalem for the feast. Shemu'el heard voices speaking a multitude of languages. The differing modes of dress and behavior astonished him.

He grinned, pointed and yelled something in his father's ear. In a crowd this size one had to shout to be heard. He cataloged every sight, sound and smell as they walked, planning to relate each detail to Rivkah when he returned. Shemu'el kept his eyes on their destination, the pillars of the colonnaded walkway.

Today, he thought, would be an unforgettable day.

The scene changed in the blink of an eye. The multitude of voices around him became the shouts of an angry mob. One moment Shemu'el, his brothers and father were walking across the crowded courtyard. The next instant they found themselves trapped amidst shouting protestors. The men around them raised their arms, clenched their fists and screamed curses.

Frightened people raced past them on every side. Shemu'el looked up and saw the reason. A phalanx of Legionnaires, arms drawn and shields raised, marched straight at them. The hobnailed soles of the soldier's sandals clattered against the paving stones like rain on a rooftop.

The troops collided with the mob. Slowing, but never stopping. They continued their advance, slashing and shoving their way across the courtyard. Panic rippled through the crowd as bloodied protestors fell to the pavement.

Shemu'el glanced around in terror. His brothers were no longer beside him. Where had they gone? He shouted their names, but the cries of a thousand strangers drowned him out.

Yo'el's hand closed around his son's. His father's touch gave Shemu'el the reassurance he needed. They must stick together; there was strength in numbers. He looked across the courtyard hoping to see his brothers. They must find Caleb and Yhonatan and escape this craziness.

A soldier bore down on them from the left.

Too late, Shemu'el shouted a warning to his father.

The Roman snatched the *tallit* from the boy's arms and tossed it aside.

Shemu'el watched it unfurl on the dirty pavement, recalling how lovingly his mother had sewn each stitch.

Then out of the corner of his eye, he saw the soldier's *gladius* slice across his father's face.

Yo'el screamed in pain and clutched the side of his head. Blood trickled between his fingers, painting red streaks on his cloak. He moaned and crumpled at Shemu'el's feet. A widening pool of blood formed beneath his father's head.

Trembling with fear, Shemu'el knelt and placed his hand on his father's shoulder. "Abba, speak to me," he begged. "Say something."

An approaching shadow forced Shemu'el to look up. Another soldier lumbered toward them, clubbing anyone who dared cross his path. Shemu'el threw himself over his father. The soldier looked down at him and laughed. Only then did Shemu'el realize that he, not his father, had been the soldier's intended target.

This was not the way things were supposed to be. They had come in peace, why were they being attacked? How could things have gone so terribly wrong?

"No!" Shemu'el screamed. He instinctively lifted his arm, shielding his face.

The soldier's upraised club became an approaching blur.

His arm exploded with pain. The force of the blow threw him back. His head struck the pavement and everything went black.

~ 15 ~

Abba called.

I hurried home, my eyes on the black smoke rising like a dirty smudge on the northern horizon.

Shemu'el's brother, Caleb, came down the path leading from our house. He avoided my gaze and turned away without acknowledging my greeting. He took several steps, then glanced back. Our eyes met. His haunted look terrified me. Then I noticed the bright bruise on his forehead…and his cloak. Why was it soiled and torn?

A pall of silence descended over the settlement. Children stopped laughing. People whispered.

If Caleb was here, it meant they had returned from Jerusalem. Shemu'el was now a man. The festivities should have begun. I baked a plum cake especially for his party. Why was no one celebrating?

I ran my eyes around the settlement looking for Shemu'el, checking every house, bush and shrub. Where was he? Fear clawed at my stomach. My mind raced. I looked again at the smoke rising on the horizon. Tears welled in my eyes.

My father came to stand beside me, his footsteps silent upon the grass. "Come to me, my little dove," he whispered.

My legs no long wanted to support me. I took a staggering step and collapsed into Abba's waiting arms. He carried me to the back of the house, sat me in his lap, and rocked me the way I rocked little Yonah when he fell and skinned a knee.

I took a deep breath. "Tell me. I must know what happened."

"Dissidents staged another protest at the Temple. The Procurator, Sabinus, panicked and sent in troops. The Romans set fire to the cloisters."

What did any of this have to do with Shemu'el? The cloisters housed the Temple's business and administrative functions. The Temple treasury and the counting rooms were there, along with the court of the Great Sanhedrin and…and the rooms where the scribes copied scrolls and…and… My bottom lip quivered. And the place where young men went to be examined by the teachers and scholars of the Law.

Shemu'el!

My lips moved, but no sound came out. Tears rolled down my cheeks. I sniffed and wiped my nose on the sleeve of my tunic.

"What happened to Shemu'el?"

My father held me tighter. "The boys became separated when soldiers parted the crowd. Caleb and Yhonatan were forced out of the courtyard and down the steps. Shemu'el rushed forward to protect his father. The last thing Caleb saw was a Roman soldier clubbing him."

His words made me shiver. I felt as if my stomach might be sick. "Please tell me they all survived."

"Yhonatan twisted his ankle when he fell on the steps. Until it heals, he must limp to get around. A soldier tore Caleb's cloak. They knocked him down and he cracked his head on the pavement. Yo'el was attacked with a sword. Kind strangers carried him to safety and a physician stitched the wound on his face."

I tugged his sleeve. "Shemu'el!" I cried. "What of Shemu'el?"

"The men came back for Shemu'el after they carried Yo'el to safety. By then the fire burned so hot that it drove them back. His brothers watched the roof collapse upon the dead and injured. The Temple cloisters sits in ruins, still smoldering as we speak."

The smoke in the north sky.

"No!" I screamed. "Do not tell me Shemu'el is gone. Tell me he is lost; I will search until I find him. Tell me he is blind; I will be his eyes. Tell me he is lame; I will support him when he walks. Tell me anything, but do not tell me that he died." I covered my ears and rocked from side to side. "Do not say those words; I cannot bear to hear them."

Abba's words had pierced my heart like a sword. We loved

each other. Shemu'el must not be under a building.

He planned to take me for his wife. Shemu'el must not be burned up to ashes.

Kriah symbolizes a heart ripped apart by grief. I grabbed my cloak and tore the left side, the side next to my heart. I had finished making it just the week before and wore it for the first time that day. Aunt Tamar would be displeased, but her displeasure meant nothing to me then.

"*Adonai natan, Radonai lakach. Yehi shem Adonai merorach*—God has given, God has taken. May the name of God be blessed," I shouted as the cloth parted.

Abba carried me into the house. He washed my face with a cool rag and laid me on the bed. I wept late into the night, wept until I had no more tears. He brought me melon slices when my mouth grew parched and swabbed my puffy eyes with a cloth.

Totally spent, I craved nothing more than dark, dreamless sleep. But that was not to be my fate. Demons tormented me while I slept. I wandered through dark passageways searching for Shemu'el. I called his name and heard it echo back at me unanswered.

Over and over again I relived Abba's words, watching Shemu'el fall beneath the Roman's club. I opened my mouth and yelled warnings that were never heeded. I ran to him, but could never reach him. The heat of the flames licked at my face, the smell of charring timbers filled my nostrils.

Each time, I awoke with a jerk to find Abba's reassuring hand on my shoulder.

~ 16 ~

A soldier noticed the boy quivering on the ground and snagged his injured arm. "Up you slacker."

Roused from his stupor, Shemu'el cried out in agony as white hot pain surged through him. His eyes snapped open. The Temple courtyard was in a state of panic. People ran past headed in every direction. Everything around him had become a jumble of fire, smoke and chaos.

"I'll show out what happens to Jews who defy Caesar's army," the soldier said, jerking him to his feet.

Shemu'el whimpered in pain and pointed to the ground. "Please, Sir, release me. I beg you. My father needs me."

The big man glanced down at Yo'el's unconscious form. He kicked him and, when Yo'el remained unresponsive, gave Shemu'el a push. "Too late for him. Now go."

Shemu'el scooped his soiled, bloodstained *tallit* off the pavement and hugged it to his breast as he staggered away with the soldier. Turning, he snatched a final, fleeting glance of his father. Shemu'el cradled his broken arm to his chest and stumbled over the bodies of fallen Jews, struggling to keep pace with the trooper who clutched his collar.

The man thrust him into the hands of waiting soldiers and left without a word. They pushed and prodded Shemu'el and his fellow prisoners along Solomon's Porch and out the Temple's north gate where additional soldiers waited. Forming a line, they passed the young men along one to the next.

First, they searched the prisoners for valuables. Rivkah's *shrika* tumbled out of his bag along with the few coins Shemu'el brought for his offering. A brawny soldier looked it over for a moment, then held it high for all to see.

"Toys." He laughed. "Our little man plays with a child's toy."

Shemu'el became their scapegoat. The other soldiers joined in, jeering and ridiculing him. When they finished, the soldier dropped the whistle back into his bag with excessive daintiness and tied it to Shemu'el's rope girdle. He gave him an affectionate pat. "We would not want you to lose your toy."

They ignored the tattered *tallit*. Shemu'el managed to stuff it inside his tunic as they shoved him along. A soldier reached to clamp his wrists into manacles, but stopped when he noticed Shemu'el's broken arm.

He swiveled his head, catching his superior's eye. "This one has only one good arm. No one buys a lame slave, better I give him a stiff kick and send him on his way."

"Keep him. Quintus must have known about the arm when he brought him to us."

The soldier locked the manacle around Shemu'el's right wrist, leaving the left side empty, then he hung a metal plate around the boy's neck identifying him as a slave. They chained the men in pairs and shackled each pair to the pair ahead. The line of prisoners grew, linked together like fish on a stringer.

When they added the last man to the chain, a mounted Centurion shouted, "On to Sebaste," and pointed the way with the handle of his whip.

The sad caravan lurched forward, stumbling north toward Samaria. Soldiers armed with *flagellum* patrolled each side of the column, eager to use their multi-tailed whips to encourage any whose pace lagged. And so, with neither examination nor ceremony, Shemu'el bar Yo'el became a nameless slave, a spoil of war.

Shemu'el stared straight at the man's back ahead of him as they marched. Had his father died in the Temple courtyard? And what of his brothers? Did Caleb and Yhonatan escape? They were not part of this train of human misery, that much he knew. He released a withering sob. In the blink of an eye he'd lost his family, his home and his dreams of life with Rivkah.

A voice beside him said, "I am Yu'dah, son of Jepthah."

Shemu'el glanced at the man walking beside him. He guessed him to be the age of his older brother, Yhonatan. His gray eyes remained on the back of the man ahead, never wavering.

Yu'dah spoke again out of the side of his mouth, his lips scarcely moving. "I come from Marisa. I am a metalworker."

Shemu'el knew Marisa. South and east of Bethlehem, it lay in a valley beyond the mountains that fed Solomon's Pools. "I am Shemu'el, son of Yo'el. We raise lambs for the Temple in a settlement near Bethlehem."

Yu'dah walked at a crooked angle and, at first, Shemu'el thought him lame. Watching his feet, he realized the true reason. Yu'dah did it to create slack on the chain that bound them, making it easier for Shemu'el to cradle his injured arm.

"Do your legs hurt when you walk as you do?"

"It is nothing," Yu'dah replied.

"I thank you for your kindness."

Yu'dah smiled for the first time. For an instant their eyes met and he said, "This chain makes us brothers. We have nothing but each other."

"Why were you at the Temple?"

"A group of us came for *Shavo'ut*." He made subtle motions with his head. "Ahead in the striped cloak is my friend, Gideon, a vine-dresser." Yu'dah's voice quivered as he said, "My wife, Salome, is heavy with our first child. Her time draws near, so I made an offering and prayed she would have an easy delivery." He gave a wrenching sigh and shook tears from his eyes. "And you?"

"I came to be examined by the priests, to become a man."

Yu'dah shot him a wry look. "You are a man now."

When they crossed the border, groups of Samaritans massed along the sides of the road, mocking and taunting them. They spit and threw spoiled vegetables at their traditional enemies, the Jews. Shemu'el and the others stared straight ahead as they marched through this gauntlet of abuse, trying to maintain whatever shreds of dignity the Romans had not already taken away.

The man ahead of them overheard them talking and joined

in. As the day wore on, snippets of conversation and shared confidences bonded them tighter than the chains.

It was dark when they made camp outside of Sebaste. The soldiers gathered around a fire, eating, drinking wine and laughing. Exhausted, Shemu'el collapsed in a heap, rousing only long enough to gulp a dipper of water when it was offered.

Each step jarred Shemu'el's arm and, by day's end, he'd taken thousands upon thousands of steps. With night came the chill. He hugged his broken limb and shivered uncontrollably.

"Come," Yu'dah said to those around him. "Our injured brother needs our warmth."

Chains clanked as men scraped along the ground creating the slack Yu'dah needed. He moved against Shemu'el, pressing his body to him. The man behind Shemu'el did the same. Nestled between them, his shivering slowed and then stopped. Together, the men whispered the *Ma'ariv*, evening prayers, then drifted into fitful slumber.

The next days passed in a pain-clouded blur, one the same as the other. They rose early and fought like dogs for whatever bread the Roman's threw to them. At the Centurion's command they plodded off, slowly baking under the merciless sun.

"I cannot go on." Shemu'el could barely speak. The sun was high overhead and his lips were cracked and dry. He raised his red-rimmed eyes to the sky. "End my suffering, Lord. Take me now to be with my fathers."

Yu'dah heard him and commanded, "Do not relinquish the gift of life so easily. You must survive." His voice broke as he shouted, "We all must survive. We owe it to those we love."

The men around him cheered encouragement.

Hearing the uproar, soldiers armed with flagellum rushed down the line. The soldiers would be upon them in an instant.

With seconds left, Yu'dah caught Shemu'el's gaze and held it. "If not for yourself, then live for Rivkah," he whispered.

The men had lapsed into silence by the time the soldiers

reached them. They strode past threatening and cursing. The metal tips of their flagellum clacked when they shook it in the men's faces before they withdrew.

Imagining Rivkah's kisses on his parched lips, Shemu'el lifted his head, threw his shoulders back and forced himself to take another step...and then another...and another.

Each night the Romans clustered around their bonfires enjoying good food, good drink and good company. Beyond those comfortable circles of light, wretched clumps of men clung to each other seeking solace and warmth among their peers.

They eventually entered the hill country of Galilee. Crowds gathered there, too, but not to mock. These were Jews and they expressed heartfelt sorrow for the men. When they passed Nazareth, the entire village paused to wail and weep and beat their breast as the men paraded by. Children from the village ran alongside, slipping into the line to hand the men small tidbits of food then scurrying away before the guards noticed.

"Where are we headed?" Shemu'el asked. The chewy date from the child's hand tasted sweeter than any he had ever eaten.

Yu'dah gauged the sun against the mountains. "We are heading northwest...toward the Great Sea."

The following afternoon they reached Ptolemais and followed the coast road north into Phoenicia. Two days later they stumbled into Tyre, hungry and shivering in the cold sea wind. The constant marching had left even the strongest of them haggard and footsore. All through the day the weaker ones dropped from exhaustion.

"Another moment's rest, savor it," Yu'dah said.

They'd grown accustomed to the chain's restrictions over the long march. He and Shemu'el rocked from side to side in unison like a pair of dancers, easing the kinks out of their tired muscles.

"*Baruch dayan ha'met*—Blessed is the judge of truth," Shemu'el said.

Together they bent forward, stretching their backs and legs, and intoned the prayer for the dead. Soldier's shouts echoed around them as they unchained the man, pitched him into the sea and re-coupled the caravan. Neither man rent his garment. With such a high attrition rate, doing so would have left them in tattered rags.

Each man tossed over the cliff represented a loss of potential income. The soldiers, accustomed to transporting battle-hardened soldiers, treated the young men as they would foes captured in battle. And now their prisoners were dying like flies, forcing the Centurion to institute a new policy.

The soldiers fed them well that night and housed them in a large barn. The walls broke the wind, but bedding down on dirty straw, amid animal droppings and vermin brought the prisoners scant comfort.

Shemu'el had just nodded off when the glare of a torch woke him. He blinked into the darkness, hearing the steady drip, drip, drip of water off the eaves and squinting at the shadowy figures in the doorway.

The man with the torch spotted Shemu'el and stepped over sleeping prisoners to get to him. He thrust the light close to his face, blinding him.

"This is him, the one you wanted," he said over his shoulder to the older man behind him.

~ 17 ~

I mourned Shemu'el as if I were his widow. True we were never officially betrothed, but in spirit we were. If he had lived, Shemu'el would have taken me for his wife. He said so. During *Shiva*, the period of mourning, I put ashes on my head, wore sackcloth, and went barefoot.

Abba gave me no more than a questioning look. He respected my feelings, even if most of the people in our little settlement thought I acted strangely. Let them roll their eyes and whisper behind my back. What did I care? I mourned the man I loved.

For a week, I spoke only when spoken to and grieved while I watched the sheep, weeping and wailing, "Ho, Shemu'el," again and again. At night I recited Torah verses on Shemu'el's behalf.

One day Sarit, Shemu'el's mother, called me over. "Come, my child. We must talk."

Sarit took me by the hand and led me to a quiet place. She ran her hand over my hair then rubbed her thumb and forefinger together.

"Ashes, Rivkah?"

"Yes, ashes."

She lifted the hem of my sackcloth dress. "And sackcloth, too. Why?"

"Because I mourn your son, Shemu'el."

"But you mourn him as if you were his widow. Is there something I should know?"

I gave her a confused look. "I do not know what you mean."

She rested her arm over my shoulder and leaned close to whisper, "This is not something a young maiden normally does."

"Do I dishonor his memory?"

"No. I only wonder why you mourn him as you do."

"Because I loved Shemu'el."

"That is all. Because you loved him?"

"Yes."

"And Shemu'el, he loved you as well?"

"He told me so the day before he left for Jerusalem."

Sarit ran her tongue around her cheek and stroked her chin. "And did the two of you ever act on these feelings of love?"

"Before he left for Jerusalem, after he said he loved me, Shemu'el kissed me." I bowed my head, staring at my bare feet. "On the mouth as lovers do. And I kissed him back."

I found a piece of loose skin beside a fingernail and picked at it. Was there no end to her questions?

"Kissed, and no more?"

Confused, I raised my head and stared into her face. Her gray eyes reminded me of Shemu'el's. "What else is there?"

"He went to Jerusalem to meet with the scribes and teachers, to become a man. You are a young maiden soon to be a woman." She lifted her arm, tossing her palm to the sky. "Surely you know what else there is."

A flock of little birds fluttered in my stomach. How could she accuse her own son of such things?

"No, never...never." I buried my face in my hands. "It was not as you imagine; Shemu'el wanted me for his wife, not his harlot."

"I imagined nothing, child," she said in a voice soft as rose petals. "When you have lived as long as I have you will understand that men are men and love makes women foolish." Putting a finger under my chin, she lifted my face and dried my tears with the hem of her sleeve. "You truly loved him."

"Yes. I truly loved him."

"So did I, child. So did I." She pulled me into her arms and hugged me close. "From now on you shall be the daughter I never had and together we will honor the man whom we both loved."

I called her *Imma Sarit* ever after. In time it seemed the most natural thing in the world. This was, after all, what I would have called her had Shemu'el and I married. How could I have known this simple endearment would return to haunt me?

I clung to my grief like a jealous lover. As time went on I felt my loss gave me nobility and wore my pain as a queen wears her crown. Abba was gentle with me then, much gentler perhaps than I deserved.

Many days I survived by pretending Shemu'el had not died. I would tell myself he went on a trip, a very long trip from which he would eventually return. Sitting in the shade of our fig tree, I narrowed my eyes and watched the road, imagining Shemu'el about to top the rise. I smiled and wondered what he would be wearing. I pretended to have anticipated his return and imagined my hair tied with ribbons, a necklace around my neck and rings in my ears, perfume applied to my neck and bosom.

He would break into a giddy run when he saw me. I would rise, smiling. And Shemu'el would sweep me up in his arms. Closing my eyes, I imagined breathing in the manly smell of his body. Then we would kiss as we had that day in the field, not caring what anyone saw or thought. We would smile and laugh again and lie on our backs staring into the sky and talk about nothing important.

Sometimes my fantasies seemed almost real. For that brief instant a tiny ray of hope lit my world before the darkness of despair returned to snuff it out.

When Imma died, they say my father nearly destroyed the left side of his cloak. A month later, as is the custom, he stitched it up. Even now, it is difficult for me to picture him as a young man who had just lost his wife, his infant daughter in the care of his brother's wife, sitting alone laboriously mending his torn cloak.

Abba once told me the tear in our heart never completely goes away. Like the garment, it too, can never be as it once was. He still had that cloak, clumsy mend and all, tucked away at home.

When the time came, I mended mine. I never wore it again. The cloak lies with my things, a reminder of what might have been. Another secret pain Abba and I shared.

Over the years, many of the shepherds encouraged my father to take a new wife so he could have sons. He always resisted. One day, as we ate our evening meal, I asked him about it.

"Why have you never sought another wife like Uncle Chayim says you should?"

He sat quietly, stroking his beard for a long time. A deep sadness crept into his eyes.

Seeing the pain I caused made me regret asking.

"Wives come easily to men of wealth and position," he said, at last. "But a shepherd's life is not an easy one. All I had to offer was hard work and drudgery."

"Other shepherds marry. You married once."

"True, I could have." He sighed. "But my bride would soon realize that my heart belonged to a woman long dead. Would it be fair to do this to the woman I married?" He looked down at the tabletop. "No. Far better I remain unmarried."

Abba's words brought both pain and comfort. I, too, had the thoughts and feelings he described. I learned then my pain was not as unique as I believed it to be.

"Do you wish we had a woman in the house?" he asked.

"Sometimes, but mostly I worry about you getting lonely. The Lord God said, 'It is not good for a man to be alone.'"

Abba gave the hearty laugh that never failed to fill my heart with delight. He drew me into his arms and kissed the top of my head.

"Ah, my little dove, there is no need to fret. I am not alone; I have you. The day your mother died, the light in my life went out. I felt certain I would never smile again. But you made a liar of me. Someday you too will laugh and smile again."

A good daughter believes what her father tells her, but that day I did not believe his words. How could it ever get better? He knew as well as I that even in laughter the heart aches.

That night in bed I asked myself why God poured out his wrath upon us? Was this what Miryam meant when she said, "*In addition to happiness, God's plan sometimes brings heartache and sacrifice.*"

But Shemu'el and I tried to keep the Law. Neither of us

were sinners. How was it possible to be so sure God smiled upon you one day, and be just as certain you were cursed the next?

I had begged God to make Shemu'el mine. Hearing him say he wanted me for his wife seemed the answer to my prayers. I even had names picked out for our first three children, two boys and a girl. A boy first because I knew that would be what Shemu'el wanted.

As foolish as I was, I assumed bad things only happened to other people. Evil people who deserved it. Shemu'el and I were somehow different. If you were righteous, the Lord gave you what you wanted. Or so I believed.

I knew better now.

~ 18 ~

The grizzled soldier thrust the torch close to Shemu'el's face. When Shemu'el tried to rise white-hot pain shot through his injured arm. He winced, hugged it to his chest, and collapsed onto the dirty straw.

"Why did it take over a week for me to hear about this?" the officer demanded.

The man groveled and muttered an indistinct reply.

Shemu'el squinted into the light, trying to identify the two figures hovering above him.

"Unchain him."

The soldier handed the older man the torch. Kneeling beside Shemu'el, he fiddled with the lock, fuming and cursing.

Shemu'el felt a hand touch his. He turned and saw Yu'dah lying beside him in the shadows.

"*Shalom Aleichem*, my brother," he whispered. "May the Lord smile upon you."

Shemu'el blinked back tears. "*Aleichem Shalom*. I will never forget your kindness."

The chain linking them dropped away. The man began work on the manacle around Shemu'el's wrist.

"Live," Yu'dah said. "Live each day for Rivkah."

"As you will live for Salome. May God bless her with a son."

Several hard twists released the manacle. The coarse metal bracelet had rubbed an ulcerous sore on Shemu'el's wrist.

"Get him out of this muck and into the air," the older man commanded.

The man prodded Shemu'el with a hard kick. Ignoring his pain, he clambered to his feet. His leg muscles, aching from five days of walking, knotted with cramps. He wobbled and stumbled in circles. The guard grunted obscenities under his breath and threw an arm around Shemu'el to steady him. They staggered out of the barn together like friends returning from a night of heavy drinking.

The guard fixed the torch into a holder near the doorway and left to continue his rounds. Shemu'el sagged against the doorway, gulping fresh air. The stink of the barn clung to him like a damp cloak. Gravity tugged at his weary legs and he slid down the post into a sitting position.

The older man watched without comment.

Shemu'el glanced up at him. He had short gray hair, clean-shaven cheeks and a large frame tending to middle-aged flabbiness.

He knelt and touched the boy's left arm. "How long has it been like this?"

Shemu'el jerked away. Throwing his right arm over his left, he spun on the ground and turned his back to the stranger.

"You must let me examine it."

"Your soldiers have done quite enough already." Shemu'el had noted the insignia of a Centurion in the dim light, though the man did not wear a soldier's uniform.

He made no attempt to reach for the arm as Shemu'el expected. Instead, the man took a step back and squatted, putting them eye-to-eye.

"My name is Evodius Scipio. I am the *Medicus Cohortis*, a healer. A guard, seeing your injury as you marched, requested that as physician to the cohort, I examine your arm. How long ago was it injured?"

"In Jerusalem...five, six...perhaps eight days ago." He shook his head, trying to clear the cobwebs. "I no longer know the days or hours."

Shemu'el's shoulders relaxed. These were the first friendly words exchanged with a Roman since the melee in the Temple. "I raised my arm to protect myself and a soldier struck me with his club."

"As I suspected. I treat many such injuries in battle." Using his own arm to demonstrate, Evodius said, "The forearm has two bones. One of them is broken here, at the point of impact. It is not too late to correct the damage."

The heavyset man placed a hand on his bent knee and grunted as he heaved himself up. He extended a hand and smiled. "Come."

The physician, Evodius, grasped Shemu'el's right forearm

with a firm grip and pulled him to his feet. He led him to the tent that served as his surgery.

"Atticus," he shouted, "we have our patient."

The tent flap snapped back and a round black face appeared in the opening. "The one with the lame arm?"

Evodius nodded and transferred Shemu'el to the younger man.

"He reeks," the black man said, blinking his eyes and wrinkling his nose.

"Indeed he does. Wash him before we begin."

The young black man, Atticus, led Shemu'el into the tent and positioned him beside a table. He removed Shemu'el's filthy cloak, taking care not to jostle his injured arm. He studied the dirty *tallit* wound around the man's rope girdle, then pointed to the cloak on the ground with a question in his eyes. Shemu'el shook his head and put a hand over his heart.

"You want to keep it?" Atticus asked, incredulous.

Shemu'el smiled for the first time. "Please. My mother made it."

Atticus folded the dirty piece of cloth and sat it aside. He untied Shemu'el's girdle, tossed it on top of the cloak and pulled Shemu'el's tunic over his head. Leaving his patient in only a loincloth, Atticus gathered the clothes and left without a word. He returned a short while later with a cloth and bowl of warm water.

Shemu'el protested when Atticus loosened his loincloth. Ignoring Shemu'el's complaints, he began bathing him.

Normally having another man touch his nude body would have been intolerable. Had Shemu'el been stronger, he might have resisted. But he was in no shape to confront anyone. He stood quietly, while the black-skinned man washed him.

Atticus opened a trunk and removed a new loincloth and a short, military style tunic. He dressed Shemu'el in clean clothes and helped him onto a table.

Evodius returned with a mortar and pestle in his hand. He scraped the powdered residue of the leaves and berries he crushed into a cup and swirled it with wine. After making sure all of the powder mixed, he handed it to Shemu'el.

"Swallow it quickly, before the solids settle."

Shemu'el gulped the bitter liquid, forcing it down in a single swallow. He screwed up his face at the wretched taste and gave a violent shudder. The undiluted wine burned in the pit of his stomach.

Evodius watched his reaction and grinned. "It may taste bitter, but its effect is a sweet blessing. It will put you to sleep while I re-break and set your arm."

Behind him Atticus laid out the bandages, tools and the other items Evodius required. The room began to sway. Shemu'el gave a frightened lurch. Atticus rested a hand on his shoulder and eased him back onto the table as he drifted into unconsciousness.

Atticus positioned the dozing patient on the table for Evodius as he had done many times before. As he did, he noticed Shemu'el's right hand curled into a tight fist. He gently pried his fingers open and chuckled at what he found. Men often slipped into the world of dreams grasping a ring, a coin, tiny statues of a god or goddess, perhaps some talisman for good luck. Instead he found a child's toy, a whistle.

Shemu'el woke to the smell of roasted meat. His eyelids fluttered, then closed against the light. He heard the indistinct sound of voices, punctuated by coarse laughter and profanities. Opening his eyes again, he stared at the orange glow of the goatskin tent stretched above him.

His left arm throbbed. When he tried to move it, he noticed an unexpected heaviness. Understanding seeped back. He recalled Evodius and the bitter mixture he gave him to drink. He felt his empty right hand against his leg and walked his fingers around the bed, searching for what it last held.

"Looking for this?" Atticus asked.

Shemu'el jerked at the sound of his voice.

He held the whistle he removed from Shemu'el's hand between his thumb and forefinger.

"I must have it. Give it to me, please." Shemu'el made a feeble grab for it.

Atticus took a step back and raised the arm holding the *shrika*. "You are not ready to be moving around yet."

He put it to his lips and blew into it, making it squeal. Chuckling, he threaded a thin strip of leather through the blowhole and brought it out the slot. After knotting it, he fit it around Shemu'el's neck.

"There," he said with a pat. "You have a new necklace. It will remain safe while you heal."

Mention of his injury drew Shemu'el's attention back to his left arm. It lay across his chest, swathed in a hard white crust.

"The bone in your arm had begun knitting itself back together. If it healed that way, you would have been a cripple." Atticus demonstrated by crooking his finger at an unnatural angle. "We re-broke it," he straightened the finger, "and put it back the way it should be." He flexed the digit into a right angle, imitating an elbow.

Shemu'el tapped the hard surface of his cast. "What is this?"

"Once we got the bones back where they belonged, Evodius bound pieces of a sapling to your arm and secured them with strips of cloth. Then I dipped more cloths in plaster and laid it over them, encasing the arm." He knocked a knuckle on the hard cast. "This will hold everything in position. After it mends, Evodius will break off the plaster and free your arm."

Atticus took a large square of cloth and folded it into a triangle. After helping Shemu'el sit up, he looped the sling around his neck.

"This will help support the weight," he said, knotting it behind Shemu'el's shoulder.

"Will I be able to use it? When he removes the plaster, I mean."

"Yours broke right here." Atticus tapped his own forearm midway between the wrist and elbow. "This usually fixes it."

Shemu'el raised his right hand. Several layers of cloth were tied around his wrist. "And this?"

"I applied salve to the open sore and bandaged it. Cradling

your arm while you walked created pressure points that festered. Expect to have a scar."

"You have both been very kind to me. Thank you."

Atticus accepted the compliment with a smile. "All part of the job. Hungry?"

He took a plate from the table and handed it to him. Despite the pain in his arm, Shemu'el dug into the food. "Where are we headed?" he asked between bites.

"Antioch on the Orontes."

"You make it sound like there's another Antioch lurking about somewhere else."

Atticus chuckled at Shemu'el's ignorance. "About fifteen more. Like families, nations develop a fondness for particular names. In their desire to honor a patriarch, a family ends up with fathers and sons, cousins and uncles all carrying the same name. Similarly, Seleucus Nicator, Alexander's General and founder of the Seleucid Empire, scattered 16 lesser and greater Antioch's throughout his land."

Shemu'el thought about what he said, then gave an understanding nod. "A bit like the Romans who have burdened their Empire with an abundance of Caesarea's."

"And as far as the arm goes?" Atticus said. "I am sorry to say kindness had little to do with it. You see, my friend, a crippled slave brings very little on the auction stone."

~ 19 ~

"This Caius put those that met him to flight, and took the city, Sepphoris, and burnt it, and made slaves of its inhabitants."
—Josephus, Wars of the Jews, Book 2, 5:1-69

Thoughts of Shemu'el never left of my mind. I saw him in the clouds drifting across the afternoon sky and among the stars scattered in the heavens at night. I had always loved looking up at the moon. Now when I stared at the moon, it kindled memories of the night we crept out to look down on the Roman encampment. How could I have known the same soldiers whom we watched would be the ones who killed my dear Shemu'el?

Liat also reminded me of him. Her name meant *You are mine*. He was mine too, at least for a short while.

It was the season of fall lambs, the month of Tishri, and Aunt Tamar released me from womanly bondage to stay in the fields. Because of the cold we dressed in heavy lambskin cloaks with the fleece left on and turned against our bodies for warmth.

My little flock continued to prosper. Three of the ewes among Abba's sheep were now mine. One, born the previous spring, was not yet old enough to breed. The other delighted me by producing twins. The third, and matriarch of my flock, Liat, had yet to drop her lamb.

"Have you seen Liat?" I peered anxiously into the clusters of sheep scattered across the dark meadow.

Abba pointed to our left. "She is over there."

A big sigh of relief. It worried me each time she wandered into the shadows.

"Could I have foretold the future," Abba said, watching me relax. "I would have chosen another lamb for you that day three years ago."

"I am glad you did not. When I look at Liat she reminds me of the day Shemu'el and I rescued her."

He grunted his displeasure. "My point exactly."

"Last week, when we were shopping in Bethlehem, I saw Shemu'el in the marketplace."

Abba looked surprised for a moment, then smiled. "And it turned out not to be him."

"No, it was not him," I admitted. "But for just a moment, my heart leapt with joy. Will it always be like this?"

"In some ways, yes. Do you recall how each spring the fresh pasture grows tall enough to swallow the sheep and billowy clouds move beneath the sun casting shadows over the fields?"

Yes, I knew.

"On such days a warm wind moves the grass, making it ripple like waves upon the sea. And when I glance across the field I sometimes see your mother rushing toward me with open arms. She is happy and laughing just as she was the day she ran to tell me she was with child."

He wrapped an arm around me and pulled me close when I sniffed.

"Such is the way with the dead, my little dove. The ones we love are never truly gone, they live on in our hearts. Memories of those we have loved sustain us, even while they haunt us."

"The Psalm says, 'Precious in the sight of the Lord is the death of his faithful ones.' Each night I pray the angels carried Shemu'el to Avraham's bosom."

"I'm sure they did. He was a righteous young man who obeyed the Law. I know you allowed yourself to imagine he would someday take you as his wife. It is a normal thing for a young maiden to do. And perhaps he would have. But he is gone now and dwelling upon things that can never be is not healthy. The time has come to put those thoughts aside."

Our eyes met.

"Do you understand what I am telling you?"

"Yes," I said in a tiny voice.

Abba smiled. "Good."

I forced a smile because my father expected it. Because it bothered him, over time I trained myself not to speak of Shemu'el. But inside, nothing changed. Thoughts of Shemu'el filled my heart and I continued to see him everywhere I looked.

Even though part of our beautiful Temple lay in ruins, the unrest continued. We learned of the next incident from Sidonius a few weeks later.

The goat kid bleated and nervously circled as I milked its mother. Releasing one teat, I patted his head. "Do not fret, little one. I will only steal enough for cheese. Trust me, there will be plenty left for you."

The far off jingle of bells caught my attention and I glanced up from my milking. A heavy-laden camel appeared around the bend. A plump man in a dusty traveling robe and elaborate turban rode toward me. One-by-one his caravan of six more camels, each linked to the other by ropes, came into view.

It was our friend, Sidonius, a Phoenician Jew and trading merchant. He and Abba were old friends. Sidonius insisted there was no better, or more tender meat, in all Judea than a roasted kid from Abba's flock.

He visited each time his caravan passed our way. He would purchase a kid, sometimes paying in cash, and other times bartering with us for the useful items or delightful trinkets he transported.

Hurrying to finish my milking, I untied the goat and patted her on the rump, sending her scurrying across the yard. I rose and waved.

Sidonius' dark eyes danced as he returned my greeting.

He waited while I carried my bucket into the house and strained the milk into a bag. After tying it shut, I tossed the bag's strap over my shoulder. Throughout the day it would shake with each step I took, separating the milk into butter and buttermilk. The next morning I would strain off the buttermilk and knead in a bit of *leban*. This starter turns the buttermilk into more *leban*. We eat some as yogurt right away. The rest gets strained through a cloth and hardened into cheese.

Sidonius' little caravan drew up along the road in front of our house. My younger cousins in the next house dropped what they were doing and ran to stare at the camels. He barked a sharp command and his camels all knelt. Heaving his bulky frame out of the saddle, Sidonius dropped to the ground.

"*Shalom Aleichem*, Sidonius," I said, as he shook the dust off his traveling robe. "Abba is just over the hill with the sheep. Shall I fetch him for you?"

Sidonius removed his plain traveling robe and tossed it over his saddle. Pulling a more colorful one from a saddlebag, he unfurled it and drew it around his shoulders.

"That would be very good." Sidonius patted his ample stomach and gave a deep chuckle. "You must know why I am here?"

We both knew the answer to that question.

"This whole trip my friends and I talked of nothing but the night we would feast on one of Yaakov's tender kids. But first..."

He reached into the one of the baskets dangling from his saddle and poked his hand into a sack. He approached me hiding one hand behind his back. Sidonius paused and looked down at me.

I lowered my eyes modestly.

"You have grown since last I saw you, Rivkah. You have become quite the lovely maiden."

His words caused my cheeks to warm.

"But you are not so old that you no longer like the sweets, hmmm?"

"There is nothing better than sweets."

He opened his hand revealing a chunk of Persian candy. Sidonius brings me some each time he visits. He knows it is my favorite.

"Is this meager offering sufficient payment for your work as my messenger?"

"Yes. Oh, yes."

I took the sweet from him and carried it over to my cousins. They each got a bite. I took tiny nibbles as I walked. It would have been easy to pop the whole thing in my mouth and chew it up in one enormous bite. Instead, I ate slowly, making it last and last.

Abba selected a kid from the flock and brought him forward for examination. "Satisfactory?"

Looking pleased, Sidonius produced a rope from inside his robes and fashioned it into a halter. As they turned to leave, Abba glanced back over his shoulder. "Rivkah, gather the flock and bring them back to the house."

I whistled for the sheep as the two men headed back up the path. They were so different. Abba, tall and strong, in his coarse shepherd's robes and Sidonius, shorter and rounder, in a striped robe rivaling Joseph's coat of many colors. The goat skipped along behind them at the end of Sidonius' rope.

My father took me by the hand before the dust from Sidonius' camels settled. "Come, my little dove, we must talk."

He had tears in his eyes. What could have happened to upset him so much? We huddled together beneath the fig tree and Abba repeated Sidonius' sad tale.

"I had hoped with Herod dead, peace would settle across our land. But pent-up anger burns in the hearts of many men. Our country remains a pot ready to boil. On the surface things appear calm, but underneath the unrest builds."

He stared at the ground for a moment, then took a deep breath. "You know Sidonius comes from the region of Tyre and Sidon far to the north beside the Great Sea?"

"Yes, Abba, I know."

"His route takes him past the town of Sepphoris, a Jewish city in Galilee not far from Nazareth. A group of Sepphorian dissidents led by a man they call Judas the Galilean raided the Roman arsenal. They drove off the troops and stole their weapons and equipment. With Herod dead and no successor on his throne, they hoped to rebel and drive the conquerors from our land." He shrugged. "A sweet, but hopeless dream, I fear."

My mind raced, wondering what tragedy befell the residents of Sepphoris.

"Word of their rebellion reached Quintilius Varus, the Roman Governor of Syria. He gathered troops from the surrounding territories and sent them to put down the insurrection. The rebels, of course, stood no chance against these trained warriors. As a warning to anyone else who might consider such an action, they burned the city. Sepphoris is no more."

"What of the people? All the innocent men and women and their children?"

"Gone. Hundreds and hundreds of people are gone. They were rounded up and sold as slaves."

Turning away from me, Abba grabbed the right side of his robe in his muscular hands and gave it a sharp tug. As the fabric separated, he cried, "*Baruch dayan ha'met*—Blessed is the judge of truth."

He buried his face in his hands and wept. My heart ached as I watched tears trickle between my father's fingers and heard his muffled voice intone the prayer for the dead. Abba had not been this distraught since the incident in Jerusalem cost Shemu'el his life.

Inching closer, I tried to console him by putting my arm over his shoulder and patting. "All is not lost. Someday they will be free again. By Jewish law they can only be held as slaves for seven years."

My father looked into my eyes and shook his head. "True, such a law affects Jewish slaveholders. But Sidonius said those who attacked Sepphoris came from Berytus and Arabia. These foreigners, the ones who carried away our kinsmen, are not bound by our Law."

I rested my head on Abba's knee and we wept together.

Many nights I woke from dreams of Shemu'el to find my cheeks damp with tears. After wiping my face with the sleeve of my gown, I would snuggle against Abba for comfort and try to go back to sleep.

I had a bad feeling that day when I saw the plume of black

smoke on the horizon. An inner voice told me it came from Jerusalem, that Shemu'el was somehow involved.

I often wondered, did Shemu'el struggle with the soldiers? Did he try to flee? Was he still alive when they threw him into the burning building? The thought made me shudder. What would it be like to have flames all around you?

Shemu'el had been burned at the Temple like the lambs we sold to the vendors in Annas' market. And like them, he was innocent.

Yo'el's face gradually healed. He said the scar on his face reflected the scar on his heart. Although I bore no external marks, where my heart once lived now there was nothing but sadness and pain.

They told me the fire left nothing but bones. A pile of blackened, broken bones. The priests prayed over them and then they buried them in a pit. Sometimes at night, when I awoke in darkness, I thought of Shemu'el lying in a pit amongst all those strangers.

Then demons returned to torment me and sleep would not come.

~ 20 ~

Shemu'el traveled the rest of the way to Antioch with Atticus and Evodius. He could not be sold until his arm came out of the cast, so he stayed on with them while it healed.

"Good news," Atticus said with an impish grin. He raised two fingers. "Actually, two pieces of good news. First, the plaster wrap comes off your arm today. Though I must warn you, it will look white and shriveled and the skin will peel. Start using it slowly, they are always stiff."

Shemu'el smiled. Without Atticus the adjustment to his new circumstances would have been much harder. Having someone close to his own age made all the difference and the dark man's upbeat personality never failed to lift his spirits.

During his convalescence Evodius assigned Shemu'el simple tasks in the surgery and *pharmacia*. He found the routine interesting and the hours passed quickly.

"And the second?"

Atticus grinned. "I believe Evodius has decided to keep you on as his personal slave. Actually, I am certain of it."

Shemu'el's expression did not meld with the other man's happy tone. "Being a slave is nothing to smile about. It is an atrocity."

"Is that so? Seems you told me the Hebrews were once slaves in Egypt."

"That is my point. They were and God granted his people freedom. I am not supposed to be a slave to anyone."

Atticus pulled a stool over and sat beside him. He peered over Shemu'el's shoulder as he worked. The job of maintaining the surgical implements fell to him since it was one of the few tasks a one-handed person could do. He washed them at the end of each day and left them on a cloth to air dry overnight. The following morning, he returned them to their cases.

He opened a case and began arranging the *specilli*, probes of various length and width. One-by-one, he placed them in the cloth-lined drawer. The *scalpri*, sharp surgical knives, lay one drawer down.

Atticus began pre-sorting the items for him to pass time. "I doubt that your god, or any other god, ever planned on slavery. Sometimes things just happen."

Shemu'el shook his head as he took an instrument from his friend's hand. "Nothing just happens. Everyone and everything moves according to God's almighty will."

"Very well, have it your way. Then it is the will of your god that you stay on with us. Either way, it is a good thing."

Unci, curved hooks for pulling muscles aside, went into the next case. Alongside them were *spatulae*, flat metal separators used to hold wounds open. In the drawer below were a variety of *extrahere*, V-shaped instruments for extracting arrowheads.

"And now I suppose you will tell me why my remaining here as slave is a good thing."

"No. I will tell you a story instead." Atticus jumped up and circled the room, rubbing his hands together in anticipation as he arranged his thoughts. "This is a story of a little, dark-skinned Ethiopian boy who left home early one morning with a jute sack slung over his shoulder and some of his mother's millet cakes in a bag. He walked into the mountains and began harvesting cinnamon stems, which his father would pound, peel and dry for the spice buyer.

Several members of a rival tribe, anxious to control the cinnamon trade, fell upon this lad while he worked and spirited him away. They bound him hand and foot and threw him in his sack. These scoundrels took him to the slave market in Axum. Now it just happened, or perhaps a god willed it, that a wealthy Egyptian by the name of Abasi went shopping that very day."

Atticus paused long enough to hang his cloak on a peg. Enthralled by the story, Shemu'el spun on his stool, ignoring his work.

"Abasi had particular notions about the type of slave he wanted. He preferred boys, the younger the better. You see, he bought them for his pleasure. Then, when he tired of them, he returned them to the auction stone and purchased a new plaything."

Atticus undid the leather girdle he wore and tossed it over

the peg. Shemu'el's interest in the story offset his reluctance to be in the room while Atticus disrobed.

"How could this man know whether a boy would submit to his unnatural desires?"

"He had no way of knowing. That is why Abasi kept a leather scourge beside his bed to encourage them when their enthusiasm lagged."

Atticus jerked his tunic over his head and turned his back. Shemu'el blanched when he saw rows of raised scars crisscrossing his friend's back. After giving Shemu'el sufficient time to examine his scars, Atticus pulled the tunic back down.

"Abasi may have been a brute, but he was not a killer. When the whip failed to elicit any enthusiasm in this particular lad, Abasi gave up and returned the dark-skinned lad to the auction stone. His life changed for the better that day for a Centurion took pity and bought him. This Roman physician treated his injuries and nurtured him, allowing him to earn his keep by running errands and performing other menial tasks. As the boy matured, he apprenticed him and instructed him in the healing arts."

Atticus stared into Shemu'el's shocked eyes. "Am I glad to be Evodius' slave, to serve a man who treats me more like a son than a slave? The answer is yes. Every day I thank the gods I am here instead of with Abasi."

He rested his hand on Shemu'el's shoulder. "Trust me, my friend, it is good news to hear Evodius has chosen to keep you on, very good news indeed."

Shemu'el returned to the instruments, his mood still glum.

Atticus noticed and asked, "They have slaves in your country, do they not?"

"Not like the Roman world, but yes, among the wealthy."

"Hmmm." The black man crossed his arms and smiled. He had made his point, won the argument. "Then I fail to see the difference."

"We have laws given to us by God governing the treatment of slaves."

Atticus rolled his eyes. "Why does this not surprise me? It

seems this Yahweh of yours has little time for anything else but making rules to govern even the most minute details of men's lives."

"Our Law grants a Jew certain rights even if he is a slave. For instance, if a man sells himself into slavery to pay his debts, he must be treated as one would treat a hireling. Slaves are freed after seven years of service. And, if a slaveholder takes a maiden to his bed, he must marry her."

Atticus stroked his jaw. Shemu'el's last statement intrigued him. "Suppose this slaveholder takes a boy to his bed instead? What must he do then?"

"He must leave town," Shemu'el replied. He dropped another instrument into the drawer and smiled over his shoulder. "If his neighbors found out they would stone him."

The last case held the items Evodius seldom used, such as *rhissagra*, the hooked forceps for extracting teeth and *trepannes* for drilling into the skull. The previous day Shemu'el had watched Evodius treat a serious head injury. When he saw the man's bloodied head, he tried to demur, but the older man insisted he attend the surgery.

He gulped and swallowed hard when Evodius took a *scalpri* and sliced across the man's scalp. Atticus stood on the opposite side of the table, firing questions at his mentor as he mopped away the blood and fluids that seeped out of the man's damaged cranium. Evodius drilled into the man's skull, inserted a pry and gently lifted the fractured bone.

Shemu'el watched in awe as the injured man's body relaxed once the piece of bone no longer pressed into gray-pink brain tissue. The Legionnaire's ragged breathing steadied and his limbs ceased their trembling.

Evodius watched too, smiling with satisfaction. He delegated the suturing and bandaging to Atticus and departed. The whole process left Shemu'el weak-kneed. As soon as the door closed he sank onto a stool and hung his head. Ignoring him, Atticus chattered excitedly as he closed the wound.

A hunting party bagged several deer on Mount Silpius. In thanks for Evodius' treatment several months earlier, one of the men gifted him with a haunch of venison. Evodius separated the leg from the tender rib meat, roasted the ribs with vegetables, and invited his two slaves to share the feast.

The three of them ate until they could eat no more. Shemu'el leaned back, watching the wine in his goblet spin in lazy circles. The flickering lamplight on the stucco walls of Evodius' quarters and an excess of rich food lulled him to sleepiness.

The other two men glanced at each other, grinned and patted their stomachs.

"A wonderful meal," Atticus said. "I will never have to eat again." Licking his greasy fingers, he tossed a well-gnawed bone onto the stack. The rib clanked against the pewter platter and settled into a pool of congealing meat juices.

Evodius cleared his throat, snapping both men out of their stupor. He stared across the table at Shemu'el. "There is something I have been meaning to discuss with you."

Shemu'el straightened on his stool and rested his left elbow on the table. He enjoyed the feel of the wood on skin that had spent weeks in a cast.

"Have you ever considered becoming a physician's assistant?" Evodius asked.

Atticus shot him a look of encouragement and gave Shemu'el a nudge under the table.

"No I have not, Sir."

Atticus' face fell.

Evodius chuckled. "An honest answer. Very refreshing." He glanced at the black slave out of the corner of his eye. "Surprisingly, some people have claimed it has been their lifelong ambition."

Atticus started to speak, then decided not to. He shook his head and waved the thought away.

Evodius laughed and pelted him with a leftover piece of bread.

"In my defense," Shemu'el said, "my father and his father's

father before him for generations were shepherds. I aspired to no more. However, I am not without experience. I have tended the sheep's needs when they are sick or injured."

"I invited you into my surgery yesterday because I wanted to see your reaction when I opened a man's skull. Blood and brains have a way of weakening some men's resolve."

"And did I pass your test."

"With colors flying. I have seen an *internus* faint at the sight of a man's skull being pried apart." Evodius nodded with satisfaction. "You also show a real aptitude in the *pharmacia*."

Shemu'el smiled at the compliment. "I enjoy helping Atticus compound the pills and tonics. And I find the plants interesting. A shepherd must lead his sheep to good pasture and prevent them from eating anything that might harm them."

"There are many jobs in Caesar's legions far worse than ours. Gruesome as it may be at times, I would rather put people together than rip them apart."

"I agree," Shemu'el said.

"This is not the type of work a man can be forced into doing. It takes hard study and patience along with a healthy dose of empathy. If it is your choice, I would be pleased to make you my slave and add you to my staff."

Shemu'el raised his cup in a toast. "Thank you, Sir. I would like that very much."

"And so it shall be. Henceforth you shall be known by the Roman name, Marcus."

~ 21 ~

"At this time it was that a certain shepherd ventured to set himself up for a king; he was called Athrongeus."
—Josephus, Wars of the Jews, Book 2, 4:3-60

We tried to tend our flocks and go about our lives. But, as Abba said, the country remained a pot ready to boil. Within a year of Shemu'el's death, the tension bubbled over in Judea.

The sound of running feet outside our window startled me. Excited voices of men, women and children resounded in the settlement. Shouts to hurry came through the open window.

"What is happening?" I asked when Abba ran in from the garden.

"Chayim said everyone is rushing to the glen. A great thing is happening. Athrongeus, a shepherd and a dynamic man, waits there to speak to us."

"What will he say?"

Abba dusted his hands and reached for his cloak. "Perhaps we should go and find out for ourselves."

The sloping hillside created a natural amphitheater. Athrongeus stood on the path, pacing and smoothing his beard as he waited while everyone found spaces on the grass. Never had I seen anyone so tall. He towered over every man in the crowd and his dark, deep-set eyes glowed with excitement, reminding me of banked coals in a brazier.

Once everyone found a seat, he pushed his sleeves up revealing rippling forearms and strong hands. His eyes roamed the crowd searching out the youngsters. "Who among you is the strongest?"

Every boy's hand shot into the air.

He grinned and scratched his chin as he chose. Athrongeus selected Hadar, a five-year-old.

"You," he said, curling a finger, "come forward."

With his mother's coaxing, Hadar rose and crept forward. His steps grew slower the closer he got. Athrongeus appeared less intimidating when the boy sat in the safety of his mother's embrace. Beginning at the man's feet, Hadar's eyes slowly moved up his tall frame. By the time he finished, his little head tilted back and his mouth gaped open.

This giant of a man smiled down at the youngster. He stooped, picked up a dry twig and handed it to the boy. "Can you break this?"

Hadar gritted his teeth and bent the twig with all his might. It snapped in half on the first try. He grinned and offered him the broken pieces.

Athrongeus took them and tousled the boy's hair. "Yes, he is indeed a *strong* boy."

Hadar swelled at the compliment.

The crowd watched in silence as Athrongeus examined the splintered ends. He held them aloft, turning so everyone could see.

"A single stick is easily broken, even by a boy. But could this lad break a bundle of sticks?" He turned to Hadar and motioned with his hands. "Go. Gather more sticks. Have your friends help."

Children scurried around giggling as they gathered every stick they could find.

Athrongeus' bundle grew larger by the minute. When he had enough, he produced a piece of twine from inside his cloak and bound them together.

He extended the package to Hadar. "Care to try and break this?"

The boy shook his head and scurried back to his mother's arms.

"What of you men? Can no one break this bundle?" He passed in front of the crowd extending it to each man with a questioning lift of his eyebrow.

Some of the younger men took his challenge, but failed.

Athrongeus put the bundle aside, apparently forgotten. Gathering his robes, he sat in the grass. He leaned forward and propped his elbows on his knees. "Truly I tell you, my friends, each of us is like that single twig. Alone, we are easily broken. Only by banding together do we become strong."

His fist shot into the air and his voice rose to a shout.

"Rome grinds us to dust like wheat under the millstone. God's chosen people were not created to live in bondage. Caesar and his puppets must be stopped."

He grabbed the bundle of twigs and leaped to his feet. Raising his bundle of sticks above his head, he shouted, "This bundle is Rome. And this is what I shall do to them." He wrapped his powerful hands around the bundle and snapped it in two. Scattering the pieces at his feet, he spit on them and ground them beneath his heel.

The people applauded and hollered their encouragement.

Athrongeus paced back and forth, gesturing as he lectured the spellbound crowd. "In the books of the Torah it is written, 'Their king shall arise from among them, and their deliverer shall be of them and with them. Exalted shall be the kingdom of the King *Mashiach*.'"

The crowd gasped. Had they heard what they thought they heard? Did this man, Athrongeus, lay claim to the title *Mashiach*? Busy conversations buzzed around me. Tingles of excitement swept through the people. Could it be? Could it be?

We Jews had been crushed under the boot of oppression for centuries. We endured wars and destruction, captivity and slavery. Yet each time the nation picked itself up and rebuilt, sustained by the hope of God's promise of the *Anointed One*, the *Mashiach*. Were those ancient prophecies at last coming to fulfillment?

Athrongeus' voice grew whisper soft. "I am a herder of sheep. A shepherd born in Judea. I come from among you; I am one of you."

He bowed his head for a moment, letting everyone make the connection to the prophecy he quoted.

"The prophet Ezekiel wrote, 'I Myself will bring near a child from the dynasty of the house of David, which is likened to a tall cedar, and I will raise him up from his children's children; I will anoint him and establish him like a high and exalted mountain.'"

He let these prophetic words sink in, giving everyone time to turn to his or her neighbor in agreement. The words of additional prophets rolled off his lips. His listeners sat captivated as he quoted Baruch, Enoch, Jubilees, Isaias, and Zephaniah.

Then Athrongeus paused.

The crowd leaned forward, eager for his next word. They had seen lightening flash across the sky, now everyone waited for the thunder. And it came with a crash.

"Is there anyone here who is not familiar with the writings of Ezra?" he asked. "He wrote, 'the lion whom you saw...roaring and speaking up at the eagle and reproaching him for his unrighteousness, this is the *Mashiach*.'"

Athrongeus knelt in front of me and took my hand. "Tell me, young maiden," he asked, "whose graven image, whose golden eagle, did Herod affix to the entrance of our holy Temple? Which empire did this blasphemous eagle represent?"

"Rome."

He dropped my hand, leaped to his feet and raised his fists to the sky. "Shepherds of Judea, I come before you gathering an army. My brothers and I plan to engage the enemy. Will you join us? Who amongst you will become part of my unbreakable bundle?"

"Me," a voice in the crowd answered. "And me," said another. Here and there, men leaped to their feet, voicing their desire to join Athrongeus' quest to overthrow Rome.

"I will," cried a familiar voice behind me.

I turned to see Uncle Chayim on his feet with his fist in the air. Abba also turned. He shook his head and snatched Chayim's cloak, jerking him back down.

Abba put his face close to my uncle's. "You will not do this thing, brother. I forbid it!"

Chayim yanked his cloak out of my father's hand. "I am not your child. I make my own decisions."

I watched in shocked silence. I had never seen these two brothers argue before.

Abba's voice softened. "I beg you, think before you act. Do not be so bold, Chayim. There is much danger here."

"I appear bold because you are so meek. Someone in this family must rise up and throw off the yoke Rome puts around our neck. I will, even if you will not."

"This can come to no good end. You are a married man with responsibilities, think of Tamar and the children. They depend upon you."

"If this man is the *Mashiach*, the Lord's heavenly host will protect them."

"And if he is not?"

Chayim left us to join the group of men clustering around Athrongeus without bothering to reply to Abba's question.

I watched him walk away knowing in my heart my uncle was mistaken. Abba was not meek; he was wise. How could Uncle Chayim not see the wisdom of my father's words?

~ 22 ~

Several months after Marcus' apprenticeship began a soldier came to their surgery soliciting Evodius' aid.

"I know you are busy, Sir," the soldier said, bowing, "and I regret bothering you. Perhaps you remember me asking your advice for my son. He was hunting with his older brother and received a gash on his foot. We bandaged it as you suggested, but it throbs and festers. I could not bring him to you; he can no longer walk upon it."

"I will come see him later today along with my assistants," Evodius said.

The three men rode in a carriage along Antioch's main thoroughfare, the *Via Caesarea*. Marcus had not ventured beyond the walls of the Citadel, the base camp of *Legio XII Fulminata,* since his arrival. This was his first view of Antioch in the daylight and he stared, eagerly taking in the new sights.

Evodius guided the horse onto the street of Herod and Tiberius, heading toward the city's eastern entrance. He made a final turn. Their path now paralleled the Wall of Justinian. A short time later, Evodius reined the horse to a stop beside the wide stone-paved plaza that formed the city's marketplace.

"It is not far now," he said. "We will do better on foot."

Atticus loosened the *loculus* stored behind their seat while Evodius secured the horse's lead to a hitching post. These leather traveling bags carried tools, equipment and extra clothing when the army was on the march. They had brass rings at each corner allowing the quartermasters to secure them to the baggage carts.

Atticus heaved the bag out of the wagon. Inside, medical instruments clinked and jangled. Since his arm was fresh out of the cast, Marcus carried a lighter satchel containing healing salves, medicines and extracts.

Stalls and stands were clustered between the columns that defined the perimeter of the spacious courtyard. Hungry buyers lingered in front of a row of smoking braziers. A round little man in a grease-stained apron scurried around flipping skewers of marinated venison, beef and goat's meat over charcoal fires.

An enterprising seller of wine had located his stall next to the one selling meat. Skins of wine, soaked in water to cool by evaporation, hung dripping in the shade of his awning.

From long habit Evodius pressed forward, ignoring the people crowded around the stands. Shoppers fell back at the sight of the Legio's insignia, creating space for the men to pass. With the crowd and smoking braziers at their back, the three of them entered the open courtyard.

Evodius led the way and Atticus and Marcus fell into formation behind him. Their hobnailed sandals clattered in unison against the paving stones as they crossed with long strides.

A raised block of stone stood at the center of the court. Men milled around it six deep, nudging and shoving for position. One glance showed Marcus the reason for their interest. A lovely young woman stood on the sale block. Beside her, a shouting auctioneer solicited bids from the crowd.

She had dark hair and crisp, sculpted features. She must be a Jew like himself, Marcus decided. Her skin appeared too dark for a Greek. Hands bound and head bowed, she quietly wept. No veil covered her hair and no clothing covered her nakedness.

Though he knew he should not, Marcus stopped and stared.

Evodius continued on without him for several steps before realizing his newest apprentice had abandoned him. The older man retraced his steps and rested a hand on Marcus' shoulder.

"Quite the beauty, heh?" Evodius whispered.

Marcus blushed and mumbled apologies for his behavior.

"Have you never seen a slave market before?"

Marcus admitted he had not. Because of his broken limb, he had gone from prisoner to slave in a private transaction. He felt his anger rise when the auctioneer prodded the girl with a stick, forcing her to turn as if she were a donkey. The crowd of men responded with hoots of appreciation.

Evodius gave a manly chuckle. "I wager there are some

other things you have never seen as well." He pointed over the stalls that lined the far side of the square to a two-story, whitewashed building with red tile roof. "You will find me in that row of apartments there," he said. "Stay if you wish. Enjoy the diversion she provides."

Marcus fell back in step. "No. I sin when I look upon her with lust."

They had nearly crossed the square by the time the auctioneer completed the sale. He delivered the girl to a buyer who, to everyone's disappointment, threw his cloak around her.

It was then that Marcus noticed a line of men waiting their turn on the block. His eyes were drawn to a tall man shackled hand and foot. Though his face bore several bruises and one eye had swollen shut, Yu'dah stood straight and tall, head high.

Marcus grabbed Evodius' arm. "Wait."

The physician looked back in anger. "The girl is gone. What is it you want."

"Please, can we stay?"

"I came to lance a foot, not gawk at slaves."

Marcus pointed. "That man, could the Legion buy him?"

Seeing the chains, Evodius shook his head. "I want nothing to do with that scoundrel."

"You are mistaken."

Evodius' expression hardened. "I think not. Only a troublemaker comes to the block in shackles."

"But I know him," Marcus pleaded. "He was a prisoner from Judea like me...a God-fearing man, a skilled metalworker. Surely the Twelfth Legion could use such a man."

"I do not tell the *Legatus* how to run his army, just as he does not tell me how to run my surgery."

"Then buy him yourself." Marcus' voice betrayed his growing desperation. "I swear you will never regret it."

"I require only two slaves, which I already have."

Marcus tightened his grip on Evodius' sleeve, preventing him from leaving. "I beg you. Do not let them sell him to someone who will further abuse him. He deserves better."

"Deserves?" Evodius laughed. "A slave deserves nothing

save what is given to him."

Marcus' chin dropped to his chest. "Is there no way I can convince you to ransom him?"

"Very well," Evodius said. "Since it so important to you that this man be a physician's slave, we will arrange it. I require just two slaves, so he shall become my apprentice and you can stand on the block in his stead."

Dumbfounded, Marcus stared at Evodius' back as he stormed away. Then his eyes returned to Yu'dah. Fate and Roman chains had forever linked their destinies. He might well have been one of those the soldiers pitched into the sea were it not for Yu'dah's continuing encouragement.

He buried his face in his hands and prayed. Lifting his eyes, Marcus glanced at his friend again. He owed Yu'dah his life; was he now being asked to give his in repayment?

In a strange twist of fate, it occurred to Marcus that he probably owed his life to Evodius as well. Two men, the same debt. One he loved. The other, at that moment, he hated.

A grim expression hardened Marcus's face. Only a sadist would require someone to make the choice Evodius suggested. To even consider it bordered on insanity. He wanted him to negotiate a deal with the Devil.

Yet how could he live with himself if he deserted his friend...his brother?

~ 23 ~

"...while he did himself act like a king...and at this time put a diadem above his head...and became their leader killing both the Romans and those of the king's party, nor did any Jew escape him, if any gain could accrue to him thereby."
— Josephus, Wars of the Jews, Book 2, 4:3-62

Athrongeus' army of dissident Jews overwhelmed Herod's guards and the Roman soldiers garrisoned at Jerusalem. When the soldiers retreated, they claimed the city.

"What do you have to say of Athrongeus now, Yaakov?"

Home from Jerusalem and flush with victory, Uncle Chayim was in a gloating mood. He watched Abba's jaw tighten, took a sip of wine, and chuckled deep in his belly.

"No more sheep for me," Chayim said, swirling his cup. "I am captain over fifty men. I have earned a place of honor in the new kingdom."

My father stared at his food, saying nothing. He took a loaf into his hands and tore it apart, sending crumbs flying.

Chayim smiled and patted my head. "I remembered you, little one."

He dug in his purse and handed me a child's necklace, gold with polished stones that changed colors when turned in the light.

"They are called opals," he explained. "It came from Mariamne's palace. Perhaps it was worn by one of Herod's granddaughters, a Hasmonean princess." My uncle winked. "I appropriated it for you."

Abba snatched it from my palm before I could say a word and threw it back at his brother. "We have no need of your spoils. Speak the truth. Or have you forgotten how? You *stole* it for her. A greedy man brings nothing but trouble to his family."

Ignoring Abba's outburst, my uncle gathered the children around him in a circle. "I wish you could have been there. Herod's troops fled before us like frightened hens." His face crinkled into a smile and his hand swept out in a wide circle.

"Afterwards all of Jerusalem assembled in the Temple court waving palms and shouting praises. Trumpets blew, cymbals rang, and the priests burned great amounts of incense. We marched through the Temple gates in a line, the footmen first, then the captains. And, finally, proud as David before the ark, Athrongeus himself. Jerusalem's conqueror wore a purple robe embroidered with gold thread and a diadem upon his head."

"Where did he get such riches, Abba?" my cousin, Elisheva, asked.

Her father laughed. "From Herod's palace, of course. Athrongeus is now the king."

"King of what?" My father snorted. "King of the Temple court?"

"He is King of all Israel and Judea, King of the Jews."

"Holding Jerusalem does not a king make," Abba laughed. "If you doubt my words, ask Absalom."

As the moon rose that evening I heard my father and his brother arguing in the garden. I crept across the dark house and knelt beside the window, silent as a mouse.

"Athrongeus asked you to rout the Romans from Jerusalem," Abba said. "You have done what he requested. Let him keep his diadems and purple robes. Come home where you belong, where you are needed and loved."

"Listen to yourself, Yaakov. Your timidity has become so ingrained that nothing but meekness comes off your tongue." I heard the pride in my uncle's voice when he said, "Athrongeus made me captain over fifty men. Jerusalem is only the start. There are more battles to be fought, victories yet to be won."

"True enough, but who will win them, Athrongeus' army or the Romans?"

Chayim's laughter came easily that night. "Do not speak of what you do not know, my brother."

"I know this night I am thankful our father rests in his grave. Better he sleep with the dead than witness his son's folly."

"You can no more speak for our father than you can speak for me." I heard a rustling as Uncle Chayim hefted his traveling bag onto his shoulder. "It is time for me to be on my way."

There were tears in Abba's voice. "Chayim wait," he begged. Listen to me. The same womb birthed us both. Your blood runs in my veins and mine in yours. I speak to you as only a brother can. Put aside this foolish scheme before it consumes you. Do not leave your wife a widow."

I listened to Uncle Chayim's angry footsteps as he stomped away and heard my father whisper. "*Shalom Aleichem,* my dear brother. May the Lord cure you of this madness before it is too late."

Having seized Jerusalem, Athrongeus and his brothers seemed at a loss as to what to do next. Meanwhile, the Romans regrouped in the north and west, leaving no one to police the countryside. Robbers, thieves and mischief-makers took control of Judea. Roving bands of criminals raided people's homes and stole their belongings claiming they were collecting taxes for King Athrongeus.

The shepherds in our little settlement took to pasturing their flocks far from home. Abba combined Chayim's flock with ours and led the sheep into the mountains near Solomon's Pools, the reservoirs that fed Jerusalem's aqueducts. He forbade me to go to the fields with him, saying it was not safe. I remained at home by myself doing womanly chores and listening to Aunt Tamar's laments.

Some things make themselves known by their absence, the empty shelf where a jar normally rests, a missing tooth in a youngster's smile, or a brown-legged sheep that is not there.

The bleating of sheep chased away my loneliness. Abba had returned. Leaving my spinning, I ran to a window and pulled aside the hide. I leaned an elbow on the sill and rested my chin on my arm, watching Abba come up the path ahead of the sheep. The look in his eyes made my throat tighten.

One after another, he counted them into the sheepfold. My eyes scanned the sheep as they passed in front of him, watching for Liat's one brown leg. The last of the sheep crossed the threshold and he dropped the gate. Not a brown-legged ewe among them.

"Liat," I cried, racing toward him. "Where is my Liat?"

Abba caught my hand and led me to the back of the house. He settled us on the paving stones surrounding the olive tree and sighed.

"Liat is gone, my dove. Stolen."

"Stolen? But how?"

"Ruthless men roam the hills unfettered taking anything and everything they can. That is why I insisted you remain here at home."

"And you…you just gave her to them?" I asked, weeping.

"If a bear or a wolf had threatened Liat, I would have put myself between them. But a lone shepherd with his *shebet* is no match for three men armed with swords. I herded the sheep into a defile for safety. Liat, as is her way, wandered off."

I sank to the ground beside him. Curling my hands into tight fists, I pounded the hard earth. "Shemu'el saved Liat from the lion. She was the last thing I had to remember him by and now she's gone, too."

He patted my shoulder. "I am sorry this bad thing had to happen."

Then and there, I decided anyone who viewed Athrongeus as the *Mashiach* must be crazy in the head. Many others agreed with me, although most were afraid to say it out loud. The women whispered about him when they came to the well. I knew very well what they thought. My eyes may have been on the clothes I washed, but my ears still worked.

"Have not the priests and scribes always taught that the *Mashiach* will be holy and righteous?"

"They have." Abba tugged his beard and frowned the way he always did when searching his memory. "Our sacred writings say it time and time again. 'The *Mashiach* shall be a righteous king, and there shall be no unrighteousness in his days,' and 'there will be singing with everlasting joy,' and 'the souls of the wicked shall wither.'"

"Where does it say the *Mashiach* will let his men roam the countryside stealing a girl's sheep?"

Abba shook his head and chuckled. "You know the answer. Nowhere. Clearly, this man is a *sheker*, a pretender, a false *Mashiach*. Athrongeus and his ilk will eat the fruit of their ways and be filled with the product of their schemes. He brings not peace and victory for our people, but only further pain and death. What he has begun can only come to a bad end."

"The angels in the field said Yeshua was the *Mashiach*. Could Yeshua be a *sheker*, too?"

"No, my little dove. The heavenly host were sent by the Most High Lord. God never lies and neither would they."

"Then why did Uncle Chayim follow Athrongeus? He was in the field with us that night. He saw, he heard."

"Memories fade over time and men grow impatient. Jews have looked forward to the coming of the *Mashiach* for generations. Yeshua is still a child whose time has not yet come. If he's truly the *Mashiach*, we will know it someday. Meanwhile people like Chayim want change now and will follow anyone who promises it."

"What is going to become of Uncle Chayim?"

My question brought tears to my father's eyes.

~ 24 ~

Marcus stood staring across the courtyard at Yu'dah. Atticus came to stand beside him, dropping the heavy *loculus* with a clank. Together they watched Evodius walk away.

"He demands a transaction worthy of Beelzebub," Marcus said, his voice low and harsh.

"Do not be hasty in your judgment. I know Evodius well. Our master is too wise to ever suggest such a bargain. He meant only to test your mettle."

"Is this the Roman way, jest while a man's life hangs in the balance?"

"What would you have him do?"

Marcus stamped his foot on the cobblestones. "I would have him buy this man, just as he bought you and me."

"If Evodius bought every slave who deserved a better fate, he would soon find himself with more slaves than Caesar has soldiers." He took Marcus by the arm and pointed to Evodius, now far ahead. "Come, our patient waits."

Marcus stared at the pavement as they walked. Suppose Atticus was mistaken. What if Evodius had not meant it as a test, but a serious proposal? How, he wondered, would he have responded?

They passed the line of slaves and Marcus again spotted his friend bound in chains. He knew he must go to him, speak words of comfort, repay the kindness Yu'dah had shown him.

"Wait," Marcus said. "I must speak with him."

Seeing the determination in his friend's eyes, Atticus made no attempt to dissuade him. Instead, being wise in the ways of the Roman world, he hatched a plan.

"Very well," he said. "Pretend to be interested in making a purchase. We wear the insignia of *Legio XII*; use its power."

The two men walked toward the line. "Check his teeth as you speak to him under your breath," Atticus advised.

"His teeth? Yu'dah is a man, not a pack animal."

Fate spared you a turn on the sale stone. Take it from one who has stood there twice, a slave with rotted teeth seldom brings a good price."

"I saw no one checking the maiden's teeth."

"There was no need." Atticus grinned. "Her physique said it all." He gave him a slight nod. "Follow my lead. Watch and learn."

Marcus stared into Yu'dah's gray eyes. Neither spoke.

Atticus snapped his fingers and motioned to the auctioneer. "You there," he shouted. "Unchain this man."

The auctioneer scurried over, keys jingling. "The one who consigned him warned me that he was dangerous."

Atticus spat at the auctioneer's feet. "And I say he isn't."

The man hesitated. His eyes shifted from side to side, looking everywhere except at the black man standing in front of him.

"Do you fear him?" Atticus asked. "You seemed brave enough when you prodded a helpless girl with your stick. Perhaps a taste of the *flagellum* will help you reach a decision."

Rather than face possible lashes, the man raced to Yu'dah and unlocked his shackles. The auctioneer hurried past Atticus lugging the chains. He caught his foot in the loops. Tripping, he lurched forward. The heavy links prevented him from using his arms to steady himself. At the last instant Atticus reached out and caught the man, saving him from certain injury.

Atticus waved away the man's words of thanks. "Go. I wish to examine the slave in peace." He waited until the auctioneer moved aside then, in a loud voice, said, "You there, come forward."

Pretending to jerk him out of line, Marcus rested his hands on Yu'dah's shoulders and squeezed. "How are you, brother?" he whispered.

"Better thanks to you and your friend."

"Over here where we can better see you." Marcus gave him a shove.

The two men led Yu'dah away from the line and stood in

front of him, blocking him from view. Behind them the auctioneer's voice rose and fell as he gathered bids on the next man in line.

"You seem to have found a good home with the *Medicus*," Yu'dah said, as Marcus examined him. "I am glad for you."

"And you?"

"My first taste of slavery has been less sweet than yours. Still, my fate rests in God's hands," he said. Though he strained to appear brave, he couldn't hide the fear in his voice

Atticus grabbed Yu'dah's chin and turned his head. "Open. We must check your teeth."

Marcus peered into Yu'dah's mouth, all the time whispering encouragement.

Atticus pushed between them. "Let me see that eye." After examining Yu'dah's injuries, he ordered salve from the case Marcus carried. His voice dropped to a tight whisper as he smoothed slave on the injury. "This will ease your pain and reduce the swelling. It should heal quickly without lasting damage."

Atticus glanced at Marcus. "Evodius waits. Check his feet before we leave."

Grabbing his *loculus*, Atticus approached the auctioneer. "I will recommend this man to the *Medicus Cohortis*. We are here tending patients and may be delayed. If his turn comes before we return, record the buyer's name on a tablet." Atticus stared into the man's eyes. "I *will* return for that tablet, if not today, then the day after. Choose your buyer carefully. The Centurion would not be pleased to find out the man had suffered further abuse at the hands of his new owner."

Atticus and Marcus crossed the square at a brisk pace. They squeezed between two stalls, passing a painted Egyptian woman hawking jars of lotions and scented oils. She also had cosmetics, henna to dye the skin and hair, kohl, which darkened the eyes, a pink powder, *rubeus*, to color the cheeks, and bright red *carminium* for a woman's lips.

Marcus gave Yu'dah a fleeting backward glance. "What will become of him?"

"We have done what we could. Pray he finds a better home the second time around. Your friend is a slave, no different than you and I. For a slave, control always rests in another's hand." Atticus shrugged. "Does a piece of driftwood tell the waves which way they must roll?"

"Still, it seems unfair for me to be a physician's apprentice while another is forced to dig in the ground, break rocks, or carry heavy loads."

"Perhaps. But you believe this god, Yahweh, of whom you so often speak orders your life, correct?"

"I do."

"Well, if such a mighty personage concerns himself with the smallest details of your day-to-day existence, why do you imagine he would overlook this other man's needs?"

W eeks became months and the months became years. The Roman slave Marcus found himself immersed in an alien environment. His rudimentary Latin, which all Jews developed to survive in a Roman culture, grew and expanded. He became as fluent, if not more so, in Latin as he had been in Aramaic. As a physician's assistant, he also learned to read and write Greek and developed a working knowledge of Egyptian hieroglyphics.

Antioch on the Orontes had little in common with either Bethlehem or Jerusalem. It was the capitol of an important province and the largest city in the Empire after Alexandria and Rome itself. Greek in design and Roman in attitude, it offered a cosmopolitan atmosphere that the Herods and other client kings mimicked, but never duplicated.

The longer he lived the Roman lifestyle, the harder it became to maintain his Jewish identity, practices and beliefs. The Romans of Antioch did not respect the Jewish *Shabbat* as they did in Judea. Despite his best efforts, new ideas and different ways slipped into his routine almost unnoticed.

Atticus, by comparison, partook of the Roman lifestyle to the fullest extent. He attended all the festivals, visited the baths and coliseum regularly, and drank deeply of what he called the *fruits of Aphrodite*. Following each new adventure, he regaled, and sometimes shocked, Marcus with his tales.

Despite its reputation for licentiousness, Antioch was also home to a large population of Hellenized Jews. To someone raised in the shadow of Pharisaic Jerusalem, they seemed at times hopelessly liberal. Despite that, as much as possible, Marcus kept the *Shabbat* and worshipped at one of the city's Synagogues whenever he could.

"No more excuses. This year I refuse to take no for an answer." Atticus poked a finger into the center of Marcus' chest. "You *will* participate in the Saturnalia celebration."

"I do not wish to romp naked and debauch myself in pleasures of the flesh."

Atticus raised an eyebrow. "To each his own, but Saturnalia is not like that at all." He searched for an analogy. "You once told me of your festival of...of..." he snapped his fingers. "...of *Bikkurim*. Saturnalia resembles your celebration of first fruits."

"I will not offer sacrifice in the temple of a Roman god."

"No, no...nothing like that. It's lighthearted, fun and carefree." He winked. "The best part is the slaves become masters and the masters become their slaves."

To Marcus' great surprise he found himself enjoying the Saturnalia celebration. The festivities lasted a week and during that time he and Atticus ruled Evodius.

They were loath to demand anything harsh of him because of the kind way he treated them. Their requests consisted of having him serve them dinner at the banquets and occasionally making him re-order the surgery at the end of day. It was a charade they all enjoyed and, when their roles returned to their pre-Saturnalia status, all three looked back and laughed.

~ 25 ~

"But Varus sent a part of his army into the country, against those that had been authors of this commotion...but such as were the most guilty he crucified; these were in number about two thousand."
—Josephus, Wars of the Jews, Book 2, 5:2-75

It is said when the *Mashiach* comes he will bring the heavenly host with him to vanquish his foes. All Athrongeus had was the ragtag group of rebels he and his brothers recruited.

Quintillus Varus marched into Judea with three Syrian legions and besieged Jerusalem. The fight quickly went out of the rebels and, once Varus had them on the run, he chose to make an example of them.

Small bands of soldiers scoured the countryside searching out Athrongeus' followers. With so many soldiers about, the gangs of thieves and thugs left Judea. Abba relaxed his restrictions and let me accompany him to the fields again.

"We Jews have always stoned those convicted of crimes," I said, unpacking my sack. "Why must the Romans crucify instead?"

We sat together on the hillside eating our noonday meal while the sheep grazed in the pasture below.

"Crucifixion is not a method of killing at all, my dove; it is a means of torture. The victim's eventual death is as much a side effect as the intent."

My father read the confusion on my face. "Crucifixion is largely bloodless. The victim is not beaten beforehand because a beating would lessen the time he suffered on the tree."

"But they nail them to the cross." The words made me shudder. I turned the pomegranate in my hand, then sat it aside. I no longer desired its blood-red seeds.

"True, but those wounds, while horribly painful, are not lethal. Men have survived crucifixion if removed soon enough. The Romans intend to inflict as much suffering as possible on the way to death." He paused, swallowed, and looked down at his food. Abba, too, had lost his appetite.

I recognized the truth in his words. The strongest men hung on for three days gasping for breath like beached fish. When the poor souls finally succumbed, it was because they no longer had the strength to pull themselves up to breathe.

In Jerusalem people sometimes jeered and cursed criminals on their way to the cross, but decent people avoided the place of crucifixion. Most were appalled to see anyone treated with such cruelty.

"This is a bad time," Abba said with a sigh. "Varus cannot get enough crosses. He has dispatched parties of soldiers, *carpentarii*, throughout the countryside cutting trees."

"Judea is a dry place and trees take years to grow. What will we do if Varus cuts all our trees?"

Abba lifted his eyebrows and shook his head.

"Are not torture and death punishment enough? Why must men hang on the cross naked?"

"If mere killing satisfied Caesar, they could dispatch them with a sword. No, first he wishes to humiliate his enemies." My father looked at me keenly, reading my mind. "Turn away whenever you see crosses in the distance. Best an innocent maiden not pass rows of naked men strung beside the highway."

I knew of what he spoke. Driven mad by thirst and pain, the men ranted and cursed, scandalizing women and children who could not help but hear.

A lucky few had families who removed their bodies for burial. Most of the men were far from home and continued to hang, their blackened corpses bloating as they putrefied in the sun.

Crows plucked out their eyes and jackals and hyenas fought over their flesh and bones. The stench of rotting corpses filled the air. Our skies blackened with vultures slowly wheeling as they searched out their next meal.

Athrongeus was gone and hundreds upon hundreds of good men lay dead, yet the slaughter continued. When we thought it could get no worse, it did. A thousand years would not be enough time to forget what happened next.

Chayim's absence weighed heavily upon Aunt Tamar. Ruth, the cousin whom Tamar nursed beside me, married the winter before Athrongeus came. She moved south to Bethsura, her husband's village. I recalled how happy Uncle Chayim looked dancing with his newly-wed daughter on her wedding day.

The world seemed a bright place that afternoon. Then Athrongeus' delusions drew him away from family, flock and fields. Now, like the rest of the rebel army, Chayim was on the run.

His absence worked a hardship on us all. Abba struggled to keep track of both flocks. I divided my time between helping Abba with the sheep and assisting Tamar with woman's work and the children.

I felt discomfort at the last new moon. My time rapidly approached; soon I would be a woman. The thought worried me. Not the natural processes that I knew must accompany it, but the societal pressures it would bring to bear.

I did not feel ready...able, to wed. Even in the grave, Shemu'el still held my heart. Yet, there would never be enough hands to do all the work until Uncle Chayim returned.

Or I married.

Tamar circled the small room, nervously rubbing her hands together. Restless without a man in the house, she spent many evenings with us. This was a time when a family had to pull together.

"The fighting has all but ended. The legions are beginning to withdraw." Her mouth trembled. She forced her lips together to keep from crying. "Where is Chayim? Why has he not returned?" It was a question she asked over and over again.

Abba put his arm around her. "Chayim loves you and the children."

"Then why has he not come back to us?"

Not wishing to upset her, my father spoke soft and slow.

"Fear keeps him away. As a captain, he must know there is a price on his head. He worries Rome's soldiers will harm his family if he returns."

His words made her sob. "Will I never see him again, Yaakov?"

"We must wait them out. Like all predators, they will eventually tire of the hunt. Then, and only then, can the rabbit safely emerge from its hole."

"Perhaps today will be the day my Chayim returns," Tamar said, smiling.

She greeted me this way every morning, more for her sake than mine. Let her have her dreams. I understood the pain of longing for a loved one.

Little Yonah overflowed with energy that morning. As an excuse to get out of the house Tamar suggested we join Abba for his noonday meal. We walked with care. One never knew where, or when, you might come upon a row of crosses. As a precaution, Tamar walked far ahead and I trailed behind with the children. If she spotted crosses, she could warn me to cover the children's eyes.

She signaled a stop. "Legionnaires," she said.

We placed the children between us, covered our faces and huddled by the side of the road. I rested my hand on Yonah's shoulder, ready to grab him in case he bolted.

Five spear-carrying soldiers rounded the curve. They had barely passed when Yonah curled his mouth, preparing to hurl an insult at them. I clamped my hand over his lips and, tightened my grip on his shoulder. After the soldiers left, Tamar grabbed him and shook him. "What is wrong with you?"

"Romans are pigs," he snarled. "I wish I had a sword like Abba." He waved his arm, thrusting an imaginary weapon. "Together we would kill them all."

He was still at an age when boys imagined war an exciting adventure. I invited the children to join me in singing a Psalm as we walked. It seemed better than cursing Romans.

Tamar crested the hill well ahead of us.

We had 30 cubits to go when her anguished shriek raised

the hair on the back of my neck.

I placed Yonah's hand in Elisheva's. "Something has upset your mother. Sit here on the ground until I return." I stared into Elisheva's eyes. "Do not move and, no matter what, never let go of your brother's hand."

Yonah craned his neck. "Why do I have stay?"

"Because I said so." I pointed at the grass. "You had better be here when I return."

I found Tamar on her knees in the middle of the road, tearing at her clothing. A shiver rippled through me. Chayim's lifeless body hung on a cross beside the road.

The injustice of it! I wanted to scream to the heavens, shriek and wail as Tamar did. The husband, father and uncle who never uttered an unkind word had been stolen from us.

But Tamar needed me to be strong and so I was. Burying my pain, I dropped to my knees beside her and put an arm around her shoulder. She fell against me sobbing his name.

Tamar's head snapped up. She stared at me, her eyes wide with fright. "The children," she gasped. "They must not see him like this."

Rising, I tugged her hand. "Come. We will tell the men and they can bring him home."

She jerked away and shook her head. "No! I will not leave him to the birds and beasts."

Tamar whipped off her veil. Her hair streamed in the breeze as she ran toward the cross, screaming and waving the veil. Two crows sat above him on the crossbeam. Seeing her, they gave a defiant caw. She snapped the veil at them sending them flapping away.

"I should return to the children," I said, checking the road.

My aunt ignored me.

She trembled when I took her in my arms. I wished with all my heart I could stay, but knew I must leave. My eyes scanned the road again. Yonah and Elisheva could come over the hill at any moment.

"I am going," I whispered. "I will not be long."

Deaf to my words, Tamar stared up at her dead husband

and mouthed prayers.

I had to make her hear me. Re-checking the road, I gave her a shake.

She turned, seeming to listen, but not really hearing.

"I cannot stay, Tamar. The children are waiting."

She gave a slow, distracted nod.

"I will notify the men and send them back with tools." I hurriedly kissed her cheek and turned to leave.

Her voice called me back. "Rivkah."

My eyes went to the brow of the hill, then to her. "Yes?"

"Tell them he did it out of love. Chayim wanted a better life for his children. He—"

I patted her hand and strained my ears for approaching footsteps. "I know, I know. Elisheva and Yonah...please, I must leave."

Tamar ignored me after that.

I left her then. I had to; the children must not see what I had seen.

I gave a backward glance as I hurried away, watching Tamar move as if in a trance. She stumbled forward and collapsed against the cross. Weeping, she pressed her cheek to Chayim's discolored legs and hugged them.

~ 26 ~

Marcus had barely shut his eyes when a tap at the door intruded on his prayers. Expecting a medical emergency, he tossed aside his blanket and rose. He snatched up the cloak he tossed over a chair moments earlier and tugged it on as he crossed the dim room.

When he cracked the door open the spicy-sweet perfume of lavender and myrrh wafted in. Marcus peered into the face of an olive-skinned woman. Her unveiled hair was curled into ringlets and rinsed with henna until it glowed dark red in the lamplight.

The lamps that hung from the posts along the balcony silhouetted her body through her gauzy gown. The sight of her curves made Marcus' pulse race. He stared eagerly, his eyes traversing her every hill and valley.

She watched with a satisfied smile. "You are Marcus?" A foreign accent slurred her words.

With intense effort he forced his gaze back to her face.

She had darkened her eyes with kohl, dusted her cheeks and painted her lips.

"Yes," he replied. "What do you want?"

She chuckled deep in her throat. "Open the door and you will see."

Instead of waiting, she placed her hand around the edge of the door and eased it back. Tiny bells sewn into the hem of her skirts jingled with each step she took. Once inside, she closed the door behind her.

After glancing around his plain, second-floor room and at his simple furnishings, she said, "I am called, Zeeta."

Marcus quickly lit two more lamps. Added to the small nightlight he always left burning, they gave the room's rough, plastered walls a warm glow.

Behind him, this woman, Zeeta, threw the bolt on the door.

A wave of panic shot through him. Though he could easily overpower a woman as slight as Zeeta, Marcus did not feel safe being alone with her.

"How can I help you?"

She smiled and stepped closer. They nearly touched. The sachet dangling like an amulet between her breasts flooded his nostrils. Its strong aroma made him lightheaded and unsteady, as if he'd gulped a cup of strong wine.

"I do not require help." She ran her tongue across her lips, seductively. "I am here to help you."

Taking his hand, she tugged him toward the bed.

They had reached the bedside table before Marcus stopped her. When she was outside, he imagined her to be about his age. In the lamplight, he saw she was not as young as he had taken her to be. Skillful application of makeup obscured telltale signs of aging.

"No wonder you shake," she said when his hand quivered. "You are hardly more than a boy." She gave his hand a motherly pat. "Have you never been with a woman?"

He bit his lip, then shook his head. "Why have you come to tempt me to sin?"

"Your patron, Evodius, sent me as a gift. A reward for work well done, perhaps?" She touched his cheek and her lips formed a pout. "He senses you need what Zeeta gives. Relax. Enjoy. I will teach you all you need to know about pleasing a woman. You may be a boy now, but when I leave you will be a man."

"I do not need you to instruct me in your wanton ways."

The coarse laughter of the gatehouse guards drifted in through the frayed piece of hide that provided his only window covering. Had they seen her enter his room? Could they be watching and speculating now?

He would be defiled if he lay with this gentile. The Romans called them *meretrix*, in Aramaic she was a *zonah*. Call her what you like, Zeeta was a heathen prostitute.

"You are nothing but a harlot."

She smiled. "And you desire what I offer."

"Be gone!"

Instead, Zeeta reclined on his bed. Rolling onto her side, she supported her head with a hand. She swept her gown aside and walked her fingers along her bare leg. "They tell me you are a physician, familiar with a soldier's body."

Marcus supposed he was.

She tugged the gown higher. "Have you ever explored the mysteries of a woman's body?"

Marcus spun around, showing her his back. He must rid himself of this woman, he thought, but how? As a slave, he had no rights. He could be punished if he threw her out and she complained of rough treatment. These women expected payment. How much had Evodius given her? Would he be upset if Marcus sent her away, wasting his *sistertii*?

Zeeta rose from the bed and pressed her breasts into his back. Slipping her arms around him, she slid her fingers inside his cloak and stroked the soft hair on his chest.

"Even brave men are fearful their first time," she whispered. She rested her chin on his shoulder and licked the side of his neck. "Trust me. Your fears will melt like summer snow. Lose yourself in Zeeta and soon you will think of nothing but passion."

Her breath smelled of the same cheap wine the common soldiers drank to excess. Marcus repeated his demand that she leave.

"What if—" She put her lips close to his ear and whispered a suggestion.

Marcus recoiled in horror. He grabbed her by the arm, spun her around, and dragged her to the door. Throwing it open, he shoved her out. "Leave and never return, daughter of Satan," he shouted.

Zeeta staggered forward and fell against the wrought iron railing that enclosed the upper balcony. Hair askew, she pushed herself up and spewed curses at him as she stormed away.

Marcus stood in the doorway listening to the tinkling of her bells grow ever fainter.

After Zeeta left, he washed his face and returned to bed, but found no answers there. Above all else he wanted to remain true to the Laws God gave Moshe. Now every decision was as dangerous as a two-edged sword.

He was two people, Shemu'el, whom they would not allow him to be, and Marcus, whom they demanded he become.

Marcus arrived early the following morning. He was at his table grinding medicinal herbs when Evodius entered the surgery.

Smiling, Evodius crossed the room with long strides. "Did you get the present I sent you last evening?"

"The woman, Zeeta? Yes, she came to my room."

"I anticipated smiles and dreamy expressions."

Marcus concentrated on his work. "She is a harlot."

Evodius laughed. "You expected me to send my sister?"

"I did not expect anything. You considered it a kindness, I know, and it is not my desire to insult you." He took a deep breath. "But I sent her away untouched."

"She was not to your liking?"

"That would be one way to put it." The pestle made loud, clinking noises as Marcus drove it into the marble bowl with increasing force.

"Perhaps I should be the one to apologize. I did not realize you preferred boys. There are a number of attractive young—"

Marcus slammed the pestle down on the table and spun on his stool. "I do not desire boys. To lie with a man as one lies with a woman is detestable before God."

"Your god."

"The one and only, the Most High God."

Evodius gave him a good-natured smile. "Well, I'm glad we have that cleared up." He pulled out a stool and sat beside Marcus. "I suggest you not spread these ideas of yours around too freely. You see, most Romans consider it a matter of preference, not morality."

"So I have noticed."

His mentor rested an arm on the preparation table. "Think of it this way. At a banquet some partake of only the lamb, while others only the veal." He put his hand on Marcus' shoulder and gave it a squeeze. "However, my experience is that most eventually try a slice of both. Perhaps we can find another woman more to your liking."

"No...thank you. It is better to drink from your own cistern. I do not wish to have relations with a woman who is not my wife."

"Fine by me, but one final word of advice. You will find that Romans are generally accepting of other people's gods. In return, they do not want their beliefs challenged either. You are a long way from *Palestinia*. When among Romans, do as they do."

That evening, after the sun went down, Marcus pushed aside the ragged piece of hide that covered his window. He stared at the rising moon in the eastern sky and thought of the previous evening. He contrasted Zeeta's brazenness to Rivkah's gentle innocence. Recalling the tender look in Rivkah's eyes when she said she loved him, he remembered their kisses and drew his fingers into a fist.

Marcus clenched his fingers tighter and tighter until the place where the bone in his arm had knit throbbed in protest. He relaxed his fingers and glanced at the moon a second time. How he longed for the connection he felt when he held Rivkah in his arms.

"Oh God of the universe, who knows all things", he silently prayed, *"could it be that at this moment Rivkah also looks up at this same moon and dreams of the man she lost?"*

~ 27 ~

Quintillius Varus and his legions left Judea when Archelaus returned from Rome. By then the damage had already been done. Several thousand men had been crucified, my Uncle Chayim among them.

We learned that Caesar Augustus, like Solomon hundreds of years before him, sought a solution by dividing the item in dispute. In our case it was a kingdom being argued over, not a baby. And, since there were three claimants, not two, he cut it into three parts.

Ethnarchs and *tetrarchs* now ruled us instead of kings. Archelaus, Herod's designated heir, received Samaria, Judaea and Idumea. Fitting, perhaps, since the Herods were not Jews, but Idumeans. Herod Antipas ruled over Galilee and Herod Phillip over Iturea, the region north and east of Lake Gennesaret, which the Romans called the Sea of Galilee.

How many more tears, O God, must your people shed? We inhabit such a meager remnant of Solomon's kingdom and yet they split us like cordwood. If you break a loaf into too many pieces, you end up with nothing but crumbs.

I examined myself as I bathed. I had grown taller over the past several months and my chest swelled with the beginnings of breasts. Sometimes the changes in my body made me feel odd, as if I scarcely knew myself any longer.

As Miryam promised, the cycle of my womanhood came upon me. Aunt Tamar and I had discussed what to expect. A neat stack of rags waited on a table beside my bed in readiness.

Now that I was a woman, other things changed too. A scarf or veil would cover my hair anytime I left the house and my sleeping mat moved into the small room on the east side of the house. I had slept beside Abba all my life, but no longer. It was not proper for a woman to sleep next to her father.

Most of my friend's mothers held special rites and

ceremonies for them when they achieved their maturity. Rachel's mother celebrated with flavored wines, honey cakes and scented oils when she received her first blood. During my *niddah*, I lay in my room by myself with the hide pulled tight over the window to shut out the light. I spent my time of separation in the dark, alone and forgotten, hugging my cramping abdomen and quietly crying. I felt as bereft as an orphan. Perhaps that is what came from not having a mother.

When my time ended I walked to the *mikvah* alone and slipped beneath its cleansing waters as all women were required to do. A moment later I broke the water's surface weeping uncontrollably with great, heaving sobs.

This was the time when Shemu'el should be going to Abba to ask for my hand. But Shemu'el was nowhere to be found. What good is womanhood with no husband? I climbed out, toweled myself dry and returned home. I spoke to no one about what had happened to me.

All I had beside my bed for comfort and company were broken dreams of Shemu'el and regrets over what might have been. Receiving a reminder each new moon that I would never bear Shemu'el's children depressed me terribly. As the time approached, my moods made me flighty and hard to live with. I snapped at Abba for no reason and sometimes burst into tears.

He ignored it all and never complained.

I often thought of Shemu'el and tossed and turned in my little room, unable to sleep. When the tension became too great, my fingers found their way beneath my gown. But in the darkness of my room, it was always Shemu'el's hands touching me. Afterwards, I would turn aside and sob myself to sleep.

A few months later, while we sewed, Rachel pulled her tunic tight across her bosom. "We are ready for a man," she said.

"True enough, but I'll never have the man meant for me."

"How do you know? You have always said matches are *b'shert*."

"They are, for every man there is a woman and for every woman a man."

"If matches are made in heaven; there is always hope. God will reward you in his own good time. Just you wait and see."

I shook out the cloak in my lap and measured it for width. Along with sewing tools, my basket contained several pieces of knotted twine. Each one represented the measurements of a different garment, some for me, and some for Abba.

We cut tunics straight on all four sides, so their strings had just two knots. One for width, and one for length. A woman hid, or emphasized, her shapeliness by the width of her tunic and the way she tucked the material when she tied her girdle about her waist.

Rachel's comment of *wait and see* lay in the back of my mind, festering as I worked. I glanced down at my sewing and frowned.

Which knot had I used to measure?

Cloaks had more knots allowing them to gradually become wider toward the bottom hem. Keeping two sets of strings for the sleeves allowed me to sew them straight, or wide with flowing cuffs.

I reached into my basket and grabbed a string without looking. It tangled with the others, forming a jumbled bird's nest. I bunched the cloth into a ball and threw it on the floor.

Rachel did not have to say the words to mean them. "So you are saying Shemu'el was not the man God intended for me?"

Rachel gave me a surprised look.

"The words are out of your mouth," I shouted, "too late to take them back now.

"Well, I..." Her hands fluttered in her lap like a bird with a broken wing. "I did not mean it to come out that way." She gave a self-conscious laugh, began to speak, then stopped. "I meant—" She sighed. "Sometimes you can be too sensitive."

Rachel returned to her sewing pretending nothing had happened. "Have you seen the grapes this year? They are as big as apricots."

Why must everyone tell me the same thing with different

words? I knew the *Torah* as well as anyone. God commanded mankind *Be fruitful and multiply*. A man without progeny was incomplete. A childless woman unfulfilled. The Most High richly blessed Avraham when he promised, "*Your descendants shall be like the stars in the heavens.*"

Now that I was a woman, I would be expected to marry. I would have done so eagerly had it been Shemu'el waiting for me beneath the marriage canopy. But it was not to be.

Winter rains greened the fields. The trees and vines flowered. My friends and I plaited our hair with flowers and draped blossom necklaces around our necks. We danced and sang in the fields as maidens did each spring. Rachel and the others watched the young men's eyes as they danced.

But I paid them no heed.

Following the new moon, my friend, Devorah, wed Shaoul, a young man from our settlement. I felt many eyes watching me at the wedding feast. I knew the thoughts that lay behind those kindly glances. Yes, Rivkah was now a woman.

She will be the next to marry.

I knew I would not. My heart beat only for Shemu'el. I did not linger long on thoughts of marriage that day, or on other people's expectations. After all, Devorah was older than I.

The small difference in our ages seemed half a lifetime to me then. Marriage was not something to be worried over. Not yet. Those decisions lay in the future, a future that seemed to me as distant as the stars at night.

I had no wish to marry.

~ 28 ~

"Will you go? You'll enjoy it, you always do."

"Attend another of your Jewish festivals? Of course," Atticus replied. "I treasure new experiences." He grinned and rubbed his hands down his legs, kneading the muscles in anticipation. Unable to sit still, he jumped up and paced the room.

"Do I need a special robe? Should I prepare offerings?"

"Nothing is required but your presence."

Atticus grinned. "Will this at last be the one festival that resembles a Roman feast? Give me a hint. How many girls will there be at the temple?"

"No girls and no temple."

"But after the meal can we dissipate our manly desires?" He sounded concerned, yet still hopeful.

"No women."

His face fell. "Not even one or two dancers to distract us? They need not disrobe if that is not the custom."

"How many times must I tell you? The Romans celebrate with lewdness and debauchery, not the Jews. Relations between men and women are restricted to the marriage bed."

Marcus moved beside his friend. "Tomorrow is the last day of *Sukkot*, the Festival of Booths. It commemorates the period when the Israelites wandered in the desert. We are going to my friend's home to share a meal under their tent."

"Such strange practices. Eating under a tent constitutes a festival?" Atticus laughed. "I shall remind you of this the next time you complain when Evodius tells us we are spending six weeks in the field with the troops."

The next evening they walked to the Jewish sector of the city where Ehud and Chava, two of Marcus' friends from the Synagogue, had set up their booth on the roof of their home. Inside this two-sided enclosure made of tent cloth their children strung palm fronds, myrtle boughs and willow branches around the top and down the sides, creating an oasis of greenery.

They hung lanterns at the inside corners and decorated the

interior walls with bunches of freshly picked grapes and short branches of ripe figs and olives. Woven grass mats covered the floor.

Atticus looked it over, smiled and nodded approvingly.

The streets were dark by the time the men left. Like soldiers on a march, they maintained a brisk pace, matching their steps. They exited through a former gate in the old Seleucid city wall and turned onto Antioch's main thoroughfare, the *Via Caesarea*. The wide road teemed with carts and wagons, donkeys and oxen, all transporting goods into the city. As they walked, a sampling of the best of tomorrow's market rolled by.

Marcus glanced over at Atticus. His dark-skinned friend seemed unusually subdued. "Well, what did you think?"

"These festivals of yours are curious occasions."

"You prefer the Roman ones?"

"Oddly enough, I do not. And I fail to understand why." Atticus stopped and crossed his arms. "I should prefer them, but I no longer do. When I go to a Roman festival I usually set off with great anticipation, but invariably return vaguely disappointed. Nothing ever measures up. Dissipating your lusty desires is supposed to bring satisfaction, yet in the end it does not."

They began walking again.

Marcus smiled. "You might say it has become wearisome and meaningless. The eye is not satisfied with seeing, nor the ear filled by hearing. All streams run to the sea, but the sea is never filled."

"Exactly," Atticus said. "You are the first person to understand how I feel. You have also experienced this feeling that something in life is missing...always beyond your grasp?"

Marcus made no comment, but continued paraphrasing *Ecclesiastes* as they walked. "You feel there is nothing new under the sun. Nothing of which it can be said, 'Look, here is something new.'" He spread his arms, showing his empty palms. "All was here before us and will be here after we are gone. We spend our days trying to catch the wind."

Atticus seemed ready to burst. He grabbed his friend's arm. "Now that we have discovered this great truth, what shall we do about it?"

"We have not discovered anything," Marcus said between chuckles. "Solomon felt the same way nearly a thousand years ago."

"Amazing." Atticus shook his head. "And he never attended a single Roman festival. Stranger still are *your* festivals. From the outside they appear to offer no special attraction. They are simple and sedate yet they always leave me feeling uplifted and energized."

"The Lord who instituted those festivals is far wiser than even Solomon."

Atticus moved his hands in front of himself as he struggled to shape his thoughts. "You Jews have found something no one else has. This powerful faith, this Yahweh you worship, the inner meaning of your feasts and festivals, like a puzzle it has begun to fit together for me."

"Congratulations. You are becoming what we call a God-fearer."

"Is that a good thing?"

"Absolutely. A God-fearer is someone who honors our traditions and participates in the festivals. A first step in becoming a proselyte, one who fully accepts and lives the beliefs and regulations of Judaism."

The dark shape of Mount Silpius rose in the distance. At the base of the mountain stood the Citadel, home to them and the soldiers of *Legio XII Fulminata* whom they served.

Atticus touched his fingers, ticking off the feasts and festivals he had attended with his friend. "The year is drawing to a close. It appears we have come full circle, been to them all."

"All but the Seder during *Pesach*," Marcus corrected.

"When will we attend that one?"

"Ah, my friend, it is not that simple. Only those who have been circumcised can participate in the Seder meal."

A look of fright swept over Atticus' face. "God-fearers must be circumcised?"

"No. That only becomes necessary when you become a full proselyte."

He breathed a sigh of relief. "Good. I choose to remain a God-fearer for a while longer then."

Lacertus rose from the surgery table and rolled his shoulders, stretching and flexing. The husky soldier smiled at Marcus. "The injury causes me no pain. You made an excellent repair."

He reached for his gray soldier's tunic and tossed it over his head. Straightening it, Lacertus buckled his leather girdle and holstered his weapons. He placed a foot on a stool and wrapped the ties of his *caligulea* around his calf. He tied the other sandal and glanced up at Marcus.

"Never have I seen such work. When the man's sword struck me, I expected to be paying the boatman to ferry me across the River Styx. I had already passed into the hands of the gods and yet you snatched me back." His cloak fanned out in a circle as he tossed it over his shoulders. "What kindness can I do you in repayment for giving me back my life?"

"You owe me nothing. I serve Caesar just as you." Marcus put away his instruments and smiled. "What lies ahead?"

"I have been re-assigned," he said, locking the clasp of his cloak. "I leave Antioch and *Legio XII* to join the troops at Fortress Antonia."

His words made Marcus' pulse race. "In Jerusalem."

"Is there any other?" Lacertus asked with a laugh. "Even though I am healed and strong as ever, Decimus, my Centurion, no longer trusts me in combat."

"You will not be accepted there as you are here in Antioch."

"So I hear. No soldier goes to Judea voluntarily. Most mark the hours until they move on."

How much Marcus would have given to trade places with Lacertus. The soldier turned to the door, but stopped when

Marcus spoke.

"Wait. Perhaps there is something I would ask of you."

"I am yours to command. Speak and I will obey."

"I would have you carry my words to someone in Judea."

Marcus snatched a wax tablet and stylus off the table and quickly scratched out a map. "Here," he said, marking an X, "is Jerusalem. To the south less than a half-day's walk is the village of Bethlehem."

He indicated its position on the tablet. "Beyond Bethlehem is a small settlement of sheepherders. There you will find a young maiden, Rivkah, daughter of Yaakov, the shepherd."

Their eyes met and the legionnaire nodded his understanding.

"Tell Rivkah thus: Shemu'el lives as a physician's apprentice in Antioch on the Orontes and longs for the day when he can return the *shrika* you entrusted to him years ago."

He had the man repeat his words back to him twice, then handed him the tablet on which he drew the map.

"I will do as you ask," Lacertus said. "If this Rivkah sends a reply, I will forward it to you through a courier." He clasped Marcus' forearm and squeezed. "You gave me back my life; I will not fail you."

~ 29 ~

If Shemu'el had to die, I always wished we had been betrothed first. If we were, it would have made me his widow. People respected a widow's feelings for the dead. As Shemu'el's widow, Abba, Rachel and everyone else would stop pestering me to marry. Then came the day when I didn't want to be his widow.

"*Shalom Aleichem*, Caleb. How are you this fine afternoon?" I had not seen Shemu'el's brother for some time. Even though Mother Sarit and I visited regularly, the men of the family avoided me.

"*Aleichem Shalom*, Rivkah," Caleb said. "You are looking well today."

I smiled politely, accepting his compliment.

"Is your father at home?"

"In the backyard resting. Shall I call him?"

"No!" His response came quick and loud. Caleb moved his hands apologetically. "Uh, no...that will not be necessary."

He glanced over his shoulder and stared up the road. Seeing his father, Yo'el, walking toward us, Caleb took a deep, cleansing breath and waved. "Yaakov is at home, father."

He gave a start when he turned and saw me.

We talked moments earlier. Had he forgotten I was there?

He shot a nervous glance back at his father coming up the walk. "My father and I will talk to Yaakov now," Caleb said. "Goodbye."

Father and son disappeared around the side of the house leaving me standing in the doorway to wonder. I was still there when Abba appeared at the back door. "The sheep need to be checked, Rivkah. Go and tend to them."

Abba waited on the porch when I returned. "Never have I seen such a beautiful afternoon." He stared up at the puffy clouds, gave a happy sigh and smiled.

Something about his behavior felt odd.

"Why not close the door and come sit with me on the hill. We will watch the sheep together like we did when you were a little girl. Bring a snack. We can talk."

"Are you feeling well?"

He stroked his cheek. "Why do you ask?"

The only way to find out what Caleb wanted was to go with him. I packed a few things and followed Abba to a soft spot on the hillside. The sheep grazed in the grassy meadow around us. I offered him a cake of raisins.

"Thank you, my little dove." He popped some in his mouth and chewed. "These delicious raisins are nothing compared to your sweetness." He kissed my forehead. He sighed and leaned back on the hillside, interlocking his fingers behind his head.

"I had a good visit with Yo'el. Caleb, too. He is a nice looking young man. I think he resembles his mother. What about you?"

I answered with a shrug.

"I have noticed Caleb working hard to build his flock. What about you?"

"What did Caleb and Yo'el want, Abba?"

He frowned. My father hated it when I refused to let him play his little roundabout games.

"They came to discuss an offer of marriage Caleb intends to make."

I brought my hands together in surprise. "How wonderful. I wish him happiness. Who does Caleb hope to marry?"

Our eyes met. My father's guilty look was answer enough.

"Not me," I said, forcing a laugh. "No. Caleb does not wish to marry me."

"He is a good man, Rivkah."

The unexpected sternness in my father's voice told me this was a battle I had already lost. Oh God, help me. Caleb would make someone a good husband. Someone, but not me.

"I do not wish to marry Caleb, Abba."

"I have always promised to select a good man for you, and I have."

"No. Tell me you did not." The look on his face told me he

did. I stared into my hands.

He rocked forward onto his knees, leaning close. "You already call Sarit, *Imma*."

I wished for a clever reply to toss at him, but I had none. My head drooped down until my chin touched my chest. Is this how a condemned man felt when they passed sentence?

"Caleb knew Shemu'el intended to take you for his wife. That is why he came to me. It was the honorable thing to do. He is, after all, Shemu'el's brother."

"So is Yhonatan," I sobbed. "He has not come to our door proposing marriage."

"Yhonatan already has a wife, Caleb does not." He leaned forward, pressing his argument in earnest. "Can't you see, the blood, the heritage, the lineage, it is all the same. This way Shemu'el would not have to die. He can live on through you and Caleb. You know the Lord created the Levirate marriage to insure a man's lineage."

At that moment I was not certain why the Lord did anything. Abba had me trapped as surely as if he were catching a bird in a net. You have me, I thought. Go ahead, pluck out my feathers and roast me for dinner. I began counting the stitches on the hem of my cloak.

"Caleb is doing what a good brother should do."

Tears dripped down my cheeks. Forty-six stitches from the seam to the first stripe. "Shemu'el and I were never betrothed."

"He is a hard worker. He will provide for you and your children."

Twenty-seven to the next stripe. "Caleb owed me no obligation."

"You are all I have."

My tears darkened the stripes in my cloak. A knot. Funny, I could not remember the thread breaking there.

"He will give me the grandchildren I long for, Rivkah."

"But I do not love Caleb," I whispered.

Abba spat my words back at me. "Love? What is love compared to respect and security and a place in the community?" He thumped a fist into his hand. Shemu'el is gone; waiting accomplishes nothing. A sapling bent when it is young never straightens. The longer you wait, the harder it becomes. Eventually you wait too long and never marry."

I turned and stared at him through my tears. "Like you did after Imma died?"

The color drained from my father's face. He rocked back on his haunches as if I had punched him. He gave an angry snort. "We are discussing Caleb, not your mother. But we have nothing to discuss. I have already given my approval."

What could I do? Trying to demean Caleb in my father's eyes was impossible. My mind raced. Chayim had been gone two years and still our families struggled to get the work done. Another man in the family would make all the difference. *If this is the match you want for me, I will accept it Lord. If not, show me a way out.*

Abba opened his mouth to speak, but my raised hand stopped him. The Lord had answered my prayer.

"Caleb and I have not shared the cup," I said. "The *kiddushin* remains unsealed."

"But...but you were not here." His eyes narrowed. "Do not try to change what has already been done. I will not go back on my word, Rivkah. One way or another, you will marry Caleb."

Fear squeezed my chest making it difficult to breathe. *Time*, I thought. I needed time to think this through.

"Aunt Tamar is too busy to trouble herself with a maiden's concerns," I said. "You are right, Abba. I already call Sarit, Imma. Since she is the only mother I have, I must discuss this matter with her."

~ 30 ~

Marcus tossed a cloth over the material on the table when he heard the latch turning on the *pharmacia* door. Trying to appear as if he had been working, he snatched up a mortar and pestle and began grinding.

Atticus came through the door smiling. "A good morning to you, my friend."

Returning his greeting, Marcus continued working the pestle around with determination.

"The soldiers of cohort seven are going to stage some games this afternoon," Atticus said. "Foot races, wrestling matches, javelin throws, perhaps a sword fight or two." He rubbed his hands together. "Evodius is still in Rome. What say we spend the afternoon as spectators? If anyone asks, we can tell them we need to be there in case someone is injured."

Marcus concentrated his attention on the grinding. "I have never been fond of combat, real or imagined."

Atticus pretended to walk toward the other side of the room. As he passed behind Marcus, he peeked to see what he was grinding with such gusto. He laughed and rested his hand on Marcus' shoulder. "That becomes a more efficient process if you first place some material in the mortar bowl."

Embarrassed, Marcus slid them aside.

His friend's eyes went to the lump under the cloth. "Hmmm. And what do we have here? No doubt something you did not want Atticus to see."

The black man folded back a corner of the cloth. His eyes widened when he saw the gleam of polished metal. "A *scalpri?*" He picked it up and examined it closely. "No. Not a *scalpri* after all." Atticus rubbed his jaw as he stared at the instrument's tiny, V-shaped tip.

"It is a carving gouge," Marcus said. He opened a drawer. "See. I have a complete set in various sizes."

"Amazing. And all with the Legio's insignia on the handle."

"I borrowed the *scalpri* from Evodius' instrument chest and had them forged into gouges. *Scalpri* are formed from Damascus steel, the only material strong enough to make fine cuts in the hard wood of a myrtle tree." He lowered his eyes. "I know I should have asked."

"Your secret is safe with me. How often do we bend one on the battlefield, or drop them on the tile and damage their tips?"

"Those were the ones I borrowed."

Atticus smiled. "You worry too much, my friend. A *scalpri* with a broken tip is useless. Besides, a few knives more or less are of little consequence. You have found a good use for something that would otherwise be discarded."

Hearing this, Marcus relaxed.

Atticus turned the gouge in his hand. "Damascus steel is notoriously hard to work. How did you manage to modify these blades?"

"I could never have done it myself. Yu'dah made them for me."

"Amazing. When I received the auctioneer's tablet saying that Yu'dah went to Gregorius the goldsmith, I assumed he spent his days pounding gold and forming silver chain."

"He does. But, like us, when the master's demands have been met, he is free to pursue his own interests."

"And what would those interests be?"

"Some time ago a woman from the Governor's household came into the shop with a broach in need of repair. Gregorius examined it and declared it damaged beyond repair. Yu'dah asked if he might try. He fixed the broach so well that the repair could not be detected. The woman who brought it in was a handmaid to the Governor's wife."

"The broach belonged to the Lady Domita Lepida?"

"It did. And she rewarded Yu'dah generously."

"So now, in addition to making necklaces, bracelets and pins, he also repairs them."

"Right again," Marcus said. "The wealthy women of Antioch wear a path to the shop. Gregorius is happy to let him pursue this pastime since he knows those same ladies will return looking for something new to purchase."

"As most women do. What a providential occurrence."

Atticus grinned. "If one did not know otherwise, they might believe some powerful personage were ordering Yu'dah's fate."

"Yu'dah hopes to accumulate enough to purchase his freedom."

"A noble goal indeed." Atticus' attention returned to the gouge. "Back to this instrument. You have such an assortment, what are they for?"

"I use them in my carving."

Atticus lifted the cloth a tiny bit. "Which, no doubt, would be lurking under here. May I see?"

"I prefer to wait until I am finished and satisfied with its appearance, but I suppose it makes no difference."

Tossing the cloth aside, he removed the carved bowl and handed it to his friend.

Atticus examined it, turning it this way and that, and smiling approvingly. "What will you do with it when it is finished?" Atticus asked, passing a finger over the delicate stalks of wheat that circled the bowl's exterior.

"A few months ago I described my work to Ophelos who has a woodshop in the marketplace. He sells his goods to a number of traveling merchants. He gave me two rough-cut bowls to work on as a test. When he saw my work, he agreed to buy all I produced." Marcus lifted an eyebrow. "Like Yu'dah, it is a way for me to earn a few coins."

"When will you deliver this piece to him?"

"I have to apply the polish first. I was just getting ready to do that when you happened in."

Atticus pulled a stool alongside and watched with interest as Marcus blended the sweet almond oil into melted beeswax.

"Now we must wait and let it cool a little," he said, putting the pot aside.

Atticus looked the bowl over a second time while they waited. "Can I give you some advice?"

Marcus scooped-up a dab of polish on his rag and smoothed it over the wood with practiced swirls. Each time he did this his mind returned to the afternoon when Rivkah sat with him in the field watching him polish a bowl he'd carved.

"*Taste it,*" he'd said, offering her the pot.
"*Will it make me sick?*"
"*Go ahead.*" He caught a dab on his fingertip and licked it off. "*See. There is nothing in it to hurt you.*"

Shemu'el gave Atticus an expectant glance. "Your advice?"

"Not every buyer has your discerning eye. A bowl is a utilitarian vessel, not a work of fine art. When the artist is paid by the piece, artistry should not be his criteria. A smart man makes as many pieces as possible."

"What you say may be true for some, but I could not be satisfied delivering less than my best."

"Walk the stalls. Look at what others produce. Have you ever taken a look at some of the clay figurines of gods and goddesses? They are crude, faceless things, poorly done... produced by the hundreds from a mold."

Marcus stopped polishing and, running his tongue around his cheek, thought for a moment. "I could produce more bowls if they came to me scraped and sanded. That would be a fair compromise. I will discuss it with Ophelos."

Atticus rose to leave. "Pack a *loculus* with some instruments and medications. If we hope to convince anyone that we are on a mission of mercy, we should look the part."

Marcus finished buffing the polish and tucked his tools and materials away in a drawer.

Halfway through the door, Atticus glanced back. His face glowed with anticipation. "Besides the games they will have beer and wine, roasted meats, salted fish and other tidbits."

~ 31 ~

I stopped at the well on my way to Imma Sarit's to splash cool water on my face and make myself presentable. The beginnings of a plan began coming together. Please Lord, I prayed, don't let him have announced our betrothal to the whole settlement. If he had, turning back would destroy both our reputations.

Voices and laughter greeted me when I reached Rachel and Binyamin's house. Like most of my friends, Rachel had already married. I went to the backyard where she and her sister, Avigail, were hard at work pressing raisins into cakes. Rachel looked up at the sound of my footsteps. The smile on her face fell away when she saw my expression.

"What is it, Rivkah?"

"May I speak with you alone?"

Avigail rose to leave, but I waved her down. "Stay. I am in no mood to sit still. It is better if Rachel and I walk as we talk."

"Tell me what has you so upset?" Rachel asked when we had gone far enough that no one could overhear us.

I answered her question with a question. "Do you recall last spring when the young maidens danced in the vineyard?"

She did.

"Afterwards you spoke of a certain young man who watched Avigail with keen interest."

"Caleb," Rachel said, confirming what I already knew.

"And Avigail, does she still dream of being his wife?"

"She speaks of nothing else...Caleb this...and Caleb that, morning, noon and night until I am ready to scream."

"Has he spoken to her about marriage?"

"He has dropped a few little hints and he sometimes carries her water bucket for her. But Caleb is very shy, you know." Rachel stared into my eyes. "Why do you ask?"

"Because I think Avigail should have what she wants."

"Has he said something...something I should know?"

"Go press raisins," I said, patting her hand. "For better or worse, you will know all soon enough."

Imma Sarit saw me coming and ran to meet me. Throwing

her arms around me, she kissed me on both cheeks. "Rivkah, my daughter, it is good to see you." She smiled and winked. "This time next year you will be my daughter in truth."

She gave me a strange look when I didn't respond with glee. Like Rachel, she had known me long enough to read my face. "Tell me what troubles you, my child."

"Caleb and his father came to see Abba today."

She hugged me again. "I know, I know. It took lots of work for me to convince both Yo'el and Caleb that this was the right match," her eye gleamed with satisfaction, "but I did it."

The ground dropped out from under my feet. I never considered the possibility that Caleb's proposal had been Sarit's idea. Perhaps she would not be the ally I hoped.

"Why have you come?"

"A young woman should talk to her mother when contemplating a marriage proposal and you are the only mother I have."

"You are about to be betrothed. Why the serious look?" She laid her hand along my cheek and brushed my hair aside. "This is a joyous occasion; perhaps we should celebrate with a cup of wine."

I could not even manage a smile. Avoiding her eyes, I hung my head.

"The men are in the fields. Come, we will sit in the shade and you can tell me what it was that stole your smile."

"A man once had two sons. Both boys loved their father very much," I began. "The man had a small shop where he fashioned clay into useful objects and from the time the boys were young they worked beside their father. The shop was small and stuffy and, because they had to cook the pots and lamps in an oven, unbearably hot in the summer. But still the man thanked the Lord that he had a way to support his family and asked for nothing more."

Sarit sat with her hands folded in her lap waiting for me to continue.

"Now, the first son loved being outside. He craved the sun on his face and the wind in his hair. Even as a young boy he dreamed of some day becoming a shepherd. His younger brother shaped pots on the wheel with joy in his heart. He found working with his hands most rewarding.

"One day the man called the two boys together. 'You have both grown to be men and soon you must take wives and make your way in the world,' he told them. 'My shop is small and cannot support you both. So, my first son, you shall become a potter like me.' Then he turned to the younger boy. "And you I will apprentice to a shepherd.' Now, because both boys loved their father very much, they did what he asked of them."

I stared into her eyes. "My question for you is, will either of those boys ever be truly happy?"

"Caleb's marriage proposal?"

The tears I had been holding back flowed like a river. She rocked me as if I were a small child. When I regained control, I took her fingers in mine.

"I want to honor Shemu'el's memory and, with Chayim gone, Lord knows we need another man in the family. Abba longs for grandchildren, and rightly so. Caleb is a good man, a hard worker."

"But..."

"But I don't feel the love for him I felt for Shemu'el."

"With time you can learn to love, my daughter."

"I know Caleb has many admirable qualities and, if this is what must be, I will respect and care for him as a wife should. Someday, I may even come to love him." I lifted my face and looked into her eyes. "Do you want Caleb to be happy?"

"Of course. All mothers desire happiness for her children."

"Even those children she adopts?"

"Yes, the one I adopted. I want both of you to be happy."

"Then do not force your shepherd to throw pots. Caleb should marry the woman he wants...someone who also wants him. Not the one his parents want."

Sarit stroked her chin as she thought. "And you know of such a girl?"

"Rachel's sister, Avigail. She longs for Caleb the way I longed for Shemu'el."

"Why has he never said anything to me about this?"

"Caleb keeps his own counsel. You asked him to approach Abba and he did. He is a good son and will do whatever you ask of him."

Sarit laughed and shook her head. "He is a foolish boy." She took my hand and we rose together. "Do not trouble yourself over this any longer. I will see that all is made right."

She dabbed at my eyes with the hem of my veil. "You look much prettier when you smile."

Abba pushed the food around on the plate. "You and Caleb, it could have been a good thing," he said, refusing to look at me. The enthusiasm had drained out of his voice. He waited.

When I didn't respond, he took my hand. "I thought because he was Shemu'el's brother you would find him acceptable. I only wanted what is best for you, my dove."

"Thank you, Abba," I said through the lump in my throat.

The whole settlement celebrated Caleb and Avigail's betrothal. We had a party. Everyone danced and smiled and laughed and congratulated the lucky couple.

Everyone except Abba.

I had snatched away his dream never imagining the price I would pay for my defiance.

~ 32 ~

Marcus continued carving and finishing bread bowls two or three at a time for Ophelos the woodworker, accumulating his payments in a small leather sack.

"How would you like to come along when I deliver bowls?" Marcus asked.

Atticus glanced around the well-ordered surgery. The two of them had spent the last week cleaning and organizing. In anticipation of Evodius' return from Rome. They wanted things in good shape when he arrived.

"Why not?" Atticus said. "Very little is happening with the Legion on maneuvers. We can stop to see Yu'dah while we are in the markets. My lady friends delight in the pins he makes."

Marcus handed him a *loculus* stuffed full of bowls. He slung an identical bag over his shoulder. "One for you and one for me."

"How many of these are we delivering?" Atticus asked as they walked.

"Twenty."

"I thought you did two or three at a time."

"Normally I do. The last time I delivered bowls Ophelos had twenty blanks waiting for me. These last few weeks I have worked late into the night completing them."

"Why so many?"

"He received word that a Byzantine trading ship is on its way. They are expected to dock at the *insula* sometime next week."

Atticus shifted the bulky *loculus* on his shoulder. "I hear the seas have been calm. They have undoubtedly reached *Pieria Selucia* already."

"Surely." Marcus quickened his pace. "That is why we must get these to Ophelos. He offered me a bonus on any I delivered before their arrival."

"Your little sack will overflow once you turn these in," Atticus said.

"As a reward for helping me, after we drop the bowls off, I will treat you to the roasted meat on skewers that you enjoy so much. Wine, too...and sweet cakes to celebrate."

"Good." Atticus swept the arm of his cloak across his sweaty brow. "Even a pack animal must eat."

Ophelos inspected the bowls one-by-one. "You have done well, my friend. Very well, indeed. And right on time."

He reached under the counter and removed his cash box. "Facing a deadline, some men skimp on quality in an effort to make as many as they can. Not you. Each bowl is as fine as any you have produced."

Marcus smiled, accepting the compliment.

Ophelos glanced up at the gleaming bowls on his shelf, then rubbed his fingers together and sniffed the residue. "I have forgotten," he said, pretending to be confused, "what is it you put into that finish of yours again?"

"You did not forget; I never told you." Marcus chuckled. "Some secrets I must retain. Otherwise you would have no use for me."

"Never worry, I will always buy your bread bowls. No one carves as you do."

The woodworker counted out a stack of silver *denarii* on the counter and matched it with an equal amount of brass *sestertii*. "For your work," he said, and pushed them across to him. "And, as a bonus." He grinned and filled Marcus' hand with copper *quadrans*.

The men picked up the empty *loculii*, preparing to leave.

"Wait," Ophelos said. "I have blanks enough to fill those sacks of yours. Take some back with you."

Marcus shook his head. "Not today. First, I must recapture the sleep I lost doing those."

"That purse of yours swells. What do you intend to do with all that money?" Atticus asked, as they ate.

"It is not as full as it appears.." Marcus counted out stacks of coins onto the tabletop. He swept a stack into his hand. "My tithe against what Ophelos paid me."

He slid the coins into a square pouch riveted to the leather military girdle he wore. Soldiers utilized them to carry small tools, extra arrowheads and flints.

Marcus made a second stack. "And this is my second tithe, which I shall give to the poor." He removed a single silver *denarius* from his sack, stood it on edge and spun it. He watched it twirl until it began to wobble, then snatched it up before it toppled over. "And this," he said, flipping the coin into the air and catching it. "Is my Temple tax." He added it to the others and latched the pouch.

He pushed away from the table. "Time to get your pins. Before we leave, let's get some roasted meat to take to Yu'dah."

Atticus placed two pins on the counter. "I will take these."

"But they came from the same mold," Yu'dah said. "Perhaps your lady would prefer something different."

Atticus winked. "The pins may have come from the same mold, but the ladies did not."

"It is hard enough to please one woman, how does a man keep two happy?"

"First, and foremost," Atticus said with a laugh, "by never letting either of them know the other exists."

A melancholy look painted itself over Yu'dah's face. He rested a hand on Marcus' arm. "Like my brother here, I would consider myself doubly blessed to have one woman to cherish. I only pray she is there when, at long last, I make my way back to her."

"How is your plan to purchase your freedom working out?" Marcus asked.

Yu'dah frowned. "Not as well as I anticipated. For a short time Gregorius allowed me to keep the money from the repairs. Then, as my reputation grew, he changed his mind. Now he takes all that I receive."

"Everything?"

Yu'dah swirled the strip of meat around in the sauce,

making patterns. "The women usually slip me a coin or two when he is not looking, but I am still a long way from my goal."

"Would this help?" The coins in Marcus's sack clinked together when he dropped it in front of him.

Yu'dah loosened the tie and stared into sack. "What have you done?"

"Assured your freedom."

"But you worked hard to earn this money. I cannot let you do this."

"I already have," Marcus said and crossed his arms with a self-satisfied grin.

Yu'dah ran around the counter and grabbed him by the shoulders. "I cannot believe this." He hugged him tightly. "You have given me back my life."

"As you gave me mine when we were chained together."

"You worked so hard for that money, how could you give it all away?" Atticus asked as they trudged back to the Citadel.

Marcus shrugged. "We must always listen for the *Kol Yahweh*, and when it comes it must be obeyed."

Atticus gave him an incredulous look. "You heard the voice of the Lord? Your God, Yahweh, spoke to you in the goldsmith's shop?"

"Not as I hear your voice now, but in a way, yes."

"But now you are without funds."

"If God wishes me to be wealthy, he will see that riches come my way. In the meantime, Ophelos always needs bread bowls." Marcus thought for a moment. "Remember the day Yu'dah waited in chains?" His voice grew soft, almost lost in the sounds of the street. "I was horrified when Evodius offered me the chance to stand on the block in his stead. Today, God showed me a way to do that." He smiled. "Better one man return to his family than two remain slaves."

Marcus, Atticus and the newly freed Yu'dah shared a final good-bye. Yu'dah drained his cup and threw his pack over his shoulder. Turning to Marcus, he said, "I can never repay you, brother."

"Be safe as you travel."

"I will name my next son, Shemu'el, in your honor."

"And someday when I have sons, one of them shall be called Yu'dah."

Yu'dah turned his staff in his hand, anxious to leave. He paused, having struck upon the one thing he could offer Marcus in repayment.

"On my way, I shall find your settlement and reassure Yaakov's daughter of your love and tell her what a fine man you are. My tales will go on and on late into the night. And only when I have told all there is to tell and answered her every question will my task be complete."

Marcus rested a hand on his shoulder. "That is very kind of you, but return first to your wife and see the child you have never seen. You need not go to Yaakov's home; a Legionnaire already carries a message to Rivkah for me."

Yud'ah stopped at the gate for a final backward glance. He waved, then disappeared around the corner.

Atticus found Marcus in the *pharmacia*. "I have two pieces of news."

"You always say good things come in pairs."

Atticus' lips tightened and he shook his head. "Not this time, my friend. Not this time."

"Give me the good news first. A taste of honey to coat the bitterness."

"On my way across the compound I passed the *Tribuni*. He said that *Legio XII*'s campaign was successful. They are headed home."

"Evodius returns. Good news indeed." Marcus swirled his tongue around the inside of his mouth. "There. I have coated my mouth with honey in preparation."

"You had better sit down."

Marcus put aside his work and walked to the table where his friend sat.

"The *Tribuni* also shared news he received from *Palestinia*. The contingent headed for Jerusalem met an unfortunate fate. While passing through Sebaste, they were set upon by brigands."

"*Cananeans*. Zealots," Marcus said, bringing his fist down on the tabletop. "The same sect whose actions so infuriated Quintilius Varus that he destroyed the town of Sepphoris. They are hot-blooded fools, revolutionaries who will be the downfall of Judaism. Were there casualties?"

"Three from a party of twelve."

Atticus waited while his friend bowed his head in prayer.

"Strange how the death of a Roman soldier upsets me," Marcus said. "I was raised to consider them all vicious heathens. To hate them. Yet coming to know them, I realize they are just men like any other. Some good, some bad.

"I am sorry to be the one to tell you that Lacertus was among the dead," Atticus said.

Those few words snuffed out the happy glow that had been lighting his life, pitching him into darkness and despair. He shook his head and gave an anguished sigh.

Marcus glanced across the surgery, idly watching dust motes drift in and out of a streak of sunlight. He could almost see Lacertus standing there...full of life, happy and healthy.

Big, jolly Lacertus whom he labored to save was dead. The grateful Legionnaire headed to Fortress Antonia with his message to Rivkah.

Unable to sit still, Marcus leaped to his feet and paced the surgery. He never should have been so quick to turn aside Yu'dah's offer, he thought, cursing his foolishness. Yu'dah offered him a treasure more precious than gold and he cast it away without a second thought. Now he had no one to call on Rivkah.

How could a single day make such a difference?

~ 33 ~

Caleb and Avigail married the next spring in the month of Adar Beth. In keeping with *machzor*, the nineteen-year cycle of leap years in the Jewish calendar, the priests added a second Adar to our calendar that year. The rains had been sparse the preceding winter and the flax, barley and wheat reflected it. Grapes, too, were thin and pinched. Winter had barely ended and the pasture grasses already showed brown tips. Despite the expectation of lean times to come, our settlement celebrated with the happy couple.

The following month my younger cousin, Elisheva, married. All my friends were now married and many had children. Even their younger sisters were taking husbands. Everyone, it seemed, had someone.

Everyone except Rivkah.

Elisheva and her husband built a small home beside Tamar's. Things became easier for us all now that the family finally had the man it needed. Abba took a well-deserved rest, but, at the end of the day, he still lacked a grandchild to bounce upon his knee.

The maidens in our settlement gathered at the well and chattered to each other like magpies. Their gossip held little interest for me. Why should it? A man's casual glance no longer made my heart race or my cheeks redden. I had once held love in my hand, a love as sweet as honey in the comb, and lost it. Though I would admit it no one, not even Rachel, inside I felt empty as a woman past her prime.

Years ago, in the garden, Rachel had stretched her tunic tight and laughingly said we were ready for a man. Shortly thereafter they began coming to my door. I read the disappointment in Abba's eyes each time I spurned a match. At times he looked so sad it made my heart ache.

I was still young then and felt no need to hurry. And Abba,

being patient and kind, never put into words what tore at his heart. At first he hinted and skipped around the bush, making it into a child's guessing game. When that failed, his words became more explicit.

"You know better than I that you are no longer a child." As he spoke, Abba opened his hands like someone begging alms. "You are all I have. Each day I grow older, and so do you. You must marry, Rivkah."

"When the time is right, Abba."

I knew how a piece of cloth felt when someone ripped it in two. I so wanted to please him, yet Abba saw only a daughter who refused to honor her father's wishes. I was not blind; I noticed the gray whiskers coming into his beard. How could I make him see that I, too, longed to marry? Tossed and turned at night and ached for a man...for Shemu'el. I still found it easier to look back than ahead.

"When the time is right," I said again, turning away with a dish.

That night neither of us made any attempt to muffle our voices or soften our words. The walls of our little house echoed with our shouts. Half the settlement must have heard us.

"For everything there is a season, a time for every matter under heaven." Abba slammed his fist against the tabletop. "I am a patient man, Rivkah. I have given you ample time to weep and mourn; now you must give me my time with grandchildren."

I fell to my knees before him and took his hands in mine. "I promise on Imma's grave I will give you grandchildren aplenty. I beg you to trust me. Can you not see? Someday the right man will appear and the Lord will whisper in my ear, '*This is your beloved, the man I intended for you.*' Until then, I must wait."

Like an almond buried within a date, Abba began by wrapping his demands in sweet words. When sweetness failed, he had turned to bitterness and shouts. That, too, failed. Only one choice remained.

The time came when my father said the words no daughter wanted to hear. "I will wait no longer, Rivkah. You have spurned many good men. You could have had Caleb, but instead you crept behind my back. You and that woman you call Imma conspired to undo the knot I tied."

A stillness settled over the room. His eyes were narrowed, his expression cold.

"Avigail is now with child," he said, his voice a harsh whisper. "A child that could have been yours, a grandchild that should have been mine." He took a deep breath. "Since you refuse to make a choice, I shall make it for you."

We both knew that after age twelve-and-a-half a girl could reject any match. I stared at him in disbelief, not comprehending the meaning of his words.

"The priests will not allow it. I am long past the age of consent."

He avoided my eyes then. "I will select a good man," he said, as much to himself as to me. "A man who will provide for you and your children." His face hardened. "When all is said and done, you *will* marry him. And no priest will be able to object."

I felt my chest tighten. His harsh words raised panic within me. I swallowed hard, forcing down the bile that burned the back of my throat.

Our eyes met across the room. He seemed as shocked by the implication of his words as I. But words once said can never be unspoken. His threat lay between us like a deadly serpent we were both afraid to touch.

"You would not," I said, finding my voice at last. "You are my father. Surely you would not do this thing."

Abba left the house without a word.

My pulse pounded inside my ears. I began to shake. He had said all he needed to say. We both understood the threat coiled beneath his words. Under the Law, the *kiddushin*, the betrothal contract, validated a marriage.

There were two ways to execute a *kiddushin*. Normally the man negotiated a marriage contract with the bride's father, but, if he lay with the woman, that, too, bound them together. The priests added this second provision to protect a maiden taken against her will. A man could not steal a woman's virginity without marrying her.

But had the priests ever imagined that a chosen bridegroom might commit this dreadful act with the blessing of the girl's father'?

Could Abba actually condone such a thing? Did he want grandchildren so badly that he would allow someone to attack his only daughter? Consign her to a life of shame? Make her the subject of gossip around the well?

Abba promised he would select a good man. A good man who ravished his bride when she spurned his advances? It was an impossible combination.

I thought about my father's words long and hard. As if my life hung in the balance. Because it did. Knowing wisdom is better than weapons of war, I prayed for wisdom. The wisdom of Solomon...and the courage of David.

It is the way of men to meet force with force. I could not drag Abba to a decision like a reluctant calf being hauled to market. No, I must always make him think the choice his, not mine.

Instead of force, I relied upon a woman's wiles and a woman's ways. Subtle hints and soft words disguised my intent. I needed to open only the tiniest gap in the thicket. He would enlarge it for me, then, like a frightened deer, I could bound away and make my escape.

I never defied my father again. To do so would have been folly. I remained respectful, speaking humbly, as a maiden ought. All the while my words sowed seeds of doubt. Seeds to grow in the fertile field of Abba's imagination.

The Lord never made a perfect man. This simple truism became the strongest weapon in my arsenal. I judged each man carefully, searching for the single trait that would diminish him in my father's eyes. Once I found it, quick as an archer, I loosed my deadly arrow.

"This man seems fine enough," I would say, my voice sweet as spring wine. "Does his tendency to idleness concern you?"

Of another I might innocently suggest, "No one works harder than he." Then I bit my lip, pretending concern and reluctantly added, "Yet he lacks your godliness. Will he teach your grandchildren to walk the path of righteousness?"

Or "He is certainly most handsome, almost too handsome. At times he seems puffed-up with pride. What do you think?"

Had Abba not cared for me so deeply, my arrows would have fallen short of their mark. As it was, he decided against the men, not me. I was careful not to gloat over my victory, for to do so would have exposed my plan. Instead, each time I smiled to myself and recalled Miryam's words of warning, "*Rivkah, you and I both know the men in the family make the marriage arrangements.*"

Did they?

Some nights I felt guilty exploiting my father's kindness. What kind of a daughter uses her father's love as a weapon against him? But there seemed no other way. The Psalmist wrote, "Deliver me, O Lord, from lying lips and from a deceitful tongue." I left it for God to judge my actions...the God who pardons sins and delights to show mercy.

In the end, as much as I wanted to please my father in this one thing I could not. And, though he threatened to force me into a marriage against my will, he could not.

~ 34 ~

Marcus glanced up when he heard the wheels of a Roman baggage cart in the courtyard. He knew it was Evodius returning from several weeks' work at a field hospital.

Quirinius, the Governor of Roman Syria, had dispatched an expeditionary force to the eastern frontier to investigate reports of rebel activity and where the army went their physician went along. In his absence, Evodius left his two slaves, Marcus and Atticus, in charge of the barracks hospital.

Earlier that morning a request came in to tend a man injured in a construction accident. They rolled the dice and, since Atticus lost the toss, he answered the call. Marcus had been under apprenticeship to Evodius for over eight years, Atticus even longer. Both men had become skilled and practiced in the healing arts.

Marcus opened the door and found his mentor trying to lift a heavy traveling case. He ran to help.

"*Ave!* Welcome home." He read the fatigue in the older man's eyes. "You look tired, worn out. Let me take care of these for you."

"Happily." Evodius thumped a fist against his breastbone and stepped aside. "Something I ate has upset me greatly. I suffered with indigestion the entire trip."

Marcus looked him over again, closer this time, doing a quick diagnosis. "You are flushed." He touched his mentor's forehead. "And you skin is damp and clammy. Go inside and sit down. Rest. I will mix up something to soothe your stomach as soon as I take care of the luggage."

Marcus grabbed the straps and heaved one of the cases out of the wagon. Nearby soldiers grabbed the others and followed him toward the door. When Marcus turned his attention to Evodius what he found alarmed him. The old man slumped in his chair, gasping for each breath.

"Come, let me get you into bed."

"Too late," Evodius wheezed. "I am already dying."

"Not if I can help it."

"There is nothing you can do."

Supporting him with one arm, Marcus helped him rise. Together they swayed and reeled their way across the room. As they walked, Marcus recalled another time years before when they staggered along together. Evodius had been the stronger one then, and he the boy with the lame arm. Now their roles were reversed.

Evodius collapsed in a heap, landing like a sack. Marcus leaned over him. He undid the girdle and the leather harness that crossed the man's chest. "Where does it hurt?"

The physician's right hand circled the left side of his chest, moved across to his left arm and up along his neck and jaw. "Feels as if an elephant is sitting on my chest," he groaned.

"Have you had similar pains before?"

"Off and on for the last year or so, but never this bad."

"And why have you never told us?"

"To what end? There was nothing you could have done. This is the way my father died." Evodius' eyes searched the room wildly. "The gods are coming for me," he whispered. "I feel their presence hovering all around me."

Marcus placed two fingers on the man's wrist and felt his pulse racing. He pressed an ear against his chest. While he listened, Marcus recalled studying an Egyptian scroll which read, "Shouldst thou examine a patient with stomach disease suffering from pains in the arm, in the breast and left side of the stomach say, '*Death threatens.*' If the pain moves to the neck and jaw say, '*Death is near.*'"

Marcus swabbed his mentor's clammy skin with a cool, damp cloth. Then, leaving it folded across Evodius' forehead, he rushed into the surgery and scanned the shelves for some herb, root or extract to give him. He grabbed a package of dried digitalis leaves. A tea made from the ground leaves and water strengthened the heart. He decided against it, knowing too large a dose sometimes proved fatal.

Instead he pulled down a bottle containing a dark liquid, draught of willow bark. Each spring, during the Matronalia Festivities, he and Atticus collected fresh, sappy willow bark, boiled it and let it steep for several days. Then they filtered and bottled this bitter decoction. Mixed with wine, it served as a general pain reliever. It sometimes lessened chest pains in cases similar to Evodius'.

Slipping the arm Evodius had set years earlier under the older man's head, he lifted him slightly and fed him small sips of the potion. When he emptied the cup, Marcus returned to swabbing his forehead, chest and arm. The pain gradually subsided. Evodius took a deep, cleansing breath and smiled for the first time.

Marcus covered him with a thin blanket, gathered his utensils and tiptoed away. He was gone only a short time when Evodius screamed in pain. Marcus rushed out of the apothecary and into the bedroom. He found him on his side clutching his chest and retching. Marcus grabbed a pan. Evodius vomited into it then sank back into the pillow with a weary sigh.

His breath came in frantic pants. The gray pallor of impending death replaced his normally ruddy complexion. Marcus put his hand on Evodius' ankle checking for a pulse. He barely detected one. He pressed his ear to the man's chest again and heard the frenzied palpitations of a dying heart struggling to live.

Atticus dropped his bag in the doorway and ran to join Marcus at Evodius' bedside. "What has happened?"

"*Palpitare*," Marcus whispered. "He returned complaining of difficulty breathing and pains in his chest, neck and left arm. I gave him willow extract in wine. It worked momentarily then he vomited it up. He's had similar chest pains for more than a year. I am afraid his time has come. The *Malakh HaMavet*, the Angel of Death, hovers waiting to whisk him away."

After a quick examination, Atticus nodded his concurrence. There was little they could do for their master.

"I considered giving him digitalis, but rejected it in favor of draught of willow."

"A good decision at the time," Atticus said, "but I think we should try it now. Desperate situations call for desperate measures. We know digitalis strengthens the heart. What do we have to lose?"

The two men stared at each other. Evodius' life hung in the balance.

Marcus ran to the apothecary and pulled down the package of dried digitalis leaves. He removed two, paused, then returned the smaller one to its container with a frown. The first rule of the Hippocratic oath stated *Do no harm*.

He dropped the leaf into the mortar and attacked it furiously with his pestle. Once he reduced it to a fine powder, he added boiling water to make a paste, which he further diluted and strained into a cup.

The mixture steadied Evodius' heartbeat. The two men took encouragement from the growing strength of the pulse in his extremities. The final outcome, they knew, had always been beyond their control. The two slaves prayed over him as he slept. Putting him in God's hands, they would watch and wait, alternating shifts throughout the night.

Marcus blinked in the dark. He saw the shadow of someone sitting at the end of his bed. The clank of spear against shield that typically accompanied the changing of the guard echoed in the courtyard beneath his window.

"How long have you been here?"

"Just a few minutes."

Believing it was his turn at Evodius' bedside, Marcus put his feet on the floor. "Why did you not wake me?"

Atticus hung his head. "There is no hurry."

"Evodius has left us?"

"Sextus Evodius Scipio, our master, our mentor and our friend, now belongs to the ages."

Marcus rent his tunic and intoned, "*Adonai natan, Radonai lakach. Yehi shem Adonai merorach.*" Seeing Atticus' confused expression, he explained, "The prayer for the dead. God has given, God has taken. May the name of God be blessed."

The two men sat quietly for several minutes letting the reality of Evodius' death seep in. At last Marcus raised his eyes, glanced over at his friend and voiced the question on both their minds.

"What will become of us now?" His voice was soft, almost lost in the thump of soldier's footsteps in the outer courtyard.

The black man's normally cheery face grew somber. He rubbed his jaw, shook his head and shrugged.

"Could we end up on the sales block?"

"Very possibly. They sell slaves here in Antioch each week. Funds transfer more efficiently than people do. Easier to sell us here and remit the proceeds to whatever family Evodius left in Rome."

Life had been good for them. So good, in fact, that they'd ceased to think of themselves as slaves. And now, the unexpected death of one man brought their precarious situation into sharp focus.

Marcus' first impulse was to bolt from the room. Leave before anyone knew of Evodius' death. Cast off every badge of slavery and run as far and fast as he could.

Atticus read his thoughts and shook his head. "Escape is not an option, my friend. They would take our absence as a sign of complicity. We would be pursued, caught and end our lives chained to an oar in the bowels of some Roman galley. Better we stay here and face our fate."

Not only was escape futile, Marcus realized it was also unmanly. Better to stay and face the consequences, whatever they might be. God, he knew, had a plan for him. He might be able to hide from the Romans, but no man hid from God.

Atticus rose. "It would look better if we both went."

They arranged and prepared the body, and at first light, left to notify the *Medicus Legonionis* of Evodius' demise.

Marcus paced the small room, adjusting and re-adjusting his sash. Although not as outwardly concerned, Atticus also fretted over his appearance. They requested, and were granted, permission to join the honor guard accompanying Evodius' funeral cortege. The previous evening both men knelt by the well washing their finest garments. Returning to their quarters, more properly, the quarters of their former master, they carefully hung the clothing to dry.

They accompanied the body to the funeral pyre and stood at attention while Evodius' superior, the *Medicus Legonionis*, gave the eulogy. When he finished, he touched a flaming torch to the oil-soaked wood saying, *"Atque in perpetuum ave atquevale...* Now and for all eternity, farewell."

A lump formed in Marcus' throat and tears welled in his eyes as he watched all that remained of Sextus Evodius Scipio disappear in a mighty rush of flames.

~ 35 ~

It had been several years since disturbing dreams of Shemu'el haunted my sleep, but that morning I awoke, cheeks damp with tears, feeling unsettled and upset. I dressed and began my day hoping work would drive the vivid images from my mind. The more I struggled to forget, the stronger the memories became.

Why now, I wondered. Now, that I had finally managed to pull my shattered life together. Finally gathered all my hopes of life with Shemu'el, stuffed them into a chest, and locked the lid.

Like cobwebs in a corner, the confusing jumble of images from the previous night returned no matter how many times I brushed them away. Anxious and distracted, I grabbed a bucket and went to the well. Hoping the sun and air would refresh me.

Rachel was at the well when I arrived. "You do not look like yourself today, Rivkah. Are you feeling well?"

I mumbled a reply hoping it would satisfy her. When that failed, I tried to laugh it off.

She insisted I tell her what was wrong.

"I had a disturbing dream last night," I admitted, under her persistent questioning. I dipped my bucket and sat it aside.

She nodded knowingly. "Shemu'el. Still you haunt him."

Strange words. I always imagined *him* haunting me.

Rachel's hands moved and swirled in the air between us. "There in *Sheol*, Shemu'el remains in a state of conflict. Each time he tries to move on, a tie to the past yanks him back. When will Rivkah put him aside and let him peacefully rest in Avraham's bosom?"

"It was not about Shemu'el. This was nothing like the dreams I had before. There was no smoke and ashes, no shouting, no bodies."

Rachel had always been prone to superstitions. Carrying a child in her womb made her even more so. She grabbed my arm, spilling my bucket, and dragged me over to a grove of myrtle trees. She settled herself in the shade and glanced up expectantly. When I did not move to join her, she pounded the grass indicating where I was to sit.

Rachel unconsciously stroked her swollen belly as we talked. A habit she developed as the time of her fulfillment drew near. "Tell me about the dream. Was it about me?"

She seemed disappointed when told it was not. "Perhaps I ate too many cucumbers at supper." I laughed, hoping Rachel would let the matter drop.

"This is nothing to joke about. Dreams have power. Remember the prophet Daniyyel in Babylon?" Rachel waved a finger in front of my face, covered her eyes and moaned the words mysteriously written on Belshazzar's banquet room wall, "*Mene, Mene, Tekil, Parsin.*"

"There were no words written upon my wall."

She refused to be dissuaded. "What about Yosef in Egypt, interpreting the Pharaoh's dream? The Lord has always spoken through dreams. Tell me...tell me." She moved her hands as if she could draw the words out of me.

"All right. I became a bird. An eagle, I think, although I could not see myself, of course. I flew higher than you can imagine. Though I am afraid of heights, I felt no fear."

Eyes down, Rachel rocked from side to side, rubbed her belly and murmured, "Hmmm...hmmm," as if she were a seer. Her head snapped up when I paused to take a breath. "Continue," she commanded.

"I soared above the earth swiveling my head, seeing from horizon to horizon. I looked down on our little settlement, on Bethlehem, the Temple and Jerusalem...every city, great and small, in all of Israel."

Rachel listened with rising interest.

"Then I rose higher still." I lifted my right arm...wing. "The Judean Mountains were below on my right." I raised the other wing. "And on my left the Great Sea stretched out until it touched the sky, blue meeting blue."

Rachel bubbled over with excitement. "Mountains and the Great Sea, what do you think it means?"

I shook my head and shrugged.

"Ahead of me, the setting sun rested on the horizon. I detected movement far off in the distance. I watched a cloud of dust rise as if thrown up by a sirocco. Yet there was no wind; everything remained still. I looked again and noticed something at the head of the dust cloud, a black speck at first...hardly visible. Then, in an instant, I saw it was a man on horseback galloping toward me, coming ever faster and faster."

The color drained from Rachel's face. She inched away and hugged her belly, trembling. Tears appeared in her eyes.

I took her by the shoulders and shook her. "Rachel, what is it?"

"An omen. You have seen the day of the Lord," she said in a deathly whisper. "The prophet Yo'el wrote, 'They have the appearance of horses; they gallop along like cavalry. They leap over mountaintops like a crackling fire consuming stubble, like a mighty army drawn up for battle.'"

Tears dripped down her cheeks. "Better if I had not asked about your dream. Better that I not know. We are coming to the end of days and here I am with child." She looked around, her eyes wild with fright. "What will I do when the Lord sweeps all this away. What about my baby?"

"No! It was a dream. A silly dream and nothing more."

Rachel stared into her lap for a long time. When she raised her eyes she had a peculiar expression on her face. "If this was no vision, then it is a message. God has heard your prayers and sends a man to love you."

Rachel took my hand, as if she intended to read my palm. Instead, she began interpreting my dream. "Here is how you will know him," she whispered. "The horse represents power. He will be a man of power. The sea and mountains represent distance. He comes from far away. He rushes to you burning with love and when he takes you in his arms your spirit will soar like an eagle."

~ 36 ~

A few days later, I heard hoof beats on the road. The afternoon was hot and I had been grinding barley into flour with my veil slipped back onto my shoulders. I stopped to pull it over my head, covering my hair, before rising to see who it was.

The hoof beats led me to expect a soldier. Instead, a handsome young man tied his horse in front of the house and walked toward me. I brushed flour dust off my cloak as he approached. He took the long, confident strides of a man accustomed to getting what he wanted.

"*Shalom Aleichem*. My name is Tyro, I seek Yaakov."

"*Aleichem Shalom*. He is not here. I am his daughter."

"I came to purchase a kid."

"A kid? You rode your horse all this way just to buy a kid? Surely other people besides us keep goats."

"My father insisted."

He arched his back and pushed his stomach out imitating his father's ample girth. He took wide steps and moved his hands around his head, adjusting a turban he did not wear. He paused to stroke his beard then shook a finger. He gave a stern look and made his voice deep and authoritative.

"Tyro, my son, you must stop near Bethlehem and purchase a kid from Yaakov. There is no more tender meat in all Judea than a roasted kid from his flock."

Becoming himself again, he smiled and threw his hands in the air. "I could not disobey my father, could I?"

"You seemed to imitate the merchant, Sidonius."

"You know my father?"

"I have known him all my life. He brings me pieces of Persian candy."

Tyro clapped his hands with delight. "You must be Rivkah. My father's description did not do you justice."

His words made my cheeks burn.

He noticed and grinned.

I jerked my veil across my face "Abba is with the flock. Do you want me to tell you the way?"

"In a moment. But first I have something for you from my father, a gift." Tyro ran to the horse and removed a package from his saddlebag. "Sweets," he said, waving the package in the air.

"Would you like some?" I asked when he handed it to me.

"I would happily eat a mountain of Persian candy to remain in your company."

My eyes went to the package in my hand, then back up to his with a smile. "Sorry. There is not that much here."

"Then I shall chew very, very slowly."

The candy turned us into children. We sat in the side yard resting our backs against the twisted trunk of an olive tree, laughing and joking as we ate.

"You must be a rich man," I said, licking my sticky fingers.

Tyro seemed pleased. "What makes you think that?"

"You have a horse."

"True, but...?"

"But other than the army, few people own horses. They cannot graze among the brush and brambles the way goats do. Asses make better pack animals and oxen pull heavier loads. Camels traverse the desert without water. The only thing you can do with a horse is ride it."

"Have you ever ridden a horse?

I fanned my hand in front of my face and shook my hand. "Oh no, just a donkey. I would be afraid to climb high up onto a horse."

"Only by being on a horse can you understand how thrilling it is. The speed...the rush of wind in your hair." He grinned and snapped his fingers, "There is nothing like it."

"Are you a merchant like your father?"

"If you mean am I tethered to the lead rope of a camel train, the answer is no. There are easier ways to make a living. I finance the journeys of other traders. In exchange, they transport my products at no cost. I have contracts with the best weavers and dyers in Tyre and Sidon. Cloth bearing my mark trades at a premium throughout the Empire."

Tyro sounded like a powerful man. I heard Rachel's voice echo in my mind whispering, *"A powerful man with a horse."* I cleared my throat and swallowed. "What brings you to Judea?"

"I have a debt to collect in Jerusalem." He crinkled his dark eyes and smiled, showing me sparkling teeth. "Sometimes I am forced to remind people that I lend, not give. When I finish in Jerusalem I will head for the Nabatean capital, Petra, the city of stone."

"I have never heard of it. Your father spoke of many places, but he never said anything about a city of stone."

"And if my father failed to mention the clouds in the sky, does that mean there are none?" Too excited to sit still, Tyro leaped to his feet and paced as he spoke. "It is one of the most fascinating cities I know. Petra is hidden away in the middle of the desert and carved from the surrounding mountains."

"How do they survive in the desert?"

"Oh, they have secret sources of water." A wave of his hand brushed my question aside. He lowered his voice. "The city itself is hidden. In places the road into it is barely wide enough for a camel to pass." Tyro extended his arms as if pressing against opposing walls. "No wider than this."

Buildings carved from mountains, water in the desert, secret passageways? It all sounded unbelievable to me. I squinted up at him and chuckled. "You strike me as a teller of tales."

He tossed his head back indignantly and crossed his arms. "Every word is the truth. If you do not believe me, I will take you there."

"How? Your horse cannot travel in sand."

"I plan to stable him in Jerusalem and contract the services of a camel driver. I will stop for you on the way back."

"You expect me to ride off with you across the desert?"

What ideas he had. This Tyro person was unlike any man I had ever met. Nothing seemed impossible to him.

"Very well. Two camels then." He read my look of skepticism and added, "And two tents. Yours shall have a lock upon it to keep me out at night."

"A lock on a tent?" I shook my head. "Come, we better find Abba so you can purchase a kid before your tales exhaust me."

When we passed Tyro's stallion, it whinnied, pawing the

dirt and tugging against its reins to reach him. He stopped to pat the horse's neck and whisper in its ear.

"He wants to go with us. Pegasus behaves like a petulant child at times, especially when he is disappointed," Tyro explained, as we left.

"Your horse told you he wanted to go with us?"

He threw me a glance. "The sheep and goats communicate their needs to you, do they not?"

"You are right, of course they do."

We went only a short distance when Tyro reached down and took my hand. Thinking he meant to steady me on the uneven ground, I made no protest. But when the path leveled out, his fingers continued clasping mine.

I tried to pull away.

His grip tightened.

Jerking free, I spun to face him with hands on my hips. "Why are you taking liberties with me? I do not know you and would not allow it if I did."

Rather than being shamed, he seemed amused. "I could not help myself, Rivkah. Your beauty overwhelmed my better judgment."

Something about Tyro both frightened and fascinated me. We walked on in silence, two cubits apart, giving each other wary sidelong glances. Our eyes met. When he smiled, I forced myself to look away. What was it about this prideful son of Baal that attracted me so?

The details of the dream I had the previous week came rushing back. The city of Tyre *was* a great distance away...on the Great Sea. And Tyro came on a horse...searching for our home. For me. I suddenly found it hard to concentrate. Stilling my mind, I listened for the Lord's voice. All I got for my trouble was the chattering of sparrows in the thicket.

"Are you still angry with me?" Tyro asked. "No real harm was done."

His words snapped me out of my reverie, forcing me to become myself again. Dream, or no dream, an inner voice warned me to be wary of Tyro.

~ 37 ~

"Why would Quirinius want to meet with us?"

Atticus considered the question for several long moments, then shook his head. "I cannot imagine what he could want with us. Neither of us have even been in his palace, much less had an audience with the Governor. Last night in desperation I went to the temple and made an offering at the Oracle of Carmentis, the goddess of prophecy."

"And?"

"And...nothing." His face slumped in disappointment. "Have you prayed to this wise Solomon you sometimes speak of?"

"Solomon was a king, not a god," Marcus reminded him. "You know we Jews worship only the one God who reigns from everlasting to everlasting."

"And what does He say about all this?"

"The Almighty does not speak to men through oracles; he puts his law in his followers' minds and writes it on their hearts. He expects us to step forward trusting that He will guide us. Many times the path itself only appears years later when one looks back."

The men's status, which remained undefined after Evodius' death, would soon be clarified. Since the funeral they spent their days providing medical care to the cohort as they always had. They anticipated the imminent arrival of Evodius' replacement and devoted any free time to cleaning and organizing the surgery. First impressions were lasting ones. Both men wanted this new physician, whomever he might be, to think well of them.

Did Quirinius plan to notify them of their new superior? Marcus wondered. He immediately rejected the thought. A Governor had better things to do with his time than converse with slaves. Such an announcement would come from the *Medicus Legonionis,* or more likely, from one of his assistants.

The day before they were told to prepare for a meeting with Quirinius, the Roman Governor of Syria. No more.

Marcus and Atticus took a quick breakfast with the troops then rushed back to their quarters. They were afraid to leave the surgery unattended for more than a few minutes. If the Centurion sent to fetch them arrived and found them missing, he might report them as runaways.

"Could this have anything to do with Evodius' death?" Marcus asked. They had debated the matter endlessly since the previous afternoon. "We were, after all, in attendance."

Atticus opened his mouth to reply, but the Centurion's knock cut him short.

The surgery lay on the south edge of the city in the Citadel, a fortress built into the Wall of Tiberius. Several miles to the north, the Governor's palace stood on the *insula*, a large island formed between separate arms of the Orontes River. The island had once been the capitol of the Seleucid Empire. Now it served as the administrative center of Rome's Syrian Province.

Marcus stepped outside and drew his cloak against the wind. He glanced up at the dark clouds hovering above Mount Silpius and frowned. A great day all around, he thought. One well suited to his mood.

He and Atticus left their quarters accompanied by the Centurion and boarded a carriage. To reach the bridge, they traveled the *Via Caesarea*, a wide, stone-paved street that bisected the city of Antioch. Roman law forbade vehicles on the thoroughfare during the daylight hours to prevent congestion.

Foot traffic parted at the sound of the approaching horse, allowing the driver to maintain a brisk pace. Because the carriage flew the legion's banner, merchants and shoppers along the route gawked as the carriage rattled by. Deep in thought, Marcus hardly noticed the rhythmic click, click, click of the horse's hoofs on the road's square cobblestones.

Midway, in the heart of the city, they passed Herod's Stoa. This colonnaded walkway with its long row of matching pillars paralleled the city wall of Seleucus I, which enclosed the oldest section of the city. King Herod built the Stoa in fawning tribute to his patron, Tiberius Caesar.

Each time Marcus passed under its elaborately decorated roof the same thought crossed his mind, this magnificent structure in a Roman city untold miles from Jerusalem, had been paid for by the sweat and toil of the Jewish people.

Despite his hatred for everything Herod represented, he usually stopped and ran his hand along one of its polished columns. Touching them gave him a momentary, if ephemeral, connection to the land and people he loved.

The Centurion accompanied them up the palace's wide marble steps and presented his orders to the guard. After transferring his charges, he saluted and left. The guard led Marcus and Atticus down a long, mosaic-tiled hallway with frescoed walls. They stopped at a table where a gray-haired man sat working.

He glanced up at them with a look of disdain. "I am Quintus, one of the Governor's administrators. We have arranged a meeting between you two and Gnaeus Valerius, a staff physician assigned to the *Legio III Gallica*." He rose and flicked a finger. "This way."

Head high, Quintus walked several paces in front of them. Everything about the man's manner told them what a sacrifice he made conversing with lowly slaves. He directed them to a small anteroom and huffed away.

Valerius entered immediately after. "As an impartial observer, I have been asked to evaluate your medical capabilities," the physician explained. Seeing their startled expression, he added, "Merely routine in cases such as this."

They both remained on the edge of their seats, straining forward as the questioning began. He quizzed each man about his medical training, presenting symptoms and asking them to make a diagnosis and suggest remedies or medications. They discussed the proper way to deal with the various wounds and fractures typically seen by a military physician. He inquired about the time they'd spent with Evodius and the instances when they functioned without his direct supervision.

"Now let us turn to the recent death of Evodius Scipio." He gave them a reassuring smile. "None of the medical staff doubts that you both did all you could. Still, the Governor felt an inquiry the appropriate way to proceed."

He directed most of his questions at Marcus since he was the one caring for Evodius. Valerius interrogated him regarding each of his mentor's symptoms and the treatment he provided. He seemed relieved when told Evodius experienced similar episodes for more than a year. As the meeting progressed, the men noticed his demeanor gradually soften from inquisitor to that of colleague.

He left and they relaxed for the first time. This welcome change in Valerius' attitude indicated they had cleared their first, and most important, hurdle. What came next neither man could imagine.

~ 38 ~

Pain pressed hard against my heart the day Shemu'el died. But, no matter what I believed then, a heart is not made to grieve forever and there are only so many tears to be shed. Like a butterfly emerging from its casing, I changed over time. Thoughts and dreams of Shemu'el stayed where they belonged, in the past.

As much as I tried to deny it, I was just a woman...a lonely woman ready for love.

Tyro returned two days after he bought the kid.

I put down my half-sorted bucket of figs. "If you were not happy with the kid you purchased, you must take it up with Abba."

He made an elaborate gesture of surprise. "Your father offered me no guarantees. How can you imagine I would expect a refund? Even if the animal he sold me was nothing but inedible gristle, it is no concern of his, or yours." He gave a disappointed shrug and dug his toe in the dirt. "Once a bargain is struck, there is no going back on a man's word."

"So you were not satisfied."

"Is that what I said?"

"You said—"

He put a finger to my lips, cutting me off. Tyro wrapped his arm around the trunk of the tree beside me and swung in a lazy circle, chuckling.

"Rivkah, Rivkah...Rivkah. I said *even if*. Merely a hypothetical example." He grinned. "My father knows well of what he speaks. The innkeeper seasoned the kid with mint sauce and we had a feast. It was delicious," he said, smacking his lips.

"I see you are not only a teller of tales, but a deceiver as well."

His eyes twinkled. "A jokester, perhaps, but not a deceiver. In my occupation one learns to listen to each word carefully. A camel could pass through the loopholes some merchants try to insert in their contracts."

I straightened my cloak and carried the figs back to the house.

Tyro trailed behind me. "Rivkah, wait! I meant no harm. It was merely a small joke, something we could laugh over. Why must we always start off with the wrong foot? Here, I brought something for you."

His hand disappeared inside his robe and reappeared with a package.

It was not more sweetmeats. He handed me a long gold necklace with an amethyst stone set in a starburst medallion.

"I, I cannot take this." I said, staring down at the chain's golden links dripping between my fingers. "It must have cost quite a lot."

He shrugged. "It is only money. I have more. We did not part on the best of terms and I wanted to make amends." He lifted the necklace out of my hand and spread the chain, making a circle. "Go ahead, try it on."

I lowered my head and Tyro draped the necklace around my neck. I had never owned anything so extravagant. I glanced down and blushed. The heavy medallion hung in the center of my chest, pressing in my tunic and emphasizing the curve of my breasts.

He smiled and nodded appreciatively. "I instructed the jeweler to make the chain extra long. I wanted the pendant to rest between your lovely breasts, the place I long to lay my head."

"Why must my every encounter with you end in seduction?" I removed the necklace and threw it back at him. "Have you no honor?"

"Would my desires be honorable if I were your husband?"

I froze. His words left me speechless.

"I am helpless. You are beautiful. I see you and I want you. I cannot be satisfied until I have you."

"And what if I do not want you?"

He grinned. "How could you not want me? Every woman does."

"You are arrogant beyond measure." I covered my eyes. . "I cannot abide those who have a haughty look and a proud heart."

Tyro staggered back clutching his left side. "Your dart has pierced my heart. Help me, Rivkah. I am mortally wounded."

Despite my best effort, he made me smile.

"You are beautiful beyond words," he said, instantly recovered.

"And you are as full of gas as a goat in the onion patch."

Tyro took my hand and tugged me down the walk. "Walk with me, Rivkah. Walk with me and we can talk."

He untied his horse and gripped the reins with the other hand. The big animal clopped along behind us as we walked. Tyro spoke of his travels and the places he would take me. The fabulous things we would see and do, the sea voyages we would take to far off lands, the home he would build for us above Tyre with a terrace overlooking the Great Sea. The servants, my fine gowns, jewelry, and banquets. He painted an enchanting picture.

He stopped and turned to face me. "Have you ever seen Solomon's Pools?"

"No. They are in the mountains. Abba once took the sheep there to shield them from Athrongeus' raiders, but I did not accompany him. He said they were lovely with many trees and remarkable views."

"Would you like to see them for yourself?"

"It is too far away."

"Nonsense. My horse will take us there."

I took one look at the horse's tall back and shook my head. "No thank you. It would be too dangerous. No one could get me on top of that huge beast."

Tyro stepped beside the horse and stroked its neck. Pegasus wore a Parthian saddle similar to the war horses that accompanied the Magoi the morning after Miryam and Yosef fled to Egypt. The saddle had a metal loop hanging from a strap on each side. Tyro put his foot through a loop and used it to climb into the saddle.

He grinned down at me and spread his arms. "See how easy it is?"

After that things happened very fast. Tyro leaned so far over I feared he was about to pitch off. He slipped his arm around me and scooped me up. One moment I was standing beside the horse expecting Tyro to fall to the ground at my feet, the next I found myself in Tyro's lap looking down at the ground.

"What have you done?" I shrieked. "Release me. Put me down."

Tyro threw his head back and laughed. He snapped the reins and made a clicking sound with his tongue.

The horse ran away with me still in Tyro's lap, swaying and screaming.

"Hold on," Tyro said. He dug his heels into the horse's flank, making it gallop.

Trembling with fear and certain of impending death, I wrapped my arms around him tightly and buried my face in his chest.

Bethlehem seemed to be nothing but scattered blocks of tan rock from the plateau near Solomon's Pools. I gazed awestruck, finding it hard to believe those familiar buildings could appear so small.

Tyro pointed south where something sparkled on the horizon. "Look at the sun on the Temple walls."

The horse's gait no longer frightened me. Tyro was right, the speed and wind blowing past your face were exhilarating. He reined the horse to a stop and I remained in his lap with his arms around me, unafraid. He leaned down and kissed me.

I felt an unfamiliar warmth flow through me. I returned his kisses until he tried to do more.

My hands closed around his. Our eyes met and I whispered, "Please do not ruin this wonderful afternoon."

For once Tyro neither argued, nor objected.

Tyro offered me the necklace again on the way back from Solomon's Pools. I agreed if he had the chain shortened to a modest length.

He slipped it back into his cloak, promising to return it on his next visit.

Unaccustomed thoughts ran through my mind as we returned home. Tyro had implied he was interested in marriage. Was it true, or merely another of his ploys?

I glanced up at him. His handsome features glowed like polished bronze in the sunlight.

The horse stepped over a hole, rocking the saddle. His arm automatically tightened around me.

Tingles of excitement coursed through me.

I had forced myself to forget how it felt to be in a man's arms...the longings a man's touch created. Questions crowded my mind. Could I lie with Tyro, giving and accepting, as a wife must do?

Could I lie with him and not think of Shemu'el?

~ 39 ~

The Governor's office displayed the lavish decor expected of an important Roman official. The walls were made of the whitest marble. Even in the sunlight, Marcus scarcely detected a vein of color in it. Ornate Persian rugs dotted the green Numidian marble floor. The choice of flooring struck Marcus as particularly ironic.

Caesar's sharp sword, which sliced Herod's kingdom into three pieces after his death, had also divided the kingdom of Numidia down the middle. They grafted the western half onto the province of Mauritania and the eastern portion they added to Africa Nova, much as the kingdom of the Jews became an appendage to the province of Syria.

Quirinius remained seated when they entered. "Gnaeus Valerius says all aspects of your performance were satisfactory," he said with a thin smile as they saluted and took their places.

Both of the men nodded politely.

The middle-aged man sitting across from them, portly and balding, wore the *toga praetexta*, the purple trimmed toga of a Roman consul. The two slaves, dressed in plain military tunics, sat ramrod straight with their cloaks neatly folded in their laps.

The Governor picked up two scrolls, absentmindedly rapping them against the edge of the table as he spoke.

Marcus noticed them on the desk when they arrived, but took them to be standard bureaucratic communiqués. Now as the Governor fingered them, he wondered if he had been mistaken. Could they be more important than he supposed, perhaps even the purpose of this meeting?

"Sextus Evodius Scipio named me Executor of his testament," the Governor said. "In it, he stipulated that his slaves, you two, be freed upon his demise. I have your certificates of manumission here in my hand."

A thousand thoughts crowded Marcus' mind when Quirinius said, "Marcus, slave of Sextus Evodius Scipio, I declare you to be a freedman, a Roman citizen." He handed him the scroll. "Congratulations. Henceforth you shall be known as

Sextus Evodius Marcus."

The Governor turned to Atticus and repeated the process.

Believing this to be the conclusion of their meeting, both men hurriedly saluted and prepared to take their leave. At the Governor's, "Not yet," they dropped back into their seats.

He motioned them over to a table beside a tall window. Beyond it a balcony, bounded by a wrought iron railing, overlooked the harbor. Marcus watched a ship ease out of its slip and glide down the Orontes River on its way to the port of Selucia and the Great Sea. Sunlight gleamed on its sails; the morning's threatened storm had passed.

A servant appeared with a tray and poured three cups of wine. Quirinius raised his saying, "To Evodius Scipio, a fine physician and trusted friend to all who knew him. The best of men. May the gods be kind to him."

After they toasted their dead patron, the Governor produced two leather pouches, each drawn together and tied at the neck with a leather cord.

"As well as being a just man, Scipio was also a generous one. His testament stipulated that, along with your freedom, you each receive a stipend. He did not want to turn you loose without ready funds."

The silver coins inside clinked as he slid the sacks over to them. He smiled, watching the two men grasp them eagerly. They shifted in their chairs, each eyeing the bag he lovingly held on his knee.

"I will save you the agony of waiting," Quirinius said. "Marcus, yours contains 100 denarii. Atticus, yours 150. Hardly a fortune, but sufficient to keep you in bread and meat while you transition into new circumstances."

He brought his fingertips together and leaned forward. His voice took on an almost fatherly tone. "It has been my experience that after the sudden euphoria of freedom wears off, a freedman's first thought is, 'What do I do now?' Well, I am here to offer a solution. The Roman Army can always use skilled physicians and you two trained with one of our best."

He paused for a sip of wine.

Both men quickly lifted their cups to join him.

"Gnaeus Valerius assures me both of you are qualified medical officers. Therefore, on his recommendation, I am prepared to offer you the position of *Medicus Ordinarii*. You will be an officer of the order and, although not a command position *per se*, you will have the rank of Centurion." He let this sink in before adding, "The starting pay for Centurions is 3,750 denarii per annum."

He turned and stared into Atticus' dark brown eyes. "What say you, Sextus Evodius Atticus? Will you accept my offer to serve *Roma Alma Mater*?"

Atticus pondered Quirinius' offer briefly, then grinned. "Yes, Sir. I think I would like that. I would like it very much."

And so, the deal was struck. Atticus glanced around the room with a satisfied smile, slightly overwhelmed by his sudden, and unexpected, rise in status. Rome's newest *Ordinarii* watched as the Governor turned to his longtime friend and asked, "I make you the same offer, Sextus Evodius Marcus. What say you?"

Marcus swallowed hard. It was a tantalizing prospect. Nearly four thousand denarii. A veritable fortune in Judea. And many Centurions earned much more. As the senior *Medicus Cohortis* and medical officer to the *Legio XII Fulminata's* largest cohort, Evodius had earned 12,000 denarii per annum.

True Marcus would live a soldier's life, but seldom would he be in mortal danger. He could complete his term of service at a relatively young age and retire. Retirement entitled him to a grant of land. He could, perhaps, earn a promotion as Evodius had done and become *Medicus Cohortis*...even *Medicus Legionis*.

Then in the depths of his memory, he heard Rivkah ask, "*Yes, what say you, Shemu'el bar Yo'el?*"

His decision came in an instant. How could he have imagined himself a Roman? He had dreamed of this moment every day since they drug him out of Jerusalem in chains. Wealth and position meant nothing next to Rivkah.

Marcus knew what he wanted, and it was not a medical posting with a Roman Legion. He'd had his fill of gore on battlefields with the stench of death and cries of pain. The thought of a lifetime littered with bloated corpses sickened him. But, realizing that rejecting the Governor's offer out of hand would seem impolite, he pretended to give it long and thoughtful consideration.

Clearing his throat, he said, "I thank you for this generous offer, Sir. It is gratifying to know you deem my skills worthy of such a post. Unfortunately, I must decline. First and foremost, I long to return to my home in Judea."

"Judea. You are a Jew then?"

"I am."

"And how long have you been away?"

"I left Jerusalem over eight years ago."

"I must warn you, you will not return to the same country you left." Quirinius' expression turned pensive. "The situation there has deteriorated greatly. Caesar recently ousted that fool Herod Archelaus and exiled him to Gaul."

"So I have heard."

"Coponius now rules the territory from Caesarea, an Imperial Prefect under my jurisdiction. Yet knowing this, you still wish to return."

Sextus Evodius Marcus rocked the sack of coins on his knee. "Yes. Yes, I do. I have very little choice. You see, a Jew carries his homeland in his heart wherever he goes," he said, putting a finger to his chest.

"Truly spoken. I suppose no Jew ever truly leaves *Palestinia*, do they? One and all, they flock back to Jerusalem from all over the world for your festivals. Especially the one when they roast lamb and eat flat bread with bitter herbs." Quirinius chuckled. "When they are not rioting in the temple."

"Yes sir, when they are not busy rioting in the Temple," Marcus replied after a long and painful pause.

"But you could return for the festivals from here in Antioch. Many Jews do. I sense there is more here, something you have not told us."

"There is." Marcus said, nodding. "Perhaps a woman awaits my return." His voice sank to a soft whisper. "Or, perhaps not."

"You have surely seen enough of the soldier's life to know time waits for neither Caesar nor slave." Quirinius lifted his eyebrows. "Think again. A bird in the hand is worth two in the bush."

"I cannot refute your logic, Sir. Still, all these years I have wondered. Now, at last, I can know."

"And knowing is worth more to you than a commission in the Roman Army?"

Head high, Marcus faced the Governor squarely and replied, "Yes Sir, it is."

~ 40 ~

An afternoon ride to Solomon's Pool changed everything. Freed from his fear of rejection, Tyro became a different man. He put aside his bravado and boasting and became attentive and caring. His work still required travel, but he stopped to visit every chance he got.

As for me, the happiness Abba promised would return at last did. I felt like a child again and caught myself smiling for no particular reason. In the evenings I enjoyed relaxing under the trees and watching mother birds feed their babies. Wild flowers bloomed in my formerly drab world.

One day I mentioned how lovely the meadow looked. Rachel insisted nothing had changed. How wrong she was. As I lay in my bed that night with moonlight painting a white stripe across the covers, I thought about these new feelings. The unimaginable had happened.

Yes, perhaps Rivkah *could* love again.

People in the settlement noticed the change in me. How could they not? Some days my feet barely touched the ground. I danced through each day eagerly counting the moments until Tyro's return.

Abba changed too. Each time Tyro left my father stood with his arm around my shoulder watching the road until the hoof beats faded away and the dust settled. Over evening meals he and Tyro sometimes became so engrossed in conversations that they ignored me. Maybe it should have upset me, but it didn't. Abba seemed to have found a son he never expected to have.

Tyro brought gift upon gift each time he came. Fine cloth, perfumes, ointments, jewelry and enameled pins shaped like butterflies or flowers for me, tools and little curiosities for Abba. The things he brought made my father's eyes sparkle. What is it about mechanical devices that interests men so?

My father began dropping blatant hints like, "If there is anything Tyro wants to discuss with me, I am never too busy to speak with him." Or, "The woman who weds Tyro will indeed be a lucky bride." Or my favorite, "A man's life is not complete unless a grandchild rests upon his knee."

Tyro's presence in my life healed the rift between my father and me. We understood now that during those stormy years we had both sought the same thing, happiness.

People in our settlement speculated on Tyro's frequent visits. All sorts of rumors grew up around us. The most common one being that I had waited all these years for a rich man and finally caught one. In reality, I never aspired to riches, only love. Better a poor man whose life is blameless than a rich man whose ways are perverse.

Occasionally I would overhear snippets of gossip at the well speculating on what a woman did to catch a man like Tyro. Why must some people always imagine the worst? It was not the first time tongues wagged about me, and probably would not be the last.

"We are approaching a time when your father and I should talk," Tyro said.

He had been away on a sea journey and it was good to have him back. We strolled hand in hand in the vineyard, treasuring the limited time we had together. Soon he would leave again for Petra.

"Only when you are ready," I said. "There is no hurry. I will be here waiting each time you return."

He plucked off a cluster of ripe grapes and we ate them as we walked.

"You sound as if you have reservations."

I read the disappointment in his eyes and sought to reassure him. "Reservations? No. Concerns, yes."

He took me in his arms and we kissed several times.

I put a hand to his cheek and stared into his eyes. "We are so different, you and I. You have known only comfort; Abba and I have struggled to survive. You have seen the world; I know only Bethlehem and Jerusalem. Surely this must concern you."

Tyro smiled. "Should it?"

We walked in silence for several minutes. Gathering in a deep breath, I turned to face him.

"Tyro, there is something I should explain about myself. I am no longer a young maiden. You surely have wondered why I never married. A number of years ago there was a young man whom I loved very much."

The words I wanted seemed to stick in my throat. Why had talking about Shemu'el suddenly become so difficult? I looked away and chewed my lip, searching for the right thing to say. "I expected to one day marry this man and—"

Tyro's lips against mine stopped me. When we parted he took my hands in his and kissed my fingertips. "You owe me no explanations. Forget the past and concentrate on the future."

We began walking again.

I longed with all my heart to do just what he said. When Shemu'el told me he wanted me for his wife it filled me with happiness, not concern. I never worried about a thing and had been more than content to let the future play itself out one day at a time.

Now I worried. Why? Tyro had professed his love for me over and over. I was hardly more than a child when Shemu'el took me in his arms. Had my inexperience blinded me to the realities of life...or was there something else? Something that my heart felt, but could not name.

Tyro ruffled his fingers through the grape leaves as we walked and grinned. "Perhaps we are not as different as you imagine. I, too, have been with other women." He snapped his fingers. "There, you see. Your worries vanish like dust in the wind."

"You loved another woman?"

Tyro patted my hand. "No, little bird, you are the first woman I have truly loved."

"But you said..."

"I said I have been with other women. Does the ram love each ewe in the flock?" He gave me a knowing wink. "A man need not love a woman to lie with her."

I now knew the source of my uneasiness. Tyro named what

I had only felt. His words, intended to bring comfort, pierced my heart like a sword.

Rachel glanced over at me. "Do you recall the caravan that passed through the first day of the week on its way to Arabia?"

"Yes."

We knelt beside the well washing our clothes. I sloshed a tunic in water and looked over at her expectantly. Now that she had my attention she could let time drag and tease me. She enjoyed doing this sometimes.

"Yes, Rachel, I remember the caravan that passed the first day of the week on its way to Arabia," I said, slapping the cloth down on a rock. A water droplet hit her face, causing her to blink.

Rachel grinned; she had succeeded in upsetting me.

"My Binyamin went to their camp to offer them a kid."

"And did they buy it?"

She looked surprised. "Well, of course."

"Good for Binyamin," I said, returning to my washing. Two could play her game.

"Do you want to know what he saw while he was there?"

"Camels, tents, a fire?"

"All that, of course...and your trader friend, Tyro."

Rachel had my attention now. Why hadn't Tyro stopped to see us? Everyone knew Abba's kids were the best. What was he doing buying from someone else?

~ 41 ~

Marcus poured olive oil into a cupped palm, rubbed his hands together and smoothed the oil across the lower portion of his face and upper neck. Taking a step closer to the polished bronze mirror, he began at his ear and ran the shaving blade along the side of his jaw. Every dozen strokes or so, he stopped and drew the blade back and forth across a leather strop, refreshing its edge. Once he dispatched his overnight growth of beard, he carefully cleansed the blade and returned it to his *loculus*.

He was cleaning his hands on a cloth when Atticus stormed into the room waving a scroll. "My posting," he said with an excited grin. "At last, I know where I am headed."

Marcus pulled down an amphora of wine they had put back to toast this occasion. He filled two goblets and smiled as his friend took a seat opposite him.

"Well, how long are you going to keep me in suspense?"

Atticus chuckled. "Make a guess."

Since their meeting with Quirinius, the two of them had spent every free moment speculating on where Atticus might be assigned. There were, they discovered, more dreadful places within the Empire to garrison soldiers than either of them ever realized. Atticus dreamed of a posting to either Africa Nova, or Mauritania, both of which would put him close to the land of his birth. But somewhere in the northwestern frontier seemed the higher probability.

"Britannia?" Marcus suggested, knowing it was Atticus' first choice on the frontier.

A down-turned thumb.

"Gaul?" It seemed likely. The Gaelic provinces were home to multiple legions.

A frown and a shake of the head.

Marcus next thought of the region both of them agreed would be the worst possible posting. It had everything a soldier did not want, extreme isolation, inclement weather and ongoing border skirmishes with hostile tribes. It was hard to imagine Atticus this excited over Germania, but he tried it anyway.

"Germania Magna?"

Atticus slapped his hand onto the tabletop. "No, praise Fortuna!" Rising, he made an elaborate bow. "I give you Sextus Evodius Atticus, the newest *Medicus Ordinarii* assigned to *Legio V Macedonia*. I am headed for Thessalonica."

He snatched his cup off the table and raised it high. "Be forewarned voluptuous Aegean maidens. Fathers lock your daughters away. Evodius Atticus will soon be on the prowl."

"Congratulations on a great appointment." Marcus smiled and clapped him on the back. Wine splashed from both of their cups, though neither cared. "When do you leave?"

"The day after tomorrow."

"Hmmm." Marcus lifted an eyebrow. "No time to post warning notices in Thessalonica."

"And when do *you* leave?"

"Day after tomorrow. Once you leave I no longer have a place to stay."

Atticus clasped his hand. "We have been through a lot together, my brother." He drew him into a hug. "I will miss you greatly. What route do you plan to take?"

"Down the coast road to Jaffa, then east to Jerusalem. It takes longer, but I have no desire to pass through Samaria ever again."

"It is exciting to think about. Each of us seeing so many places we have never seen before."

"Actually," Marcus said, studying the cup in his hand, "I am more excited about seeing the places I *have* seen before."

"How long until you reach your home?"

"A month, perhaps a month-and-a-half."

"This is unbelievable. Surely you do not plan to walk?"

Marcus leveled a look at him. "I did it once before, or have you forgotten?"

"Forgotten the bedraggled boy with the broken arm? Never." Atticus sipped his wine, swirling it in his mouth as he remembered the day they met nine years before. "What will you eat? Where will you stay?"

"I plan to glean the fields as I go and sleep under the stars.

"Strange words coming from someone who recently invited me to celebrate *Rosh Hashanah*, the coming of the Jewish New Year. Look around you, man. The fruit trees are still in flower, anything left on them from last fall rotted in the winter rains. The barley remains soft and milky, the heads of wheat bright green. The only creatures capable of gleaning those fields move about on four legs."

The truth of his friend's words left Marcus speechless. How could he not have realized the impossibility of what he proposed? In his eagerness to leave the Romans and return home, he had tossed aside all common sense. He folded his arms, resting his elbows on the rough wood of the tabletop, and hung his head.

Barley harvest was several weeks away and Atticus left the day following the morrow. If he remained in Antioch until the grain ripened, he would have no funds left for his trip.

"My sack contained 100 *denarii*. I gave 25 of them to the goldsmith who fashioned this ring for me." The new ring sparkled when he turned it in the light. Marcus' voice grew soft, sinking almost to a whisper. "For my bride...just in case."

He raised his foot and showed Atticus the half-worn sole of his sandal. "If I am to walk 500 miles, I will need a new pair of *caligulea*. That leaves nothing for *cauponea*."

"You do not want to stay in the *cauponea* anyway," Atticus said with a disgusted shake of his head. "Some of those inns are foul places, infested with lice, thieves and harlots." He gave a disappointed sigh. "We have been together nearly ten years, Marcus. Have I taught you nothing of the Roman way of life?"

He recalled some of the orgiastic festivals Atticus had dragged him to over his protests. "More than I ever intended."

"Perhaps, but not the right things. Let me assist you on this trip."

"No. I refuse to take your money."

Atticus smiled across the table at him. "Good. I had not planned on giving you any."

"If not you, then who? Someone must finance this trip you are proposing and I have already told you I lack the funds."

"Let's reason together. Just a week ago the Governor

offered you an appointment as an *Ordinarii* with rank of Centurion. Clearly he thinks highly of you. You chose Judea instead. What did he tell you about Judea?"

"That Archelaus has been exiled and the prefect, Coponius, now rules."

Atticus pounded the table. "Think man. If Coponius rules Judea, dispatches must pass back and forth between Caesarea and Antioch every day. Let Caesar pay your way; he owes you at least that much." Leaning forward, his voice took on a conspiratorial tone. "Now, here is what you do. Go to Quirinius and offer your services as a courier. It gives you a *diploma*, the Imperial passport, and the use of a horse."

Years before, Evodius had insisted both men learn to ride, a necessary skill for a *Medicus*. One or the other of them frequently strapped a *loculus* filled with instruments and medications to one of their saddle horns, mounted up and rode cross-country to where the troops were bivouacked.

"Couriers are supplied with fresh mounts at every *stationes*."

Marcus leaned back in his chair. Interlocking his fingers behind his head, he stared at the ceiling. "Imagine how much faster I could travel on horseback."

"Precisely. And at the end of each day, your Emperor gratefully provides his courier with food, wine and lodging in a *mansio*. At the very least you can rest contentedly instead of sleeping with one eye open. You will reach Caesarea inside of a week without spending a single *sestertius*. Whatever is in that sack of yours will carry you the rest of the way in comfort."

Marcus' brow knitted. "I have never felt entirely comfortable taking advantage of my position like this."

"I know." Atticus smiled. "It is one of your faults I have learned to overlook."

T he two men said little as the carriage rattled along the *Via Caesarea* on its way to the *insula*. Atticus sat tall and proud, displaying the uniform of his rank. True, he wore none of the silvered armor of a Centurion and he holstered only a small dagger, instead of the usual *gladius*, but he looked resplendent in his new white tunic with a leather harness criss-crossing his chest. On his head Atticus wore a pounded brass, crested helmet and he had a crimson cloak draped around his shoulders.

Marcus looked plain by comparison in a common gray cloak and *bracae*, the leather breeches of the cavalry. When they reached the Governor's palace, Atticus waited with the driver while Marcus dashed up the marble steps taking them two at a time. He disappeared inside and emerged several minutes later. Burdened with multiple diplomatic pouches swinging from both shoulders, he lumbered back down the broad stairway.

A strand of copper wire secured each pouch Marcus carried. Inserted through a forged bronze staple which protruded from a slot in the flap, both ends of the wire were threaded through a small lead disk. Then a smashing hammer blow impressed the Imperial seal into the lead, rendering the pouch tamperproof.

It seemed beyond belief, almost a dream come true, Marcus thought as he descended the stairs. He, a newly-freed slave, had become a Provincial courier armed with a *diploma* from Tiberius Caesar granting him unlimited access to the Imperial highways. Nothing stood between him and Caesarea but roadway interspersed at regular intervals by *stationes* stocked with fresh mounts and *mansiones* for nightly lodging.

Once he delivered his pouches he would be on his own, free to proceed to Bethlehem and recapture his life. In the long and circuitous transition from Shemu'el bar Yo'el to Sextus Evodius Marcus and back again, he decided this must be the strangest chapter of all.

From the palace they went directly to the harbor where a frigate waited to carry Atticus to Thessalonica. Marcus followed his friend up the gangplank. Once on board, he lightened his load by transferring several of the dark leather pouches destined for Rome to the Captain of the ship.

Marcus and Atticus faced each other, both struggling to give words to their feelings. The deck gently rocked beneath their feet and deckhands scurried around them storing cargo and supplies. They were as much like brothers as two friends could be. They clasped forearms for a moment, stared into each other's eyes and hugged.

"But for you I surely would have perished," Marcus said. "You gave me back my life."

"As God willed I should," Atticus replied, "because without your words of wisdom my life would have had little meaning."

"I will always treasure your friendship."

"And I yours. I feel certain we shall meet again, my brother."

"If we do meet again, best it not be in Judea. The Roman military is hated there."

"How very odd," Atticus said with a wry smile. "We are so loved everywhere else."

Marcus chuckled and took a step back, preparing to leave.

Atticus touched his arm, stopping him. "Tell me, as a God-fearer, if I were to pray to Yahweh, would he hear me? Would he know who I am?"

"The Lord God of Israel calls you by your name. He knew you when you were still in the womb."

"And the woman whom you hope awaits your return, what is she called again?"

"Rivkah." The name stuck in his throat.

"Rivkah...Rivkah." Atticus repeated the name, listening to its lyric tone as it slid across his tongue. "Each day I shall pray to Yahweh. I will implore him to help you find this Rivkah whom you love so deeply. I shall also pray that each morning since you have been gone she has looked afar off hoping to see your figure on the horizon and each night she has fallen asleep listening for the sound of your footsteps."

The Captain called to make ready. The sails snapped in the wind as the deckhands hoisted them up the mast. The ship, eager for the sea, strained against the ropes holding it to the dock.

"Before you go let us make an oath, friend to friend, brother to brother." Atticus took Marcus' hand between his. "As we go our separate ways there will be moments when we reach a fork in the road and must decide which path to follow. On our honor let us pledge to each other that at such junctures we shall always choose the harder road, knowing that in the long run we will be better men for it."

Marcus wrapped his other hand around the dark hands holding his, squeezed and nodded his agreement. "Goodbye, my brother. *Shalom Aleichem.*" Marcus leaped onto the dock as they threw off the last of the ropes.

"*Aleichem Shalom,*" Atticus replied. He waved as the ship eased away from the dock.

~ 42 ~

I called the stray ewe a second time. There was still no sign of her. I blinked my eyes. Everything around me seemed to have changed. The fields I saw were not my own. They looked different, strange.

Where was I?

After wandering for some time I came upon a lake. Tired and thirsty, I knelt at its shore and scooped a handful of water. When I raised my head I noticed a stag standing on the far bank. It stared across the water at me and our eyes met. It had no fear. Like one of my sheep, it seemed to know me.

The stag approached the edge. I expected it to bend and drink. Instead, it stepped into the water. In it waded, further and further. The water grew deeper, eventually reaching its chest then its shoulders, yet it continued toward me. It took another step and, to my surprise, disappeared beneath the water.

I noticed that, though ripples in the water distorted its appearance, I could see the stag swimming under the surface. I blinked in shock and surprise. Its shape began to change; it no longer had horns. The stag gradually became a man, a man swimming toward me with powerful, determined strokes.

Quaking with fear, yet unable to move, I knelt there on the bank. The water in front of me erupted in a giant splash.

The creature, now a man, rose up, stepped onto the bank and shook the water out of his hair. He looked down at me and smiled. It was Shemu'el!

I gasped and swooned, collapsing onto the grass.

My eyes opened to the darkness of my little room. I felt the covers of my bed clutched in my hand. The grass, the lake, Shemu'el...had all vanished like smoke in the wind.

If I had not already agreed to go to the traveling fair with Ruth and Elisheva, I would have stayed home. I got very little sleep after my strange dream and the memory of it continued to trouble me.

Beside me, my cousins chattered about what they hoped to find.

Perhaps this fair will prove to be a good thing, I thought, as we walked. I needed something to divert my mind from its current unrest. Lifting my head, I threw my shoulders back and promised myself I would visit every stall.

I wandered the rows of merchandise aimlessly, examining the merchants' wares with little interest. Coming upon a table offering wooden bowls, I slowed. The sight of them re-kindled memories of a girl sitting cross-legged in the grass watching the young man she loved carve stalks of wheat around the outside of a bowl.

The tears in my eyes made it difficult to see the bowls arrayed in front of me. First the dream and now this. It took so little to knock me off balance, I thought, resting a hand on the table, while I struggled to regain my composure.

Taking a deep, cleansing breath, I looked at the bowls again. My body went rigid. Sitting there among the other bowls was one with stalks of wheat circling its exterior.

Could it be...could it be?

I looked around. The stall's owner paid me no heed. Facing the opposite direction, he was deep in negotiations over a pair of beaded necklaces.

I ran to the table and seized the bowl. I held it close, letting my fingers slide along its smooth surface, tracing each stem. Caressing the exquisite kernels, I remembered the sharp knife and careful strokes that carved them. I ran a fingernail along the thin grooves forming the spikelets at the top of each head of wheat.

Shemu'el carved it. I did not know when; I did not know how. I just knew he had. Only he carved so realistically. Only he could draw such beauty out of a lifeless chunk of wood.

I rubbed my forefinger and thumb together, feeling a long forgotten slipperiness.

"*Taste it,*" I heard Shemu'el say with laughter in his voice. "*There is nothing in it to hurt you.*"

I put my fingers to my tongue and tasted the almost

forgotten sweet nuttiness of almond oil blended into beeswax.

A touch on my arm caused me to jerk around in surprise. It was Elisheva.

"Rivkah, are you all right? You did not answer when I spoke to you." She studied my face with a worried look. "You appear to have seen a ghost."

"Perhaps I have," I whispered. My hands shook when I extended the bowl for her to see. "Shemu'el carved this bowl."

"That cannot be. Shemu'el died years ago."

"Do you think I have suffered all these years and do not know that?"

"I'm sure there's another explanation. Meanwhile, you need to calm down. I will be at the next table if you need my help."

Elisheva left me there clutching the bowl. My head swam. What did it mean? I pressed the wood to my face breathing in the slight perfume of its polish. I closed my eyes and stroked it against my cheek, feeling the places where Shemu'el's hand had been.

"Have you ever seen anything so beautiful?" the merchant asked.

I gave a start and pressed the bowl to my bosom.

"You seem to like it." His tone was tentative, friendly...open-ended. "I have never seen one with such intricate carving. Perhaps you wish to make it yours?"

Unable to make my mouth form words, I nodded numbly.

As we haggled, I tried to negotiate carefully. But in my heart I knew I would pay any price to own the bowl. Give everything in my purse...all the coins I had buried in a jar in the backyard, my sheep, the very clothes upon my back.

I would gladly give it all and more. No way could I let this piece of Shemu'el slip through my fingers. No one would ever take him from me a second time.

I paid the merchant, wrapped the bowl and placed it in my bag. As I walked away from his stall the hustle and bustle of the marketplace dropped away. Fear swirled in the pit of my stomach. I asked myself the terrifying questions that had hung in the back of my mind since the moment I saw the bowl sitting on the table.

How had it come to be here? What did it mean?

I retraced my steps and waited patiently while the merchant finished with a customer. He gave me a surprised look.

"Is something wrong? Have you changed your mind about the bowl?"

I shook my head. "I wondered if you could tell me where the bowl came from. How did you acquire such a piece?"

"I do not know where it came from."

Were I a man, I would have grabbed his cloak and shaken him. Instead, I tried to exhibit the comely behavior and feminine demeanor befitting a daughter of Avraham.

"The bowl sat on your table, how can you not know?"

"Things come and things go." He shrugged, showing me empty palms. "I buy and I sell."

"Where did you last purchase bowls?" I asked, desperate for the tiniest of clues.

"I bought some a few days ago in Jerusalem."

"From Leandros, the woodworker?"

"No." His lips curled into a sneer. "His wares are too costly." He tugged at his beard, searching his memory. "I bought bowls from a Samaritan." He thought for another moment and frowned. "But that bowl was not part of the lot."

"And where before then?"

"If I knew, I would happily tell you. As I said, I buy and I sell. If another merchant offered me a good price, I would part with everything on the table this afternoon."

The man's expression said he wished I would go away.

I stayed.

"Think! Surely you would remember such a unique piece. You admitted you have never having seen one like."

"We met a trading ship at the port of Seleucia. It had come from Antioch."

"Antioch, then." I held my breath, waiting...hoping.

"But that means nothing. Ships and caravans transfer merchandise from one end of the empire to the other, and beyond. The ship of which I spoke traveled from Byzantium to

Pontus and Bithynia. On its way to Antioch, it stopped in Athens, Corinth, Crete and Cyprus." He threw up his hands. "I will swear the bowl came off that ship, if it brings you peace. But how they came by it only the gods know."

I thanked the man and left.

I had come to the fair seeking diversion, hoping to release the turmoil created by my strange dream. The dream was all but forgotten by the time we headed for home. I had a much deeper mystery to ponder now.

The interior finish of a wooden bowl gradually wore away with use. Housewives routinely re-oiled their bowls to keep the wood from splitting. But they used olive oil; no one would blend a finish such as Shemu'el used to refurbish their bowl. Yet the finish on this bowl remained fresh, as fresh as if Shemu'el had applied it only a few weeks earlier.

What did this mean?

The merchant insisted the bowl's origin could never be determined. Perhaps not, yet the bowl had no significance to anyone except me. Could it have been intended as a message? A message meant for me and me alone.

And if so, who sent it...and why now when Tyro spoke of marriage?

~ 43 ~

Marcus paused on a hilltop and watched the frigate glide across the turquoise waters of the Great Sea. By the time the square sail of Atticus' ship shrank to a white dot on the horizon, he had lashed his baggage to his four-horned Roman saddle and strapped the pouches tightly around his body.

A trade wind ruffled his hair, sending a rush of exhilaration coursing through him. Grinning, he spurred the horse.

Homeward bound at last.

Faster, then faster still, he urged the horse forward. Each step, each clop of horseshoe against pavement put him one step closer to his destination. Weaving around slow moving carts and wagons, whisking past chariots, on he rode.

The sun hung low in the western horizon by the time he reached the *mansio*. He dismounted with a groan and handed the reins to the slave in charge of the stable.

"Your first time carrying dispatches?" the man asked.

The groom reached under the horse's belly and loosed the saddle. Pulling it off along with the blanket beneath it, he led the horse into a stall. He removed the dark stallion's bit with a practiced hand and swung the gate closed. Grabbing a bucket, the man scooped water from a trough.

Shemu'el rubbed the small of his back and stretched "How could you tell it was my first trip?"

"I have seen it many times before. New riders always overdo it on their first day." The man laughed. "Rest easy at dinner tonight."

Shemu'el gave him a wry nod and limped away. The slave's voice brought him to a stop.

"The *mansio* has a small *therma*. Lucius, the big man in charge of the bath," he spread his arms and rocked from side to side illustrating the man's bulk, "has an ointment. It will help." He gave a friendly wave and resumed brushing the horse.

Marcus limped inside, sunburned and saddle-sore. Every

joint in his tired body ached. After a quick meal, he put aside his usual reservations about public nudity and granted himself a long soak in the steaming bath.

He had no trouble identifying the man whom the slave had called Lucius. He was easily the fattest man Marcus had ever seen. His bare feet slapped against the damp stones as he jostled between the pools covered only by an oversized towel tied about his waist.

The *mansio* was not fully-occupied that evening and, when most of the regulars left, Lucius wandered over to where Marcus soaked. His rotund stomach and flabby chest glistened with sweat. He wiped his balding head with a towel and eased himself onto the stones beside Marcus, dangling his toes in the water like a child.

He noticed Marcus surveying his girth and chuckled. "I am a man of surprising dimensions, am I not?"

Marcus answered with an uncertain nod.

"You have ridden hard today, perhaps harder than you anticipated." It was more a statement than a question.

"How could you tell?"

Lucius' belly shook when he laughed. "I have attended these baths for many a year. The older riders, they have buttocks tough as a stonemason's hands. I noticed when you came in," he said, "your cheeks were red as a baboon's." Ignoring Marcus' embarrassed frown, he continued. "Soaking only draws more blood into the area. What you need is a salve."

"I was told in the stables you have something."

He grinned. "Something better than any salve." He clapped and a half-naked Egyptian slave girl appeared in the doorway. "I have Nefertari. She will massage all your troubles away." Lucius put his face close to Marcus' ear and whispered, "Her name means *most beautiful*. A good choice, heh?"

"Caesar provides his couriers with massages by Egyptian slave girls?"

"Caesar supplies the ointment; you pay for the girl," Lucius said with a shrug.

"I think not."

On the way out Marcus secured a jar of salve and carried it back to his room. He preferred to apply it himself rather than submit to the ministrations of Nefertari.

He grunted in pain and eased his aching body onto the bed. Positioning himself on his stomach, spread-eagle, he sighed with pleasure when a gust of cool night air swept across his fiery skin. Sleep overtook him before he completed his evening prayers.

The morning sun blazed through his window when Marcus re-opened his eyes. He was up and out in a hurry, pausing only long enough to fold a blanket and lay it across the saddle for padding. His initial exuberance spent, he rode slower on this his second day as Caesar's courier.

At Ptolemais, he left the coast road and detoured southeast toward Sepphoris. Among the satchels strung about his neck he carried one addressed to Herod Antipas and several others for the commander of the Sepphorian garrison.

On the way, Marcus stopped at Asochis to water his horse and stretch his legs. After the horse drank its fill, he entered a small shop to purchase a midday meal. Asochis was a Jewish city and the people there spoke Aramaic rather than the Latin or Greek he had grown accustomed to.

"How much for some loaves, dried meat and an amphora of wine?" Marcus asked in Aramaic.

The shopkeeper, his back to the door, did not look up from his work. "Today is your lucky day, my friend. I have some wonderful salted venison. Delicious and just a single *sesterius*."

"And if we added a cake of raisins?"

"That would be another—" The man's eyes widened when turned and he saw the Imperial seals on the satchels Marcus carried. "Excuse me, Sir," he said, bowing deeply. "I did not realize to whom I was speaking. For Caesar the price would be ten *quadrans* for the meal and one additional for the raisin cake."

Marcus swiveled in both directions inspecting the shop. "Caesar? There is no one here but me."

"Did I say ten? Make it nine including a cake of dates."

"But a moment before it cost more than a *sesterius*."

A spark of fright glimmered in the man's eyes. "You toy with me, Noble Sir. I beg forgive me. I made an honest mistake." He displayed his empty hands. "I am just a humble shopkeeper toiling to feed his family. Seven *quadrans* and I will include some of my wife's goat cheese and a second raisin cake."

Marcus slapped down two *sestertii*. "One raisin cake, and feed the cheese to your children. They need it more than Caesar ever will."

Marcus carried his food to the outskirts of town where he found a quiet spot for his horse to graze. He settled himself gingerly, wincing when he encountered a hidden tree root, and stared across the wide valley at Sepphoris as he ate. Herod Antipas' capital, his city on a hill, gleamed in the noonday sun.

Like the Temple, Sepphoris had been in flames when he last saw it. Could it have been over eight years since its ugly black smoke blotted out Mt. Tabor? At that moment it seemed as if it were only yesterday.

The Roman column that took him to Antioch had threaded their way through a procession of Sepphorian residents. Innocent families who, like him, were being led into slavery. He remembered the hollow look in the children's eyes as they trotted alongside their mothers.

There had been another chain gang that day. Not of slaves, but rebels on their way to execution. Those foolish few who believed capturing the armory of a rural outpost could somehow weaken Caesar's grasp on their homeland. Their miscalculation cost them their lives and their neighbors their future.

While he rested, Marcus dug his hand into his traveling bag and extracted a cloth-covered bundle. He folded back the wrapping and studied the small bowl in his lap with a satisfied smile. He added a few final touches with his knife then worked almond oil and beeswax into the grain of the wood.

Marcus spent the night in a Sepphorian *mansio*, changed horses and returned to Ptolemais the way he came. Thus far, he'd retraced the path he marched shackled to other prisoner slaves.

He felt tingles of excitement as he wheeled his horse back onto the coast road and headed south to places never before seen.

The road curved south from Ptolemais, hugging the edge of the Great Sea. After about an hour it veered north, skirting Mt. Carmel. Marcus stopped to rest at the tip of Cape Carmel. Water surrounded him on three sides and the rolling foothills of Mt. Carmel lay to his back.

Staring out at this endless expanse of water, he felt the first tendrils of fear. What if this trip were in vain? For eight years the desperate hope that he could somehow reclaim what was lost had sustained him. But here, free of the trappings of his enslavement, alone except for his horse and the call of the gulls, a harsh reality set in.

What possessed him to set out on this fool's errand? He had no chance of finding Rivkah unmarried. Tradition demanded she marry. Yaakov wanted grandsons; he would have insisted on it. Could he bear seeing Rivkah as the wife of another man?

Marcus drew his cloak tight against the sea breeze and reined the dappled stallion to his left. First things first. He must reach Caesarea before nightfall, he thought, touching his spurs to the horse's flank.

~ 44 ~

"Abba, come eat."

My father left the sheepfold, washed and came into the house. "When will Tyro return from his trip?" he asked, taking his first bites.

"Soon. He promised to share the Seder meal with us. He told me to reserve the best lamb you had."

"So he intends to purchase it and eat it with us?"

I smiled and nodded.

"This year we shall have free lamb." Abba grinned. "I suppose he will pay too much just as he does with the kids."

"It is his way of helping. He is a generous man."

I watched my father tug at his beard as he thought. Somehow, without me noticing, it had become the color of slate. His hair had also grayed. In spite of these signs of age he looked happier than he had in years. I knew then that, if Tyro asked, I must not turn him down. This much I owed my father.

"Something tells me Tyro plans to talk to me before he leaves." He looked at me expectantly.

Avoiding his gaze and the question it implied. I picked up a knife. "Would you like more cucumber?"

Rachel arrived with a baby on her back and a bag of yarn under her arm. She handed Nahum to me while she unpacked. His tiny hand closed around my finger, causing more pain than he could ever know.

The same thoughts returned each time I held him. How would it feel to hold my own son? When would I, if ever? I always imagined Shemu'el being the father of my children. Was it now to be Tyro instead? Speak Lord, my ears strain to hear your voice.

Rachel settled him on the bed and came into the front room. She unpacked her bag of yarn. It was the seventh hour, the heat of the day. A good time for babies to nap and their mothers to work indoors.

We were alone this afternoon. Abba finished his noonday meal and left to visit a neighbor about a ram he had for sale. We spent many afternoons weaving. Working together meant extra hands, which made light work.

"Can you believe the roads?" Rachel took her accustomed place beside the loom. "It is not just the pilgrims coming to Jerusalem for the *Pesach*, this year everyone is passing through Bethlehem for the census. It reminds me of when we were little girls."

The same thought had crossed my mind. The busy roads, the crowded inns, it all felt familiar. The last census was the time of the angels and Yeshua's birth. Twelve years, where had the time gone? After exiling Archelaus to Gaul, Caesar placed the government of Judea into the hands of a Roman prefect and asked Quirinius to conduct another census.

"You sound surprised," I said with a laugh. "Is there anything the Romans enjoy more than counting?"

Rachel took the shuttle from me through the maze of warp threads suspended from the top of the loom. As I handed it to her, my hand brushed against the threads, vibrating the weights holding them taut. The clay weights clicked and plinked against each other, creating a melodious sound. What we called *The Song of the Weaver*.

"I know one thing the Romans enjoy more than counting," Rachel said. "Collecting taxes from the impoverished inhabitants of their empire."

"Perhaps, like us, they must count heads and then, knowing how many sheep they have to shear, estimate their revenue."

She shook her head. "Everything I have seen says they approach it from the opposite side. Those who rule decide what they wish to spend. Then their overseers determine how much each of us will cough up to provide it."

"If only Abba and I could do that with our sheep." I glanced at the ceiling, doing imaginary calculations. "Yes! Why not raise the price of lambs and eat wheat bread this year instead of barley loaves."

"You dream too small. Why wish for plain wheat loaves?"

Rachel thrust her shoulders back. "I demand semolina, the finest white flour."

"Of course. And a fatted calf at least every other week, gold bracelets for our wrists and carved ivory combs in our hair. We need not breed more lambs, we will simply raise the price."

"And servants...never forget the servants."

The longer we continued this game the more uneasy I became. To me, our conversation sounded more and more like Tyro's promises.

It was nearly time to begin preparing the evening meal when we finished tying off the threads. Nahum's hungry cries interrupted, calling Rachel away. I removed the cloth and began re-stringing the loom with her yarn. We alternated our work when we wove. The next piece off the loom would be hers.

She planned to make a new *tallit,* as a present for her husband, Binyamin. In her bag were many skeins of un-dyed yarn, all a uniform white color. She carefully selected only the lightest fleece when spinning. Along with them she put in one blue skein. I began by stringing the blue threads at each side to form the border.

Prayer shawls had a blue border reminding the Jew of the second day of creation when God separated the waters into the seas below and the firmament above. Seeing this border, a man knew the presence of the Most High Lord surrounded him at all times. When finished, Rachel will tie *tzitzit*—tassels, at each corner. Bound into each one will be a *techelet* cord.

Only the Phoenicians knew how to produce this royal blue dye. It is far too expensive for us to buy. Sidonius, the merchant, brings us *techelet* yarn. He also sells whole bolts of cloth in royal blues and purples for Tyro. Of course, no one but the very rich could ever afford such a thing.

Rachel returned with Nahum at her breast. She eased herself into a sitting position, resting her back against the wall as he nursed. I watched in silence until Rachel looked up and caught me. Jerking my eyes away, I resumed tying the yarn that dangled from the loom.

"Who were you thinking of Tyro, or Shemu'el?"

She knew me too well.

"Truthfully, both. One I wanted and could not have, the other I can have, but am not sure I want." Gathering the clump of blue threads between my fingers, I attached a clay weight to the bundle.

"You are nearing your twentieth birthday, Rivkah. What will become of you?"

"All is in God's hands." Sometimes Rachel worried more about me than I worried about myself.

Ignoring the fussing babe in her arms, she continued to pester me. "You should have married long ago. It is not because you have lacked for offers."

"There have not been that many."

Rachel sat Nahum in her lap and began ticking off names on her fingers. When she ran out of fingers and still had names, she spread her hands in front of my face like spider webs.

"People talk."

"Really? And what do they say?"

Rachel busied herself with Nahum, pretending to have forgotten our conversation. She shifted him in her arms, adjusting and re-adjusting, ignoring me.

"What do they say?" I asked, a second time.

She took a deep breath. "They say many things. Losing Shemu'el made you crazy in the head and you will never marry. You are destined to wander the streets as a beggar. You will grow old before your time and die childless, carrying Shemu'el's memory with you to the grave."

I concentrated on the loom. It was all *lashon hara*. Malicious gossip I had heard many times before.

"Do something before it is too late." Rachel's voice sounded strained, as if she might burst into tears. "And what about Tyro? You say you are unsure. What is there to be undecided about?"

"I have found out that Tyro has been with other women," I said, lowering my eyes.

"And this surprises you?"

"I had different expectations for my husband."

"Well, you need to change those expectations. He has probably been with lots of women. Men have needs, Rivkah."

"And women do not?"

"It is not the same and you know it."

The next words out of her mouth cut like a knife.

"Men like Tyro sample other women before *and* after marriage. You must learn to accept it."

"Like you would if it was Binyamin?"

"Binyamin is different," Rachel muttered.

Her bitter expression told me she did not find the thought of *her* husband with another woman nearly as acceptable.

"Why the face? Many women would be happy to marry Tyro. He is young, good looking and wealthy. Not comfortable, wealthy! You would have servants, fatted calves and more semolina than you could ever eat."

"Better humble among the poor than proud among the wealthy."

"Oh, pooh! In the end you will reject him for the same reason you have rejected all the others."

"All my life I have believed a marriage is *b'shert*."

"And Shemu'el was that man, the one meant for you?"

"He and I were part of God's plan, yes."

"And now he is gone and there can never be another?"

"If the Lord wants me to have another, he will let me know."

"What about the prophecy...the man on the horse coming from afar? The Lord spoke to you of Tyro."

"There was no prophecy, just a dream and a silly dream at that."

"Do you expect this man to come with a tag that says, *For Rivkah, from God*?"

"Trust me. I will know, just as surely as I knew all the others were not the one." Without intending to, I folded my hands over my heart. "When the man appears, the Lord will whisper to me, *This is the one, your beloved*." I looked around the plain room. "Meanwhile, Abba and I get by. We are not uncomfortable."

"Your father will not always be here. You need a husband. Do you not wake in the darkness of morning desiring the caress of a man's hand? Shemu'el is gone, Rivkah. You can never have him. Find what happiness there is with someone else, someone who will care for you when your father is no longer here."

"Many are the afflictions of the righteous, but the Lord delivers him out of them all."

"Quoting Psalms does not get you a husband."

"Perhaps not, but right now this cloth has to be folded."

Rachel frowned and shook her head.

I sat the cloth aside. "Very well, will this make you happy? Listen, Rachel, I am going to say what you long to hear." Making my voice sad and pathetic, I wailed, "Life is no good without a husband. I must do what Rachel suggests. I will marry the next man who asks for my hand." I gave her a smug look. "Are you happy now?"

"Tyro will not wait. He can have anyone he wants."

The folded cloth went on a pile of others, some hers and some mine. They all required finishing.

"Devorah and Shaoul are going to Bethlehem tomorrow. I plan to go with them and take these bolts to the fuller." I winked at her. "Who knows? By day's end, perhaps I will be betrothed."

~ 45 ~

Caesarea, Herod's former capital and home of his most ornate palace, became the seat of Roman government in *Palestinia* following Archelaus' exile. Herod designed his city by the sea to be thoroughly Roman with baths, theatres, a coliseum and swimming pools.

Marcus delivered the last of his satchels and turned in his horse. A meal and lodging awaited him at the *mansio*, and then he was on his own.

Curious, he traversed the city's mosaic sidewalks. Rows of columns, white Italian marble and pink Egyptian granite, supported roofs covering the promenades. He marveled at the splendid buildings and strolled the esplanade fronting the sea.

While walking through its gardens, he heard giggles and turned in time to watch a young couple slip behind a tree and share secret kisses. They seemed oblivious to everything but each other. He ached inside. Could he ever feel so carefree again?

There were two huge statues at the end of the pier. On a whim, Marcus walked out to examine them. Along the way he passed huge warehouses filled with merchandise brought by merchant vessels from all over the Empire and the Far East.

He sat on the great stone blocks which formed the jetty protecting the harbor and watched the cresting waves break over this manmade barrier. He sighed. Was his quest for Rivkah any different, he wondered, from these waves crashing blindly against immovable barriers? Tomorrow the sea would be much as it was today, or yesterday.

Would that be true of his life as well?

The cosmopolitan atmosphere of Caesarea reminded him of Antioch. He found himself feeling pangs of nostalgia for the city he left behind. It shocked this former sheepherder to realize how accustomed he had become to the Roman lifestyle.

The following morning Marcus found a merchant heading to

Jaffa and paid for a seat in his cart. Jaffa, like Caesarea, was a port city. He could have found transportation there among the many pack trains and caravans shuttling cargo to Jerusalem, but he preferred to walk.

Living with the Roman Army had taught him the value of good planning. Before leaving Antioch, Marcus formulated some vague ideas about the best way to handle his return. Twelve hours on the road would give him time to refine his strategy.

Long years with the legions conditioned him to the gait of the Roman soldier. When he left Jaffa heading east toward Jerusalem he maintained a steady pace of 3.6 miles per hour regardless of the terrain. Most people allowed two days for the trip. Knowing a single day's hard walk would put him there by nightfall, he left in predawn darkness and pushed toward his goal.

A man in a plain cloak and military tunic joined the surging crowd when the *shophar's* blast signaled the opening of the Temple gates. Marcus looked to his right as he crossed the outer court and slowed to stare at the scaffolding. Even after all these years, the fire's damage had not been completely repaired.

He stopped first at the offering bowl and deposited his tithe, ten denarii, one tenth of what Evodius left him. The night before, he set aside a similar amount for his second tithe, money spent within the city's walls. It went for lodging, meals and the bread, both leavened and unleavened, which he purchased from the innkeeper for his sacrifice.

Next he stopped at the market of Annas and selected a lamb. His heart skipped a beat when, upon examining it, he saw what at first glance appeared to be Yaakov's earmark. On closer inspection, Marcus decided he was mistaken. True, it looked very similar to the one he remembered, but it had one additional notch.

After paying for his lamb, he followed the worshippers through the Beautiful Gate into the Court of the Israelites and to the place of sacrifice. There he offered the Lord a Peace Offering in thanksgiving for his freedom and safe return. He prayed his journey not be in vain and, as unlikely as it seemed, that he find his beloved Rivkah waiting.

The Law required the bread and lamb of his sacrifice be eaten that day, or the next. Wanting to dispense with this requirement as quickly as possible, he had purchased enough bread for a crowd. Returning to the outer court, he invited all those begging alms to join him. After eating his portion, Marcus emptied his purse and divided the last of Evodius' money among his guests.

From here on, everything rested in God's hands.

Yaakov watched the muscular young man raise a hand to shade his eyes and scan the grassy fields. Even at a distance, his short dark hair and clean-shaven cheeks marked him as Roman. A traveler, Yaakov decided, someone who had lost his way.

Seeing Yaakov, the man waved. He headed toward him with a wide grin, traipsing through the tall grass still silky-wet with dew.

The stranger wore a knee-length, gray military tunic beneath his cloak and his confident, precise gait spoke of time with the Legions. Seeing the thick sandals of a Roman soldier laced above his ankles, solidified Yaakov's conclusion.

The man carried a *loculus* slung over one shoulder. These large, squarish bags had bronze rings at their corners. Yaakov had seen piles of such bags tied to the Legion's baggage trains. This odd young man modified his by stringing a strip of leather through two of its rings, creating a shoulder strap.

The young man paused at the edge of the slope, leaving a dozen cubits between them.

The old shepherd rose from the rock on which he sat and smoothed his robes. "*Ave*," Yaakov said. Assuming the man to be Roman, he used the standard Latin greeting. Living in an occupied country demanded certain deference when encountering the military.

The young man surprised him by replying, "*Shalom Aleichem*. May I join you?"

"Come ahead, stranger." The sudden appearance of such a person here in the middle of nowhere greeting him as a Jew piqued Yaakov's interest.

The young man extended his arm, grabbing the elder man's forearm in the manner of the Roman Legion. "I am called Marcus."

"My name is Yaakov. You are a soldier?"

Marcus smiled as if he made a joke. "Never, although I have lived the soldier's life. I spent the last nine years in service to Sextus Evodius, *Medicus Cohortis* to *Legio XII Fulminata*."

"But the Syrian Legions are in Antioch," Yaakov glanced around, "and here you are in Judea."

"True enough. I left Antioch when I became a freedman following Evodius' death."

"So you are a sojourner?"

Marcus gave an absentminded nod. He seemed more interested in the sheep grazing on the lush pasture than in their conversation.

"How can I assist you?" Local custom demanded all travelers be offered hospitality and given accurate directions. "What is your destination?"

"My destination? I am already there," the young man responded with a happy laugh. "I dreamed of such a lovely place as this. And now, here it is." He lifted his hands to the sky as if praying and turned in a circle.

Yaakov leaned his head back, measuring the position of the sun. "My stomach tells me it is time to eat and the sun agrees. Would you join me for my noonday meal?"

"Thank you. I would like that."

The two men walked side-by-side leading the flock home. As they traveled the familiar road, Marcus regaled his host with details of his trip from Antioch to Bethlehem. When they reached the house, he waited while Yaakov counted his sheep into the sheepfold.

Yaakov dropped the gate and smiled. All of his charges were home safe and sound. The sheep and goats clustered under the trees seeking shade while the men headed into the house. Once inside, Yaakov produced a basin of water and towel so Marcus could wash.

"I suggest we eat outside," Yaakov said. "There is a refreshing breeze."

Flat stones set around an old fig tree created a small patio where Marcus reclined in the shade while Yaakov arranged their food on a low table. It was a simple meal, the semi-soft goat cheese Rivkah kneaded with herbs because her father liked it best that way, barley loaves baked early that morning before she left for Bethlehem, smoked fish, olives pickled in wine vinegar, and assorted dried fruits.

When Yaakov finished placing the food on the table, Marcus dug into his *loculus* and produced an amphora of wine. "Galilean wine," he said. "Let it be my contribution to the meal."

Yaakov nodded his acceptance and disappeared into the house. He returned carrying two cups and a small pitcher of water. After a short blessing, he poured a little water into each cup. Marcus filled them the rest of the way with his wine.

Marcus scooped up the last bite of cheese with his bread. "I believe this cheese is the best I have ever eaten." He folded the thin bread over between his fingers, spreading the soft cheese.

"My daughter, Rivkah, makes it."

The mention of Rivkah's name sent Marcus' pulse racing. He steeled himself, vowing to follow the format he developed trudging the dusty road to Jerusalem.

"You have no wife to cook for you?"

"Hadassah, my wife, died many years ago. I have chosen not to remarry," Yaakov said, matter-of-factly, anticipating the unspoken question.

"And now your daughter, this Rivkah, she is grown?"

Yaakov popped an olive in his mouth and gave an

affirmative grunt.

This simple acknowledgement unleashed myriad emotions. For years Marcus surreptitiously studied every woman he saw, watching and wondering. He watched them walk and asked himself, *Is that the way Rivkah steps?* He would see them laugh with their friends and think, *Does Rivkah laugh with her friends that way, too?* Seen them nursing their infants and envied the husbands who held them at night.

When she was young, Rivkah had looked up to him. What would she think of him now? She would have married, of course, but still he knew he must see her.

Marcus took a deep breath and reached for his cup. It was time. He took a swallow of the sweet spring wine and, steeling himself for disappointment, posed the question he came so far to ask.

~ 46 ~

"Now his parents went to Jerusalem every year... And when he was twelve years old, they went according to custom..."

—Luke 2:41-42

There are certain things in life we are better off not thinking about. Among these is the fact that every piece of cloth for every cloak and tunic I made went through the fulling process before I stitched it into a garment.

No directions are needed to find the fuller's shop. Follow your nose and the stench will lead you right to him. The only place worse is the leather tanners. Both shops sit at the edge of town as far removed from the respectable businesses as possible.

The wool Rachel and I spun into yarn retained its natural greases and fats. Dyeing and rinsing removed some, but not all of it. To do this, the fuller treads the cloth in a vat of stale urine. How he acquired so much urine is another one of those things best not pondered.

The fabric also shrank while the fuller did his work, tightening the weave. After he washed and rinsed the cloth, the fuller put it on a stretcher to dry. Then he pounded it with a wooden mallet to smooth the finish and soften the cloth. The change was remarkable. He returned soft, flexible material ready for stitching.

We maintained a rotation. Each time Rachel or I dropped off newly woven fabric we picked up the previous batch. I left him four bolts, paid him for his work and stuffed the finished material into my bag. After a quick good-bye, I hurried away. Best not to linger at the fuller's shop.

It was market day in Bethlehem and merchant's stalls lined the main street. The exotic smell of incense hung heavy in the air and I tasted imported spices on the wind. When the breeze changed direction, the sweet, flowery scent of perfumes and ointments wafted by.

A familiar voice caught my ear while I examined the vegetables. Hearing it brought a smile to my face.

"Yeshua, you may look at the vendor's stalls, but do not wander far. We are leaving for Jerusalem as soon as your father has registered."

I sat aside the leeks and spun around. The years fell away; I recognized Miryam immediately.

"*Shalom Aleichem*, Miryam. I gave up hope of ever seeing you again."

A puzzled look crept over her face. She scrutinized me for several moments then asked, "Do I know you?"

"Yes. It is me, Rivkah."

"My little friend Rivkah?" She tapped the side of her head. "Of course. We are in Bethlehem, how could I not have known?" She pulled me into her arms and kissed my cheeks. "*Aleichem Shalom*. You are all grown up. How is your father?"

"Fine, and Yosef?"

"His business is good." She looked for him over the heads in the crowd, but could not find him. "He will be sorry he missed you. He went to register for the census. It seems fate brings us together under the strangest of circumstances."

We stepped between the stalls, moving out of the foot traffic so we could visit. A tall, boyish young man interrupted our conversation. "Imma, one of the merchants sells sweetmeats. May I have a few coins?"

I looked from the boy to his mother. The resemblance between them was unmistakable. Miryam gave a nod of acknowledgement to my unspoken question as she dug into her moneybag searching for small coins to give her son.

"I remember holding you the night you were born," I said. The startled expression on his face delighted me. His eyes had the same bottomless depth I remembered. I took his hand in mine. "Many times I have wondered what became of you, and now I see my precious Yeshua has grown tall and handsome."

He swallowed hard and stared at the ground, moving his foot in endless circles as young men do when they are embarrassed.

His fingers quivered and I thought he might bolt like a frightened calf, but he never pulled away. He had large, strong hands. Callused hands. Hands accustomed to hard labor. His shoulders relaxed when I released his fingers and his eyes returned to Miryam. He seemed more interested in watching his mother dig among the coins in her purse than reminiscing with a stranger.

"I used to play with you when you lived behind your father's shop." I pointed down the street. "Right there, around that corner. Has your father taught you to be a builder?"

"Yes. I help him every day." His confidence returned now that he was on familiar ground. "We live in Nazareth, but often work in Sepphoris. The two cities are quite close. At night I can see the lights of Sepphoris from the hill behind our house."

"I heard Varus' armies destroyed Sepphoris."

"Oh, they did," he said. "Large parts of the town were mostly ash and rubble the first few times we went there. Of course, I was small then. I could do no work, I just carried my father's tools. Herod Antipas, the tetrarch of Galilee, rebuilt the town and made it his capitol. He constructed an enormous palace. The new Sepphoris is a very Roman city with baths and theatres, even a coliseum where they hold games." His eyes narrowed. He frowned and shook his head. "Not a good place for a Jew."

Yeshua seemed content talking about carpentry, although I noticed his eyes wander back to Miryam's bag from time to time.

"The last time I saw you, you were leaving Bethlehem for Alexandria. I gave your mother a *dreidel* to take for you. I carved it from an olive burl and a special friend of mine cut the letters."

A wide grin lit his face at my mention of the *dreidel*.

"You must be Imma's friend, Rivkah. I played with it many, many times in Egypt. It still rests on a shelf in our home."

Miryam dropped several coins into his palm and admonished him to buy enough for everyone.

He turned away, took several steps and looked back. "*Shalom Aleichem*, Rivkah," he said. "I regret that I do not remember you, but I had a pleasant visit."

I wished him well.

"He is a good boy." Miryam smiled as she watched Yeshua

weave through the crowd pursuing his sweets. "After we have registered, we are going on to Jerusalem for the *Pesach*. It will be the first time Yeshua sees the Temple. He plans on presenting himself to the scribes and teachers to be examined on his knowledge of the Law."

"I could tell he was excited. He will surely do well."

"Yes, he will," she said with a mother's pride. "There is little he does not know. Yeshua studies the scripture more than anyone I have ever known."

She ran her eyes over me approvingly. "The years have flown by and you have matured into a beautiful woman. It seems I recall you talking about a certain young man who had stolen your heart. How does the story end...are you now married with children of your own?"

I shook my head. "No. Shemu'el died some time ago. We never married." I tugged my veil aside to blot my eyes.

"Oh, Rivkah. I am so sorry." Miryam pulled me into her arms and hugged me tightly. "Surely there will be another."

"Yes, I believe I have recently met him."

She smiled and patted my hand.

A man hurrying out of an alley almost knocked me over on my way to meet Devorah. I stumbled and caught myself against the wall of a building. Looking up, my expression changed from anger to surprise.

"Tyro?"

"Sorry, Rivkah. I was not watching where I was going."

"This seems to be my day for seeing old friends. I had not seen Yeshua and Miryam in over ten years. But you, on the other hand, visited my home just..." I laughed and counted the days on fingers. "Just nine days ago. You are early for the Seder, but welcome. Abba will be glad to see you again."

Tyro glanced from side to side and rubbed his palms along the side of his robe. "Ah yes, the Seder." He took a deep breath. "My plans have changed. I will not be able to eat the Seder meal with you and your father."

"But you are already here."

"I am not staying. I stopped to take care of a pressing matter and now I must leave."

Tyro usually talked and talked, but that day he had very little to say.

"Is something wrong?"

"Wrong? Why would you say that?" Taking my hands in his, he gave them a half-hearted squeeze. "No, I am just preoccupied. I will be back this way soon, very soon...but after the *Pesach*. When I return, we can have a nice long talk."

Before he could rush away a young woman joined us. "There you are, Tyro," she said in an exasperated voice. "I searched everywhere for you. I might have believed you were hiding from me."

Her name was Keren and the pained look on Tryo's face told me all I needed to know.

"How are you acquainted with my Tyro?" Keren asked, looping her arm through his.

"His father and mine have been friends for many years."

"Perhaps you should rejoin your mother, Keren," Tyro suggested.

"She is still in the perfumery. The smells made me ill."

"Is your family new to Bethlehem?" I asked.

Tyro urged her to leave again.

She shushed him. "No. I come from Jaffa. My parents sent me away to stay with my aunt in Bethlehem until Tyro and I could be married because, well..." She lifted her eyebrows and patted her bulging tunic. "We are going to live in Tyre after the wedding."

"No doubt you will have a lovely home. How did you two meet?"

Tyro tugged Keren's arm.

She smacked his hand away. "What is wrong with you? I want to visit. My aunt keeps me indoors all day. This is my chance to see the sun and talk to someone close to my own age."

Keren turned to me. "My father is a tailor. Tyro came into

his shop to offer him cloth. I saw him and, well, he just swept me off my feet." She giggled. "One day we went for a ride on his horse and I just could not tell him no."

Tyro jerked her aside. "Go tell your mother to hurry up. Now!" He gave her a shove, sending her on her way.

He watched her disappear into the crowd then turned to face me. "This is not what you think. What choice did I have when she turned out to be with child?"

"I suppose you will tell me she accomplished it all by herself."

He glanced around and made soothing motions with his hands. "I would have told you, but I have been busy dealing with this...this problem." He lowered his voice. "I intend to speak to your father, honestly I do. First I must deal with Keren. Give me a little time. In two, maybe three months, I will come for a visit."

Were my ears deceiving me? Had he just asked me to wait while he married someone else?

"Thank you, Tyro."

He gave me a confused look. "What are you thanking me for?"

"For helping me make up my mind."

He grabbed for my arm when I turned to leave. "Rivkah! Rivkah, wait. We talked about this. Remember the day in the vineyard? I thought we understood each other. About me and other women."

"Oh, I do. Now."

"I swear, little bird, I love only you. The Law allows a man more than one wife. In a few months I will come and see your father. I swear it before the Lord himself. Forget about Keren. After we marry, I will give her a writ of divorce." His eyes flicked from side to side and his voice dropped to a conspiratorial whisper. "Trust me, I can easily do it. Her family worried more about their reputation than Keren's security. It will cost me practically nothing to rid myself of her. Then we can be together just as you wanted."

Tyro continued calling to me as I walked away.

Devorah and I hardly spoke on the way home. She and Shaoul knew something happened in Bethlehem to upset me, but were kind enough not to pry.

Tyro's actions put my life into perspective. The time had come to face the facts. Rachel was probably right. I had spent too much time dreaming of things that could never be.

I could have had Caleb. For all intents and purposes I had been betrothed to him, yet I conspired to undermine Abba's work. And there were others, too, whom I cast away as carelessly as a tree sheds its leaves.

Abba once warned, "*Eventually you will wait too long and never marry.*" But I would not listen. In my stubbornness I clung to memories of Shemu'el instead. In the end, that was all I would have, memories.

Without intending to, I had married myself to a dead man. Now I must pay the price for my foolishness. I was destined to be an old maid, spending my years with only my shadow as a companion. I would become a laughingstock, a withered prune. Childless.

Unwanted and unloved.

~ 47 ~

"Your daughter has no doubt married," Marcus said, "and given you many grandchildren for your old age."

His heart leaped in his chest when Yaakov sadly shook his head. "I have no grandchildren. My Rivkah has never married."

He could scarcely contain himself. This was more than he dared hope for. Marcus examined the plate of fruit, pretending only passing curiosity in their conversation. He selected several dried plums and slowly chewed the sticky fruit.

"May I be so bold as to ask why she has never married?"

"Do not imagine my daughter has some defect, or that she is not pleasing to the eye. My Rivkah is a lovely creature, a delight to behold."

"I would never think such a thing. Excuse my inquisitive nature, but most young women look forward to marriage and children. Why has no man sought her hand?"

Yaakov's laugh came from deep in his belly. "If I had a *denarius* for every man who sought Rivkah's hand, I would be a wealthy man. They all want her, but she does not want them."

"Because…"

"Because as a girl she set her heart on one particular young man."

Scooping up the last of the cheese, Marcus nodded knowingly. "An old and sad tale, but unfortunately a true one. This man rejected her and chose another for his wife?"

"Worse than that, far worse. He died."

Marcus slumped forward in shock, only catching himself when his elbows hit his knees. "Died? He died?" He did not have to feign astonishment at hearing of his own demise. "No. Uh, I mean how did he die?"

"He was in Jerusalem." Yaakov shifted on the ground as he began the tale. "Shemu'el, was his name. A local boy. His father's name was Yo'el. He had two older brothers, Caleb and Yhonatan. They were all good boys, the kind any man would want as sons. They worked hard, never troubled people. They lived nearby. His brothers still do."

"But what became of Shemu'el?"

"He was at the Temple to fulfill one of our customs. You see, in order to achieve manhood, a boy must go to the Temple and present himself to the teachers for examination." Yaakov chuckled. "I remember being terrified when my time came. But they ask only cursory questions; it is more formality than substance. A simple rite of passage."

"Yes, yes. I am familiar with this practice." Marcus gestured with his hands. "So this young man went to Jerusalem. Tell me more."

"Did you know that King Herod profaned our Temple by placing the golden eagle of Rome on the front wall?"

"Everyone does. What did Herod have to do with Shemu'el?"

"When Herod fell ill, two Rabbis incited their students to storm the Temple and rip down this graven image. They assumed he could not respond since he lay on his deathbed. They were mistaken; he had them all burned alive. The following *Pesach*, the Jews protested and Archelaus, Herod's successor, unleashed his troops and slaughtered 3,000 worshippers."

Marcus had tired of indulging his host. "My friend, I know all of this. Please, the matter of Shemu'el's death."

"But you said you came from Antioch."

"I did, but word spreads."

Yaakov began again. "It was a period of great unrest. Caesar appointed a man named Sabinus as temporary procurator after Herod died. Archelaus was gone to Rome at the time. Then came *Shavo'ut*, the Feast of Weeks—Pentecost. Meanwhile, Quintilius Varus, the Governor of Syria—"

"I came from Antioch, remember?" he said, stopping him.

"So you did. So you did. Where was I?"

"Shemu'el went to the Temple to be examined during *Shavo'ut*."

"Yes. And on the day Shemu'el went to Jerusalem, there was another protest. The boy had nothing to do with it, mind you. He was a good-hearted lad, a mere shepherd boy there for his examination. The last time his brother, Caleb, saw Shemu'el a legionnaire was clubbing him to death. Then the soldiers set fire to the Temple cloisters incinerating everyone."

Marcus chewed his lip. "Where is this unfortunate youngster buried?"

Yaakov lifted his arms, displaying empty palms. "He disappeared amid the ashes and bones of hundreds of others. He was one among many, all burned beyond recognition. His family had no body to bury. All those blackened bones were placed in a common grave."

Marcus sat in stunned silence. It made sense. He recalled looking over his shoulder at the flames as the soldiers led him away in chains. What other conclusion could they have come to? He smiled to himself. All these years he had been dead and never even knew it.

"Why have you not arranged another marriage?"

"Each time I presented a proposal, she cast it aside. Her answer was always the same, 'Marriage is *b'shert*. If God destines someone to replace Shemu'el, I will recognize him when he arrives.'"

Would she? Marcus wondered, brushing the crumbs from his lap. Would she know him after all these years?

"A few men still try, but they are not a good match."

"No one but this Shemu'el will do?"

Yaakov smiled. "There may yet be hope. A prosperous young man from Phoenicia has been coming by to see her. I can tell he has made up his mind. He plans to share the coming Seder with us." His eyes sparkled. "Things are about to change; I can feel it in my bones."

With both the meal and the story concluded, he gathered the plates and dishes. After carrying things back into the house, he and Marcus rested in the shade letting their meal digest.

"You have heard my story, what about you?" Yaakov asked, giving him a sideways glance. Despite his strange appearance, he found himself liking this Marcus person.

"I have no wife." Marcus drained the cup of wine and licked the remnants from his lips. "I sleep alone."

"Even slaves marry."

"And to what end, to produce more slaves thereby enriching their master? No thank you. I have lived a chaste life."

"There is no one here but the two of us. We are both men; there is no need for pretense. You said you and this Ethiopian assisted the Physician. You must have traveled with the army, slept in the soldier's encampments. Surely women visited."

"Every camp has its followers, if that is what you mean. Yes, they came and I sent them away." Noting Yaakov's astonished expression, Marcus explained. "The Romans view relations between a man and a woman differently than we Jews do. Their world presents abundant opportunities for illicit romances, trysts and dalliances. They find no shame in adultery."

He turned to face the older man.

"What I say now, I say as one man to another. Has my lust never been stirred? Of course it has. And late at night, have I ever ached for a woman's soft body beside me. Yes, again. Still in my heart of hearts I knew if I gave myself over to my baser instincts I would prove myself unworthy of the woman I wanted for my wife."

Yaakov gave him a confused look. "How can you deem yourself unworthy of someone who does not exist?"

"Oh, she exists. With every breath I took I dreamed of the day I could hold her in my arms."

"And this is the purpose of your journey? You traveled all the way from Antioch searching for this ideal woman?"

"In a way, yes." Marcus toyed with a twig, peeling away its bark. "Perhaps my search has ended this very day."

Yaakov's back stiffened. "Do you mean what I think you mean?"

"I know your daughter is pleasing to the eye and sought after by many men. You admitted as much. The meal she left proves she is a good cook and homemaker. Why should I not want her for my wife?"

"No! It is out of the question. The Romans murdered Shemu'el. My daughter will never be the wife of a Roman soldier."

"A Roman *physician*. I have been a citizen of Rome just a

few weeks, I have been a Jew all my life."

"She will still refuse you."

Marcus chuckled. "Have I finally met a man foolish enough to presume he knows the mind of a woman?"

"I will not consider it."

"But you have not heard my offer."

"There is no need to. I will not send my daughter away to live among strangers."

The more agitated Yaakov became, the more Marcus' voice soothed. "What if I agreed to live here?"

"Among shepherds?"

"Why not?"

Yaakov's answered with indistinct muttering.

"This Shemu'el, this young man your daughter loved, how did he earn his bread?"

"He was a shepherd." Yaakov swept his arm in a wide arc. "Like all of us here in this settlement."

"So if I were a shepherd, then would I be acceptable?"

"No, no, no. You are taking my words and twisting them. I have already told you she wants Shemu'el." He fluttered his hands at the young man. "Go! If you are not Shemu'el, she does not want you."

Marcus bent forward. "I must tell you something."

The older man leaned closer.

"You are being unfair to both me and your daughter. You say Rivkah has spurned all offers of marriage, yet you refuse to hear mine. How do you know today might not be the day she changes her mind? I can offer more than anyone has ever offered before."

Yaakov glanced at Marcus' worn sandals. "I told you a rich man is interested in her hand. You will not be able to match his bride price."

"Are we discussing your daughter, or a sheep? It sounds as if you intend to auction her to the highest bidder."

Yaakov straightened. Grabbing the sides of his cloak, he gave them a hard tug. "How dare you insult me in my own home. I only meant he will surely make a generous offer."

"And just as surely I will offer more."

"This man is very wealthy."

"He can never offer what I do."

Yaakov's eyes narrowed. "Is there something you have not told me?"

"There is much yet to be told."

Yaakov started to respond, but Rivkah's voice stopped him.

~ 48 ~

"Abba, I am back. The cloth turned out beautifully, but we need to talk, there is something—"

I froze in the doorway with the cloth in my hand. The stranger beside him lifted his head at the sound of my voice. His eyes moved across me, staring shamefully. A smile curled his lips when he saw me blush. His audacity seemed boundless.

Instinct told me to treat him the same as any goy who stared, glare at him, cover my face with my veil and turn away. For unexplainable reasons, I could not do that. His gaze felt warm and reassuring, his smile honest and accepting.

"I was not aware you had company."

"This is Marcus, a sojourner from Antioch."

"*Shalom Aleichem*, Rivkah."

When he looked into my eyes it felt as if he saw into my very soul. What was so unnerving about those eyes? I never felt the presence of any man as intensely as I did this stranger. Stammering my apologies, I retreated into the house.

Abba rose and followed me in.

With Marcus safely outside, I found my tongue again. "What is a Roman doing in our home?"

I turned my back and busied myself storing the food I purchased in Bethlehem.

"I told you. He is a traveler from Antioch, a sojourner."

The cups and plates from their meal sat in front of me. Abba already fed the man, what more were we required to do? "Fine. Then let him continue on his way."

"There is something else, my dove. He has asked to take you for his wife."

My stomach dropped. The words I threw at Rachel the previous day returned to taunt me. I swallowed hard. Had I actually promised to marry the next man who asked for my hand? No, it was a joke. Something said without any forethought. No one could expect me to honor such a commitment...could they?

"Surely you misunderstood."

"He refuses to take no for an answer."

Blood rushed into my cheeks. "He is either possessed by an evil spirit, or crazy in the head. I will not marry a *goy*. If you do not tell him to go away, I will."

"He claims to be a Jew, a freedman. If you give him a chance, you will find he is a very nice person."

"Why should I care to find out?"

My eyes flicked around the room searching for something I could use to drive him off. A rod or a staff would have done nicely. Why were there never weapons around the house when you needed them?

My father took my hand. He patted it the way he did when he wanted to calm me. "So what if he is a crazy man? Let him make his offer and refuse it. Even a fool deserves kindness."

"Another day perhaps, but not today. I am not feeling very kind right now. Send him away."

"Marcus says he came all the way from Antioch. Let him have this one moment." My father looked down at me the way he did when I was a child. "Would it hurt to humor the poor soul?"

Neither of us heard Marcus' footsteps as he came through the doorway. We turned together when he coughed to announce his presence. He had the strap of his satchel over his shoulder. For an instant I allowed myself to believe he was leaving.

"Yes," he said, giving me that disarming smile of his. "Why not humor the poor soul?"

"Very well, have it your way." I cast aside the cloth I picked up to wipe the dishes and headed for the door. "I will wait outside while you and Abba talk."

"Rivkah?"

I froze. He spoke my name with unbelievable tenderness.

"You just walked all the way from Bethlehem. You must be tired, probably thirsty. Can I draw you a cool drink, get you something to eat?"

"I stopped at the well before coming home ."

"Please do not rush away. Having you leave would be like extinguishing a lamp at midnight." He swept his hand in the direction of the front room. "Since the decision will ultimately be yours, why not stay?"

Abba nodded his encouragement.

At that moment it would have been easy to convince me they were co-conspirators. Left with no choice, I swept my robes under me and sat down at the far side of the room.

Marcus smiled.

A flicker of recognition swept through me. No, it could not be. Do not even imagine it, I told myself. Over the years, I encountered Shemu'el everywhere, had seen bits of him in a thousand strangers. Was it surprising that I saw him in this crazy Roman? It would take more than a charlatan's charm to win me over.

"Who will represent you?" my father asked, settling onto a stool.

"I am of sufficient age to represent myself," he said. "Though having never been through this before, I must ask your indulgence. I will do the best I can." His eyes sought mine. "I understand from your father you have been through this many times. If I stumble, feel free to correct me."

Marcus reached into his satchel and extracted an amphora of wine. Its twin lay empty beside their dishes from their noonday meal. "To share at the acceptance of the betrothal," he announced, putting it beside the other.

He circled the room nervously, gathering his thoughts. "As I understand it, there are three points to be addressed: the bride-price paid by the bridegroom, the bridegroom's present for his intended and the groom's surety, the amount the bride will take away from the marriage should it end in divorce."

Marcus looked from me to Abba, seeking our concurrence. "With your forbearance, I would like to address the last item first. If she becomes my wife, I offer Rivkah a surety of one thousand talents of gold."

The blood drained from Abba's face. His mouth fell open. Lord forgive me, there was nothing I could do but chuckle at Marcus' ridiculous offer.

"Do you take us for fools?" Abba screamed. "Who do you think you are, Solomon?" He rose from the stool, waving his hands in the air. "A thousand talents of gold is a king's ransom. Caesar's daughter would merit only a fraction of that. There is no way a man like you could gather such a sum."

Marcus rubbed his chin, weighing Abba's challenge. He winked at me. "If that is true, then I suppose I would be forced to spend the rest of my life with her. For if we wed, there would be no way I could afford to divorce her."

Despite my best effort, I found myself smiling at his curious logic. Abba was right. He was hard not to like.

"Earlier, before you arrived, I told your father I would offer a bride-price greater than anyone has ever offered before."

Marcus reached into his satchel and extracted the metal tag he wore as a slave. The chain jingled as he tugged it out reminding me of the bells on Sidonius' camels. He extended it to my father.

Abba contemplated it in silence, refusing to accept it. "What do you take us for? You expect me to part with my beloved daughter in exchange for a worthless scrap of metal? She is my life, all that I have."

"Truly spoken, and you deserve an appropriate bride-price for her. This sweat-stained, tarnished tag, this mark of shame and disgrace is what I give."

He held it in front of Abba's face, demanding he take it.

"A life for a life. When they took my life from me I got this plate in return. This plate and the few tools in my *loculus* are all that I have." Marcus drew himself up to his full height. "Therefore, Yaakov, as my bride-price I offer you everything I have in this world. Has any man even offered half as much?"

Abba snatched the tag out his hand and pitched it aside. "How dare you? It seems my daughter was right, you are a madman."

Before Marcus could reply, my father grabbed him by the arm and dragged him to the door. "Out!" he shouted. "Be gone, you crazy fool."

"Wait! Patience, please." Marcus gave me a desperate glance over his shoulder and wrenched free of my father's grip. "We agreed the decision would be Rivkah's to make. I have proposed my surety and offered my bride price. Now let me give my intended her presents and then, if she refuses me, I will be on my way."

Without waiting for Abba's response, Marcus fell to his knees in front of me and took my hand.

"Today God has smiled upon me. Each night I dreamed of finding you and now I have. If the world were mine, I would give it to you. Alas, I am a former slave, a freedman with neither money nor assets. My purse may be empty, but my heart overflows with love."

He gently unfolded the fingers of my right hand. "Here are my presents to you, lovely Rivkah." Marcus' hand disappeared into the satchel. "A ring of gold, a symbol of my unending love. I had it made for you in Antioch," he said, slipping it on my finger. "And this, which I once promised to return." He placed the small *shrika* I gave him to take to the Temple in my outstretched palm.

My father shot off the stool. "A fancy stick? You insult my daughter by offering her a twig?"

Abba continued ranting, but neither of us heard him. I had already thrown myself into Shemu'el's arms. My father watched in stunned silence as we hugged and kissed. I looked up at my father with tears of joy streaming down my cheeks. "Please, Abba, I beg you. Accept his offer. I wish to be this man's wife."

If we do nothing else, we Jews revere our traditions. Shemu'el swept off his cloak and draped it over me. Many men do this at a betrothal. It is a symbolic way to claim the woman as Boaz did with Ruth.

I rested my hand against Shemu'el's cheek and repeated Ruth's immortal words. "Wherever you go, I will go, where you stay I will stay. Your people shall be my people, and your God my God. Where you die, I will die, and there shall I be buried. I swear a solemn oath before the Lord our God: nothing but death shall pry us apart."

Then the stranger with his Roman appearance and strange ways rose and approached Abba. Standing tall and proud, he said, "I, Shemu'el bar Yo'el, request the right to take your daughter, Rivkah, to be my wife."

~ 49 ~

The sun left my life the afternoon Abba told me that Shemu'el had been killed. And, like a plant deprived of sunlight, I withered.

It became easier to look back than ahead. Many nights, when the pain seemed too much to bear, I prayed death would overtake me. Death, I thought, would surely be better than the torment I felt. When death never came, I assumed my prayers had not been answered. Believed it further proof the Lord had turned his face away from me.

But, as Miryam said years earlier, *"God's ways are not our ways."* Sometimes God's "No" can be a greater gift than his "Yes."

Tears of happiness ran down Abba's cheeks. Never have I seen my father so joyful. When he hugged us for the last time, Shemu'el and I retreated to the shade of the same olive tree I climbed as a little girl and began planning our future together. Too excited to sit still, we drifted over to the sheepfold. Shemu'el ran his fingers through the sheep's thick wool as we talked.

"I meant what I said, you know. I truly am a shepherd without sheep. I still have my medical instruments and carving tools, but there is no living in that here. Perhaps I can become a hireling, paid to watch someone else's flock."

"An excellent idea. I know of a flock in need of a shepherd."

He gave me a strange look.

"Have you forgotten Liat and the lion? She gave me many lambs and those lambs had more lambs and they had still more."

I stretched up and kissed him. "I have had much longer to build my dowry than most. Never worry, my love, you shall not be without a flock just as I shall not be without a husband."

"I must see my family and tell them of our good fortune."

"You have not seen them yet?"

A look of guilt washed over Shemu'el's face. "God forgive me, no. The Torah says, '...a man will leave his father and mother and be united to his wife, and they will become one flesh.' More than anything I wanted to find you. When your father told me you had not married, nothing else mattered."

It became my sad task to tell him his father had been dead

for two years. I also told him of the girls his brothers married and the children they had.

"I must go to them. Will you accompany me?"

"I can wait here if you prefer to meet with them alone."

He tugged my hand. "Come with me. We have been apart too long. I never want us to spend another moment apart."

I fell into step beside him.

We found his mother sitting on the porch shelling beans.

"*Shalom Aleichem*, Rivkah. It is good to see you, my daughter." She wrinkled her brow and squinted at the man beside me. "Tell me, why do you hold the hand of that Roman? Who is this strange person you have brought to my door?"

"He is my betrothed."

Her eyes widened in disbelief. She put her hand to her heart and murmured a prayer. "Tell me it is not so. Surely you would not marry a heathen."

It seemed cruel to delude her any longer. I rushed to her, took her in my arms and kissed her cheek. Putting an arm around her shoulder, I led her to where Shemu'el stood.

"Imma Sarit, this is my betrothed, your son Shemu'el. The man we both believed dead."

She gave me a harsh look. "The Lord will punish you for tricking me by saying my Shemu'el lives when he does not."

"I would never do such a thing."

Mother Sarit inched closer. Afraid to trust my words, she looked him over carefully. She circled him. This man looked nothing like the boy she lost. He did not even look Jewish. And yet…and yet there was something about him she could not deny. No matter what her eyes told her, her heart wanted to believe the truth of my words.

An incredulous whisper rose from deep within her as she reached to touch his cheek. "Shemu'el? You are my Shemu'el? My son come back to me from the grave."

He wrapped her in his arms. "Yes, Imma. Your son lives."

The standard Jewish betrothal lasts one year. Ours lasted three months, which was three months longer than either of us would have liked.

When Yo'el died Yhonatan and Caleb divided his flock. Without intending to, they had disinherited Shemu'el. They tried to make it right by offering him his choice of their flocks. He refused, saying they owed him nothing. To make it up to him, they agreed to help him build his house.

One day, on the way home from the well, I saw the end of a large wooden beam rise over the brow of the hill. An instant later Simeon appeared, sweating and grunting as he struggled to carry the heavy timber on his bare shoulder. He and Gavriel, who followed on the other end, stopped beside me. They had forsaken their cloaks and girded their loins for strenuous work.

"You both look exhausted. I raised the bucket in my hand. "Have some cool water."

Simeon caught Gavriel's eye. They counted together, "*Alef, bet, gimmel,*" and released the log on three. It rolled off their shoulders and thudded to the ground.

I studied the long, freshly-peeled log. "That is too large for two men. You should get some help."

Simeon grunted and shook his head as he emptied the dipper. He sucked in a deep breath and passed the bucket to Gavriel. "We can manage," he said, while his friend gulped the cool water.

Simeon rolled the beam with his foot. "Have you ever seen a more beautiful piece of wood?"

"It's lovely. What do you plan to do with it?"

They gave each other a look and chuckled. "Now that you have seen it, there is no use pretending. If you do not recognize it now, you soon will. It will support your new roof."

"We cut eight of these cedars far up in the hills where Varus' *carpentarii* never ventured," Gavriel said. "Each one straight and true, perfectly matched, as similar as peas in a pod. They are our gift to you and Shemu'el. After we deliver this one, we plan to go back for another before nightfall."

"Why not rest? You are both scraped and bleeding."

"Just scratches from the branches."

Simeon filled the dipper, bent and poured it over his head. Gavriel repeated the motion and handed me the empty bucket. Grunting, they heaved the log back onto their shoulders and trudged away toward the site where Shemu'el and the men were stacking rocks and blocks for the walls.

"Hey, Rivkah," Gavriel called over his shoulder.

When I looked up, he grinned. "Better draw some more water, little shepherdess. Your bucket is empty."

The whole settlement spent every free moment helping us prepare. Ours was more than a wedding, it was a communal celebration of Shemu'el's safe return. While he, his brothers and the rest of the men built the house, the women of our settlement gathered every afternoon to assist me.

It was a time of gaiety, spontaneous laughter and discussions about the relations between men and women and married life in general. One afternoon, Devorah, the least inhibited of my friends, suggested we make a trip to Jerusalem.

"We must visit the sellers of cloth and purchase some fine Egyptian linen." She winked. "We shall select the very sheerest of fabrics to sew you a gown. One so fine that when you light a lamp it will reveal your nakedness."

These married women giggled like girls at Devorah's suggestion.

"I do not think I will require sheer gowns," I said, lowering my eyes.

My embarassment only increased their laughter.

Devorah rose from the floor and snapped her fingers. "We must get some of those little cymbals that fit on your fingers, too." She danced across the room to the rhythm she created.

The other women clapped their hands, picking up her beat. She removed her headband and twirled it on one finger. Her auburn hair cascaded down her back as she circled the room, hips swaying. "That is how you do it," she whispered.

Stopping in front of me, she ran her hands over her body seductively. Dampness glistened on her forehead. She took a deep breath and swept a hand over her face, brushing hair away from her eyes. "To make a fire, you must first strike a spark."

After retying her hair, Devorah returned to her stitching as if nothing had happened.

Growing warmth began at my neck and crept into my cheeks. I could not believe she expected me to display myself in a sheer gown like some Babylonian whore.

Devorah noticed my discomfort and motioned to the others.

Rachel crossed the room, waving her hands to shush them. She dropped to the floor beside me. "Rivkah, look around you. These are your friends, your sisters. We do not laugh at you, we laugh with you. We all felt these same things on the eve of our wedding." She patted my hand. "Save the flimsy gowns for when Shemu'el grows old."

Aunt Tamar invited me to walk with her several days before my wedding. We moved aimlessly enjoying the evening breeze and the setting sun. Tamar combed the heads of grain with her fingers when we stopped beside a field of barley. She took my hand. "I am so happy for you, Rivkah."

I smiled.

"Tell me, will you disappoint Shemu'el on your wedding night?"

"I hope not. We love each other very much and have waited a long time for this moment."

"True, but men have expectations of their bride."

It took me a moment to discern her meaning. "If you wonder if I remain a virgin," I said, "the answer is yes." She'd insulted me and my harsh tone reflected my hurt. I jerked my hand away. "What do you take me for, an adulteress, a harlot? How could you even imply such a thing?"

"I had to for your sake. You are older than most brides, Rivkah. There are ways to make certain your wedding cloth has a stain upon it."

"You need not lose any sleep over my wedding cloth."

She surprised me by taking me in her arms and hugging me. "You have always been too sensitive. For years I ached watching you trod your rocky road. Yet you remained as unyielding as the old gnarled trunk of a grapevine."

"What is it you want from me?" I asked, resisting her embrace.

"Let me love you. Why must you build a fortress around your heart? I am not your enemy. Open a gate; let me in."

I had the sudden realization of love rejected, help refused. No gate opened as Tamar wanted. Instead, like at Jericho, my whole wall tumbled down. I sobbed into my aunt's shoulder.

"Forget what you imagined," she whispered. "I meant something different. You spent a lot of time alone with the sheep and bands of soldiers patrol the countryside. Bad things can happen when a woman is by herself."

She had every right to be concerned. With so many Roman soldiers around a young woman was always at risk. In an instant she could be pulled behind a bush and her virtue stolen from her. How could I have ever faced Shemu'el if such a thing had happened to me?

What times we lived in. Many young couples in Judea chose to consummate their union before the wedding, often right after the betrothal. In this way a man's right to his bride's purity could not be stolen from him. I whispered a prayer of thanksgiving. God had protected me, preserving me for my husband.

~ 50 ~

I gathered my hair into a bundle and tucked it under my chin. The Law required a woman be completely submerged, even her hair. A smile, a deep breath, and I sank beneath the *mikvah* waters. This would be my final time to perform this cleansing ritual of immersion as a maiden.

When I came up, my damp skin glistened as the water sheeted off me. Reborn and purified, I shook the water out of my hair and shivered with anticipation. When I came to the *mikvah* next month it would be as a married woman.

In our world weddings demanded a certain amount of surreptitious planning. Not only must someone prepare the food and beverages, but the families had to agree on a proper date. Relations between a man and his wife were prohibited during her monthly cycle. This time of *niddah*, or separation, extended an additional seven days beyond. Thus, women were *tamei*, ritually impure, for about twelve days each month.

Young men, being young men, wanted their new bride available to them for as long as possible after the wedding. Couples accomplished this by scheduling their marriage close to the bride's purification.

As our preparations neared completion, Mother Sarit called on me making discrete inquiries. I named the date I planned to go to the *mikvah*, and smiled to myself as I watched her leave. In most cases, the day on which the groom would appear to claim his bride became a poorly kept secret.

In our little settlement weddings took place on the third or fourth day of the week. This allowed sufficient time after the *Shabbat* to make ready and time for celebrating prior to the day of preparation for the next *Shabbat*.

We Jews love nothing as we love our traditions, and marriage is the most traditional event of all. One or more messengers typically notified the bridal party of the groom's pending arrival.

Our morning began with a tiny rap at our door. Abba opened it and found Caleb's three-year-old daughter, Yohanna, staring up at him.

"Prepare! The groom comes to get Aunt Rivkah," she shouted. She scurried back to her mother's arms without so much as a good-bye.

Every so often another child appeared with a similar message. The boys and girls gradually became older and their presentations more elaborate. They treated us to whistle serenades, bell ringing, cymbal tapping and tambourine rattling all morning.

Rachel and Devorah, my attendants, arrived at the fourth hour to wait with me. Devorah concentrated on smoothing my white linen cloak and worrying. Rachel passed the time by fussing with my hair, tying and retying my blue ribbons...blue for good luck.

"Tell me, Rivkah," Rachel asked as she re-tied the ribbon for the third time. "You always said the Lord would tell you when the right man came along. Did he? When Shemu'el offered marriage, I mean."

I laughed. "To tell the truth, I was so busy throwing myself into his arms and kissing him that I forgot to listen."

We were getting close now. The messages were carried by young men, not children.

I began to pace.

A hard rap on the door startled us. A loud male voice announced, "Hark! Yonder comes the bridegroom."

Caleb and Yhonatan blew their trumpets. I hurriedly kissed Abba, hugged Rachel and Devorah and tugged my veil over my face. Brides wore veils because nearly two thousand years earlier another Rivkah had veiled herself when she married Avraham's son, Yitzchaq. A veil symbolized modesty, saying soul and character were more important than beauty.

My attendants lit their lamps. The door swung back and Shemu'el stepped in. He had let his hair and beard grow and appeared more Jewish than Roman. He looked handsome in his wedding garment, so very handsome.

His brothers set up a *chuppah* in a clearing near Mother Sarit's house. Like all Jewish couples, we stood under this tent without sides as a reminder of the time when our ancestors wandered the desert in search of the Promised Land.

Normally Shemu'el's father would have officiated, but since Yo'el died, Shemu'el asked Abba to take his place. My father stepped under the *chuppah*, turning to face Jerusalem.

Before we joined Abba under the tent, Shemu'el lifted my veil. This was done because of the trick Laban pulled on Yaakov when he switched daughters, forcing him to marry Leah first. We had not seen each other since the day before yesterday. Would he still recognize me?

The veil lifted.

Surprise! It's me, not Leah.

Shemu'el grinned and took his place under the *chuppah*. I walked three circles around him. Rachel accompanied me with a lamp. Now there were as many interpretations to this tradition as there are rabbis. Some say it shows how central the groom is to the bride's thoughts and very being. Others say she basks in his shadow and he in her luminescence. Still others mention the Song of Songs which refers to a woman as an enclosing garden. Some refer to Jeremias, who wrote, "...a woman surrounds a man." No matter, it is a nice tradition.

Afterwards, I stepped into the circle I created, making us a community of two. As his queen, I stood on Shemu'el's right. For the Psalms say, "a queen shall stand at your right side."

The guests formed a semi-circle in front of us. Tradition demanded the person officiating read the *ketubah* before the wedding. Reading the marriage contract made it a matter of public record. Abba turned and faced our friends and relatives.

"As required, I now proclaim the *ketubah* between Shemu'el bar Yo'el and Yaakov bar Yonah for the hand of Rivkah bat Yaakov."

The guests inched closer, the better to hear. The reading of the *ketubah* was everyone's favorite part of a wedding, the time when the secrets were revealed. Tension and expectation filled the air. How much did he pay? What presents did he bring? What surety did she have?

All sorts of fanciful tales passed around the well in the few short weeks since Shemu'el's return. He had not been a slave at all; he had served the Governor of Syria as his private physician. He brought bags of gold coins with him. The bride price had been so large that Abba would never have to work again. After the wedding we would leave for a Roman province where Shemu'el had a commission waiting. It was hard not to laugh when listening to such silliness.

Abba's voice boomed, stilling the crowd. "First, the bride price. The groom offers the bride's father all his worldly possessions."

The crowd gasped. Unbelievable. Unheard of. No wonder Yaakov had been smiling so much.

Abba raised his hand displaying the slave tag Shemu'el gave him the day he came to our house looking like a Roman. "Which consists of one slave identification plate."

The crowd's excitement turned to dismay. A slave plate? There must be some mistake. What happened to the bags of gold? They looked at one another. No one seemed to know what to make of it.

Both of us scanned the sea of stunned faces with repressed grins.

Undeterred, Abba continued. "The groom brings his bride the following presents: a gold ring worth 100 brass *sestertii* and one exceptionally well-carved, heirloom *shrika* of inestimable value."

Abba held up the little whistle for all to see. He looked ridiculous standing there holding the hollowed-out twig. Somewhere in the crowd a child giggled. Their mother shushed them then snickered herself. People looked around, stared at the ground, glanced at the sky, anything to keep from laughing.

Shemu'el and I caught each other's eye. Our sides quivered as we struggled not to chuckle.

Abba pushed on. Just one more. "Finally, the bride's surety. Should he ever divorce her, the groom promises a payment of one thousand talents of gold."

Shock silenced the crowd. This was one day they would always remember. A *ketubah* like no other. What to make of this? No gold, no commissions, no easy life, nothing. Nothing but love.

People looked at one another. Rivkah and Shemu'el had nothing but love. They smiled. What else did anyone need? The Lord will provide the rest. Laughter spread from one person to the next, joyous laughter that swelled the heart and refused to be contained. It surrounded us, growing louder and louder. We all laughed until we cried. I believe God's angels in heaven laughed with us that day.

When the crowd quieted Abba poured the cup of wine and Shemu'el took my hand. "Rivkah bat Yaakov, be sanctified to me with this ring in accordance with the laws of God and Moshe." He slipped the ring onto the finger of my right hand and we sipped from the cup.

Then Abba read the seven blessings: a blessing on the vine, a blessing for creation, a blessing for the creation of human beings, a supplication for Zion, a supplication for the couple, a blessing for the joy of the married couple and, finally, a blessing for a long married life.

We shared the cup again, draining it this time.

Shemu'el and I had crossed the second bridge on our way to marriage. First the betrothal, then the ceremony. I nervously awaited the third and final step, when we lay together as man and wife.

~ 51 ~

We stepped out from under the *chuppah* and our friends and neighbors descended upon us with kisses and hugs and congratulations. As groomsmen, Caleb and Yhonatan now became our guards. They stepped forward, ready to conduct us to the bridal chamber.

Before we left, I removed my veil and handed it to Devorah. Then I untied my blue ribbons and shook my hair free. Little girls raced to catch the ribbons I tossed to the wind. Shemu'el's brothers escorted us away, leaving the music, food and friends behind.

Shemu'el took my hand as we walked up the path to our new home, the house he, his brothers, and the men of our settlement constructed for us. Tingles of excitement danced inside me. From time to time I stole passing glances of the exterior, but they never allowed me inside. What would this place where we would spend our lives be like?

The house was built around a cave. Like every home in our settlement a portion of the rear extended into the hillside providing a cool storage area for food. The larger front portion, built of blocks and bricks, had a flat roof accessed by an outside stairway along one wall. I imagined summer evenings lying on the roof in Shemu'el's arms and staring up at the heavens.

A sloping roof shaded the front porch. We stopped under it and Shemu'el, that is, my husband, Shemu'el, kissed his fingertips and touched them to the *mezuzah* on the right side of our doorframe. I did the same, marveling at its shiny newness. Over time the one on Abba's doorframe had weathered to a dark burnish.

The *mezuzah* reminded us our homes were always under God's protection. A metalworker in Jerusalem made these small scroll cases out of cast bronze. It had a raised letter *shin* on the outside, the first letter in the name *Shaddai*—Almighty. Inside the case was the *klaf*, a small parchment inscribed with the *Shema*.

Then Shemu'el scooped me into his arms, elbowed the door

aside and carried me across the threshold. Our home was lovely, all I dreamed it would be and more. Like the *mezuzah*, everything was bright and new. The smell of fresh-cut timbers and new plaster competed with the warm scent of sandalwood. Before coming to get me Shemu'el had taken time to put scented oil in the lamps.

With me still in his arms, he eased the door shut with his heel. His brothers moved to the end of the walk to stand guard, making sure no one disturbed us. I watched my husband's eyes move around the room. He seemed torn between putting me down there or carrying me to our bed. Poor Shemu'el. He was stuck holding me like a farmer with a sack of grain and nowhere to sit it.

I leaned back and pressed my lips against his.

"If you distract me now, I may stumble and fall," he said.

"So long as you land on top of me, I will not mind."

Shemu'el carried me to the bed and eased me down upon it. He scattered pillows around the edges where it met the wall and a new linen sheet was spread across the bed, our wedding cloth.

The book of *Devarim*—Deuteronomy, commanded such a cloth be placed over the wedding bed on the first night. The bridegroom later presented it to the bride's parents as surety against him slandering her and saying, "I took this woman, but when I came near her, I did not find in her the tokens of virginity." In such a case, the parents could present the cloth to the elders and they would punish the man for his lie.

Shemu'el circled the room adjusting the skins covering the windows. A squat ointment pot and bottles of scented oils waited on a table beside the bed. There was also a plate with fruits and nuts, wine and two cups.

I scooted back against a pillow. My dark hair, loosed of its ribbons, rippled across my shoulders. I watched him move about the room as he tended to last minute details, feeling somewhat like I did as a girl, slightly confused and a little afraid.

We were now man and wife. I loved Shemu'el as I could love no other man. Loved him since I was a motherless child and he protected me from bullies.

As his wife, I wanted to please him. But how to go about doing that? Oh, I knew what was supposed to happen. The way in which men and women coupled was no mystery to me. All my life I had seen rams seek out ewes when they were in season. But we were not animals and I had never been with a man. For days these worries came to me as I lay alone in my bed and imagined Shemu'el beside me.

More than one of my friends took me aside to warn the first time sometimes hurt. I knew the fire of desire burned strong in young men and at times they attacked their brides with fierce passion. Shemu'el had also spent many years living among the Romans. Everyone knew of their depraved practices, their baths, brothels and temple prostitutes. My friends repeated rumors of Roman men degrading their wives by demanding unnatural pleasures.

Would Shemu'el?

He was a good man, a kind man, a gentle man. I did not fear him, nor could I imagine him knowingly hurting me. Still I worried. I so wanted to please him. What would he expect of me?

He knelt beside the bed and studied my face.

I saw the gleam of desire in his eyes and wondered if he sensed my inner turmoil.

"I await you, *Rab*," I said in a small voice. Slaves called their owner as *Rab*, Master. A Jewish man truly was the master of his home and many wives addressed their husbands as *Rab*.

Shemu'el cupped my face in his hands and caressed my hair. "I am not, and never will be, your master, Rivkah." He bowed low. "Rather, for time everlasting I seek to be your slave. I exist only to love, serve and protect you and to bring you happiness."

He reached for a date, ate half and fed the remainder to me. We continued talking and sharing. Moving onto the bed, he folded his legs and rested his elbows on his knees.

"Remember all the silly things we used to do and say when we were children?"

I smiled and nodded.

"Even then I wanted you for my wife. There was never a time when I did not dream of you." He took my hands in his and stared deep into my eyes. "And now, at last, you are."

Shemu'el removed his cloak and loosened his tunic.

My heart beat faster.

Then he did the most loving thing imaginable. He looked at me and, in a kind voice, said, "Behold, you are beautiful, my love, behold, you are beautiful; your eyes are doves."

My fears vanished like shadows at sunrise. Hearing him speak those words of the *Shir HaShirim* both soothed and aroused me.

I answered, "Behold, you are beautiful, my beloved, truly lovely."

Word by word, verse by verse, picking and choosing as we went, Shemu'el and I voiced our love and desire for one another using the ancient words of Solomon's Song of Songs.

"How graceful are your feet in sandals, O queenly maiden." He removed my sandals and rubbed my feet with scented ointment. Sliding my tunic aside, he moved to the ankles and then massaged my legs. "Your rounded thighs are like jewels, the work of a master hand."

The touch of Shemu'el's fingers made my head swim.

"How fair and pleasant you are," he said. "O loved one, delectable maiden. You are stately as a palm tree, and your breasts like its clusters. I will climb the palm tree and lay hold of its branches."

A breeze wafted across the room, causing the lamp's flame to quiver. Light and dark shadows danced across the ceiling. The bed seemed to sway as Shemu'el undressed me.

"Oh, may your breasts be like the clusters of the vine, and the scent of your breath like apples, and your kisses like the best wine."

I recited the familiar words of scripture meaning every word. "I am my beloved's, and his desire is for me. Over our doors are all choice fruits, new as well as old, which I have laid up for you, O my beloved. Make haste, my beloved, and be like a gazelle or a young stag upon the mountain of spices," I whispered.

The words reminded me of a forgotten dream in which my stag turned out to be Shemu'el. I sank back onto the cushions as Shemu'el, my husband, my lover...my stag came to me.

When we were ready, Caleb and Yhonatan escorted us back to the feast. They blew their trumpets and announced, "All hail, Shemu'el bar Yo'el and his wife."

As a group, everyone moved aside, clearing a circle of space around us. It was time for the bride and groom to dance. Music played and people clapped in time.

My hair billowed out as Shemu'el twirled me around the circle. We stared into each other's eyes, grinning. After a short while, he led me to my father. Stopping in front of him, Shemu'el bowed and placed my hand in my father's hand.

"I present Rivkah, my wife, the woman who will someday be the mother of your grandchildren. Dance with your daughter, Abba Yaakov."

While Abba and I danced, Shemu'el took his mother's hand. They danced beside us. Then Caleb and his wife, Avigail, joined us, along with Yhonatan and his wife, Miryam. Soon everyone in the settlement danced around us, smiling and laughing and patting us as they passed.

When the music ended, Rachel and Devorah approached with cloaks folded over their arms. Rachel removed my white linen wedding cloak and replaced it with one she made. Devorah did the same for Shemu'el. It was our coronation. For the next seven days we would be King and Queen of our little settlement. Our cloaks matched, each brilliantly colored, with elaborate stitching and tassels along the bottom hem. Accompanied by our guards, my friends escorted us to our thrones.

Two chairs awaited us in the shade of some myrtle trees, the tree of fertility and life. There, among the sweet smell of their pungent leaves, we would reign over our subjects. The wives of

Shemu'el's brothers placed wreaths of woven flowers on our heads as crowns.

Tamar appeared leading a parade of children. She gathered them around her, giving them their final reminders. The youngest ones received tambourines to beat with their hands, the rest held palm branches. The children waved their palm branches in the air, beat their tambourines and shouted praises.

When they finished, Shemu'el rose and pronounced a blessing upon them and everyone there. He decreed that every child should have lots of sweetmeats to eat and for the next seven days laughter and words of love would rule the settlement.

The women set up tables on the flat below us. They brought food until the tables groaned under its weight. Large jars of wine appeared. Some of the men roasted lambs and kids on spits over a bed of coals.

The celebration continued even as darkness settled upon us. Eventually the fires turned to glowing embers and the women stored the leftover food. Then mothers carried their sleepy children off to bed. Our neighbors lit their nightlights. And the King and his Queen returned to their bed while chants of *Ma'ariv*, evening prayers, echoed across the settlement.

~ 52 ~

Shemu'el dropped onto the bed with a tired, but satisfied grin. He lay beside me, head propped up on one hand, and toyed with my hair. We stared into each other's eyes then kissed. Both of us had waited so long, spent so many years imagining this moment. Now that it had finally come, it hardly seemed real.

An owl hooted at the moon outside our window. Engrossed in each other, we nestled together telling and retelling the story of our love.

Reading his thoughts, I whispered, "Again?"

His arms tightened around me.

I kissed Shemu'el's shoulder. He gave a sleepy grunt and sighed with pleasure as my fingers kneaded the muscles in his neck and back.

"Are you ready for your morning meal, my husband?"

He yawned. "I will be by the time you have prepared it."

"Stay where you are. I will be right back."

My bare feet padded across the smooth floor. Shemu'el watched me open the door with a quizzical look. I reached out and retrieved a cloth-covered basket waiting on our doorstep.

"What do you have there?" he asked as I returned.

"A basket."

"I can see that. Whose basket is it?"

"Mine." I sat on the bed and folded back the napkin. "Now what shall we have for our morning meal?"

"Our morning meal comes in a basket on the porch?"

"Of course." I pretended everyone found his or her morning meal in a basket outside their door. I gave him a sly wink. "Surely you would not expect your Queen to cook?"

He shrugged. "Even the Israelites had to gather their manna; it was not delivered to their tents."

Each day one of my friends served her Queen by preparing our morning meal. All the young women in our settlement participated. I did it for them when they were newly married and now they returned the favor. Everyone enjoyed the surprises and it freed the new bride to concentrate on things more important than meals.

A few days before the wedding, Rachel asked if she could borrow a basket. The morning after our wedding, someone tiptoed to our door just before sunrise. They filled my basket with enough food for two, left it on the porch and slipped away. Each evening for the next week the empty basket went outside our door when we retired. By the following morning another secret benefactor had refilled it.

We women competed with each other to find the most unusual delicacies for the Queen's basket. A strict code of secrecy surrounded the whole process. The bride must never know which of her friends left what items.

Over the next few days we grew accustomed to hearing feet scurry away in the pre-dawn darkness. Some days we retrieved the basket right away and other mornings...we did not. No matter. We always enjoyed folding back the napkin to see what my subjects left for their Queen.

Being outside Bethlehem and tied to our flocks, we shepherds developed our own *Shabbat* rituals. Rather than journey to a Synagogue, we gathered among ourselves to wish each other *Shabbat Shalom* and worship the Lord. Lacking an ark with holy scrolls, we sang Psalms and then one of the older men spoke on whatever scriptural passage came to mind. A young man's first chance to address his neighbors traditionally came on the *Shabbat* following his wedding.

The men, all in *tallits*, stood in a circle chanting Psalms. We women and children sat off to one side on the grass. When they finished, Shemu'el stepped forward. During prayers, he wore the new *tallit* Imma Sarit made for him draped over his head. Now, as he prepared to speak, he let it slide back onto his shoulders.

Shemu'el's eyes moved in a slow circle, passing from

relative to friend to neighbor. He glanced over our heads at the humble homes comprising our little settlement. He studied the sheep and goats penned beside each house. And finally, his eyes rested upon me, his new wife.

Tilting his head back, he spread his arms to the sky in a gesture of thanksgiving. A bright smile lit his face as he cried, "How I longed to be home. And now, thank God, I am.

"The prophet Jeremias wrote, 'My eyes will watch over them for their good, and I will bring them back to their land.' Likewise, Zacherias wrote, 'Though I scatter them among the peoples, yet in distant lands they will remember me and they will return.'"

His eyes glistened as he recounted the story of being carried away in chains and taken to Antioch on the Orontes. He spoke frankly of the pain and loneliness, but also mentioned the blessings bestowed upon him by strangers like Yu'dah. Shemu'el told us of his mentor, Evodius, and of his friend and fellow slave, the one called Atticus. He described the circumstances surrounding his release, the things he turned aside in order to return.

His life, Shemu'el said, characterized the history of our people. He had been a slave. Our people were once slaves. As in Egypt, his freedom came in a miraculous way. And, like the Hebrews of old, he had found the Promised Land.

The realities of being a shepherd restricted the rest of the week's feasting to late afternoon and evenings. Each day, after the passing of the ninth hour, the tables came back out and women carried in dishes. One might imagine all of this required a great deal of planning, but we simply let things take their own course. Somehow, everything worked out fine and it made for many interesting and diverse meals.

The highlight of our wedding feast occurred the day after *Shabbat*. It began simply enough. A shadowy outline of a single figure appeared far off walking toward us. Then another person crested the hill, a woman this time. And another...and another.

Groups of men, women and children came over the rise. Conversation ceased as everyone stopped what they were doing to gaze and wonder. Rachel touched my hand. I glanced up and saw what seemed to be an invading army marching toward us. Leaving the table, I moved close beside Shemu'el. He slipped a protective arm around my waist.

Our friends and family bunched together in a tight semicircle, watching apprehensively. We stood shoulder-to-shoulder staring at this mass of strangers.

Their leader, a tall man with a narrow face and gray eyes, stared back as he silently scrutinized each man's face. His gaze settled on Shemu'el. A heartbeat's pause, then a wide smile broke over his face.

"Shemu'el, my brother," he said, lifting his arms and racing toward us.

"Yu'dah?" Shemu'el blinked in astonishment. "Yu'dah!" he shouted and ran to meet him.

The two men threw their arms around each other and hugged. Then, leaving his arm draped over Yu'dah's shoulder, Shemu'el turned to address our group.

"My friends, this is my brother slave, Yu'dah, of whom I spoke yesterday. Come and meet him. Make him, and those with him, welcome in our settlement."

Everyone rushed forward to shake the hand of the man whom Shemu'el credited with saving his life. I let the others go before me, preferring to linger at the end of the line. Yu'dah made an elaborate bow when Shemu'el presented me.

"And now you must meet my family," he said. He led us over to the people who'd accompanied him and held out his hand to a lovely woman about my age. Taking small, graceful steps, she took her place beside him.

"My wife, Salome," Yu'dah said.

Leaving her husband, she grasped Shemu'el's hand in hers and smiled. She tried to speak, but could not. She bit her quivering lip and blinked away tears. Unable to form the words that were in her heart, she dropped to the ground and kissed his fingers, washing them with tears of gratitude.

"You will always be welcomed as a great hero in the village of Marisa," Yu'dah said, helping his wife to her feet. A young boy stepped up next. Yu'dah proudly rested a hand on the boy's shoulder. "My son, Jepthah. Born while I was away." A young woman handed Salome a small child. Yu'dah smiled and ruffled the youngster's hair when she brought him forward. "And my youngest boy. He is called Shemu'el."

Yu'dah's entire family had come with him, his parents, his brothers and their wives and children, his sisters and their husbands and children...even Salome's family came to celebrate the wedding feast of Shemu'el and Rivkah. After everyone had been introduced, all the women worked together making room for the food Yu'dah's party brought.

While everyone busied themselves around the tables, Salome glided up to me carrying a package in both hands. She extended her arms, presenting it like an offering.

"This is for Rivkah, wife of Shemu'el, from the women of Marisa. May these always bring you happiness."

The young women of our settlement gasped when I opened the package. Inside was an elegant set of gold jewelry, engraved bracelets, earrings and a matching necklace. A gift fit for a princess.

"Made by Yu'dah's hand especially for you," Salome whispered. "Each woman in our village contributed a piece of her gold so that you might have them."

Shemu'el and Yu'dah chuckled when my friends clustered around me, elbowing each other aside to get a closer look.

"How did you know?" Shemu'el asked Yu'dah after things quieted down.

He laughed. "How could I not know. The whole countryside buzzes with the tale of the shepherd boy who returned from the grave to reclaim his lost love. Once we learned the date of your wedding, we knew we would not find peace in our hearts if we failed to come and celebrate with you."

It was our custom to offer hospitality to the traveler and each family in our settlement opened their home to some of the visitors. Yu'dah and Salome ate with our family. Imma Sarit, Abba and Aunt Tamar along with Shemu'el's brothers, my cousins and all their spouses, their children and Yu'dah's children, gathered in a circle around a table piled high with delicacies of every sort.

Impossible as is seemed when we sat down, all the food was eaten. As the setting sun sank below the horizon, lamps were lit and a fire started. People lounged about idly picking the last scraps of meat off the bones, chasing the remaining pickle or olives in a dish, or scavenging for any remaining crumbs of honey cakes. Men swirled their cups lazily and yawned as they watched the last sips of wine dance in the bottom.

Yhonatan looked across the table. "Yu'dah, would your family like to stay with us for the night?"

Pretending to weigh the offer for a moment, he replied, "That is not necessary." He patted Shemu'el's knee. "I prefer that Salome, the children and I stay with my brother here."

All eyes turned to us.

Shemu'el and I looked at each other, unsure how to respond. What could Yu'dah be thinking? Protocol said no one disturbed the King and Queen during their marriage feast. Men were even exempt from work the first days after their wedding.

"Unless, of course, you and Rivkah had other plans," Yu'dah added after a long pause.

My cheeks warmed. I glanced over at Shemu'el and saw he also blushed.

The people around the table elbowed each other, winking and snickering.

Yu'dah quietly sipped his wine.

I folded my shaky hands in my lap and stared into them. Shemu'el swallowed hard and stroked his beard.

Yu'dah grinned across the table at Yhonatan. "You played your part well. It worked just as we hoped it would."

Still chuckling, Yu'dah folded his legs and motioned to

those around him. "Draw closer, my friends, and I will tell you tales of Marcus the Roman slave." Lifting an eyebrow, he grinned. "Stories he prefers you never hear."

At the end of the week, our reign ended, the guests left and life resumed its normal routine. Shemu'el carefully folded our wedding cloth and presented it to my father as required. He found Abba in the yard tending a fire.

The two men hugged and Shemu'el offered him the package he brought. "Our wedding cloth, Abba Yaakov. Yours to keep."

My father stared at it for a moment, then snorted and tossed it into the flames. Right before their eyes the cloth, my father's surety, disappeared in a rush of flames and a whiff of smoke.

Abba noticed Shemu'el's surprised expression and tossed an arm around his shoulder. Pulling him close, he chuckled and said, "Why should I want such a thing? I prefer to wait for my one thousand talents of gold."

~ 53 ~

With their reign as King and Queen over, Shemu'el and Rivkah set about building a life together.

Shemu'el constructed a sheepfold beside their stable. They planted a fig tree near the front of their new home and additional fruit trees in the back. He cleared and prepared an area for a garden and set posts to support the grapevines Rivkah planted.

Their days settled into a pattern of work and worship with Shemu'el spending most of his time in the fields with the sheep while Rivkah kept house. A few months later Rivkah made the big announcement. She was with child.

The following spring she delivered a healthy baby boy. Following tradition, they named him Yo'el after Shemu'el's father. Grandfather Yaakov at last had a grandchild to bounce upon his knee.

Two years later a girl, named Hadassah for Rivkah's mother, joined the family. She was followed in turn by brother, Yaakov, sister, Channah, and another brother, Yu'dah.

Years passed and the more things changed, the more they remained the same.

The Government? The tetrarchs and prefects pursued corruption and debauchery as eagerly as their predecessor King Herod had.

Taxes? They remained high. Too high, Shemu'el contended.

The price paid for the lambs they delivered to the Temple? Despite the hard times, it remained low.

And the Levites and Pharisees continued to look down their noses at shepherds, clucking their tongues and saying they did not properly keep the Law. If their judgment ever meant anything to Rivkah and Shemu'el, it no longer did. The only judgment they feared was that of the Lord's and they knew His eyes saw into the hearts of righteous men and women.

In truth, Shemu'el and Rivkah were too happy to worry about such trifling details. After twenty years of marriage, if asked they would have said they lived a rich life.

Rich?

No, they did not have the fine home, purple robes, servants

and soft cushions she and Rachel once joked about. They dwelt in the same little house in the same little settlement of shepherds. Hardly the lifestyle of a Centurion, but Shemu'el and Rivkah knew that a small house could hold as much love as even the greatest mansion.

Over the years Shemu'el learned to de-emphasize his time spent with the Roman Army. Romans failed to understand his refusal of a Commission and when Jews heard of it they looked upon him with suspicion. Although a shepherd by trade, and happy doing it, he still maintained a private cupboard of medicinal herbs and salves in their home. He had kept his medical kit and provided for the settlement's needs.

But most days Shemu'el spent his time caring for the sheep and Rivkah spent hers caring for him and their five children. They had the things of life that really mattered: health, children, family, friends and most of all, the contentment true love brings.

~ 54 ~

It shames me to admit that none of us missed Shemu'el until Yu'dah, my youngest, returned with his father's noonday meal.

"I could not find Abba," he said, handing me the sack I gave him to deliver. "He was not there."

Panic leaped in my chest. I dropped to one knee and grabbed him by his shoulders. "What do you mean, 'he was not there'? What about the sheep?"

"Some were there, and some not. The ones I found I brought back with me. They are in the sheepfold."

My pulse pounded in my ears. I tossed the lunch sack aside, forgotten. "Come children," I shouted. "We must find out what happened to your father."

Yu'dah led us back to the spot where they agreed to meet. More of our sheep wandered the meadow aimlessly. I set Channah to gathering the sheep and kept the two boys with me. I noticed their hands resting on the shepherd's rods in their sashes and smiled to myself at their youthful bravado.

We took only a few steps when one of the boys spotted Shemu'el's waterskin hanging from a tree limb. A quiver of fear clawed at my stomach. He would not have left his water behind unless he planned on returning. This was not good, not good at all. I threw the bag's strap over my shoulder and we continued toward the rocky ridge, calling his name.

I squinted into the sun, examining every crevasse and cranny.

No Shemu'el.

I cupped my hands around my mouth and shouted for him. We cocked our heads, straining to hear a reply. My cries echoed off the dry canyon walls, unanswered.

"Let's split up. I will continue on this path. One of you go to the right, the other to the left. If you find him shout it out."

I murmured desperate prayers and followed the curving trail in silence. An inner voice tempted me to call his name, but it would only confuse the boys. In the end, the sheep led me to him. I saw them in a cluster and knew that was where he must be.

"Shemu'el!" I cried, rushing toward him. I clambered over the rocks, ignoring the dry soil crumbling underfoot. "Shemu'el. I am here. I have come, my love."

He stirred at the sound of his name. The hand he had placed over his eyes to protect them from the sun lifted a little and he blinked up at me. His mouth was so dry he could barely speak. I put my ear down close and he whispered, "Please tell me you are my Rivkah and not an angel come to whisk me away to *Sheol*."

"It is me, my love," I said, kissing him. "I am sorry I did not come sooner."

I dribbled water from the bag into my hand and wet his parched lips. I called out to the boys while he licked it away, then gave him more.

"Thank God you found me," he said, after he drank. "Otherwise, I would surely have perished."

I bathed Shemu'el's sunburned face and wet his hair to cool him.

He stared over at the sheep, pointing to a lamb. "There. She's the one. I trailed her up into this gully and found her perched on that rock." He pointed above his head. "The hillside collapsed beneath me when I climbed to reach her."

He took the waterskin and drank deeply.

"I called the sheep and kept them here until my tongue grew so dry I could no longer whistle. They began drifting away and there was nothing I could do to stop them."

"Come boys. We must move these rocks so your father can stand." The boys helped me shove aside the boulders that pinned his leg. They tumbled down into the gully, crashing against others already there.

"As the sun rose higher and higher I felt its heat and knew my time was running out," Shemu'el mumbled.

"But we are here now and everything is taken care of."

Seeing his father struggling to rise, Yaakov stepped closer and took his arm. Shemu'el rocked forward into a sitting position and cried out in pain.

"My leg," he said, wincing. "I think it's broken."

I sent the children in search of help and tented my cloak over him for shade.

"The last of the lambs must go to the Temple before *Pesach*," Shemu'el said. He took nervous bites of his bread, gnawing at it like a mouse. "Otherwise we will miss the best market of the year."

I sat on the corner of the bed feeding him parched wheat cooked to porridge. Even with raisins and honey he balked at eating it. I teased and coaxed each spoonful into his mouth as if he were a small child.

"We have the most important thing, you. As for the lambs, they are only money."

He raised his eyebrows and laughed. "Spoken like a wealthy woman."

Shemu'el dug an elbow into the bed and used it to leverage himself onto his side. He came to rest with a disheartening sigh, groaning as much in frustration as in pain.

I dipped a cloth in a basin of cool water beside the bed and swabbed the perspiration from his face.

He touched my hand. "I'm sorry, my darling. Your husband, it seems, has failed you once again."

I put my hand on his cheek, turned his face to mine and stared into his eyes. "The medicine makes you babble like a crazy man. You could never fail me. I count each moment with you a precious gift from the Most High Lord."

Kissing my silly Shemu'el, I brushed damp hairs from his forehead. Despite the scrapes, he looked much improved. My fingers tiptoed along the dressing on his leg, testing for dampness. I had applied it the night before just as he instructed.

"The plaster dried while you slept." I toyed with his bare toes, tugging on them as I did with my children when they were babies. They always giggled. He did not.

He gave me a tired, but happy sigh.

"Has the pain lessened?"

As soon as we got him home, I got the medicine in the vase shaped like the poppy pod. Even though he knew it would ease his pain and make him sleep, Shemu'el refused to take it. First, he said, we must repair his leg. He took my hand in his and ran my fingers down his calf, showing me the place where the bone had broken. Abba and Caleb restrained him while our oldest son, Yo'el, pulled and rotated his foot until I felt the bone slip back into position. Shemu'el would not rest until we cut several small olive branches and secured them on either side of his leg with strips of cloth. After wrapping a cloth around his leg, I dipped additional rags in plaster and swathed his leg with them.

"Do not trouble yourself over my pain. It will pass soon enough and be forgotten. Time will knit my bone, but until then, I will not be able to walk. How can we survive?"

"Have you forgotten you married a shepherdess?" I asked, smiling.

The night before I had placed my sleeping mat on the floor beside Shemu'el. While he thrashed and moaned in his sleep, I considered our situation and determined what needed to be done.

"One of the boys and I will take the lambs to the Temple."

I met his wary glance with a reassuring smile. I planned to leave the two younger children at home and take our middle son, Yaakov, with me to Jerusalem.

"Channah and Yu'dah can take care of the house while I'm away. If they need help there is a whole settlement of family and friends to call upon. Yo'el will manage the flock and Yaakov will accompany me."

He frowned.

I watched Shemu'el's mind work. During the night I had already considered the options and developed my counter arguments.

"It will not be an easy trip. The roads are crowded with pilgrims. You may encounter dangers."

"The Lord will protect us." I patted his hand. "My rod will be tucked into my girdle. You forget, I have faced down lions with it."

Shemu'el's face relaxed. "Ah yes, the lion. I remember those foolish children as if it were only yesterday. Life seemed much simpler then."

I rose from the bed and began gathering my clothes. "I want you to rest while I'm gone. Going to Jerusalem will give me a chance to visit Hadassah and Hebel. If it is all right, I would like to stay and have Seder with them."

As much as I hated leaving Shemu'el, I knew he would be well cared for. I had not seen Hadassah, our second child and first daughter, for several months. She wed Hebel, a potter from Bethlehem, the year before and they moved to Jerusalem a short time later when the potter's guild there had an opening.

I caught myself smiling as I folded a tunic and added it to the stack. Was I a bad person for looking forward to seeing my daughter when my husband had a broken leg?

~ 55 ~

"And Jesus entered the Temple of God and drove out all who sold and bought in the Temple, and he overturned the tables of the money-changers and the seats of those who sold pigeons."

—Matthew 21:12

Our oldest son, Yo'el, and his wife and child lived in the house beside ours. He supervised things while our middle son, Yaakov, accompanied me to Jerusalem.

Normally it was a three-hour walk to Jerusalem. That day it took much longer. Sheep always slowed our progress, but we were taking yearling lambs. They were young and used to following their mothers. Could that be Yaakov's problem, I wondered, as I watched him leave the sheep to chase after a butterfly.

Shemu'el was right. Even though we started early, the roads were crowded with pilgrims heading to Jerusalem for the coming *Pesach*. Ignoring their angry complaints, we threaded our way through making apologies as we went.

We followed a familiar route, one I took many times with my father. Yaakov gave an excited shout when, at last, the city came into view. For a few moments the gold roof of the Temple sparkled in the sunlight and then, as we descended, it disappeared behind the city walls.

The Jerusalem road from Bethlehem led us to the south side of the city. Sheep had to be delivered to the northeast side of the Temple, so we followed the Hinnon Valley and circled the city walls. I stationed Yaakov at the lead and I trailed behind, catching any stragglers. The road made a wide, sweeping curve past Herod's palace and then turned a sharp corner, leading us to Tower's Pool. We stopped there to rest and water the sheep.

Refreshed, we continued north, again following the city wall. We halted the sheep at the crossing of the road from Emmaus, letting a large caravan pass. When the caravan reached the city gate they, too, had to pull aside for a procession of mourners making their way to the tombs. Yaakov and I whispered a prayer for the deceased then nudged the sheep forward. Out of respect, we averted our eyes as we passed Golgotha, the place of crucifixion.

"Not much further," I said, as much to myself as to Yaakov. We followed the well-trod path around the high walls of Fortress Antonia.

"Look, Imma," Yaakov said, pointing to his right.

I watched my son examine the massive foundation stones of the Temple Mount. Yaakov had made this trip before with his father, but like me he could not come to the Temple without being awed by its splendor. The eastern wall rose straight up from the edge of the Kidron Valley, a manmade extension of the hillside. I remembered staring up at those same walls as a little girl while I ran to keep up with my father's long legs.

We were not the only ones making a last minute delivery. Shepherds crowded around us from every direction. The flocks merged and mingled like streams blending into a single river of wool.

We came to a halt. Far ahead, barely visible beyond the sea of lambs, were the Pools of Bethesda where they washed the sheep before sending them into the market. All morning we hurried, now we would wait.

The spot was sparse, dry and dusty. Passing sheep had long since gobbled up any vegetation sprouted by the winter rains as well as the water that ran here a few weeks ago. The sheep drank the puddles down to mud and trod it into dust.

"We can eat our noonday meal while we wait," I said, pulling the bag off my shoulder.

I motioned Yaakov closer and dug in for the food I packed. Thank goodness for the waterskin slung over my shoulder. We refilled it at the Tower Pool, but it had already warmed.

The two of us rested in the shade of walls while we ate. Across the Kidron Valley, neat rows of olive trees marched up to the *gethsamne*, the oil press on the Mount of Olives. We watched their silvery leaves shimmer in the sunlight with each gust.

Yaakov pointed to the gardens down in the valley floor and commented on the beautiful roses. Years ago, Abba told me about a drain in the Temple floor beside the place where they sacrificed the lambs. The floor sloped toward the drain so blood flowed into it. Then, through a labyrinth of pipes, it emerged on the valley floor. Gardeners applied it to the rose bushes.

Some people believed the roses' bright red color came from the blood sprinkled around the bushes. Others scoffed, insisting blood nourished the bushes the same way manure nourished plants.

I had spent my life raising sheep and knew little about growing roses. Nevertheless the gardens reminded me how God brought beauty out of everything, even death. I found it reassuring to think those beautiful flowers were the lamb's final legacy. It seemed a fitting memorial to a life given for others.

We reached the head of the line. Yaakov whistled the lambs forward and directed them into a temporary pen for inspection. Off to one side, Obadiah, the overseer, sat at his table, head down, carefully recording each transaction. According to custom, when the inspector entered the pen, the name of the sheep's owner was called out for the overseer to record.

When he heard a woman's voice cry, "Shemu'el bar Yo'el," Obadiah dropped his stylus and looked up. The old man stared for a moment and then rushed toward me, robes billowing.

"*Shalom Aleichem*, Rivkah," he said, smiling.

"*Aleichem Shalom*, Obadiah."

"It's an unexpected blessing to see you. I remember when you came with your father years ago. I was an inspector then and you were so small you disappeared amongst the lambs."

He motioned at Yaakov. "And now look at your fine son, nearly a man. Why has Shemu'el not come?"

"He fell and broke his leg."

Obadiah clucked his tongue. "I am sorry to hear that and right before the *Pesach*. Will he be left lame?"

"Thank the Lord, no. When he served Evodius, the Roman physician, he learned the art of setting broken bones. He told me exactly what to do."

The inspector gave his sign of approval and opened a gate on the far side of the pen. Yaakov shooed them out and down a chute leading to the larger, general enclosure. Obadiah marked the transaction on a tablet and handed it to me.

"If you hurry, you can still return home before sundown," he said.

It was not even the seventh hour, but I knew from experience there would be long lines at the Treasury window.

"My son and I are staying over with my daughter and her husband for the Seder." Noting the worried look in Obadiah's eyes, I added, "You need not worry. Shemu'el is well cared for."

"You, not Shemu'el, are the ones at risk. If you remain in the city, be alert." He gave a sidelong glance up at the Temple wall. "The signs are all there. You know a storm is coming when the trees show you the underside of their leaves."

"Storm? What storm?"

Obadiah swiveled his head, making certain no one could overhear what he was about to say. Just in case, he lowered his voice and inched closer. "It began right after last *Shabbat*. He rode into the city on a donkey and people cut palm fronds, waved them and shouted 'Hosannas.' Ever since, he has been coming to the Temple each day preaching and stirring up the people."

"Who are you speaking of?"

"The Galilean," he said. "They are beginning to follow him. Many claim he is the *Mashiach*."

My thoughts returned to Athrongeus and his unbreakable bundle of sticks. "Again? Will they never tire of these *shekers*?"

"Two days ago he overturned the moneychanger's tables, scattering coins everywhere. Then he attacked the dove vendors and broke apart their cages."

Recalling the moment, he shook his white head in disbelief. "For an instant the fleeing birds blotted out the sun. The vendors demanded Annas reimburse them for their loss."

He wagged a finger. "Mark my word, Caiaphas watches these events closely. And you know how fickle Pilate is. Trouble during the *Pesach* could easily cost Caiaphas his position as High

Priest. He will not allow this Yeshua, or anyone else, to put him out of office unchallenged."

I turned away without another word, motioning to Yaakov to follow. Obadiah must have thought me rude, but I could never explain the conflicting emotions his warning raised in me.

Shemu'el and I knew all about Yeshua. His fame had spread throughout the land along with the wondrous miracles he performed...feeding the hungry, curing the sick, even raising the dead. We eagerly listened to each piece of news with rising interest. We were there at the beginning and now, at last, Yeshua's time had come. The *Mashiach* was about to rescue his people.

Yet the truth in Obadiah's words frightened me. Annas and Caiaphas would not take kindly to the disruption of their trade during this the most profitable week of the year. A powerful coalition opposed anyone who challenged the Temple aristocracy. More and more it seemed the Sadducees allied themselves with the Romans instead of the Jewish people.

At this pivotal moment, which side would they be on?

~ 56 ~

"And when they had mocked him, they stripped him of the robe, and put his own clothes on him, and led him away to crucify him."

Matthew 27:31

Obadiah's warning slipped from my mind as we threaded our way through the pilgrims crowding Jerusalem's streets.

Hadassah had a startled expression on her face when she opened the door and saw us. Of all the people to come knocking, she never expected to find her mother and younger brother, Yaakov, outside her door. Smiling, she rushed out and hugged us both.

We explained about her father's accident and she and her husband, Hebel, listened with somber expressions. When we finished, Hadassah glared at Hebel the way Aunt Tamar used to frown at me whenever I made a mistake.

"See," she said. "We should have stayed in Bethlehem. How many times have I told you we need to be closer to our families?"

"Sometimes you can be too feisty for your own good," I said, grabbing my daughter's hand and placing it in Hebel's. I wrapped my hands around theirs. "A woman's place is beside her husband. Hebel will prosper here in Jerusalem. The world needs his pots and bowls just as much as it needs our sheep."

And we needed a change of subject.

"How is your business, Hebel?"

"Very good, Imma Rivkah. With all the pilgrims coming to the Temple for *Pesach*, my wares sell as fast as I can make them."

Hadassah lifted an object off the table. "Look at this. Do you know what it is?"

"A lamp?" Yaakov guessed.

"True, but a lamp with a difference." She turned and prodded her husband. "Why do you just sit there downcast and tongue-tied? Tell her, Hebel."

"Many of the pilgrims camp on the hills surrounding the city. They need lamps, but the usual ones are meant to rest on a table." He took it from her and turned it upside down. "See. I make them with a wider base so they will not tip when placed on uneven ground." He pushed a finger through a loop at the back. "And this grip makes to easy to see your way along a path."

"He cannot produce them fast enough," Hadassah said, beaming with pride.

They glanced at one another and grinned like children keeping a big secret. Hebel put his arm around my shoulder and whispered, "Imma Rivkah, we have news, wonderful news."

Hadassah could not remain still a moment longer. "I am with child," she said. "Nearly three months now."

I threw my arms around them both, kissing their cheeks. My eyes misted for joy. Even Yaakov managed a smile for his big sister and her husband. It was all I could do not to rush home and shout the news from the rooftop.

The four of us enjoyed a wonderful Seder the following evening. Being the youngest person in the room, poor Yaakov had to ask the *Mah Nishtanah*. As a mature man of almost twelve, he found the whole process of asking the four questions undignified. At home it would have fallen to Yu'dah, the youngest in our family.

Instead of hiding the *afikoman*, the last morsel of matzoh, Hadassah left it in plain sight for Yaakov to find. Even she knew her brother would not crawl behind furniture searching for it as he had when he was six years old.

After our meal, he and Hebel went to the shop to stoke the kilns. Hebel had lamps baking and more to go into the oven.

At last we were alone. I took Hadassah by the hand and led her near the window. "Let me see. Let me see," I said, tugging at the hem of her tunic.

"Must you?" One look told her she would have no peace until she let me. Hadassah snatched the tunic from my hands and lifted it.

My fingers traced the faint roundness of her usually flat belly. "A woman is most beautiful when new life blossoms within her."

She lowered her eyes. "That is what Hebel says when I undress at night." She suddenly clutched my hand. "Imma, sometimes when I think about the travail of delivering a baby I grow afraid."

"We all do, my child. It is only natural."

"But I carry the name of a woman who died in childbirth."

"Yes, but your own mother delivered five healthy infants. When you were born I suggested Hadassah as a name. People warned against it. They said naming you after a woman who died in childbirth could be a curse." I squeezed her hand. "No, my child. The Most High does not work through curses and superstitions. Your name sanctifies your grandmother's memory."

I tugged her arm. "Now step into the light so I can see you better."

Seeing her standing there in her loincloth reminded me of how I looked as a young woman. I pulled up a stool and placed my hand on her belly the way Imma Sarit touched me the first time. Closing my eyes, I whispered the same prayer she said years ago. *"God of our ancestors strengthen your servant, Hadassah, and this new life growing within her. Give her an easy birth, a healthy baby and watch over them both all of their days."*

She was not the only one who regretted their move to Jerusalem.

"Will you go with me to the spice merchant?" I asked Hadassah early the next morning.

As long as we were in Jerusalem, it made sense to shop before we headed home. Spying several small cakes of dates on the counter, I wrapped several and stuffed them into my bag.

"For you," I whispered, "in case you grow hungry."

We went down the stairs and around to the back of the building where Hebel had his shop. He had the doors open, exhausting the kiln's warmth into the alleyway. The stifling heat hit our faces as soon as we turned the corner.

A small stool and his clay-stained potter's wheel sat in the center of his crowded workroom. Beside it, hidden beneath a damp cloth, a mound of clay waited to become more lamps. Rows of shelves lined the three walls. One overflowed with items waiting to be fired; the other two held his finished work.

"Hebel?" Hadassah called.

"In the back."

We found both Hebel and Yaakov hard at work feeding branches pruned from nearby olive groves into the fire. It was hot work and, even though they had stripped and girded their loins, their bodies glistened with sweat.

Hadassah swallowed hard and covered her mouth. "I cannot stay here. This heat makes me feel ill...like in the mornings."

I took her by the elbow and led her away. Over my shoulder I called, "We are going to the spice merchants."

Hebel ran after us to give her a sweaty kiss before we hurried out of the alley.

The street we followed rose steeply. We took our time, stopping occasionally so she could catch her breath. The residents of Jerusalem were a prideful lot, and my manner of dress marked me as someone from the country. Assuming we were pilgrims here for the *Pesach*, they made rude comments as they elbowed us aside.

Merchants on both sides of the street had stretched out awnings and were hawking their merchandise to passersby. These stalls forced all foot traffic into the center of the street, which was not wide enough to accommodate everyone. People bumped and jostled, yelling back and forth in a multitude of languages. I realized too late that perhaps there were better days to buy spices.

We rounded a corner and came to an abrupt stop. The street was packed with people, all craning their necks to see.

True to her nature, Hadassah began to fret. "How will we get past the crowd, Imma. We should not have come this way. What are we going to do?"

A quick glance over my shoulder showed the impossibility

of retracing our steps. The moderately crowded street had quickly filled to overflowing.

Being with Hadassah brought out my mothering instincts. "It is *Pesach*," I said, taking her hand and patting it. "The streets are always crowded during the festivals. It is also the day of preparation. Everyone is shopping for the *Shabbat*. Be patient, it will pass."

"But we can never get around all these people."

A trumpet blast made us turn. A mounted Centurion appeared with a burly soldier behind him. A murmur rippled through the crowd as they parted to let the horse pass.

It was the soldier's job to keep the street open. He swaggered along, slapping a club into the palm of his left hand. His head swiveled from left to right with each step, eyeing the people. Without warning, he leaped to one side and flailed out the club.

A frightened man jumped back, bumping into several bystanders. They all fell in a heap.

The soldier tossed his head back and grinned, revealing black stubs of rotted teeth.

The man with the horn came around the corner and blew another warning blast. Curious, Hadassah pressed forward, pushing between people and straining to see.

"Get back," I shouted.

I shielded our daughter as she grew up, perhaps more than Shemu'el would have liked. She never experienced the cruelty of Roman soldiers and, eager to watch the drama unfold, she ignored my command.

"You heard what I said to you. Get back!" I grabbed her by the shoulders and jerked her out of the street. She thumped into the wall between two open-fronted shops. The shopkeeper raced out, muttering threats as he re-stacked his merchandise.

My daughter blinked at me in disbelief, wondering why her mother had turned into a crazy woman. Neither the ugly face she made nor the merchant's shouts bothered me. She had grown up hearing her father's stories of life with the army. How could she have forgotten?

"Have you lost your mind?" I screamed.

"Have you?"

"You were tempting fate. A club like that nearly cost your father his life." My finger pointed at the ground. "Until they pass, you will not move from this spot."

She looked away, refusing to answer.

"Do you understand?"

Hadassah fumed. She had not been treated like this in many years. She opened her mouth to protest, saw my jaw tighten and gave a reluctant nod. Better that she be upset with her mother than have her head split apart by a club.

People flooded out of the side streets and customers abandoned the shops, pushing and shoving their way to the edge of the street. I glanced around and sighed. A handful of cinnamon sticks were not worth putting up with this.

~ 57 ~

"And as they led him away, they seized one Simon of Cyrene, who was coming in from the country, and laid on him the cross, to carry it behind Jesus."

—Luke 23: 26

A *Signalis*, the soldier who preceded a condemned man, came around the corner next. He carried a tall metal staff bearing a *titulus*. This plaque, which listed the prisoner's name and offense, would be nailed to the *palus*, the upright stake of the cross, for all to see when they reached the place of execution. I realized too late why this crowd had gathered. They were here to watch men being led to their death.

Obadiah's words of warning returned to me along with bitter childhood memories.

My instincts told me to turn away. Do what I always did, shield my eyes with my veil and face the other direction. But I could not. An invisible hand seemed to anchor me to that spot, forcing me to watch what I would rather not have seen.

Four legionnaires, armed with spears, formed a box around each hapless victim. Condemned men had their arms lashed to the *patibulum*, the crossbeam. Walking in such an unnatural posture made it difficult to remain balanced on the uneven pavement. They weaved and staggered with each step.

People shook their fists and screamed curses at the first man as he passed. Their jeering voices echoed off the walls of the surrounding buildings creating a deafening roar.

Hadassah saw the terrified look in the man's eyes and clutched my arm, cringing.

A group of women caught the Centurion's attention and he halted the procession. They ran into the street and put a cup to the man's lips. He drank with deep, greedy gulps, ignoring the liquid spilling out both sides of his mouth.

"What are they doing?" Hadassah asked. Even though she stood beside me, she had to shout for me to hear.

One of them refilled the cup from a jug and the woman offered it to the second man in line.

I cupped my hand around Hadassah's ear. "Merciful women of Jerusalem bring the condemned men myrrh mixed in wine. It deadens their senses and lessens the pain."

Murmurs of surprise moved through the crowd when the women disappeared around the corner. A man near them strained to see. He raised his hand showing three fingers. The mob caught his message and began chanting, "Three. Three."

Each prisoner wore a rope girdle around their waist connecting them to the soldier ahead of them. At the Centurion's command, the soldier in front of us gave the rope a hard tug as if pulling a reluctant donkey and his prisoner lurched forward.

One glance at the third man in line changed the crowd's mood. People gasped and fell silent as he came into view. Those nearest to him bowed their heads and beat their breasts.

I noticed the rope in the lead soldier's hand hung slack. Rather than tugging as the other soldiers had done, he walked slowly, pacing his steps to the man behind him. The man he led gradually wobbled into view.

His dirty, bloodstained clothes stuck to open wounds on his body. His eyes were nearly swollen shut, his bruised face unrecognizable.

Someone had jammed a horrible wreath of thorns onto his head leaving the man's hair, damp and matted. Rivulets of blood from the cuts in his scalp dripped down his face.

A reverent hush swept over the crowd. No righteous person could look at this poor man and not feel pity. Weeping women covered their children's eyes and turned their backs to the street.

Three women walked down the center of the street behind the last soldier, two of them supporting the other between them. Without their help, she could not have walked.

It had been twenty years, but I recognized Miryam immediately. The years melted away. I became a little girl again, standing at a stable door watching a young mother nurse her firstborn child. I remembered scooting back and letting her help me hold little Yeshua in my arms.

I looked again at the man passing in front of me, seeing him with new eyes.

Yeshua!

My legs buckled. I reeled, groping for support, and finally toppled against Hadassah. Only her strong grip prevented my collapse.

What had they done to my precious Yeshua?

His sandal caught in a crack between the cobblestones. He pitched forward, teetering and swaying, desperately trying to regain his balance. The soldiers around him either failed to notice, or did not care. As he toppled over, Miryam broke free of the women at her side. Arms extended, she rushed forward to help him. The women wisely grabbed her and held her back.

A groan went up from the crowd as his face crashed into the dirty pavement. The *patibulum* strapped to his outstretched arms made it impossible for him to rise.

The crowd screamed with a single voice at the injustice.

The Centurion galloped back. He eyed the crowd nervously, prepared to respond to the slightest sign of revolt.

No one assisted Yeshua as he lay face down and helpless in the street.

The Centurion leaped off his horse and prodded him with his toe. When he got no reaction, he folded his arms over his chest with a frown. He looked at the soldiers and with a flip of his head said, "Get him up."

A soldier grabbed each end of the beam and jerked him back onto his feet.

Yeshua's eyes rolled back in his head.

They released their hold and took half a step back.

Yeshua mouthed prayers as he spun in crazy circles.

A soldier reached out and steadied him before he crashed to the ground again.

A young woman darted out of the crowd before anyone could stop her. She ran to Yeshua. Not giving the soldiers a chance to react, she whipped off her veil and gently wiped his dirty face.

A gasp rippled through the crowd when they saw this grown woman brazenly exposing her hair for all to see.

Paying them no heed, she kissed his bruised cheek. Then she wadded up the dirty veil, tucked it under her arm, and returned to the curb. Still murmuring, the crowd parted to let her through. She tossed her dark hair aside, letting it ripple down her back as she walked between them.

Meanwhile the Centurion picked a man out of the crowd. "Are you a Jew?"

The terrified man nodded.

"Then get over here and help your king."

The man gave him a confused look. "I see no king. My king is Caesar. I have done nothing wrong. I am not even a resident of Jerusalem. I do not know these men."

He tried to run, but one of the soldiers collared him and dragged him into the center of the street.

"I am innocent, I tell you," the man shouted. "I have done no wrong. I am an honest pilgrim here to offer sacrifice. You are making a mistake."

One of the soldiers held the pilgrim while the others transferred Yeshua's heavy *patabulum* to his shoulders.

The Centurion mounted his horse and aimed the handle of his *flagellum* into the lead soldier's face. "That man must reach Golgotha alive," he said, glancing in Yeshua's direction. He stared into the soldier's eyes. "Let him die on the way, and you will take his place."

"Now," the Centurion grunted, "Let's move."

He pointed the way with his *flagellum*. The leather straps of his whip dangled in front of us, their metal tips clacking ominously. He glared at his soldiers once more, wheeled the horse around, and rode off.

"Innocent," the pilgrim cried as he fell into line behind the soldiers. "I am innocent."

As the procession moved on, we heard him repeat this refrain with each step.

Several members of the Sanhedrin trailed behind Miryam

and the women, speaking to the crowd as they passed.

I pushed away from Hadassah and stepped into the street, motioning the man over.

"What is it you say?"

"Ignore the *titulus*. The heathen Pilate is confused," the man said. "This Galilean is no king at all. The man is a *sheker*, a false *Mashiach*."

"And you know this how?"

He sneered at me. "I have no time to discuss the fine points of the Law with unschooled rabble."

"Yet you remain convinced he is not the *Mashiach* even though angels said he was?"

"Angels?" He glanced around the narrow street and smirked. "What angels? I see no angels." The man studied my homespun cloak. "Woman, I already told you he was a pretender. Now go and bother me no more."

A slave hovered beside us fanning away flies and the warmth of the street lest they disturb his master. I detected the scent of rose petals when the fan blew air past my face. This Pharisee smelled not of honest labor, but of sachets and scented oils like a kept woman. I ran my eyes over his brocaded cloak with its gold stitching and many tassels along the bottom hem.

He blanched when I dared run a finger along its purple binding.

Leaning close, I locked eyes with the Pharisee. "I believe it far more likely that you, not he, are the pretender here."

~ 58 ~
"There were also women looking on from afar..."
—Mark 15:40

The procession moved on and the crowd gradually dispersed. The Pharisee gave me a look of contempt and huffed away to rejoin his fellows.

I watched Miryam disappear around a corner. My heart ached for her.

Hadassah gave me a shake. "Forget the spices, Imma. We must return home."

"Not yet. There is still more to do."

She shook her head and waved her hands. "No! None of this is our concern."

"It is not far." I slipped my arm around my daughter's shoulder. "Walk with me and I will try to explain."

We trailed at a distance, following the sad procession out the city gate and onto the road that passed through Emmaus on its way to Jaffa. A hundred paces later we turned onto the path leading to Golgotha, the place of the skull. We passed it every time we brought sheep to the Temple. Even as a little girl I turned my face and averted my eyes. Unbelievably, here we were walking toward it.

Hadassah's frightened eyes jerked from side to side. "This is a place of infamy and death. This place is unclean, we will be defiled for the *Shabbat*."

"You worry too much."

"And you worry too little. We should not be here. What if someone sees us?"

"If they do, they do," I said with a shrug.

"That is easy enough for you to say. You can go home to your settlement. Hebel and I must live here in Jerusalem. What if people decide they do not wish to buy lamps from a man whose wife goes to crucifixions?"

I shot her a stern look. "Very well, return home without me. I will go on alone."

She made the same angry snort her father did whenever he

became upset with me.

The death party reached the plateau and the soldiers set about their gruesome task. The women with Miryam walked her to the edge and turned their backs, huddling and praying with bowed heads.

We reached a wide spot in the path, a resting place. From there the trail rose sharply, curving around a small hillock on its final ascent to the top.

"This is close enough for now," I said, catching Hadassah's sleeve. I could not bear to watch them pierce Yeshua's hands and feet with nails.

We sat on a boulder to wait. I noticed fresh droplets of blood on the ground in front of me. Yeshua, too, had paused here. Moving my foot in tiny circles, I brushed dust over each spot.

Scattered stalks of fescue sprouted between the rocks above us, screening our view. Unfortunately the ear hears even when the eye cannot see. The clang of a heavy hammer rang out like a gong. A man's high-pitched shriek sent shivers racing up my spine.

My daughter turned to me with the look of a frightened lamb.

My arms closed around her. She buried her face in my shoulder and I placed a hand over her ear to block out the screams. I noticed one of the women doing the same for Miryam.

The pounding finally stopped. "It is time," I said, raising my daughter's head.

She began to tremble. "Please do not make me go up there, Imma. I do not want to go."

"Neither do I, child." I took her hand in mine. "Come, we will help each other."

"What makes you seek out this awful place?"

"An inner voice summons me."

Hadassah pointed toward the summit. "We are not part of this. We could still leave."

"Perhaps you can, but I cannot," I said, taking my first steps. "I must see it through to the end for Miryam."

Hadassah stared at the mountains, blue in the distance. Her voice had a childlike quality. "Look, Imma," she said, pointing. "The sky."

From horizon to horizon the sky grew darker by the moment. True to Obadiah's words a terrible storm was surely on its way. As I watched the sky darken, the words of Amos the prophet came to me.

"On that day, says the Lord God, 'I will make the sun go down at noon, and darken the earth in broad daylight. I will turn your feasts into mourning, and all your songs into lamentation...I will make it like the mourning for an only son, and the end of it like a bitter day."

As we crested the hill each step revealed a bit more of the three crosses planted in the rocky soil. First, the top of the upright *palus*, next the *titulus*, then, beneath the *patibulum* that formed the cross, the men's heads slumped in pain. I saw the full extent of Yeshua's injuries for the first time, and shivered in sympathy.

Throughout the afternoon we hovered nearby, always available, never intruding.

Hadassah grew increasingly impatient with me. Tomorrow was *Shabbat Chol HaMoed Pesach*—the Sabbath during the feast of Passover—the most sacred *Shabbat* of the year. Today was the day of preparation and Hadassah had not yet prepared.

It was too late to return to our settlement now. Yaakov and I would have to stay over until the first day of the week. Shemu'el might worry, but he knew travel on the *Shabbat* was forbidden.

"We should have gone back to the house. It is unlawful to cook on the *Shabbat*. All of us will go hungry." Hadassah said. "What will we do, eat Hebel's pots?"

"God will provide. Our ancestors survived on his manna."

She made an unpleasant face and turned aside.

"You told me Hebel always banks his fires early on the day

of preparation. Seeing we are late, he will surely purchase a few items just in case."

I scanned the darkening sky. It felt like night already. She was right; soon it would be the *Shabbat*.

Yeshua pushed himself up and sucked in a deep breath.

Transfixed, Hadassah groped for my hand as we stood silently watching.

He turned his weary eyes heavenward and said, "Abba, into your hands I commend my spirit."

How appropriate, I thought, brushing back tears. My precious Yeshua's final words were the bedtime prayer every Jewish child learned at their mother's knee.

A huge bolt of lightening split the sky followed almost immediately by a mighty clap of thunder that rocked the ground. A great loneliness wrapped itself around us.

Hadassah sobbed into my shoulder as Yeshua's body slowly sank under its own weight.

The soldier's work was nearly complete. They had spent the afternoon drinking wine and, after three hours in the heat, they were drunk. They stood aside in a circle, laughing loudly as they emptied the last wineskin. Their commanding officer watched with a look of disgust on his face.

All afternoon a group of Pharisees stood afar off awaiting Yeshua's death. Now they approached the Centurion insisting the men not be left hanging over the *Shabbat*.

A short while later two merchants appeared with burial cloths, spices and orders authorizing them to remove Yeshua's body. The young man who had stood with the women joined the merchants in their work. The women helped by mixing the spices. Setting a ladder, the men lashed Yeshua's arms to the beam to prevent the body from falling when they released the nails in his wrists.

Left alone, Miryam crumpled to the ground beside the cross.

"I must go to her," I whispered.

"The Centurion will not allow it," Hadassah said. "He ordered everyone away."

"I will ask his permission."

My daughter's eyes grew wide. "No! Women do not approach men outside their own family."

Today felt like a day when every rule of decent behavior had already been broken. I felt the cakes of pressed dates in my bag. Removing them, I took a step forward.

Hadassah could stand no more. "Stop, Imma." She grabbed my cloak. "He is a Roman soldier, an indecent heathen, a barbarian."

I spun around to face her. "Like your father? Have you forgotten the Romans offered him a commission? We are all made by the same God."

The Centurion did not seem like a bad man. I took a cautious step forward. "I have heard you called Petronius."

"Yes, that is how men address me."

I unwrapped the pressed dates and extended my hand. "You must be hungry. Would you care for some dates?" Keeping my eyes low, I bowed my head.

His eyes moved over me.

Fear rolled across my stomach. There was no one here to protect me if he chose to molest me.

"Why have you, a Jew, approached me offering dates?"

"I bear you no animosity. When Quirinius governed Syria my husband served as assistant to Evodius Scipio, the *Medicus Cohortis* to *Legio XII Fulminata*. I understand you must do as you are ordered."

Hearing this changed his attitude. He took one of the cakes and ate several bites. "Your husband, he is a Roman?" he asked as he chewed.

"A Roman citizen...a freedman. Quirinius offered him a commission as *Medicus Ordinarii*."

I glanced over his head at the cross. They had already freed Yeshua's feet.

The Centurion finished the date cake, smiled his thanks, and took the other. "What do you want from me?"

"I wish to go closer."

"Why now?"

"I knew the man and his mother when I was a child. She is alone. I would like to comfort her."

He glanced over his shoulder at Miryam slumped against the base of the cross, then tilted his head studying the sky. Dark thunderheads encircled Jerusalem like the sides of a cauldron. Random drops pelted us and the swirling wind raised dust about our ankles.

"Pilate spoke correctly," he said. "There was no crime in him." He sighed deeply. "Truly this man was the Son of God." He stepped aside to let me pass.

I knelt beside Miryam and rested an arm around her shoulder.

My touch startled her. She jerked around. "Rivkah?"

Though she had seen me earlier, in her grief Miryam forgot I was there.

"Yes, here I am."

She gave a heaving sob. "They've killed my son."

I pulled her close and held her tight.

Miryam turned and stared into my eyes. "When the time came for my purification after Yeshua's birth, we met a holy man and prophet named Simeon at the Temple. He prophesized one day a sword would pierce my soul." Her hand clutched her side. "Truly I tell you, when that soldier plunged his sword into Yeshua's side I felt the blade enter my heart."

A shiver rippled through her. Struggling to maintain her composure, Miryam swallowed hard before going on.

"Years ago I relinquished my will to God never knowing it would come to this. Over and over Yeshua warned me this was coming, but the thought so pained me that I never allowed myself to believe it."

Beside us the men continued working to free Yeshua's body.

Miryam ran the ball of her hand across her eyes, clearing tears, and sniffed. "Do you remember that night in the stable so long ago, my friend?"

"Always."

In spite of the circumstances, the memory brought a slight smile to my lips.

"It was the first time I nursed him." She brushed back more tears and whispered, "He was such a beautiful baby."

One of the merchants spread a burial cloth over Miryam's lap. Releasing the ropes, they lowered Yeshua and placed him in her arms.

Miryam looked down at him and wept. Her arms quivered.

Already behind her, I slipped my arms beneath hers. "Here," I whispered, "let me help you."

And that was how the life I watched begin came to an end. The same invisible hands that led me to the stable many years before once again guided me to Miryam's side.

But this time my arms helped her hold him.

~ 59 ~

"...and lo, I am with you always, to the close of the age."

— Matthew 28: 20

After they took Yeshua's body away, Hadassah and I stumbled back to the house. Our appearance shocked Hebel and Yaakov.

True to my prediction, when we didn't return on time Hebel banked his fires and went to the marketplace for foodstuffs. We ate raw vegetables, but none of us starved as Hadassah had feared.

While she prepared our evening meal, I used her sewing supplies to fashion a crude tunic from sackcloth. I went down and gathered ashes at the stovehouse where Hebel cooked his pots. Returning to their apartment, I curled up in a corner in my sackcloth dress with ashes on my head and wept for Yeshua and Miryam...for us all.

Yaakov barely spoke on the walk back to our little settlement. It was just as well. I was in no mood for conversation. The image of Yeshua's dead body slumped on the cross had been seared into my memory and I saw it everywhere I looked. Over and over I relived the events of that afternoon, struggling to make sense of a senseless situation.

This was not the way it was supposed to be, I thought. How could our people have waited centuries for the coming of the *Mashiach* and then have it all come to naught? No matter how many times I went over the events in my mind, I always reached the same conclusion. Somehow, something had gone wrong. Yet that could not be; God did not make mistakes.

A bird trilled in the bush, snapping me out of my reverie. I glanced around in awe. Fields that had been bare on our way to Jerusalem were now blanketed with lilies. In the few days we were away the fields had became a sea of flowers bordered by lush, green grass. The unexpected storm awakened the slumbering earth and it brought forth its beauty.

"*And why did it storm?*" an unseen voiced whispered in the back of my mind.

"*Because of Yeshua's death,*" I thought in reply.

I looked again at the lilies dancing in the breeze. My eyes filled with tears and my heart swelled as newfound hope surged through me. Standing tall, I threw my shoulders back and grabbed Yaakov's hand. Together we strode toward home and family.

What Hadassah and I had witnessed was the beginning, not the end. Though I would still mourn Yeshua, I now understood that God had something greater in store for us. I did not know when or how it would come about.

I only knew that when it did, it would be more wonderful than anything I could ever imagine.

— *The End* —

Author's Notes

I hope you enjoyed your trip through the First Century with Rivkah.

Writing historic fiction presents a unique challenge. The principal characters, who are most often not historical figures, must be inserted into the flow of known events in a way that avoids doing violence to the historical record and stretching the limits of believability.

To accomplish this I imposed a set of rules. Except for the natural compression of time which all novels require, I adhered to the historic sequence of events. Everything is portrayed as my research indicated it probably occurred. When it became necessary to introduce historic personages, I exploited the existing gaps in the record and deduced what cannot be known. Most importantly, the story focuses less on the big events of history and more on how average people of the era were impacted by them. Here's more detail on a few of the many topics covered in the book:

Lambs for the Temple

All of those in the settlement of shepherds where Rivkah and Shemu'el lived are portrayed as raising lambs for the Temple market. There are historic references which indicate most Temple lambs came from the area around Bethlehem. Since the shepherds needed proximity to the fields to pasture their sheep, and were generally looked down upon by the higher classes, it makes sense that they clustered in their own little settlement.

The Magi

The magi have been imagined to have been everything from traveling entertainers, to magicians, to kings. My research led me to portray them as Magoi – the original phrase Luke used and the title given to members of the upper house of the Parthian Government and advisors to Phraates, ruler of the Parthian Dynasty.

What support is there for this conclusion?
1. We know they came from the East. The province of Syria formed the Eastern edge of the Roman Empire and bordered the Parthian Empire. Parthia's influence extended from there to the Indus River.
2. The Parthians had a history of meddling in Jewish politics. Prior to Herod the Great claiming the Jewish throne, they supported Herod's rival, Hyrcanus II, a Hasmonean.
3. Parthia's capitol was Babylon, home to a large residual contingent of Jews who were familiar with the Prophecies of a coming *Mashiach*.
4. We are told the Magi followed a star to Bethlehem. The Parthians themselves were Zoroastrians and strong believers in astrologic influences. Although we are never told how many there were, I followed tradition and made them three, naming them Melchior, Gaspar and Balthasar.

False Messiahs

To me, this was one of the most interesting aspects of my research. Jewish yearning for the *Mashiach* reached a fever pitch in the years surrounding the birth of Christ.

The list of Messianic Pretenders can be short or long depending upon the criteria used. (One list I found extended into the Twentieth Century. Its most recent entry being an Hassidic Rabbi who died in the 1990's.) For our purposes, the real interest lies in those who arose just prior to, or shortly after, the birth of Yeshua of Nazareth. This yields a list of thirteen individuals beginning with Athrongeus and ending with Simon bar Kokhba in 132AD.

The Bar Kokhba Revolt marked the last attempt by the Jews to establish a nation in ancient Israel. Though the Temple had been destroyed in 70AD, Jews still inhabited the territory in and around Jerusalem. Simon bar Kokhba, or Simon Son of a Star, is referenced in the Babylonian Talmud, in Cassius Dio's, *Roman History*, and in Eusebius', *Ecclesiastical History*.

It took the Romans three years to put down the Bar Kokhba Revolt. Coins minted during his reign are stamped "Year one of the redemption of Israel." His defeat led to the absolute leveling of Jerusalem and the expulsion of all Jews from the Holy Land. His critics later cynically referred to him as *bar Kozeba*, or Son of Disappointment.

WITNESS chronicles the rise and fall of the two earliest pretenders, Judas the Galilean and Athrongeus of Judea. Of the two, Judas had the greater impact. The Roman army executed most of Judas' followers after his uprising. He, however, lived to fight another day. Retreating into the Galilean hills with a handful of supporters, he waged a guerilla war against the Romans for many years. The party of the Zealots arose from his movement.

Jacob & Simon, both sons of Judas the Galilean, are listed among the Messianic Pretenders. They were crucified by the Roman Governor Tiberius Julius Alexander sometime around 47 AD. Seventy years after Judas' revolt in Sepphoris the Zealot party seized control of Jerusalem, which ultimately led to the city's destruction by the Romans in 70AD.

Interestingly enough, one if not two, of Judas' followers apparently found a home among Yeshua's disciples. Luke refers to the first as Simon Zelotes (Simon the Zealot). In Matthew and Mark the KJV identifies him as a *Canaanite*. This is an incorrect translation of the Hebrew word *Cananean*, which in Greek becomes Zealot.

It has been suggested that the name Judas Iscariot derives from the Greek word *sikarios*, dagger bearer. The Sicarii were a band of fanatical nationalists who broke with the Zealots and assassinated their perceived enemies with daggers.

Quintillius Varus

The Roman Governor Varus is interesting in his own right. After leaving Syria, he took command of the Roman forces along the Rhone (Rhine) river in Germania. He had five legions, two based in Mogontiacum (Mainz) and three which rotated their quarters winter and summer. In 9AD the three legions were enroute to their winter quarters when Varus received word of a German uprising.

He marched his troops into the Teutoburg Forest where they were ambushed by the enemy. When they realized the battle had been lost, Varus and his officers fell upon their swords. Only a cavalry commander and a few of his horsemen escaped to tell the tale. The rest of the troops were slain, making it the worst defeat in Roman history. The Roman historian, Suetonius, portrays Caesar Augustus wandering his palace at night crying, "*Quintili Vare, legiones redde!*"..."Quintillius Varus give me back my legions."

Legio XII Fulminata

Varus commanded *Legio XII Fulminata* while Governor of Syria. They were known as the Lightning (Fulminata) Legion because of their quick response in battle. They were among those sent to quell the revolt following Herod's death.

It was during this uprising that Shemu'el was captured and transported to Antioch where he became a slave. This protest took place while Sabinus was temporary Procurator. In the process, parts of the Temple were set afire doing extensive damage. The Jewish historian, Flavius Josephus, tells us 18,000 workmen labored until the reign of Nero to rebuild and repair the damage, a period of about 50 years. This means they were still working when Yeshua visited the Temple. Ironically, a few short years after they completed these repairs another revolt broke out and this time the Temple was leveled.

In 66AD, after the Zealot revolt destroyed the Roman garrison in Jerusalem, *Legio XII* and two others were sent to retaliate. They fought during the Siege of Jerusalem and supported their commander, Vespasian, in his bid to become Emperor. Under Vespasian's son, Titus, they participated in the sack and destruction of Jerusalem.

In later years *Legio XII* became a strong Christian influence within the Roman army. The story is told that during Marcus Aurelius' campaign against the Quadi, a people occupying what is now the Slovak Republic, they were surrounded by enemy forces and left without food or water for several days. Facing certain annihilation, the soldiers knelt on the battlefield and prayed. A torrential storm began immediately, sending the enemy fleeing in terror and providing them with badly needed water.

Legio XII appears again when St. Basil writes of the 40 Martyrs of Sebaste, in Armenia. Licinius condemned 40 Christian soldiers from the legion to be striped naked and left out overnight in freezing weather. One of their members lost faith and recanted. A guard, inspired by the heavenly light hovering around the men, threw his clothing aside and joined them. At daybreak their stiffened bodies were burned.

Jewish Betrothal and Marriage Customs

A significant portion of the book deals with Rivkah's attempt to remain true to her love for Shemu'el and avoid being forced into a marriage she didn't want.

Could this have happened? I believe so.

Though a girl became a woman, and therefore eligible for marriage at puberty, most didn't marry until around the age of 15 or so. Once she reached the age of 13, rabbinical law gave a girl the right to refuse any offer of marriage. Boys also came of age at 13, but since they would have been incapable of supporting a wife and family, they typically waited until about 18 to marry.

Given her trauma over the supposed death of Shemu'el, a loving father would surely have allowed her time to grieve. By the time Shemu'el returned Rivkah was approaching her 20th birthday and, though this was late, I'm sure it was not unheard of. After all, some girls never married.

—Shalom Aleichem

The Saga Continues—

Follow the lives of Rivkah and Shemu'el as they convert to *The Way of Yeshua*, face persecution in Jerusalem, and journey to Antioch with Simon Peter to establish the Church there.

Sit in with the twelve apostles as they partition the world and begin their mission of preaching and teaching. Meet James the Just, first Bishop of Jerusalem. Along with Stephen, the church's first martyr meet his persecutor, the scourge of the early church, Saul of Tarsus.

Coming soon—

DISCIPLE

Book Two of The Seeds of Christianity™ Series.

"Why do you look for the living among the dead? Remember how he told you that the Son of Man must…be crucified…and on the third day rise."

— Luke 24:5-6

Someone called Rivkah's name from across the marketplace. Turning, she saw Miryam rushing toward her with open arms.

"It is good to see you, my friend." Miryam reached to hug her. "How have you been?"

Rivkah took a step back, resisting her embrace. When their eyes met, Rivkah looked away.

Miryam touched her coarse gown. "You are wearing sackcloth."

"And you are not."

"I do not understand. Has someone died?"

"Has someone died?" Rivkah pushed her hand away and her voice grew shrill. "Yes, someone died. Your son! Look at you. You wear a fresh tunic while I am dressed in sackcloth. I have ashes on my head. You have washed your hair and anointed it with oil. Each night since his crucifixion I have recited Torah

DISCIPLE

verses on Yeshua's behalf. Why do I, merely his friend, honor the 30 days of *Shloshim* while you, his mother, have ceased to mourn?"

"Bless you," Miryam said. "It is not as you imagine. After they placed Yeshua in the tomb I stumbled home grief stricken. Friends brought me the *se'udat habra'ah* and I ate my bread and eggs of consolation alone in the darkness. Though it was *Pesach*, a time when mourning is prohibited, I sat on a stool in my room and wept for three days."

"Three days of weeping does not justify your behavior."

Miryam's eyes sparkled. "Then my room was suddenly filled with light and Yeshua stood before me."

Rivkah began to tremble. "His ghost visited you? How can this be?"

She shook her head as tears of happiness filled her eyes. "It was no ghost, my friend. Yeshua lives. His Father in heaven raised him from the dead just as he predicted. I held him in my arms. He told me not to mourn, but to rejoice."

Rivkah turned aside and covered her face. "Oh, I feel like such a fool."

"Nonsense." Miryam snatched her into her arms and kissed her cheek. "Your mourning demonstrated your love for Yeshua. You were not here in Jerusalem. How could you have known?"

Rivkah experienced the same unexpected surge of hope she'd felt the first day after Yeshua's crucifixion. She and her son, Yaakov, were on the road home from Jerusalem when she noticed lilies filling the fields.

"So the feeling I had on the road is true. His death was not the end of all that we hoped for."

Miryam took her by the hand and tugged Rivkah away from the stand. "This fruit will still be here when you return. Come home with me. I have so much to tell you."

She led Rivkah through a confusing labyrinth of streets. Leaving the stands of fruits and vegetables behind, they passed through the market of wool buyers and sellers of cloth. Turning one corner and then another, they eventually entered the bazaar of the fishmongers.

DISCIPLE

"This way." Miryam led her into the front portion of a two-story stone building.

A shipment had just arrived and they stepped around workman unloading barrels from a cart parked beside the shop's open door. The men hoisted the heavy containers onto their backs and weaved between customers to complete their delivery. After stacking their barrels of dried fish on the shop's wooden floor, they returned to the cart for more.

Curious, Rivkah glanced into one of the barrels. Shemu'el and her sons occasionally caught similar fish using worms and crickets.

She and Miryam headed for the back of the shop, weaving through a maze of merchandise. They passed crates of spicy fish sauces from Rome and Alexandria and baskets of dried fish from the Great Sea.

Miryam paused to speak to some clerks sorting fresh fish.

When they finished, the man pulled another wiggling fish out of a large clay jar and inspected it. Satisfied, he passed it to the man beside him who opened it with a quick slice of his knife and gutted it. The third man stuffed the fish with damp moss, wrapped it in grape leaves, and packed it.

"Fresh fish?" Rivkah asked with surprise. "In Jerusalem?"

A man's deep voice chuckled behind her. "Nothing but the best at Zebedee's Fish Market."

The intense young man stepped around Rivkah and Miryam to check the last fish placed in the basket.

He shook his head. "This will never do." He replaced it with a larger one. "How many times have I told you, nothing but the pick of the catch for the High Priest's household?" He brought his hands together in a loud clap. "Hurry! His servants are waiting. Caiaphas has a banquet planned for this evening."

The man's expression softened when his eyes returned to the women. "Imma Miryam, how was your trip to the market?" He put an arm around her shoulder and bent to kiss her cheek as any son would do. "You found many bargains, I hope." A spark of recognition flashed in his eyes. "And who is this with you?"

"You remember Rivkah, wife of Shemu'el. She was at

DISCIPLE

Golgotha the day they crucified Yeshua."

Miryam turned. "Rivkah, this is Yonah bar Zebedee, my new son and benefactor."

"And about the fish," Yonah explained. "During the cooler months fishermen at Jericho transfer their catch into jars of cold water. Before dawn these fish, fresh from the Jordan River, are loaded onto wagons and rushed through mountain passes to Jerusalem where they command a premium price. But in this heat they won't last forever." Grinning, he turned to help.

Miryam led Rivkah out a side exit to a stairway. "Up here," she whispered. "This is where I live now."

Leaving the hustle and bustle of the shop behind, the two women climbed the narrow stairs. They entered a simple loft with whitewashed walls and a pine floor. It had a small sitting room and tidy kitchen in front and two bedrooms in the back. Yonah's deep voice resonated through the floorboards as he directed the workmen in the shop below.

"Who is this young man who called you Imma, the one you introduced as your son?"

"Yonah was Yeshua's loyal disciple and most beloved friend. Both he and his older brother, Yaakov, were with Yeshua from the very beginning. While Yeshua hung from the cross he charged Yonah with my care."

Rivkah glanced around the plain room. "Are all your needs met?"

"I am well cared for." Miryam chuckled. "One thing we never lack for is fish. Although I must confess the smells one encounters living above a fish market differ greatly from the sweet perfume of wood shavings."

"Has Yeshua visited others as well?"

"Oh, yes. Many of those who loved him. He appeared to Miriam from Magdala when she went to the tomb on the morning after *Shabbat*. And to his disciples, of course, a number of times...both here in Jerusalem and in Galilee."

She motioned Rivkah into a seat and offered her dried fruit from a plate. "He appeared to others along the road to Emmaus." She sighed with satisfaction. "The list grows and grows."

DISCIPLE

"Where do you think this will lead?"

Miryam shook her head. "I do not know what God has planned for us. Those who knew Yeshua are ecstatic, yet terribly afraid. None of us knows what to expect from one day to the next." She rocked from side to side. Crossing her arms, she hugged herself. "But my son lives. I held him in my arms and kissed his cheek just as when he was a young man. To me, nothing else matters."

"Where are his disciples now?"

"They fear the Great Sanhedrin will order their arrest. When they tired of cringing behind bolted doors and creeping through dark alleyways, they left Jerusalem and scattered.

"Yonah, of course, remained behind because of me and the business. His older brother, Yaakov, returned to Capernaum to help their father, Zebedee. Andrew and Simon have gone back to their nets as well. Mattithayu also returned to Capernaum, not to fish, but to write."

"He is a scribe?"

"No. He was a tax collector before Yeshua called him to be a disciple. He has begun collecting all of Yeshua's sayings on a scroll. When he finishes, Mattithayu says it can be copied and distributed to keep the memory of those teachings alive."

Miryam stared into the distance, teary-eyed. "You are correct; our story is far from over. Yeshua promised to send a Comforter...a Counselor who would teach us all things."

"Who will this Counselor be?"

"No one knows. All we can do is wait and wonder. In my heart, I feel we should not be dispersed as we are now. We draw strength from each other. I am hoping that during the pilgrim feast of Pentecost his disciples will return to Jerusalem so we can again gather as a group."

For more information go to

www.capearagopress.com